A Writers Guide to the Fairies, Witches, & Vampires

From Fairy Tales and Lore

By Ty Hulse

Ravensshire.com

2014 Raven's Shire
Seattle, WA

Table of Contests

5 - The Nature of Fairies

9 - Using Fairytales to Create Fairy Characters

12 - Common Fairy Tales
12 - Extreme Mood Shifts and Multiple Souls
15 - External Dualism
16 - Fairies are Artistic
17 - Fate is an Art
18 - Wild and Extreme Emotions
19 - Overabundant Libido
21 - Playful and Disciplined
21 - Artists Love Nature and Urban Environments
22 - Strict with Their Art
23- Fairies Never Mature, but Are Always Ancient
27 - Many Fairies are Kind and Caring
34- Fairies are Often Shy
37 - Betwixt and Between
38 - Mischievous and Playful
42- Mutable, Anamorphic, Astral, Creators of Illusions
46- Fairies Can See the Future
47 - Death is a Beginning
48- Enforcers of Morality
53- Robin Hood and the Fairy Queen
56 - Immunity and Immortality
58 - Trickster Figures
58 - Murderous, Blood Thirsty, and Vampiric
65 - The Vampires and the Fairies
77 - Fairies Need Respect
81 - Emotionally Sensitive
83 - A Few More Fairy Activities
83 - Kidnapping Children Taking Slaves
84 - Hunting
86 - Fairy Food
87 - War
88 - Hunting

89 - Fairy Backgrounds

90 - The Relationship Between Humans and Fairies
93 - Humans Are Uncanny to Fairies
95 - Ancestral Spirits
106 - The Forgotten Gods
110 - Refugees
115 - Fairy Courts
117 Solitary Fairies
118 - Nature – Nurturing but Dangerous
123 - Undead Nature Spirits
124 - Domesticated Nature Spirits
128 -Banished from Court
129 - Nature Elements
130 - Half Fairy

132 -Sample Fairy Characters

154 - Witches & Cunning
156 - Defining Magic
158 - The Encounter
165 - The Witch's Life
166 - Fairies and Witches are Often Mischievous
168 - Witches Are Usually Born From Suffering
171 – Some Witches Choose to Live on the Fringes of Society
174 - Slave, Servant, and Battered
177 - The Love
178 - The Pet
178 - Friends
182 - Social Center

183 - The Fairy's Purpose

193 - A Few Witch Archetypes

220 - Using Magic

237 - Journey into Spirit World

252 - The Purpose for Enter The "Other World"

262- References

The Nature of Fairies

Rain sweeps over the dusty fields, causing the people who work the land to breathe a sigh of relief; their crops will continue to grow. Although many will still go to bed so hungry that it stunts their growth, the fear of outright starvation has been alleviated, for now. A few weeks before, when people had started to become desperate for rain to keep their crops alive, they'd gone to the rivers, or into the forests. There they'd offered either bits of cloth, votive statues, tablets, oatmeal, bread, or even animal sacrifices to the fairies in hopes that the spirits would make it rain.

This was the world of the people who told fairy tales, a world filled with constant fear and dependence on the forces of nature. People once believed everything was controlled by the spirits of nature and the ghosts of the dead, the magical beings we now call fairies. At its root, the word fairy roughly means "those that control fate" (Narvaez, 1997). It was the fairies who made it rain or storm, who caused the plague or the years of bountiful harvests. Fate in ancient Europe wasn't some abstract concept; it was something fairies made happen. What this means is that fairies were very often those beings that cared about humanity, for good or for ill. Jacob Grimm stated that:

> Destiny itself is called orlog, or else nauor (necessitas), aldr (aevum); the norns have to manage it, espy it, decree it, pronounce it. It was only when the goddesses had been cast off, that the meanings of the words came to be confounded, and the old flesh and blood causes

> disappeared. (Grimm, 1835)

The word "fairy," then, refers to a whole host of beings who control the fate of humanity. Throughout this work, we will discuss many beings from many lands, yet I refer to each of these as fairies because the word is meant to designate those who control the fate of humanity and who share certain traits in common. The word "fairy," like the word "deity" or "animal," is just a definition, one that crosses many cultures. This book is not, however, an encyclopedic discussion of fairies, but rather it is a discussion of the emotions and personality traits that people assigned to them. After all, when humans believe their lives and happiness depend so completely on something – as people once believed they depended on fairies – they ponder its nature, they worry about its moods, and they constantly concern themselves with it. So, for thousands of years, people worried about the nature of fairies. Shaman figures, such as witches and cunning, would enter the spirit realms to gain a better understanding of the metaphysical world of fairies. People would consider carefully what would make fairies happy and what might make them angry. In his memoirs, one Breton man muses that;

> At that time, with no education, the peasants, laborers, and fishermen had no other topics to talk about; they (fairies, ghosts, and spirits) were the sole matter for conversation, for chatting, whenever a few people found themselves together with nothing else to do. But I, who already knew well those tales and legends from my father and mother, and especially from the great weaver.... (Dequiqne 2011)

He goes on to say that people oftentimes argued about stories from distant places:

> But, when it came to local lore, there was not of that wrangling. Those legends, or rather accounts – for they were always real-life stories-were about personal incidents that every man would tell and that no one would want to dispute. In those times, everyone had seen ghosts, miserable souls caught in some swamp, or in a nook of some old house, or in a hollow tree trunk,

or out on a moor; everyone had seen fairies, night-washerwomen, night-screamers, and the elfin couriquets... (Dequiqnet, 2011)

So, to a large extent, people assigned some level of personality to various fairies, despite the fact that fairies often make only small appearances in fairy tales. This also means that fairies were much more than just prancy, dancy little creatures that lived in crystal palaces beneath lakes and hills. Rather, fairies were often complex beings about which people would have nightmares or tell horror stories, and to whom people would give offerings in hopes that the fairies would leave them alone. Because of this, it's easy to picture fairies as a little like gangsters, demanding that people pay them for protection and certainly some fairies were very much like this. Most, however, were generally caring and kind, going out of their way to help humanity, yet capable of having horrible tempers.

Reading about fairies, one quickly realizes that they are complex, conflicted beings. Take the Rusalka, for example. The Rusalka is a young girl – one who can never grow up, never mature, never find true love. Yet, at the same time, she is always wise and ancient, and very lustful; she was a nature spirit, who taught humans how to create civilization. Thus, she is caught forever between many opposite extremes. It is a maddening moment in time in which fairies live; between dark and light, between youth and maturity. They are forever caught betwixt and between. It's no wonder, then, that when a fairy tells someone they love them and makes an offer to allow someone to come away with them to a land of beauty where they can be immortal, it sounds both lovely and at the same time a little like a threat.

Despite the threatening nature of fairy abductions, Fairyland could oftentimes be likened to Heaven, for many humans were comforted by the idea of going to Fairyland when they died. In Rome, when a girl drowned, people took comfort in the knowledge that she got to play with the nymphs forever (Larson, 2001). Starving peasants who heard tales of fairy dances and of eternal parties must have, at times, hoped that they too would become a fairy who got to participate in these dances when they died. They must have longed for the day when they could be free of the suffering and toil of their station in life. Again, looking at the Rusalka, we see that she lives a life that is, in many ways, a girl's dream; for Russian girls were truly second-class citizens. They often gave birth while working in the fields, and the harshness of the experience caused them to develop age spots on their faces while they were still barely twenty. Their husbands would spend their money on vodka, leaving them to starve. Then, the drunken husbands would come home and beat them. At times, their husband would grab them by the braids and beat their heads against a wall or drag them up and down the stairs (Ranset, 1993).

    Rusalka, who were often said to be the spirits of dead girls, had no braids; their hair was free just like they were. They were all beautiful and sexy so that men longed for them, but the Rusalka were in control. They could not only refuse men, they could kill them if the men became too cruel. No one dared to walk on the Ruslakas' laundry when they laid it out to dry; no one dared to mock or abuse them. The Rusalka danced all evening and lived in crystal palaces, while human girls were forced to continue working (Rappoport, 1999). At the same time, in order to become a Rusalka, a person had to die, and there were no guarantees, which explains why people both feared and longed for the fairy world.

Using Fairy Tales to Create Fairy Characters

As you read through fairy tales, you'll quickly discover that the fairies in them are rarely ever the protagonists. Instead, they tend to play supporting roles; either as the villains who drain blood, kidnap babies, and do other wicked things, or as donors who provide magical aid to the hero. More difficult still to understand are the small snippets of information about fairies, bits of lore about fairies that tell people what to do, but not why they should do it. For example, some of the only information we have about the Fairy of the Apple Orchard was that one should leave an apple in the orchard, rather than harvest them all. Why this should be done, or why the fairy should care isn't specified in this bit of lore. The reason for leaving an apple in the orchard becomes apparent from other tales about similar fairies, however. In these tales, it is said that the fairy's spirit lives within the crop, so if it is all harvested, the spirit will go away. This means that the Apple Tree Man lives inside the last apple left in the orchard; they are, in essence, the spirits of the apples themselves. Further information about the Apple Tree Man can be discerned from other stories about similar beings. Thus, while there are many fairies who have no stories about them, it is possible to create compelling characters from them. In order to understand fairies as characters in fairy tales and lore, you need to step back and look at the big picture, taking your information from multiple sources by:

1 - Reviewing common traits to see if any of these fit the

fairy and the character you want to create. There are, after all, certain traits and certain underlining threads, which many fairies, regardless of their country of origin, have in common. So, while no one fairy exhibits all these traits, reviewing them can help provide you with insights into the fairy's actions and help you see beyond the simple fairy tale in which the fairy appears.

2-Research the specific fairy to see if it makes more than one appearance in fairy tales and lore. The zwerg (dwarfs) who helped Snow White, for example, have brethren who appear in dozens, even hundreds of other tales in which they help men and women get married, or give magical gifts to heroes. These Zwerg also almost always demand a show of kindness and a willingness to do hard work in return for their help. Indeed, the Zwerg themselves are often depicted as fastidious and hardworking. So, while the fact that the Zwerg allow Snow White to stay if she cleans and cooks has typically led to the interpretation that the Zwerg couldn't cook, clean, or take care of themselves, the truth is that they are far more capable of doing these things than a human is and certainly an untrained princess. They just believed that hard work is important and won't help those who don't work at least a little for themselves.

3-Give your fairy a background. After all, fairies are oftentimes immortal, or very nearly so, which means they may have lived hundreds, even thousands of years. Like anyone else, they have been shaped by this long past, by where they come from. While there are many different potential backgrounds for fairies, there are certain backgrounds that are repeated in the stories about fairies, thanks to their nature. Figuring out which of these backgrounds is likely to apply to any one fairy character will often change their entire story. For example, Rumpelstiltskin is often depicted as nothing more than an overzealous tradesman. However, if we think of him as an enforcer of morality, a former deity, or ancestral spirit, as many fairies were, then he, like Merlin, wanted the child of a king, a prince, in order to raise it so that he could save the kingdom from a tyrant. This interpretation makes sense, given that the child whom he wanted had a father who was so greedy he was willing to kill a poor girl if she didn't weave straw into gold for him.

4-Research the culture the fairy comes from, since fairies are interconnected with the culture from which they come. The fairies who aid hunters among the Kalasha people, where hunting was an almost meditative experience for nearly any male in the village, are likely completely different from the fairies that helped the hunters of England, where only the nobility could legally hunt. Hunting, among the English, was an act of rebels such as Robin Hood. The fairies that aided hunters for both these peoples would appear as beautiful women, and would both care for and aid the people in the forests, but their goals, like the goals of each of these hunters, was likely very different, and the only way to understand this is to understand the people with whom the fairies choose to interact.

5- Give your fairy some personality traits. Our personality often dictates what we do and how we choose to live. So it's possible to extrapolate a fairy's personality type and or character archetype based on the activities in which they engage. For example, the Tomte of Scandinavian is a household fairy who chooses to live on farms, to be isolated from both the fairy court and from large human cities in a place where it can contemplate the nature of the world as well as do hard work. This means that Tomte likely share many of the traits in common with farmer archetypes and/or the personality types most associated with farmers.

Common Fairy Traits

Fairies are compelling characters that have been plotting and planning for thousands, if not millions of years. They have personalities, purposes, and traits, which are often complex and difficult to understand. Thankfully, many of the fairies of Europe share certain traits in common with each other, making it easier to begin to understand them. Of course, as complex beings, no one fairy has all these "common traits," nor is any one fairy defined only by these traits. Still, these traits can give important insights into the characters and purposes of the fairies.

Extreme Mood Shifts and Multiple Souls

Fairies often exist in many forms and have many natures simultaneously, to the point that many of them seem to exhibit multiple personalities and purposes. This same thing is true of the natural world as well, where nearly everything is its own opposite. The river that brings water to the fields to help the plants grow also floods and destroys them. The same forest that provides food for the flocks is also the home of the wolves, which kill them. The sun, which helps plants grow, causes the famine that withers them away. Just as nature is a contradiction, the spirits of nature were often viewed as internally dualistic; that is, they were their own opposites. Hermes, for example, was the deity of both thieves and merchants, and he would help either as he wished

(Brown, 1990). This duality is also expressed in the Slavic beliefs about the bathhouse and the spirit that lived there:

> Peasants avoid visiting a bath at late hours, for the *Bannik* does not like people who bathe at night, and often suffocates them, especially if they have not prefaced their ablutions by a prayer. It is considered dangerous, also, to pass the night in a corn-kiln, for the Domovoi may strangle the intruder in his sleep. (Ralston, 2007)

In one story, a woman who interrupts a Bannik in a bath has her skin flayed from her body as punishment for her interruption. Yet, at the same time, Banniks protect people from evil spirits and illness. For example, a girl who was being pursued by vampire-like creatures ran into the bathhouse calling for "Grandfather Bannik, who then jumped out and risked his life to save her by battling a horde of powerful spirits" (Ivantis, 1992). For this reason, people went to the bathhouse to break the curses of evil spirits, and gain protection against them. So, on the one hand, the Bannik and Domovoi were a family's protectors; they wept with sorrow when humans were about to die and gave them blessings before their weddings. Yet, on the other hand, they were easily angered and they would kill those who disturbed them.

In the Celtic lands, house fairies would perform chores, bring luck, and protect a family. Yet, at the same time, when angered, they could go on wild rampages, becoming poltergeists. When angry, house fairies were called something different from what they had been when they were still kind (Keightley, 1892), almost as if they were a different being all together. In Iceland, the spirits of rocks protected people, making their flocks thrive; yet these highly sensitive spirits would become cruel, dangerous beings if they witnessed violence (Davidson, 1988). In Macedonia, it was believed that one could sweeten the disposition of a murderous spirit by sprinkling boiled grape juice on the ground near where they lived (Abbott, 1976).

Perhaps the best example of the multiple personality of fairies comes from the fairies that gave babies their fate, as even a little annoyance could change a normally kind and helpful fairy into a murderous monster. In one Germanic

Saga, for example, these "Norn" are all giving blessings to a baby when the youngest stands to give hers and trips, hurting herself. In her rage, she curses the baby to die when the candle beside it burns out (Grimm, 1830). The "wicked fairy" in *Sleeping Beauty* was no different from the good fairies; she just hadn't been invited to give a blessing to the child and it was the slight of being forgotten that caused her to curse the king and queen's baby girl to die. Yet, despite the fact that it was a small thing that angered her, this wasn't just a short-term change in mood, for she held this grudge for years.

    Many fairies seem to feel things much more intensely than humans do, but their sudden and often long-term changes in personality make it seem that, more than just mood swings, they have multiple personalities. In fact, in parts of Northern and Eastern Europe it's well documented that people believed that humans, and very likely fairies, had multiple souls (Czaplicka, 1914). Lecouteux (2003) has argued very elegantly that the Germanic peoples, Celts, Ancient Greeks, and Romans also once believed in the idea of multiple souls, as multiple spirits and natures of humans are often mentioned in mythology and lore. Certainly, we see that nearly every European people believed that multiple things would happen to a person when they died, that their spirit would stay in their body, grow into a tree, become a fairy, and go to the afterlife. This complexity of beliefs about the afterlife is often associated with the belief in multiple souls in other parts of Eurasia.

    If we are to assume that fairies have multiple souls, we should also presume that as mystical beings and spirits, fairies are likely to be much more "in touch" with each of these souls and/or natures, which means that it's often as if any given fairy is not one, but two or more different characters, each with different goals, and each competing for dominance. Depending on which spirit is dominant at any given time, the fairy's entire personality can change completely. As a consequence, the question of whether a fairy is good or evil can often be answered with "both." For unlike Christianity, which has dualism in two separate beings, Europe's ancient folk religions tended to have dualism within nearly every being.

    Many fairies, then, are cursed with something very similar to Multiple Personality Disorder, except that each personality of the fairy is actually a different soul, a different spirit always struggling for dominance over the others. Because of this, humans always need to be careful not to give power to the crueler aspect of the fairies' natures by insulting the fairies, while working to empower the kinder, gentler aspect. As Yeats (1888) puts it:

> Witness the nature of the creatures, their caprice, their way of being good to the good and evil to the evil, having every charm but conscience—consistency. Beings so quickly offended that you must not speak much about them at all, and never call them anything but the "gentry," or else daoine maithe, which in English means good people, yet so easily pleased, they will do their best to keep misfortune away from you, if you leave a little milk for them on the window-sill overnight.

External Dualism

While nearly every fairy had extreme emotional reactions, many of them were still very clearly externally dualistic; that is, they had their opposite contained outside themselves. In the Lithuanian tale of "Lake Peipsi," for example, there is a sacred grove of trees that contains three good and three evil fairies. In this story, the good and evil fairies oppose each other, but they cannot fight each other, not directly. So, when the wicked spirits kidnap the King's Daughter, the good spirits send her a dove bearing magical gifts to help her escape on her own. (Grautoff, 1916)

In Scottish folklore, the fairies are divided between the Seelie and Unseelie Courts. The Seelie Court are the "benefactors of mankind, they gave bread to the poor, and supplied them with seed-corn; they cheered the afflicted and comforted the mourner." The Unseelie Court, however, are wicked and cruel tormentors who haunt man and carry human souls to hell (Rogers, 1880). While in Scandinavian lore, the elves are divided into light and dark with the:

Former, or the Good Elves, dwell in the air, dance on the grass, or sit in the leaves of trees; the latter, or Evil Elves, are regarded as an underground people, who frequently inflict sickness or injury on mankind; for which there is a particular kind of doctors called Kloka män, to be met with in all parts of the country. (Keightley, 1892)

Further, according to Keightley, there were three tribes of dwarfs in one region of Germany that were similarly divided. Yet, such divisions aren't always clear, even where they existed. For example, in Greek lore, when the nymphs were angered, they would sometimes ask a dangerous and ugly hag to go take revenge for them. When Pharaonia, the King of Myrmidonia's son, attacked a grove of trees, they sent a spirit hag known as the Ravaging Hunger after him. True to her name, the ugly hag punished the man with a hunger so great that he ate and ate until he became so impoverished that he had to sell everything he owned in order to buy food to feed himself. Yet, in the end, it still wasn't enough and he died tearing at his own flesh (Larson, 2001). This case is interesting because the nymph's ugly and cruel opposite worked with them to maintain beauty, aka, the natural order of both civilization and nature. For nymphs were both the ones who built civilization and the ones who demanded nature remain intact. This means that even where there might be kind and cruel fairies as separate beings, they might still work together to maintain order.

Fairies Are Artistic

"Dancing and song are their delight" - Jacob Grimm

Fairies are lovers and creators of art, which, given their wild and eccentric nature, means that many of them are very much like either rock stars or ravers seeking their next thrill as they bounce from one wild party to the next. More than simply being skilled artists and lovers of beauty, fairies are the artists who control everything. They are the ones who control nature, deciding, for example, when the flowers bloom or the winter comes. It is the fairies who push and control the fate of humanity as well, even to the point that the talents a person possess are often given by the fairies. In Shetland, many of the songs that people knew were said to have been given to them by the fairies (Black, 1903). Similarly, the nymphs of Greek lore were often the ones who gave humans the gifts of painting, of poetry, of weaving. In Celtic lore, blacksmiths and even shipbuilders owed much of their skill to the fairies. In Irish lore, the ancestral spirit known as the banshee would give the gift of poetry to one of their descendants (Wilde, 1902). This means that fairies can create the fate of humans as a form of art.

Being artists – truly great artists as the fairies are – isn't just an action; it's often a state of being which both comes from and affects the emotional core of the artist. Because of this, many artists have certain personality traits in common and the fairies of lore tend to share many of these personality traits as well. This is why I tend to think of fairies as being a lot like stereotypical rock stars, or Mozart, or the Phantom of the Opera. Like rock stars, many fairies live in a world of seemingly endless parties in which they dance every night on hillsides and fill the countryside with their primal music. Yet, just as rock stars are known for leaving hotel rooms in shambles, and for experiencing sudden bouts of depression, fairies also will, at times, destroy huge swaths of the countryside in their wild dances and are prone to sudden bouts of horrific depression so deep that the result is a famine that leaves tens of thousands, if not millions of people starving.

Fate is an Art

For the fairies, the entire world really is a stage: we are the players, and they are the writers and directors. For example, as ancestral spirits, banshees gave the gift of poetry to people, yet this was only a tiny part of their art. Their true art was in writing the legacies of their families and the sagas of heroes. As with many fairy-like beings, including the Fees of France who set the course of "Sleeping Beauty's" life, and the Rusalka of Russia who determined the fate of children, the banshees would give blessings to newborn children, crafting their future shortly after or even before they were born. In Germanic lore, Odin not only gave the gift of poetry, he sat over the battlefields and decided which side would be the victor (which, given that he was a god of poetry, was likely in part an artistic choice), while the Valkyries, forerunners to the Swan Maidens of future lore, would decide, to some extent, who lived and who died.

As artists, fairies try to create a more "beautiful world." Of course, how they define this beauty isn't always the same. After all, beauty is more than simply in the 'eye of the beholder'; sometimes, beauty is an emotional or artistic statement to understand the nature of humanity. The same artist who admired sculptures of neoclassicism can become Picasso, who himself created scenes of war and pain, of sadness and depression alongside his works of happiness and joy. The same writers who carefully crafted jokes and allowed the boy to get the girl in their stories also kill major characters in horrible ways, just as Shakespeare did. What this means is that even artistic fairies may not seek to create beauty. They may instead be seeking to create fulfillment and understanding through horror, tragedy, and more.

Unlike human artists and poets, fairies are not limited to writing about the beauty of nature; they create it. In the same way, they are not limited to trying to understand the nature of life, love, or pain by writing on these subjects. They are able to create the events that further the understanding of these things. In other words, because of their powers and their nature, fairies manipulate humanity and nature to create the ultimate art.

Wild and Extreme Emotions

Many artists have a tendency to be prone to wild and extreme mood swings. One famous and over-the-top example of this aberration occurred when Gauguin cut off Van Gogh's ear because the latter artist attacked him for saying he was returning to Paris (Kucharz, 2009). In much the same way, fairies often react impulsively in extreme ways. They will make decisions on the fly, which can often seem out of character for them. Such decisions often get them, as well as the humans around them, into a lot of trouble. Yet the fairies have difficulty stemming their desires. The result is that fairies tend to feel emotions much more intensely than humans do. So, for example, instead of the mild embarrassment humans might feel because of their flaws or mistakes, fairies feel intense shame, which can lead to fury. When someone does something that might annoy fairies, they feel rage, or when they should feel mildly thankful, they feel euphorically grateful. So when humans give fairies the tiniest amount of help, they reward those humans with lifelong happiness, gold, or some other incredibly precious gift. However, should a human do even the slightest amount of harm to a fairy, death is often the punishment. We see this repeatedly in fairy tales. In the story of "The Three Mannlien in the Wood" (Grimm, 1812), a young girl shares her stale crust of bread with three Mannlien and, in return, they make her more beautiful every day. They cause gold to fall from her mouth every time she speaks and set it up so that she marries a prince. When the girl's stepsister refuses to share her food with them, the fairies cause her to grow more ugly, frogs to jump out of her mouth, and ultimately to die horribly.

In a spectacular display of over-emotional reaction, Rumpelstiltskin tore himself in two in the midst of his tantrum (Grimm, 1812). Fairies lose control of their emotions easily, allowing happiness to pull them into a seemingly never-ending series of celebrations, while allowing frustrations to cause them to throw destructive tantrums. Such extreme behavior means that people have to be especially careful when dealing with fairies. This is why people were careful when approaching sacred wells and entering sacred groves of trees because the fairies within them would kill over the slightest amount of disrespect (Tacitus, 2012). Like many artists, musicians, and actors, fairies crave approval. Yet like human artistic-personality types, who are among the only people who can switch from being introverted to extroverted and back again, fairies also seek extreme solitude as well as lots of attention.

The problem is that fairies, much like those with artistic personalities, are easily prone to feeling an intense sense of emptiness, an overwhelming loneliness. Because of this, fairies can become easily depressed; a fact that is historically problematic for humans because when fairies get depressed, plants stop growing, the rain stops falling (or won't stop falling), and so humans must go out and try to make the fairies feel better with songs about how great the fairy is, and with offerings. This means, on the one hand, that fairies are often emotionally dependent on the approval of others, yet, at the same time, they are easily embarrassed and overwhelmed by attention. So, like many actors, they want much of their private life to remain private, even as they seek praise from others.

Overabundant Libido

Extreme emotions also mean that fairies are often associated with an overabundant, and often dangerous, libido. The nymphs of Greece, the Nixes of Germany, the Rusalka of Slavic lands, and the Huldra of Scandinavia, as well as many other notable fairies, were known to kidnap men in order to mate with them. Indeed, both nymphs and satyrs are both well known for being extremely sexual (with the exception of the followers of Artemis, who were expected to remain virgins). Similarly, in Norway, the spirits known as Bergsrået hated having humans about and would cause them trouble in the mines where they lived. Yet these fairies were still happy to seduce and sleep with young men (Grimberg, 1924).

Women, too, were always in danger of fairy attentions. For example, Chaucer (2011) states that the disappearance of fairies means that women were able to travel more safely about, except for the friars, who during his time preyed on woman's virtue as fairies once did, implying that fairies used to attack woman the way lustful and dangerous men did. In Tuscan lore, when the Siero grow angry with a family, they will destroy the milk of their cows:

> Then the peasant, to make matters right again in his house, implores Siero to be favorable; upon which the goblin comes and knocks at the house-door, and if the contadino has a pretty daughter, cries, 'Yes, I will make you happy; but you must let me sleep one night with your daughter.' But, if he has a plain daughter, Siero laughs, and says, 'If you had a girl less ugly, and had

> mocked me less, I would have made you prosperous. But since your daughter is so plain, I cannot revenge myself for all the ill things you have said of me.' And if the peasant has girls neither pretty nor plain, then Siero calls, 'If you will remember to bless me every day, I will make you happy; but should you forget it, you will be wretched while you live. (Leland, 1892)

Meanwhile, in a Russian tale, the Spirit of the Steppes will not let the queen pass through his lands to return home unless she and all her handmaidens sleep with him. From this, the queen and her handmaidens all become pregnant. Ultimately, the queen's daughter is banished by her jealous husband to a distant land, where she is raised by the trees and the breezes (Ralston, 2004). Sometimes, the fairies even chose witches on the basis of their looks.

> But all this the time, fairies were not idle; for it was at this very season of dances and festivals, when the mortals around them were happiest, that Finvarra the King and his chosen band were on the watch to carry off the prettiest girls to the fairy mansions. There they kept them for seven years and, at the end of time they, when they grew old and ugly, they were sent back, for the fairies love nothing so much as youth and beauty. But as a compensation for the slight put on them, the women were taught all the fairy secrets and the magical mystery that lies in herbs, and the strange power they have over diseases. So, by this means, the women became all-powerful, and by their charms or spells or potions could kill or save as they chose. (Wilde, 1887)

Playful and Disciplined

Fairies are extremely playful, exuberant to the point of being childish. At the same time, however, they can spend centuries helping the same forest to grow, the same river to flow, or city to survive. Like artists, they are able to work for long periods of time on a project, often putting other professionals to shame with their disciplined work ethic.

A large part of this contrast between playfulness and discipline comes from the fact that fairies, like artists, likely live in a fantasy world of their own making. Dwelling within their minds, they often imagine what *should* be. However, unlike humans, who spend a lot of time daydreaming, fairies can use their magical powers to try to make their dreams a reality. As a consequence, they role play their often bizarre dreams while working furiously to make these dreams a reality. This also means that while fairies tend to be fairly conservative about most things, because they try to cling to perfect moments, they are at times willing to make extreme changes or take risks to fit their own artistic visions. Fairies, too, as we'll see in greater depth later, tend to be fairly distrustful of new ideas or ways of doing things. However, at the same time, they are often the ones pushing human civilization forward.

Artists Love Nature and Urban Environments

Artists love the beauty of nature, but they can also love the energy of urban environments. Fairies often blend these two extreme aspects of their nature by living in high energy fairy societies that are located in wilderness areas. The fairy kingdoms so often described in lore are very much like human courts, yet thanks to their magic, these kingdoms can grow to enormous size without interfering with the natural world, which means fairies can live in both the wilderness and their urban kingdoms at the same time. Much like club hoppers, they dance all night, fall in love with great musicians, and generally act wildly as they flit about their lives. Yet, at the same time, they often seek the solitude of nature, depending on their moods.

Strict with Their Art

It should be fairly obvious from the previous list of artist traits that the personality most often associated with artists isn't whimsical. Indeed, looking at the nature of artists throughout history, we see that they are rarely whimsical. Fairies are strict with their art, as shown by the example of the Fossegrim (a male waterfall fairy). In order to learn to play music from the Fossegrim, a person would sacrifice a he-goat to him by throwing it into the waterfall. If the fairy accepted the gift, the Fossegrim would grab the person's hands, forcing them to play the violin so violently and for so long that blood would spurt out of the human's fingertips. With their hands bursting apart and spurting blood, the humans in the tales would beg the Fossegrim to stop, to allow them to take a break, but the Fossegrim would ignore the student's cries of pain as they continued to force the human to play this way for as long as it took for them to perfect the art of playing music, to the point that the trees would dance when they played (Grimm, 1882).

The brutality with which the Fossegrim teach music shows that fairies are demanding artists and that they do not accept weakness or pain when it comes to their art. They are beauty and art lovers to an extreme degree. For many of them, then, it seems that suffering is an acceptable byproduct of making something beautiful.

Fairies Never Mature, But Are Always Ancient

In addition to their artistic nature or their multiple souls, part of what may be driving the fairies' extreme emotional reactions is the fact that many of them never truly mature. Many fairies are, after all, the spirits of dead children who never had a chance to grow up. Throughout most of Europe, people often believed that fairies were the spirits of unbaptized babies. Even in pre-Christian times, there appears to have been this idea that children who died became fairies. The Kubu of Mesopotamia was known as "the little one who never saw the sun." This was a child who never knew its mother's love, or even its own name. It died as a child, and experienced much, but never got to have a childhood (Purkiss, 2007). In Slavic lore, the Kłobuk are the spirits of stillborn babies buried at the threshold of houses, which can take the form of many different animals, including cats and magpies, in order to play and cause mischief. They, like children, seem to love their families, yet they can only express this love in childish ways, such as stealing from the neighbors in order to provide for those for whom they cared. In Ancient Greece, the epitaph for a girl who drowned in the water states *"Not Death, but the naiads snatched the excellent child as a playmate."* The implication of this epitaph is that not only will the girl become a nymph, but that nymphs seek children as playmates (Larson, 2001).

> In the traditions of the Little Russians, the Mavky, who are children either drowned by their mothers or unbaptized, have the appearance of small babies, or of young, beautiful girls with curly hair. They are either half-naked or wear only a white shirt; and on moonlit nights they rock on branches of trees, seeking to attract young people either by imitating the crying of infants or by laughing, giggling, and clapping their hands. Whoever follows their enticing voices will be bewitched by their beauty, and at last will be tickled to death and drawn into deep water. They live in woods and on steppes. Very often, they may be seen in young corn; and, by day, they walk along the fields, crying and wailing. In summer, they swim in rivers and lakes, beating the water merrily; during the fairy week, they run about fields and meadows, lamenting, "Mother has borne me and left me unbaptized." They are angry at those who allowed them to die unchristened, and whosoever chances to hear their wailing voices should say, "I baptize thee in the name of God the Father, God the Son, and God the Holy Spirit." This will set them free; but if for seven years they find no one to take pity on them, they are turned into water-nymphs. (Gray,

1918)

Purkiss (2007) stated that fairies are very much like children who will not or cannot grow up, that even ancient nymphs often seem to seek to play house with the heroes they kidnap. It is common for many fairies to prefer the company of children to that of adults. The Buffardello of Lucca Italy, for example, would only show himself to children or to girls he fell in love with. The Buffardello would care for children, keeping them safe while causing trouble for adults. The house fairies of Scandinavia, known as Tomte, would also typically only reveal themselves to children with whom they would spend much of their time. In all these cases, the fairies themselves acted very much like the children they played with; going on little adventures, causing mischief, playing games, etc. (Keightley, 1892). In Britain, Robin Goodfellow himself was a trickster who loved to play jokes on people, especially those who were conceited, and he, too, would only appear to children in the form of a curly-haired boy so that he could join them in their games (Briggs, 1978).

Yet, despite the fact that fairies so often seem to get along better with children, most of them are ancient, being thousands of years old. Further, many fairies have almost no childhood at all, for they grow up within a few years or are born ancient from the very beginning. Dwarfs, for example, had matured after three years and were ancient by their seventh birthdays (Grimm, 1882). Zeus was fully grown within a year. Elves seem to have appeared fully grown, although they could later have children. In the fairy tale of "Daughter Snow and Son Fire," a woman has a daughter of snow with the spirit of winter who was able to walk and talk within a few months of being born (Wilislocki, 1892). Further, because of their immortal nature, even fairies that had a childhood would eventually only have the slightest inkling that they were ever young at all. This situation can lead them to desire the childhood they miss or could never have. Many fairies have some of the worst cases of Peter Pan Syndrome imaginable.

Consider that when fairies kidnap adults, the fairies most often replace them with objects that are made of dirt or wood, but are enchanted to appear to be corpses. Yet, when a fairy takes a human baby, they replace the child with old fairies in disguise. So when a fairy takes an adult, it's clear that what they are after is the adult because they leave the humans very little recourse to discover the deception or to force the fairies to return the person who was taken. Yet, by leaving an elderly fairy in place of a child, the fairies risk being found out because of the actions of the elderly fairy. Further, they risk having the fairy abused by the humans, as often happened. If all the fairies wanted was the child, then they would simply replace the child with clay or wood, magically disguised to appear as a dead child as they do with adults. By replacing children with older fairies, the fairies show that they are actively seeking to take the place of the child.

In history and our own society, we can see many child actors who grew up to seemingly seek after their childhood later. They sought to create a "Neverland" for themselves. By the same token, fairies live in a world filled with illusionary castles and make-believe parties. Again, within our own society, we see that those who had no childhood or who were famous as children often grow up to be mischievous; they pee in mop buckets and such, generally getting into or causing trouble once they are on their own. For their part, fairies, too, act the role of the mischief-maker by tying sleeping people's hair into knots, leading people astray, and more.

For many people, the desire to regain one's childhood is often overwhelming and present for nearly everyone. Movies are ripe with stories of people who wish to regain their youth, or to find the happiness they never had as a child. For such people, however, the rules of society, age, mortality, as well as the fact that no matter what they do they cannot look like children, prevents them from achieving childhood later in life. Fairies, however, can change their form at will, and they don't have the same social rules as humans. This lack of rules means that fairies can force their desire for a childhood on others and can eventually get away with nearly anything. For this reason, one can think of many fairies as being somewhat akin to the ultimate former child actors in personality. On the opposite side of this coin, however, is the fact that many who never had a childhood, who never had the opportunity to grow up, seek some way to do so, seek to mature. Often, they go about trying to mature, to act grown up in clumsy ways. Many become overly sexual, thinking perhaps that this is a way for them to enter the world of adulthood. In a similar fashion, many fairies become aggressively sexual, and clumsily try to imitate the world of mature humans.

Many Fairies are Kind and Caring

In the Spanish folktale "A Sprig of Rosemary" (Lang, 1897), the main character asks Sun for help, but Sun sends her on to Moon, who sends her on to Wind. And it is ultimately Spirit of the Wind, not Sun or Moon, who takes the time to help her. In the "White Bear," a girl searches for her husband and finds help from the kind and caring East, West, and South Winds. However, in the end, she is forced to seek help from the cantankerous and often dangerous North Wind, who at first doesn't care about her. However, upon hearing that she has lost her love, he transforms into a fatherly figure and provides her with the help necessary to regain her husband (Bunce, 1878).

This story shows that the wind and fairies in general can feel fatherly or motherly towards humans, perhaps in much the same way as we can feel fatherly towards orphan children in need or will take in stray animals. Indeed, even Baba Yaga, the grouchiest and perhaps one of the cruelest fairies can still feel kind-hearted emotions under the right set of circumstances.

Beyond such feelings of kindness, the wind also seems to have a great sense of fair play, despite its destructive nature; such that if one can seek it out, it will pay off the debts its nature incurs. In a Norse tale, the wind blows away a boy's lunch over and over again until at last, in frustration, the boy seeks it out and complains, at which point the wind provides him with a magical cloth, which will never run out of food (Dasent, 1904).

One of the primary roles of fairies in fairy tales is as the donor, the one who gives advice and magical items to the hero of fairy tales in order to help them find success or love. While it's true that many of these fairies don't do much in fairy tales other than this, it would be a mistake to think of them as trivial or emotionless characters. The fairies' actions tell us something important about the emotional nature of the fairies, who are willing to go so far out of their way to help someone whom they may not know at all. In order to understand the kindness of fairies better, I've broken it down into five primary types.

Santa Claus

Fairies are thousands of years old. In other words, to them, humans are all like children, so there are many fairies who can't help but act grandfatherly or grandmotherly towards us. Thus, Santa Claus, the most famous of all fairies, is not alone in having a jolly, joyful love of humanity, and a desire to bring gifts and luck to those who need or deserve it. In Wales, for example, it was believed that the Tylwyth Teg would leave money for the maids who had done a good job of keeping a home clean. Although true to fairy form, it was also said that no one should say that they had found this money, as the fairies would be offended if anyone told what they had done. Further, just as children are likely to do with Santa Claus, the maids would leave token gifts for the fairies, including a tin full of clean water at the foot of the stairs and bread on the table (Rhys, 1901).

In Spain, beautiful little forest fairies known as Anjanas would bring presents to the poor people of Catabria and help animals they found injured in the forests. An old jolly wind spirit, which traveled with funny-looking and goofy little fairy followers known as the Basadone in Italy, would comfort and protect children during storms. The old grandmotherly fairy Baba Marta of Bulgarian lore would banish the cold of winter in order to bring spring and would also protect people from evil spirits and sickness through her magical symbol; a series of red and white bands. In Ireland, Brigit helped keep children from becoming lost and brought the secrets of healing to wise physicians, while also giving power and virtue to the herbs (Young, 1910). And we can't forget the Fairy Godmother and similar fairies who gave gifts to help to poor girls and boys in countless fairy tales across the world. In Brittany, a girl named "Little White Thorn" encounters a little bird, who tells her that he is given the right to make one poor person, whom he chooses, rich every year (Masson, 1929).

Some jolly and cheerful old fairies would even take joy in hunting down the enemies of mankind. The Chuhayster in

Ukrainian lore, for example, were white- or black-haired old men who hunted the mavok, the forest spirits that would behead young men in the woods.

In another tale, nothing prospered for a poor farmer named Rowli Pugh. His wife was too sickly to help with the work, his crops were always poor, even when everyone else's were thriving, his house was damp, his roof leaked, and more. Finally, he was so poor he determined that he needed to sell everything he had and see if he could start over. That was when the tiny fairies known as ellyll appeared. The little fairies assured him that everything would be right if he would just leave a candle out for the fairies at night. From that night on, the fairies came and did the baking and brewing, washing and mending. More than that, the farm began to prosper, the crops were good, barns were tidy, and their cattle and pigs thrived and grew fat. Then, one night, the man's wife, Catti Jones, crept downstairs to get a peek at the fairies.

> There they were, a jolly company of ellyllon, working away like mad, and laughing and dancing as madly as they worked. Catti was so amused that, in spite of herself, she fell to laughing too; and at sound of her voice, the ellyllon scattered like mist before the wind, leaving the room empty. They never came back any more, but the farmer was now prosperous, and his bad luck never returned to plague him (Sikes, 1880).

Nostalgic Old Folks

Other fairies are more cantankerous or even cruel, rather than jolly, yet they hold a nostalgic and romantic view of adventure and love. Like the old man from Pixar's *Up*, they may have always dreamed of adventure, or of having a childhood, or of romance, and so will help those who are seeking specifically after these things. Recall, for example, that in the tale of "White Bear," the North Wind was at first furious at being disturbed. But when he learned that the heroine of the story was looking for her lost love, he became grandfatherly and came to care for her, going out of his way to help her find her love. So one can see in the character of the

North Wind a cantankerous old man who still likes to read good literature and watch opera and so enjoys taking part in a good romance. In the Russian fairy tales, Baba Yaga normally devoured humans, yet when a young man lost his love, he was able to approach her for advice and a hot meal, for she felt sympathy for that (Lang, 1890). In the German fairy tale, "The Nix of the Mill Pond," a mountain fairy helps a woman find her lost love who has been kidnapped by the nixes.

Although fairies will help people directly in such stories, they oftentimes tend to prefer to teach humans the skills they need to help themselves rather than giving them aid directly. For example, when one boy is tormented by his wicked stepmother, an old fairy comes to him and says, "Your stepmother is bad to you and in ill-will towards you.... If I give you a trade, will you be inclined to follow it?" (Wentz, 1911). In this story, the old fairy gives the boy a trade of becoming a bagpipe player, rather than simply giving the boy money to get out from under his wicked stepmother. It was also common for fairies to test humans by requesting that they do work, before the fairies would reward them for being "good."

In Greek, Russian, and Roman lore, nymphs, or beings very much like them, were the ones who found humans naked, bedraggled, and starving, and taught them how to make warm clothes, how to farm food, etc. It was the fairies who taught humans how to work in these lands, and while these fairies remain to help humans, they rarely show their interference in direct ways. Many other fairies, for example, prefer to give sage advice. One such was Billy Bind, a house fairy who would give advice to young people so that they could undo the magic of witches and find love. This advisory role was perhaps the most common role for fairies in fairy tales, in which the fairy would appear for a few moments to give sage advice to the hero or provide some magical item that the hero would need to complete his quest.

Lovers of Lost Puppies

Some fairies seemed to have loved humans the way a child might love a lost puppy. I use the comparison between fairies helping humans and children who find lost puppies because, like children, the fairies feel a lot of sympathy when they see those in need, but are prone to kick a puppy that snaps at them, as they don't entirely empathize with the way humans might be feeling.

In Russian lore, for example, "Grandfather Frost" pokes and prods the heroine and the heroine's wicked sister by making them colder and colder and then asking them how they are feeling. When the heroine responds positively, he takes her in and treats her well, yet when the heroine's sister does what most people would do and gets upset that he's hurting her, he kills her in a fit of rage (Ralston, 1880).

In the Hungarian tale of "Handsome Paul," a young man greets a giant by calling him "father," to which the giant replies, "You may think yourself lucky that you called me 'father,' for if you had not done so, I would have swallowed you whole." Like a child finding an animal, the giant is kind to those he finds lost if they do something immediately to put themselves in his good graces. So instead of eating the young man, the giant feeds him and helps him reach the distant kingdom he is journeying to (Gyula, 1896).

We see similar behavior at the opposite end of Europe, in Southern Ireland, where a hunchback named Lushmore is resting when he hears some fairy music. Although the music is beautiful, the words are repetitive and simple, so he adds a part to the song. The fairies, thinking his addition is wonderful, pull him into their party and treat him as an honored guest before at last removing the hump from his back. When a different hunchback comes and tries to add to the song in a clumsy way, he's punished with a second hump. So, while fairies can feel sympathy, like children they are quick to choose favorites and punish those whom they find annoying (Croker, 1825).

Finally, my last story illustrates the conflicted emotions of a child who finds a lost puppy in earlier times. An eight-year-old boy found a puppy in the 1800s that his mother wouldn't let him keep, so he hid it away. He gave up some of his own food to feed it, which was often a hard thing to do, given how little food he had. Eventually, his female puppy grew and went into heat, causing other dogs to come about, which was bad, as these dogs would grow violent when anyone would approach them. His mother complained, saying he needed to kill the dog. Soon, the boy's friends began to tease him, saying that he needed to hang and kill the dog as his mom had requested he do. At last, the boy could not take it anymore, so he finally led the dog to the river where he tried to hang her from a willow tree. The rope broke, however, and the poor dog plunged into the water.

> The children began to laugh. Altogether beside himself because of the laugher and his own failure, Fedka grabbed a handful of stones and used them to finish off the half-dead dog. He began to feel bad about it and headed home.... (Tian-Shanskaia, 1993)

This story is significant because it helps illustrate the harsh world in which the people who believed in fairies live: A world that was capable of compassion and caring, but which didn't always value life the way we do. It also shows that while any individual fairy might have cared, like the boy, they were still subject to outside pressures.

Sympathetic Giver

It's important to understand the kindness of fairies in fairy tales because it's so easy to begin to focus on their darkness, their shockingly cruel actions, and the fact that so many people feared fairies. After all, even when discussing the kindness of fairies, I still mention their cruelty. Fairies, however, are the source of good luck and life itself and, so very often, they are willing to sacrifice a lot to help humanity.

Those who had luck with fishing and hunting were believed to gain it from the fairies. In Kalasha lore, it was believed that when a hunter was successful, it was because one of the mountain fairies sent the animals to them so that they would have food (Jettmar, 1986). In Celtic lands, humans survived very often because of help from the fairies. For example, one man asserted that:

> The gentry have always befriended and protected me. I was drowned twice but for them. Once I was going to Durnish Island, a mile off the coast. The channel is very deep, and, at the time, there was a rough sea with the tide running out, and I was almost lost. I shrieked and

shouted, and finally got safe to the mainland. The day I talked with one of the gentry at the foot of the mountain when he was for taking me, he mentioned this, and said they were the ones who saved me from drowning then. (Wentz, 2011)

In Sami lore, the daughter of the sun watched humanity's struggles, both curious and somewhat afraid of them, yet she was still able to feel an intense sympathy for humans. So much sympathy, in fact, that she gave up her life in the heavens to live among and help us (Riordan, 1991). Similarly, a man whose wife was sick and dying, and whose children were starving, and who was worrying about what he'd do and how he'd get food meets a fairy woman that tells him how he might gain a great treasure (Lauder, 1881). The Virgin Mary, who in many tales is a replacement for a fairy figure, meanwhile appears and helps a teamster get his wagon unstuck, and even gives the teamster a bush of blooming roses (Lauder, 1881).

One Hellenistic poem sings praises to the Greek fairy figures with the following words:

> For the bristly-haired Pan and the nymphs of the grotto, the lonely herder Theudotos placed this gift under the crage, because when he was greatly weary from the summer heat, they refreshed him, offering honey-sweet water in their hands. (Larson, 2001)

In one Estonian tale, a girl whose wicked stepmother is cruel to her is taken in and adopted by the fairies to live happily in Fairyland, while a clay doll glamoured by the fairies to appear like her is sent to live what would have been her life of sorrow and suffering had they not intervened (Kirby, 1894).

Three brothers who found a fairy girl determined to raise her in secret, so:

> They sought out a place, a hidden green spot in the forest. They made a house, and there they nurtured the child in secret. Year by year, she throve and grew with them. Teigue brought her berries and taught her to play on a little reed flute. When she made music on it, the

wild creatures of the woods came about her. She played with the spotted fawns, and the king of the wolves crouched before her and licked her hands. Osric made a bow for her, and taught her how to shoot with arrows, but she had no wish to kill any beast, for all the forest-creatures were her friends (Young, 1910).

Here, too, the naturally gentle nature of the fairy comes forth, for while the fathers who raised her were warriors and hunters, the fairy girl was far too concerned with the welfare of the animals to hunt them.

Related

Many fairies are the ancestors of humans. For example, the fairy that helped the girl in many Cinderella stories was her mother, and an there was an Italian witch who stated that she gained her healing powers from the spirit of her uncle. I'll go into greater detail on this in the section that discusses how fairies were once human later in this book.

Fairies are Often Shy

Many people are more afraid of public speaking than they are of death. To some extent or another, we all are likely to understand the feeling of awkwardness, of being judged, the anxiety of being around certain other people. Nearly everyone has felt the desire to hide, to duck away in certain social situations. For fairies, this desire, like almost all their emotions, can become so intense they can hardly stand it. So intense, in fact, that often when these fairies are spied on, they'll sometimes fly into a rage, killing the person who spied on them or fleeing from the place, never to be seen again. For example, Goldemar of Vollmar, a household fairy of Germany, hated being spied on so much that when a servant strewed ashes on the floor in order to see his footprints, Vollmar killed and cooked him. He then ate the servant with cries of joy before leaving the house forever (Keightley, 1892).

In another case, a man attests that:

My grandfather, William Nelson, was coming home from the herring fishing late at night, on the road near Jurby, when he saw in a pea-field, across a hedge, a great crowd of little fellows in red coats dancing and making music. And as he looked, an old woman from among them came up to him and spat in his eyes, saying, "You'll never see us again"; and I am told that he was blind afterwards till the day of his death. He was certainly blind for fourteen years before his death, for I often had to lead him around; but, of course, I am unable to say of my own knowledge that he became blind immediately after his strange experience, or if not until later in life; but as a young man, he certainly had good sight, and it was believed that the fairies destroyed it. (Wentz, 2011)

In Romania, the Sânziană would fly about, giving blessings on June 24th. During this time, men had to stay inside because the Sânziană hated for men to see them so much that they would attack and maim any who did. Further, any man who heard them speaking would go mad from it. In Brittany, a fisherman sees through some fairy disguises at a fair where they are pretending to be fortune tellers and showmen, yet despite the fact that he says nothing about them to anyone, the fairies still poke out his eye with a stick to keep him from seeing them (Spence, 1917).

With their extreme response to social situations, one could even argue that fairies have something akin to social anxiety disorder, in which certain social situations cause them to panic. However, given their dual nature, this panic can lead to rage and wild destructiveness at times. At the same time, however, these same fairies are not shy around each other. Nor are fairies shy around humans in every situation; they will dance with them, tease them, and play with them. So there is more to this than a fear of social situations.

Part of this may be the fact that fairies are perhaps more easily embarrassed by humans, fearing that we won't understand them or may judge them. In lore, humans are descended from fairies, as will be discussed further in the section on how humans are related to fairies. Yet humans choose to grow up, to mature in ways that fairies never could, so in many ways they are like children to us. Further, fairies dislike the inconstancy of mankind, presuming that we are overly judgmental and worse, that we are duplicitous. Like a child faced with the scrutinizing gaze of a scary and overly judgmental adult, fairies often feel awkward by the attention of humans.

There are more practical reasons for fairies to be afraid of humans; humans, after all, are dangerous. There are many stories about humans kidnapping fairies to force them to become their wives or to steal their gold and for fairies, like the dwarfs and leprechauns, which guard gold and other treasures. It's practical for fairies to want to avoid human scrutiny and avoid encounters that could lead humans to try to steal from them. Perhaps worse still, a human gaze, along with negative judgment, is the formula for "the evil eye." The human gaze has power. According to Briggs, "An Irishman who had captured a leprechaun could keep hold of him only so long as he did not glance aside for an instant." In other words, a steady human gaze could prevent fairies from disappearing or exercising their powers. Humans, as we'll see further, are exercisers of an incredible array of magical powers that allow them to thwart and harm the fairy folk. Similarly, people in the Ukraine are very careful with their animals because they believe that if someone looks on one of their cows with envy, the power of the person's negative emotion and their look could spoil the cow (Kukharenko, 2007). In other words, human sight has strange and magical properties that can harm others, something the fairies would want to avoid.

Further, fairies are guardians of treasures and of secrets who hate to have their secrets revealed, as that would put their treasure at risk. For example:

> The peasantry in the Lough Gur region commonly speak of the Good People or of the Kind People or of the Little People, their names for the fairies. The leprechaun indicates the place where hidden treasure is to be found. If the person to whom he reveals such a secret makes it known to a second person, the first person dies, or else no money is found: in some cases, the money is changed into ivy leaves or into furze blossoms.

Or

An old woman, who I knew, used to find money left by the fairies every time they visited her house. For a long time, she observed their request, and told no one about the money; but at last she told, and so never found money afterwards. (Wentz, 2011)

Fairies, in general, are naturally secretive. They control fate and have their schemes, which they don't want to give up. For example, in Greece, one girl that the fairies are trying to turn into a fairy as well is told, "We shall help you again, but do not tell anyone about us. Do you understand? You must not speak of us to anyone." Yet, she does eventually tell and so the fairies' plans are thwarted by a cunning woman (Gianakoulis, 1930). Other times, the fairies want to keep their secrets to avoid having them fall into the wrong hands. When a man named Robert brags about being given the location of fairy treasures, the fairies nearly crush him with some rocks. Worse still, a girl named Kaddy tells her husband how she's been given money by the fairies, and they then kidnap him and her child from her (Emerson, 1894).

Betwixt and Between

Fairies are the moment when the coin is in the air, the time it hovers twirling, caught between two choices, between two opposites. As already mentioned, many fairies are wise, ancient beings, but they can never mature, so they are caught forever between childhood and adulthood. Fairies are always caught in a world between, a journey with no destination and perhaps no beginning. That fairies dwell in a world of in-between is both a function of what they are and what they choose to do. Fairies often seem to relish being in a state of between, appearing to people during times when they are between one state and another, such as adolescence, on journeys, at crossroads, at sunset, or midday, etc.

A Scottish witch named Espeth, for example, learned

that one fairy was a human who had died at twilight, a time of in-between, and so is forever caught between the world of the living and the dead (Purkiss, 2007). In another case, a boy who is wooing a fairy maiden in Wales brings her bread, but she will not accept her gift until he half bakes the bread, for she does not want it fully cooked or uncooked, but somewhere in between (Rhys, 1901).

When oracles perform a divination by asking the fairies a question, the fairies rarely give a straight answer. Rather, they often speak in riddles and rhymes. They force the person to go on journeys instead of giving them an easy way out. It would seem that fairies love journeys, and perhaps this is an advantage of their immortal lives. For while human art is defined by endings – songs with finales, paintings with exhibition, and plays with curtains closings – many fairies do not like such destinations and, as immortal beings, they never have to actually seek an ending. Their art can be a journey that never ends, but continues forever. For example, in a Czech tale, a prince gains some fairy-like companions on his journey, at the end of which he offers to allow them to live happily and have whatever they want, but what they want is to continue to journey (Fillmore, 1919).

Mischievous and Playful

Beautiful and seductive, she moves through the trees, lithely jumping branch to branch like a squirrel. Intrigued, the boy approaches her, eliciting a welcoming smile. She whispers gently in his ear before tickling him. At first, he laughs, enjoying the attention, but she doesn't stop. She keeps tickling and tickling; harder and harder he laughs. He wants to stop laughing, but he can't. It's hard to breathe, his lungs hurt. He starts to cough from laughing for so long and so hard, and eventually, she tickles him to death.

What are we to take from the strange behavior of the rusalka, a fairy of the water and forest that performs the bizarre act of seducing men so that it may tickle them to death? Similarly, gui, the Scazzamurrieddhru who guards graveyards at night will jump on people's chests if they enter at night, causing them to laugh themselves to death.

No matter how seemingly dangerous the fairy, they always seem to have some element of playfulness, even though their play can often turn deadly. Grimm (1882) asserts that

> At the bottom, all elves, even the light ones, have some devil-like qualities, e.g. their loving to tease men; but they are not therefore devils, not even the black ones, but often good-natured beings.

Fairies spend their nights dancing on hills, singing, partying, and trying to lure mortals to join them to the fairy realm where the mortals find themselves trapped forever, or where the humans dance until their legs are so worn away, they bleed to death. Because of their strange, internally dualistic natures, fairies are extremely playful and dangerous at the same time. This means that their version of play can be wanton, even cruel, like a boy pulling the legs off a grasshopper.

Others seem to be very much like humans who like to watch reality TV. These fairies enjoy watching extreme, over-the-top emotional reactions that come from their pranks. For example, the Anguana were water spirits from the Northern Italian Wilderness who loved to follow travelers to learn their gossip so that they could spread discord among them, causing wives to believe their husbands were cheating on them and so forth.

When the villagers in Germany held festivals and carnivals, the dwarfs would amuse themselves by seeking to outsmart them. When some young men held a grand ball, the dwarfs didn't want to let the opportunity pass without some prank. So three of the dwarfs snuck into the party and pretended to be humans in order to steal the pig that was going to be used for the feast (Jergerlehner, 1907), making the fairies seem like goofy frat boys.

Of course, fairies can be kind as well, even in their pranks. The dwarfs of Switzerland began to steal sheaves of corn from humans, leaving a dead horse in return for what they'd taken. Angered by the pathetic gift, a farmer took just enough to make a little bit of the horsemeat for his dog, but when he got home, he discovered that the flesh had turned into gold (Knightly, 1892).

Fairies often pay humans with seemingly meaningless objects: leaves, dirt, mud-objects that frustrate and annoy the humans, but which then turn into gold when the humans get home. Even when fairies make overly generous payments, they love to play pranks and pull tricks. Again, in Switzerland, it wasn't uncommon for fairies to perform tasks; finishing the building of homes, the sowing of fields, and performing other chores for humans before hiding and waiting for humans to come along. Then when the humans came along:

> They saw, to their astonishment, that the work was already done while the dwarfs hid themselves in the bushes and laughed aloud at the astonished rustics. Often, too, were the peasants incensed to find their corn, which was scarcely yet ripe, lying cut on the ground; but shortly after there was sure to come on such a hailstorm that it became obvious that hardly a single stalk could have escaped destruction had it not been cut. Then, from the bottom of their hearts, they thanked the provident dwarf-people (Keightley, 1892).

Whether they are helping or hurting, humanity's fairies are often playful in their actions. They are always children, immortal, and immune from any reprisal, and this makes them seek random bouts of humor. This playfulness is exemplified by one of the fairies' most famous features, that they are mischievous. Fairies love to lead people astray. In Wales, for example, people on journeys would find themselves walking past the place they were supposed to be because the fairies hid it with illusions. All over the world, in fact, fairies love to lead travelers astray to cause them to get turned around. Similarly, the Bysen of Swedish lore were small woodland fairies that distorted people's sight so as to make them go astray, but they didn't stop there. They would tip over people's loads of lumber, knock people down, and generally cause trouble, although in this case, their mischief may have had a purpose as they were trying to preserve the forest by interfering with the woodsman in it. True to fairy form, they were also their own opposites in that they would each cut down trees as well.

In another case, a man tells how:

> I heard of a man and wife who had no children. One night the man was out on horseback and heard a little baby crying beside the road. He got off his horse to get the baby, and, taking it home, went to give it to his wife, and it was only a block of wood. And then, the old fairies were outside yelling at the man: "*Eash un oie, s'cheap t'ou mollit!*" (Age one night, how easily thou art deceived!). (Wentz, 2011)

In an English fairy tale, "The Hedley Kow," the fairy for which the story is named takes the form of a pot filled with gold pieces so that a woman begins dragging him home with her. The Hedley Kow then proceeds to take less and less valuable forms in order to tease the woman (Jacobs, 1892). The Hedley Kow played other pranks as well, for example:

> Two young men of Newlands, near Ebchester, went out one evening to meet their sweethearts; and arriving at the trysting-place, saw them, as it appeared, a short distance before them. The girls walked on for two or three miles; the lads followed, quite unable to overtake them, till at last they found themselves up to the knees in a bog, and their beguilers vanished with a loud Ha! Ha! The young men got clear of the mire and ran homewards, as fast as they could, the bogie at their heels hooting and mocking them. In crossing the Derwent they fell into the water, mistook each other for the sprite, and finally reached home separately, each telling a fearful tale of having been chased by the Hedley Kow, and nearly drowned in the Derwent (Henderson, 2011).

Fairies rarely did any real damage with their pranks. Rather, it seems that a mixture of boredom, which comes from living forever, and their childlike nature along with their lack of any real accountability means that they love to play pranks. Yet, they will often try to make up for their mischief. For example:

> Ned Judge, of Sophys Bridge, was a weaver. Every night after he went to bed, the weaving started of itself, and when he arose in the morning, he would find the

dressing, which had been made ready for weaving so broken and entangled that it took him hours to put it right. Yet with all this drawback he got no poorer, because the fairies left him plenty of household necessaries, and whenever he sold a web [of cloth] he always received treble the amount bargained for. (Wentz, 2011)

Mutable, Anamorphic, Astral, Creators of Illusions

By nature, fairies tend to be in a state of change. According to Jacob Grimm, "The freest personality is proper to gods and spirits who can suddenly reveal or conceal their shape, appear and disappear. To man this faculty is wanting. He can but slowly come and go, and in his body he must abide." (Grimm, 1882) Fairies, it seems, are easily bored and so they love the strange and absurd. They are often very much like a child giggling at goofy rhymes and weird tales with no discernible plot.

What would it be like not to have any form? To be able to change and adjust at will; to be anywhere one wanted to be? Like all things fairy, this aspect of their nature can be both good and bad, freeing but confusing. Nothing is what it seems in the world of fairies. Castles turn out to be dark caverns, and caverns turn out to be bright palaces. Fairies are in and of themselves mutable beings, always changing form and type. When a fairy pays a human for services rendered, the enigmatic creatures are never satisfied with simply paying them in money. Fairies instead pay humans with dead horses, dried leaves, twigs, or other seemingly useless items. Items which will turn to gold, should the person be smart enough to bring it home with them.

There are a number of reasons why fairies might choose to live in a world of illusions. It may be that they do it because, as artists, they seek to create a more interesting and magical world than the one that exists. It may also be that they find the confusion amusing, or it may be that they are testing human faith. Remember that fairies were once worshiped. Just as many religious figures will tell a person to do something seemingly arbitrary in order to test their faith, so too could the fairies have sought to test human faith. It may be, however, that fairies don't have complete control over how they change. Indeed, it may be that they change in order to remain hidden from or play pranks on humanity. For example, many fairy celebrations and fairs are only visible to those who are far away from them. Yet as people walk closer and closer, they begin to fade until they vanish entirely, much like a rainbow; the fairies may be there but only as a trick of light that can be seen at a distance. So it's impossible at times to catch or touch them. The Boeman of the Netherlands changed shape in order to terrify and play pranks on people, acting as a bogyman figure that lives under beds or in basements. It may even be that the Boeman has no natural form of their own without humans. This last point is interesting, as it shows that many fairies may simply be a reflection of the world around them: A reflection that shows us what we want to see. In "Religion of the Ancient Celts," MacCulloch (1911) attests that:

> With the growth of religion, the vaguer spirits tended to become gods and goddesses, and worshipful animals to become anthropomorphic divinities with the animals as their symbols, attendants, or victims. And as the cult of vegetation spirits centered in the ritual of planting and sowing, so the cult of the divinities of growth centered in great, seasonal and agricultural festivals which were the key to the growth of the Celtic religion to be found. Yet the migrating Celts, conquering new lands, evolved divinities of war. Here the old, female influence was still at work since many of these were female....
> Most of the Celtic divinities were local in character; each tribe possessing its own group, each god having functions similar to those of other groups. Some,

however, had or gained a more universal character absorbing divinities with similar functions. Still, this local character must be borne in mind. The numerous divinities of Gaul, with differing names—but judging by their assimilation to the same Roman divinity, with similar functions are best understood as gods of local groups. Thus, the primitive nature spirits gave place to greater or lesser gods, each with his separate department and functions. Though growing civilization tended to separate them from the soil, they never quite lost touch with it. In return for man's worship and sacrifices, they gave life and increased victory, strength, and skill. However, these sacrifices had been and still often were rites in which the representative of a god was slain.

In other words, the spirits that controlled human fate waxed and waned according to human worship. In Russian lore, we see this very clearly. For example, one normally beautiful fairy was transformed into an ugly hag when humans disrespected her (Ivanits, 1992). These fairies may not have been so free after all, for they might have been, at least in part, defined by the thoughts of the people who surrounded them. In this sense, when humans wished for fairies to be beautiful, powerful beings that would make their crops grow, it was so. Later, as humans wanted them to be devils or faded souls, it again became so. Finally, when humans stopped caring about fairies, they ultimately vanished altogether. We see this idea repeated in modern fairy tales. For example, in the tale of *Peter Pan*, every time someone says they don't believe in fairies, a fairy dies and we must show our belief to bring them back to life.

Of course, MacCulloch's assertion that deities and fairies altered to match human culture doesn't guarantee that they are the ones being altered. It may be that they were altering the societies that they led in order to achieve their own ends. What's most likely, however, and perhaps the most interesting possibility as far as stories are concerned, is that humans bend fairies just as they are bent by fairies. Michelangelo stated that he was simply bringing out of the rock the sculpture, which God had put in it, yet to some extent, he was clearly shaping the rock. Great directors adjust their work to fit scripts, actors, and other challenges and opportunities they are given. For a purely amorphous artist, it may be that art creates the artist even as they create their art.

Beyond the fact that fairies might change form to fit human thinking and attitude, fairies could have a number of reasons for creating illusions.

Illusions to Play Tricks

As previously discussed, fairies are mischievous; they love to play pranks on people and will often use their powers of illusion to do this. For example, when a man was traveling through Cornwall, he kept getting lost in the fog. Yet, when he stopped to ask for help, he was informed by a couple that there was no fog at all. The fairies, they told him, must be playing tricks on him by creating illusions of fog where there was non,e as well as of houses where there were forests and forests where there were houses (Bottrell, 1870).

To Imagine a Better World

As I'll discuss later, many fairies are refugees, living on bad food in rundown caverns and under people's houses. Their lives are miserable. It's no wonder that they create illusions of fabulous feasts, of soaring and beautiful castles, of great halls. For them, illusions are an escape, a way to pretend that their lives are better than they truly are.

To Play Games

As childlike beings, fairies often use their illusions to play games or to show off. One fairy girl used her powers to make animals out of ashes and soot when she was playing with a human child (Keightley, 1870).

Illusion to Teach a Lesson

Fairies are the enforcers of morality, the teachers of

humanity, and sometimes, they teach their lessons with illusions. In one case, they taught people that greed was wrong by creating the illusion of gold and jewels in order to try to get people to give up these things willingly, and to show those that didn't that such things were in fact illusions (worthless stones).

Illusions to Remain Hidden

Fairies are shy, so they use their illusionary powers to hide their homes, to turn invisible, to appear as animals, and to avoid human contact.

Fairies Can See the Future

The fairy's ability to see the future would have a huge impact on their decisions and emotions. On the one hand, the ability to see the future would allow them to make better decisions, to know if they should help some poor person, or if the person would become greedy and corrupt once the fairies helped them become wealthy. It would let them know which child wandering in the woods would grow up to become a bandit and which would grow up to become a farmer. In other words, when fairies look at someone, they don't just see who they are, but who they will become and so all the fairies' decisions and actions would be based on this.

More than simply altering their decisions, the ability to see the future means that fairies know who they will love before they meet them. Indeed, when a girl wanted to know who she would marry in the future, she would often ask the spirits to give her a vision. This means that the fairies could seek out someone who they would be in love with before they ever met them. In essence, seeing possibilities allows fairies to truly plan and shape the world. The word "fate," after all, originally meant something akin to "what fairies choose to happen." This means that, as artists of fate, they can work on a piece of art that will come to fruition thousands of years in the future, rather than simply focusing on the here and now.

Further, through their ability to see the future, fairies

could warn others to prepare for danger. The Grant, for example, is a fairy creature who would appear as a horse and run about towns to frighten people and cause a ruckus with the dogs so everyone would know in advance that a fire was about to start (Keightley, 1892).

There are disadvantages to seeing the future as well, however, for fairies must live with the pain of failure, and the pain of knowing that a loved one will die before the event even happens. This means that fairies suffer with anxiety and loss longer than any human does, so long that many banshees have red eyes from crying long and hard because they've seen their loved ones die, over and over and over again before it even happens. It may be, then, that part of the reason fairies throw such wild parties is to have some means of drowning their sorrows.

Death Is a Beginning, Not an End

For many fairies, death can be likened to birth. After all, many fairies began their journey in Fairyland as the spirits of humans who died. Their real joy and fulfillment then didn't come until after they had died, which means that they view death completely differently than humans would. When a fairy "kills" someone, they aren't always ending them, but sometimes helping them advance along their path. In other words, the fairies are taking someone to the fairy realm. For example,

> There used to be an old piper called Flannery who lived in Oranmore, County Galway. I imagine he was one of the old generation. And one time the good people took him to Fairyland to learn his profession. He studied music with them for a long time, and when he returned he was as great a piper as any in Ireland. But he died young, for the good people wanted him to play for them. (Wentz, 2011)

In this case, the fairies trained a musician who turned out to be so good, they couldn't stand to part with him, so they took him back to Fairyland with them, leaving his dead body behind. In a world inhabited by fairies, one could imagine that this is why so many great artists die young. But it wasn't just artists who were taken, as I already mentioned; it was once believed that sometimes children would live with the nymphs when they died and, as I'll explain more in the section about human spirits who become fairies, there are many humans who become fairies for a number of reasons.

Enforcers of Morality

Most fairies are obsessed with morality and traditions. They have a clear sense of how the world should work, of how people should act, and of what is right and wrong for humanity. The Domovoi of Russia, for example, would punish women for going outside without covering their heads first, or for spinning thread on Friday. Further, when the family was sloppy, used foul language, or did other similar things, the Domovoi would punish them by acting like a poltergeist. He would tangle their needlework, spread manure on the door, turn everything upside down, and generally cause mischief (Ivanits, 1992). Similarly, in Britain, "One of the principle characteristics of the brownie was his anxiety about the moral conduct of the household to which he was attached." He would report lazy servants to the master of the house, which of course often led the servants to view him with a mix of hate, fear, and respect (Douglas, 1901). In Ireland, a fairy disguised himself as a beggar to test the generosity of the royal family. And in so doing, he discovered the greedy and uncaring nature of the royal family. To punish them, he kidnapped the greedy princesses and queen, telling their greedy fiancées and husband: "Bid your daughters and your brides farewell for a while. That wouldn't have happened you three, only for your want of charity... Bad people, if they were rolling stark naked in gold, would not be rich." (Kennedy, 1891)

Oftentimes, these fairies were enforcers of morality because humans were descended from them. In Greek lore, for example, the hero Arkas came upon Chrysopeleia, a hamadryad, whose oak was falling over because of a stream that had swollen from snow melt. To save the hamadryad's oak, he rerouted the stream and, in so doing, won her affection. Together, they had two children, "Elatos and Aphidamas," from whom all Arkadians were descended (Larson, 2001). For centuries this nymph was grandmother to the people of the land where she lived and, like any grandmother with high morals, she would have expected her grandchildren to follow a certain moral code. Indeed, nymphs had some of the strictest moral codes of any divine being, even if these didn't always fit current ideas of propriety. For example, while one nymph was willing to sleep with a man named Rhoikos for saving her tree, she was not willing to put up with foul language. After agreeing to sleep with him, she used a bee as a messenger between them, a bee that later witnessed Rhoikos using foul language for which the nymph punished him horribly.

Bees were the symbol and messengers of the nymphs because they held many of the nymphs' strict ideals. Bees and nymphs are both lovers of cleanliness, neatness, and hard work. In Greek lore, bees were more likely to sting those who were unclean, who committed adultery, or did other reprehensible things that made them unclean. Those raised by nymphs were taught not only about divination and the magical world; they were taught the rural arts, how to work, and about a strict code of morality. Thus, the hero Aristaios, who was given the secret to many of the rural arts, which he then taught to others, was also taught how to live a virtuous life. Nymphs taught humans to weave and how to dress modestly, they taught humans about the importance of marriage, and how to observe divine law. It was even the nymphs who taught humans to eat healthy foods and that cannibalism was wrong (Larson, 2001).

It might seem oddly hypocritical that the nymphs should sleep with whomever they wished, or that they would run around naked, yet expect modesty from humans. One must bear in mind, however, that nymphs are thousands of years old. To them, humans, all humans, are children and most people realize that there are certain things children are not sexually ready for.

In addition to being related to humans, other fairies are perfectionists who, as artists, may be seeking to help people find the meaning of life. Or as kind and generous beings, fairies concern themselves with human happiness and believe that morality is the only way for people to achieve true happiness. Rather than sit by and lecture people, fairies tend to enforce their strict moral codes through blessings and punishments. In lore, fairies will often test people to determine if they are worthy of gifts and help, or if they should be punished. Even Santa Claus does this, deciding "who's naughty and nice," then giving rewards to moral children and, at one time, punishments to those who didn't fit within these morals.

We see this clearly in the story of the Golden Harp (Griffis, 1921), in which three men are actually "fairies in disguise who come to reward all those who gave them help." This is an act designed to help keep people moral. In said story, the fairies travel from door to door and ask for alms, and when the protagonist of the story gives it to them, the fairies give him a magical harp, which allows him to play beautiful music. However, he abuses the harp's power by using it to force a rival to dance himself to exhaustion. Because of this, the fairies come and take their gift back. The fairies' purpose in this story is clearly to make people moral rather than to reward people for good deeds done towards them.

> *"You'll have the land and food you wish*
> *for as long as you remain hospitable."*
> *(Bryuhanov, 1991) Georgian fairy to his host...*

One of the most famous fairy tests in Ireland was a lot more difficult than simply giving alms to those in need. This test was given by Cailleach, who before becoming a fairy-like being, was in lore a beautiful woman who had been used by kings and heroes, then tossed aside. After she had died childless, she became a powerful fairy, a horrifying hag, at least in appearance. In this hag form, she stopped the three sons of Eochaid Muigmedon from getting a drink of water from a well unless they kissed her. The one who was willing to kiss her, to look past her outside appearance (or perhaps was willing to sacrifice more to do what needs to be done for his people?) was proven the true heir to the throne (Purkiss, 2007).

In Celtic lore, one man asserts that;

The gentry take a great interest in the affairs of men,

and they always stand for justice and right. Any side they favor in our wars, that side wins. They favored the Boers, and the Boers did get their rights. They told me they favored the Japanese and not the Russians, because the Russians are tyrants. Sometimes they fight among themselves. One of them once said, "I'd fight for a friend, or I'd fight for Ireland (Wentz, 2011).

In the Hartz Mountains of Germany, the Princess Ilse turns a magician named Castiglione into a fir tree for approaching her with falseness in his heart. While across the border in Poland, the mining spirits known as Skarbnik would become angry and destructive if they saw laziness. Indeed, laziness is perhaps one of the greatest sins a person can commit against many of the most important fairies. House fairies, for example, grew furious at those who were slothful. The spirits of mines and other labors such as spinning would punish those who didn't perform chores. Even princesses who find themselves lost in the woods as Snow White did would need to work in order to prove they were deserving of help from fairies.

In the story of *Mother Hulda* (Grimm, 2008), a girl's wicked stepmother forces her stepdaughter to do all the work. As this poor stepdaughter is spinning outside the cottage, she drops her spindle into the well. Fearing her stepmother more than the depths of the well, the girl dives into it. Instead of splashing into deep water, however, she finds herself in another world with a woman who keeps her as a maid for weeks. Because she is so respectful, Hulda comes to be very impressed with the girl and gives her gold as a reward. When her stepdaughter returns home with these riches the stepmother becomes jealous and sends her own daughter out. Because her own daughter is idle and disrespectful, however, Hulda punishes her.

In addition to being lovers of hard work, fairies are lovers of the truth, who will almost never tell a direct lie or break a promise; even if they might distort or bend the truth or promises. Further, they expect humans to remain truthful as well and will punish those who lie. In the story of *Old Gwilym*, the fairies punish a man for spending all the money on drinking (and likely trying to hide it from his wife) by stealing his clothes and leaving him in a bramble bush

(Emerson). When a Ben-Varrey girl (a mermaid from the Isle of Man) steals a doll from a human girl, her mother tells her to bring a necklace of pearls to the human to atone for what she's done. Even the normally feared bogles could hate theft and lies.

> A Bogle, or something akin to one, appears, however, in the following narration as the protector of a poor widow. At the village of Hurst, near Eeeth, lived a widow who had been wronged out of some candles by a neighbor. This neighbor saw one night a figure in his garden, so he brought out his gun and fired it, upon which the figure vanished. The next night while he was in an outhouse the figure appeared in the doorway and said, " I'm neither bone, nor flesh, nor blood, thou canst not harm me. Give back the candles, but I must take something from thee." So saying he pulled an eyelash from the thief's eyelid and vanished. The candles were promptly restored the next morning, but the thief "twinkled" ever after (Henderson, 1879).

Finally, many fairies are known to travel about and punish those who have messy homes, or who mistreat their families, and those who act greedy or lazy are also likely to take ill, lame, or even be killed by the angry fairies. At the same time, those who are neat and tidy, kind and generous, are very likely to be rewarded. Fairies are so obsessed with morality that a lack of morality can drive them away as happened in Eastern Europe where:

> As men had departed from their old virtues, when the shepherds had thrown away their flutes and drums and songs, and had taken whips into their hands and commenced to crack them in their pastures, cursing and swearing, and when, finally, the first reports of guns were heard, and nations began to make war against each other, the Vily left the country and went to foreign lands. That is why only very few chance to see them dancing in the fields, or sitting upon a bare rock or a deserted cliff, weeping and singing melancholy songs.

In like manner, the Slovenians believe that the fairies were kind and well disposed toward human beings, telling them what times were particularly suitable for ploughing, sowing, and harvesting. They themselves also took good care of the crops, tearing out weeds and cockles; and in return for all this, they asked for some food, which they ate during the night. So long as their anger was not aroused, they would appear every summer; but when mankind commenced to lead a sinful life, and when whistling and shouting and cracking of whips began to increase in the fields, the Vily disappeared, never to return. (Gray, 1918)

What we see is that fairies were greatly saddened when humanity lost its moral center; so sad that they began lamenting, crying, and singing melancholy songs. Eventually, these fairies could not stand to remain around humanity, they couldn't stand to watch what we were doing to ourselves, so in their sorrow, they left us.

Enforcers of Fun

Of course, morality isn't all about hard work, as already mentioned. The Domovoi punished those who spun thread on Friday, which is to say they demanded that people take a break from work. Fairies often demanded that people rest and relax. On Nicholas's Day, it was shameful in Russia not to get drunk, while certain fairies of Wales were believed to hate teetotalers, who never drank (Sikes, 1880). On many days, throughout Europe, fairies demanded that people rest, that they celebrate, that they have fun. Those who didn't, who tried to look better than others by working hard on days of relaxation, would be punished by the fairies.

Robin Hood and the Fairy Queen

A few hundred years after the fall of the Western Roman Empire, a woodsman was working in a glade of trees when he was overcome by a swarm of flies. Soon after, he retreated into the wilderness for over two years. When he finally emerged from the forest, dressed in the skins of wild animals, he himself had grown a bit wilder. More than this, however, he claimed to be the Messiah. To prove this, he began to heal the sick and soon he'd gathered a group of about three thousand followers. Followers he ordered to begin robbing from the rich to give to the poor. Eventually, he was labeled a heretic, and accused of using magic to deceive people (McCall, 1979). Within this story, we see the remnants of Europe's shamanistic past cropping up, as it so often does, long after it was supposed to have been stamped out. For the story of this woodsman's journey to becoming a healer, a "Messiah," didn't begin in a church; it began in a glade of trees. But these trees were once a church, for Europe's pagans believed that such glades held the gods in them. These were not the all-powerful gods we think of today, for at times, woodsmen could terrorize these spirits' lives by threatening to cut down their tree, sparing them only in return for granting wishes. Among the Mari-El, the story of a woodsman doing this ends well (Zeluna), with the woodsman forcing the spirit of the tree to make him rich and powerful; while among the English a similar tale ends with the fairy tricking the woodcutter, as so often happens.

It is the flies in the woodsman's story, however, that point me to Europe's shamanistic past; for the souls of the dead, fairies, and other spirits were often believed to appear in the form of flies, as well as in the form of butterflies, birds, and other flying animals. So, as with many shamans of Eurasia, this man was surrounded by a swarm of something that symbolized spirits, after which he fled into the woods as if he'd become possessed by these spirits. At this point, he was no longer in control; when he emerged from the woods, he had strange powers and abilities and, as with the shamanistic sorcerers of Russia, he soon gathered an army of followers and eventually had to be stopped by the authorities from growing too powerful.

One can't help but see a bit of Robin Hood in the story

of this woodsman, who becomes the focus for a rebellion against greedy nobility and so led an army of bandits to rob from the rich and give to the poor. In fact, this story may have a lot to do with Robin Hood's tale, as nearly a thousand years later, in the fifteen hundreds, during the time of Robin Hood's first ballads bandits, poachers and rebels began springing up all over England, claiming to be "Servants to the Queen of the Fairies" (Purkiss, 2007). Even the first ballad about Robin Hood seems to allude to his own service to "The Queen of the Fairies." This first ballad, "Robin Hood and the Monk" tells of Robin Hood's great devotion to the Virgin Mary, who was often a replacement for The Queen of the Fairies in English and French lore; while in Germany, "The Key Fairy of the Grünstersburg," the Virgin is the ruler of the fairy realm (Lauder, 1881). While Robin is in the midst of his devotion to the Virgin Mary, a monk sees him and reports him to the sheriff, thus casting Robin Hood against the greediest elements of the Medieval Church, rather than on the side of the Church. Even as late as the eighteen hundreds, a beautiful maiden dressed in gray appeared to the Rebel Lord Derwentwater as he was resting under the trees. She gave him a talisman (crucifix), which would protect him against sword or bullet (Balfour, 1904). In these stories, fairies or spirits of some form order people to rob from the rich to give to the poor. More than just stories about bandits, these tales give us an important insight into the nature of the fairies, which is that fairies loved the people.

    The fairies of lore were commonly depicted as champions of the people, as haters of greed and poverty. Many fairies were, in essence, the Gods of the Harvest and the Hearth, so people believed that they were the ones who helped them to get food. Yet, despite the best efforts of the Fairies of the Harvest, people often starved, even during years that yielded a decent crop. This starvation occurred in large part because the nobility and church would take around 50% of a family's income in taxes, tithes, and various fees. Further, while fairies demanded hard work, the nobility didn't work, except to wage war, which further hurt those who did work hard. One shouldn't be surprised to find that the fairies would hate and resent the nobility. It would be a mistake, however, to think that fairies are communist in sensibility; they clearly help some people become rich and cause others to fail. Rather, fairies believe that people should be rewarded based on their merits (or based on friendship with the fairies) and often the nobility didn't merit the life they were living.

Perhaps the most interesting thing that fairies leading rebellions tells us is that fairies want to be involved with humans; they aren't, as so often is depicted, shy, evasive woodland creatures who avoid humanity. Rather, they purposefully go out of their way to involve themselves in human affairs, to manipulate and alter the course of human history, to reward and punish, and to transform the very fabric of human society.

Immunity and Immortality

Diplomatic immunity, which allows people to park anywhere they wish, drive how they wish, etc., encourages people to act differently from the way one might normally behave. Diplomatic immunity itself, however, is not true immunity, as the diplomat's job is to make the citizens of the country they are in like them or their employers. Fairies have no such needs, however, so they are oftentimes truly immune from the punishments that haunt the mortal world, even from death itself. Such immunity alters their perception of things. Nixes, nymphs, and satyrs need not fear reprisals for their actions, and so their desires are rarely ever tempered by anything. In such cases, then, a fairy becomes pure desire, mating and dancing, living for the moment because there is no need to worry about anything else. Not even the freest of humans can do this for long because eventually mortality will crash down on them, or eventually other humans will tire of their actions and they'll be restrained.

> The Russian peasant draws a clear line between his own domovoi and his neighbor's. The former is a benignant spirit who will do him good even at the expense of others; the latter is a malevolent being who will very likely steal his hay, drive away his poultry, and so forth, for his neighbor's benefit. Therefore,

incantations are provided against him some of which the assistance of "the bright gods" is invoked against "the terrible devil and the stranger domovoi." The domestic spirits of different households often engage in contests with one another, as might be expected, seeing that they are addicted to stealing from each other's possessions. Sometimes, one will vanquish another, drive him out of the house he haunts, and take possession of it himself. When a peasant moves into a new house in certain districts, he takes his own domovoi with him, having first, as a measure of precaution, taken care to hang up a bear's head in the stable. This prevents any evil domovoi, whom malicious neighbors may have introduced, from fighting with and perhaps overcoming the good Lar Familiaris. (Ralston, 1872)

Why should the domovoi act so callously towards other families and each other? After all, in life, it is unlikely that people stole from their neighbors very often, so why should they do so in death? Perhaps the answer lies in simple immunity, immortality, and a more extreme set of emotions as well as the greater connection to their conflicting souls. For unlike humans, the domovoi are essentially immune from the harm they do. They cannot be put in prison for stealing or helping their family get ahead of another family by causing trouble the way a human could be. Thus, they are more likely to act on their negative and greedy impulses than a human would. Further, as time goes on, what the domovoi cares about will change as immortality itself will greatly alter a fairy's perceptions of the world. Mountains rise and fall, trees grow and die, and even the stars shift their courses over time. Time changes so much that even for humans, growing older means that little things seem to matter less and less. After a while, the latest fashions, brands, and other such crazes are just other events that will pass. Imagine what it would be like to live for thousands of years and you will come to a closer understanding of the emotions of fairies. After thousands of years of life, very little would seem to matter. Any kingdom might simply be just another kingdom, and any mortal is just another life in an infinite string of meaningless and temporary lives. This means that the domovoi and the vampire would, over time, come to care less about outside people.

Immortality can also cause fairies to hate the new, just as elderly people are stereotyped to. In German mythology, wood wives demanded that humans not use the new recipes that called for baking bread with caraway or cumin in them. Water wives didn't like the touch of new clay pots in Welsh mythology. Dwarfs called humans fickle creatures because humans constantly changed as time passed (Grimm, 1882). Immortality also means that to the fairies, it must seem that humans are the ones who are always changing not only in mood, but in the very ways in which they choose to function. A fairy, for example, might be loyal to a household or kingdom for thousands of years while the people within the household could change their loyalties dozens of times. Being immortal alters not only what fairies care about, but what they understand to be fickleness.

Trickster Figures

Trickster characters tend to be clever and intelligent beings who are footloose and oftentimes very irresponsible. On top of this, they have strong desires for food, drink, sex, and pleasure, which can make them seem fairly selfish, as they are willing to lie, steal, and cheat nearly anyone to get what they want. Their cleverness and strong emotions also mean that fairies have a great desire for merriment, for laughter and humor. The problem is that because fairies are often selfish, they can easily become mean spirited, with their jokes often taking the form of pranks.

This is not to say of that fairies are uncaring. After all, it shouldn't be so surprising that those who seek pleasure might also seek the joy that comes from helping those in need. And should helping those in need require tricking or stealing from a wealthy being, so much the better.

Murderous, Blood Thirsty, and Vampiric

Fairies crave the taste of blood, for blood has magical energy, life, and a strange power all its own. Witches will often summon spirits with drops of blood and build good relationships with their familiar spirits by allowing them to suck their blood. In Ireland people feared that the smell of blood would make the fairies hungry (Purkiss, 2007), while in Scotland wives would set out bowls of water as offerings to the fairies so they wouldn't get thirsty and drink human blood during the night (Campbell, 1900).

The fairies who were the souls of the dead come in many forms, some not so kind. In Scotland, the restless dead, known as the sluagh, who were rejected by heaven, hell, and the fairies themselves, would fly in flocks, searching like vultures for those who were dying so that they could carry their souls away. This notion, that fairies would kidnap the souls of innocent people to serve them as slaves, was common throughout Europe.

In the story of "Lady Isabel," a woman is seduced by a handsome elf-knight who leads her off into the forest, where he tells her that he is going to murder her. When she pleads for her life, he tells her, "Seven king's-daughters here hae I slain. And ye shall be the eight o them." In one final act of desperation, Isabel has sex with the elf-knight until he falls asleep and then she kills him with his own sword, declaring that he will now be husband to all those women he has murdered (Lady Isabel).

Handsome and seductive, the elf-knight in this story plays the perfect serial killer. Yet his story isn't isolated; elves were commonly believed to play the role of seducer, kidnapper, and murderer. In the fairy tale "Childe Rowland," the Elf King kidnaps a beautiful young girl and takes her to his kingdom. Then when the hero comes to save her on the advice of Merlin, the Elf King calls out the famous lines *"Fee Fi Fo Fum, I smell the blood of an English Man,"* at which point he threatens to make the man's brains into a delicious pudding (Jacobs, 2004).

In the story of the Hobyahs, some fairies come to a house chanting, "Eat up the old man and woman, and carry off the little girl!" When eventually the Hobyahs succeed, they place the little girl in a bag and knock on the top over and over again, calling, "Look me! Look me!" before at last going to sleep, because like vampires, Hobyahs sleep during the daytime (Jacobs, 2004).

The Germanic alp (elf) would drink the blood from the nipples of children and men. Yet they weren't quite vampires, for their favored food was milk, which they would drain from cows and the breasts of women. This, however, is still much like vampires, who would also seek after milk as well as blood. Similar to many of our conceptions about vampires, the alps stalked the night because they didn't like light, so much so that even a nightlight could help keep them away. They were not destroyed by the light, however, as they did come out in the day time in order to fire their infamous invisible arrows, which caused illness in people and animals.

As magical beings, these alps used a magical hat to turn invisible and could shape-shift to take any form they wanted; however, whether they appeared as a horse or snake, their hat was always a dead giveaway of their origins. This is in contrast to vampires, who could shape-shift at will without any magical item.

The elves' dark nature is not to say that elves weren't elegant, beautiful beings. They were mentioned as a tribe of beings similar to the gods of old Germanic lore, and Loki was even called an elf. Although it's perhaps telling that Loki, the one who betrayed the other gods and is said to be raising an army to bring about the end of the world, was the god who was called an elf.

Another fairy known as the "Red Cap" lived in spots related to the tyranny that existed on the Border Lands such as castles, towers, and peel houses. This spirit was perhaps an undead reverent as well, for it was said that the foundations of the castles in the Border were bathed with human blood by their builders, the Picts. In many ways, this spirit resembles vampires very closely; he has long, prominent teeth and sharp talons, as well as strong features. Like many vampires, he's fairly territorial, attacking those who come into his territory, assaulting and killing them so that he may catch his blood in his cap. Further, he is driven away by the presented cross (Henderson, 1879).

What's important to recall in many, if not most of these cases, is that blood has power, especially for those who are dead, and many fairies are the spirits of the dead. Because blood gives power to the dead, one could also make the argument that blood is in essence vitality, so when fairies steal a person's life, when they cause someone to wither and die, they may in fact be eating away at the spiritual essence of their lives, just as they eat the goodness out of foods without touching the material substance.

Many fairies seemed to steal this substance from people, for people often pined and died after encounters with the other world. One man encountered two elle maids (elves), lost his senses, and died shortly after that. Another boy who encountered an elle maid presented a young man her breast from which to drink. Unable to resist, he did so and, because of this, he lost all his senses and nearly died. Yet, curiously, his life was saved because he ate some meat shortly thereafter, perhaps because the eating of human food helps to keep one anchored in the human plane. Yet, he never recovered the use of his reason (Keightley, 1892).

Although the elle maids in these stories drank no blood that we know of, their actions were very much like those of vampires, seducing people and then draining away their sanity and life.

One of the most common things that fairies demanded from people in return for supernatural aid was blood. People, at one time, would hang heads of animals killed during a hunt or impaled sacrifices among their branches. In Finland, people would worship in their sacred groves where they would hang the skins of sacrificial victims from the trees within a sacred grove (Frazer, 1922).

Such actions show us that tree fairies were interested in collecting pieces of the dead; on the Steppes, people hung animals from trees as these were thought to be a way to transport the sacrifices to the deities in the sky. A number of human interactions with tree spirits involved actual sacrifices. When the Rus would travel down the Dnieper River to trade with Byzantium, they would sacrifice chickens to the gods in thanks for their success of making it through the dangerous lands to the north. These sacrifices would then be placed around a giant oak tree (Davidson, 1989). Should a woodsman worry that they had accidentally cut down a sacred tree, they would behead a hen on its stump with the axe they'd used to cause it harm (Frazer, 1922). Further, Julius Caesar claimed that the Celts performed human sacrifice in their open-air, sacred groves.

It's clear that the peoples of ancient Europe believed that trees desired offerings of dead bodies as well as direct sacrifices. The question is: "What is it that these humans believed the trees got out of this? What was the purpose for these sacrifices?" A number of possibilities present themselves. First, it is possible that sacrifices of the skins and heads of animals were made at least initially for the same reasons that people would carve statues as a form of sympathetic magic meant to help insure success in future hunts. By the same token, such offerings might have occurred as a sign of respect for the animals, to help pacify them because it was believed that their spirits would ultimately be reincarnated. So in order to have successful future hunts, it was necessary to do something to make certain the animal stayed in the area. Hanging them on the local god might have been a way of insuring that this happened.

Another possibility is that it was believed that these sacrifices could provide the spirits of the trees and forests with strength, which the trees would in turn provide to the hunters and warriors in the form of luck and success. Trees needed additional strength because, like humans, fairies go to war with each other. It is also possible that the humans were seeking to provide the tree with additional strength so the tree would be in a better position to support humans in their endeavors. Still, it's important to keep in mind that people feared trees. For within the sacred groves of the Celtic, Germanic, and Baltic peoples, silence reigned supreme as even the greatest adepts feared to set foot during certain hours of the day, lest they interrupt the fairies within them. As with all fairies, people were always careful to pay tree fairies the utmost respect. As Tacitus pointed out:

> No person enters it (the sacred grove) without being bound with a chain as an acknowledgment of his inferior nature and the power of the deity residing there. If he accidentally fall(s), it is not lawful for him to be lifted or to rise up; they roll themselves out along the ground. The whole of their superstition has this import: that from this spot the nation derives its origin; that here is the residence of the Deity, the Governor of all,

and that everything else is subject and subordinate to him (Tacitus, 98).

People were afraid of trees and forests even as they were awed by them. So the relationship between humans and fairies wasn't necessarily the purely loving relationship many people think of now when they think of deity and human relations. It is rather a relationship in which the trees are extremely dangerous, even to those who respect them. That trees could crave blood is made most clear by an old punishment for those who hurt them.

> The old German laws for such as dared to peel the bark of a standing tree. The culprit's navel was to be cut out and nailed to the part of the tree, which he had peeled, and he was to be driven round and round the tree till all his guts were wound about its trunk. The intention of the punishment clearly was to replace the dead bark by a living substitute taken from the culprit; it was a life for a life, the life of a man for the life of a tree. (Frazer, 1922)

This type of punishment is interesting because it shows more than simply the brutality with which ancient groves were defended. It shows us that living animals could be used to heal the tree and potentially provide them with power. Yet it wasn't just blood to heal that fairies were after, as at other times, the fairies seem to actually have been cruel and vindictive. In one story:

> A man's wife was carried away by the fairies; he married again, but one night, his first wife met him, told him where she was, and besought him to release her, saying that if he would do so she would leave that part of the country and not trouble him anymore. She begged him, however, not to make the attempt unless he were confident he could carry it out, as if he failed she would die a terrible death. He promised to save her, and she told him to watch at midnight, when she would be riding past the house with the fairies; she would put her hand in at the window, and he must grasp it and hold tight. He did as she bade him and, although the

fairies pulled hard, he had nearly saved her, when his second wife saw what was going on, and tore his hand away. The poor woman was dragged off, and across the fields, he heard her piercing cries, and saw next morning the drops of blood where the fairies had murdered her. (Andrews, 1919)

This vindictive cruelty isn't isolated and, in fact, it's all too common for the fairies to punish any slight with death and illness. The fairies often take a terrible revenge if they are ever slighted or offended. A whole family once came under their ban because a fairy woman had been refused admittance into the house... one after another, they all pined away and died, and the ban of the fairies was never lifted from the ill-fated house until the whole family lay in the grave (Wilde, 1902).

A farmer built his house on a fairies' dancing field, even though his neighbors had warned him not to. The fairies plotted their revenge for a time, then one of their cows sickened and died. Then one of their boys grew strange as the fairies started to come around at night to pinch and beat him and, eventually, the fairies killed him. Soon after, the rest of his cattle died, and his crops went to ruin. A year and a day over, he died himself and the house was pulled down by the person who inherited the land so that the fairies' curse would be lifted (Wilde, 1902).

In a similar tale from Wales, a farmer tries to drive the fairies away by destroying their dancing ground. The fairies continually appear to him and warn him that "Vengeance cometh." Soon, his corn is burnt up, after he paid to harvest it. The man pleads with the fairies to forgive him, so they tell him that his family could have a few more generations. A hundred years later, his heir is taken by the fairies and never heard from again (Rhys, 1901).

After another boy was foolish enough to throw dirt at a fairy wrath while bored, an invisible force struck him down. He was mad for some time, bleating like a calf, and it was a long time before he recovered his senses (Wilde, 1902).

A man named Seigneur of Nann was punished by a korrigan, similar to a water nymph, with an illness that killed him, for refusing to marry her, although he was already married with two children. (Spence, 2010).

Indeed, most ailments and diseases were attributed to

vindictive or simply cruel fairies, who were accused of causing everything from cramps to tuberculosis. Further, fairies would cause bruises and pain to those who failed to keep their homes clean, by pinching the person repeatedly. "In cases where a person had been paralytically affected, and lost the use of an arm or a limb, the people believe the fairies have taken away the sound member, and left a log in its place" (Black, 1903).

When cows became sick, it was believed it was elf-shot, that the fairies hit her with an astral arrow, which left the cow injured and sick, even if the wound was only visible to those who could see the fairy realm. Sometimes, the fairies would even kill cows and steal away the real one, leaving a changeling in its place so that they could have the animal's meat for themselves. Accidents, too, were often causes by angry fairies. For example, one man tried to drive a bogle from his home by using a Bible; however, the bogle got his revenge as the man was killed in the mines (Henderson, 1879).

The Vampires and Fairies
I include vampires in this book of fairies because they are at the very least closely related creatures. Like vampires, many fairies are the spirits of the dead who blight fields, steal milk, and drain the blood from people. These wicked fairies are also banished by the light of the sun, held at bay by the sign of the cross, and are at times indiscernible from vampires.

The light cannot banish the darkness; it can only hold it at bay. But in doing so, it makes it impossible for human eyes to adjust to the night, to see what's in the shadows beyond the embers of the little fire. Compared to the darkness of night in ancient Europe, humans were tiny creatures; their civilization was a small thing. Beyond people's homes lay miles of thick forests filled with darkness, with the unknown. This darkness that lies beyond civilization is the realm of the vampire, the realm of nightmares, and what was truly terrifying for the people of the past was how easily someone could become a vampire, for they believed that a person's soul could turn to evil as easily as a candle could be blown out.

In one case, when a holy woman who was a healer and a saint died, she gave instructions not to bury her, so the village people began to panic. They believed that if they left the body out of the grave, it would likely turn into a vampire, for even a little thing, like having an animal jump over it, would corrupt the soul within it. However, if they buried the saint's body, they would incur the wrath of her vengeful spirit (Ivanov, 2003). What we see, then, is that even the gentle soul of a saint on whom the village had depended for their spiritual and temporal wellbeing was greatly feared in death. For despite her kindness, her soul could easily choose to attack them or become a vampire from something as simple as having an animal jump over her corpse. This fear was even greater because she had been a healer, for those who used their powers to perform good deeds in life were especially likely to become vampires. Because in fighting impure forces they had come into contact with these impure forces, all too often, these impure forces would win out in the struggle for their soul (Petreska, 2008). The spirit world of ancient Europe was easily corrupted, easily turned to darkness, and once a soul had gone over to the darkness, it was nearly impossible to turn them back. Indeed, it was so easy to become a vampire that even a living person's soul could transform into one as they slept.

> It is a general Slavic belief that souls may pass into a Mora, a living being, either man or woman, whose soul goes out of the body at nighttime, leaving it as if dead. Sometimes, two souls are believed to be in such a body, one of which leaves it when asleep; and a man may be a Mora from his birth, in which case he has bushy, black eyebrows, growing together above his nose. The Mora, assuming various shapes, approaches the dwellings of men at night and tries to suffocate them; she is either a piece of straw, or a white shadow, or a leather bag, or a white mouse, a cat, a snake, a white horse, etc. First, she sends refreshing slumber to men and then, when they are asleep, she frightens them with terrible dreams, chokes them, and sucks their blood. For the

> most part, she torments children, although she also throws herself upon animals, especially horses and cows, and even injures and withers trees, so that various means are employed to get rid of her (Gray, 1918).

It's likely people believed that it was so easy for anyone to turn into an evil spirit because there was so much evidence for it. Death was an omnipresent fact of life in ancient Europe. The plague, which killed a third of the people in Europe, struck during a time when people believed that evil spirits such as vampires were the cause of disease. Therefore, the people who survived the plague, along with those who were dying from it, would have believed that they were being overwhelmed by evil spirits. In their minds, plagues were the result of undead spirits and fairies slaughtering millions of people. The people of this time believed that evil spirits were responsible for more deaths than any war in history, and had brought Europe's once great nations to their knees in a few short years.

As time went on, millions more continued to die of starvation, of tuberculosis, and many other illnesses, all attributed to vampires and other evil spirits. With so many tens of millions of deaths attributed to evil spirits, it was clear to these people that the evil spirits had to be everywhere. Yet few people ever saw them, and even fewer, it seemed, could fight against them. This can be likened to a zombie apocalypse tale in which the walking dead could slip into homes through keyholes, could blight fields so no food would grow, could steal peoples food away leaving them starving, and yet almost no one could see them and even fewer people could shoot them. Worse still, as previously mentioned, nearly anyone could become a vampire, because in lore, vampires were often spirits that had left their bodies behind for a short time.

> For forty days (after death), the soul dwells on Earth, seeking for places which the deceased used to frequent when alive, it enters his own house or those of other persons, causing all sorts of trouble to those who had been enemies to the departed, and it is either invisible or else appears in the form of an animal (Gray, 1918).

Even when vampires existed as walking corpses, they were often believed to be as fast as lightning. They were supernaturally strong, and nearly impossible to kill. As a result, the most common stories of vampires in the ancient past aren't folktales. Rather, they are the stories of people who were haunted and, in essence, under siege by armies of undead monsters, constantly seeking not only the blood of the living, but their food as well. Yet because there was almost no way to fight the vampires, people rarely told stories about these massive attacks. Instead, they spent their time digging up and burning bodies to fight against them. In Greece, fear of vampires could drive whole villages to move away from their homes (Hartnup, 2004).

One of the largest vampire hysterias began in East Prussia in 1721 before spreading to Austria-Hungry. Here, a single vampire, that of Peter Plogojowitz, nearly emptied an entire village. This vampire was responsible for suffocating people in their beds, murdering his own son, and more (Hellman, 2011). Throughout Europe, whole regions would become hysterical with fear, as normally calm and thoughtful people began digging up bodies, fleeing their homes, and hanging protective herbs from their windows.

Fearing Death

> *"Dark and Joyless is our Prison-house, stone and earth lie heavy on our hearts, our eyes are fast closed, and our hands and feet our frozen"* (Ralstin, 2007).

This is how Russian peasants once described death; as a time when their souls were trapped inside their bodies still aware and suffering, trapped under the frozen ground, going mad with hunger, mad with pain and boredom. Imagine the pain and agony involved in being trapped inside a decaying body, in longing for the end that will never come.

Yet there was an escape from this prison, an escape from the agony of death, for a person's soul didn't have to be trapped inside their body. One Russian man tells his wife:

"What a beautiful bird I heard singing by my bedside tonight... It was my ghost; I cannot live long."

A person's soul could leave his or her body, and this soul would become anamorphic, able to travel quickly, turn invisible, change form. In essence, this soul was a fairy. For example:

> There exist certain men of the Celtic race who have a marvelous power that they get from their ancestors. By a demonic force, they can, at will, take the form of a wolf with large sharp teeth and often, thus metamorphosed, they attack poor defenseless sheep. But when people armed with sticks and weapons come toward them, they flee nimbly and cover great distances. When they are of a mind to transform themselves, they leave their human body, ordering their friends not to change their position or touch them in any minor way whatsoever, for if that were to happen, they would never be able to return to their human appearance. If, while they are wolves, someone wounds them or hits them, the mark on their (animal) body is found in exactly the same place on their (human body). (Lecouteux, 2003)

As already discussed, it was believed that humans could send their souls from their bodies for many reasons. Even when a person was alive, their soul might become a vampire. Many vampires were sorcerers whose souls left their bodies in their sleep and went out in the form of straw or fluff in order to enter homes through keyholes and to attack people. Similarly, the souls of the dead could leave their bodies as well (Stevans, 1903).

In one case, a woman lost two of her children before they reached their first year. The stryges (witches) had sucked their blood. When the woman's third child was born, she stood watch with a hot iron when she saw a neighbor enter the house, riding a wolf through the closed door (Lecouteux, 2003).

These vampire souls were very much like ghosts, although they couldn't pass through solid walls. Instead, they had to slip like water through cracks; if there were not cracks, however, there was no way for them to get through a wall. Further, this ghost often seemed to have material form. People could wrestle with it and kill it using the proper items, although which items differed from culture to culture. Only occasionally was the vampire an actual corpse that had managed to claw its way back from death. Whether the vampire was a soul or a corpse, it could only continue to live so long as its body hadn't decayed. So the vampire was faced with two choices; watch its body stay trapped beneath the earth as it slowly decayed away or take matters into its own hands by stealing life from the living. People believed that human spirits would choose the darker path all too often. In 2003, a man named Toma died and his sister believed that he'd become a stirgoi, a vampire, who began to attack his own niece. Such stirgoi typically began the first forty days of their undead existences as poltergeists who would move objects and make scary sounds. But soon such spirits hungered for blood. Once they began drinking blood, their spirit began to grow darker, more corrupt, even as it started to take on physical form (Taylor, 2007). That the spirits of the dead need blood is a common feature in lore. In the Odyssey of Ancient Greece, the dead are summoned by blood, which they all seek to drink. Yet he only wishes to speak to the spirit of a dead seer, so he keeps the rest at bay with a sword until the seer gets to drink the blood offering. Once he does so the seer states that:

"Any ghost that you let taste of the blood will talk with you like a reasonable being, but if you do not let them have any blood they will go away again" (Homer).

According to this story, the ghosts weren't even aware enough to recognize the person they attacked or to make any moral judgments at all. Vampires then, were corrupted spirits that sought to drink blood and, because so many different people could become vampires, they could have as many personalities as are available to people, but there is typically something darker to the vampire aspect, for they have been tainted in a number of different ways and have become corrupted. It's through the different types of corruption that happen to the vampires' minds and souls that I've developed my categories of vampires.

Corrupted

Vampires who are the souls of those who have been corrupted in some way, such as: being excommunicated, having red hair with blue eyes, being the seventh child of the same gender as the others, having an animal jump over your corpse (the animal was believed to be a devil in disguise), being buried on unhallowed ground, eating the meat of a sheep killed by a wolf and more could all lead a person's soul to be corrupted so that they would become a vampire in death. In this case, the person's soul, like the spirit of a fairy seems to be internally dualistic, having an evil as well as a good aspect. However, once the vampire's soul was corrupted, it stayed in its cruel state. Such a soul became cruel and vindictive and seemed incapable of remembering anything good that anyone had done for them, only the bad. Thus, they would seek out those they knew in life to get revenge for some wrong, slaughtering their families with abandon.

Hunter

Then there are those vampires who are in control, who hunt those they hated in life in order to stave off death or simply for revenge. Other times, the dead who returned from their graves acted as reasonable men, not as ferocious brutes.

> This did not, of course, exclude the idea that a spirit might return to seek revenge where vengeance was due; he was not necessarily peaceable; but if he exacted even the life of one who had wronged him, the act of vengeance was reasonable. (Lawson, 1910)

According to the gypsies, when a vampire returns, he notifies his wife on his first night back. Such vampires could even eventually have children with their wives. And while most vampires seemed to attack those they cared for, these vampires still seemed to care for their families to some extent. Further, the Romoni believed in temporary vampires who would come back to take revenge against those who wronged them (Tihomir, 1903). Interestingly enough, other people become vampires because of old debts and concerns they had in life. In Greece, a man whose wife refused to pay off his debts became a poltergeist-like vampire who left the wine taps running, shook people's beds while they slept, and frightened one lady so much she couldn't speak for three days, although the primary focus of his wrath was his wife, who hadn't paid his debts. Once she'd paid off the debts, he never troubled anyone again.

Even for these "good vampires," we must wonder, however, what happens when they run out of victims, or when they begin to truly suffer in their rotting corpse? Do they then accept their fate to rot away, to remain trapped in the cold heavy grave, or do they continue killing? People feared that the choice in this was often all too clear. A person can only take so much before they will crack. Those born with cauls over their heads, for example, were believed to have shamanistic powers, yet they were also believed to be very likely to become vampires simply because people believed those who could would do so.

Unfulfilled

Those who were unfulfilled when they died gained power from their desire. If this desire was strong enough, it could allow their spirit to project out from their dead body. Even our own modern folklore oftentimes uses this "unfinished business" as the reason why ghosts remain behind. Similarly, the Slavic peoples believed that those who died with an unfulfilled wish would often become vampires (Conrad, 2001). We see this idea in the stories of people who become vampire-like monsters if they die childless. Women who died in childbirth became monsters, such as mamun, which would devour newly born children or pregnant women out of jealousy. Children who died without a name (before baptism) and especially those who died in abortions were also very likely to become vampires. The Russian Drekavac is a good example of this. Drekavac were vampires who, like most others, could change shape, and would often haunt the countryside at Christmas time in the form of a bird. Similar monsters exist in nearly every country throughout the world, for children who died without a name belonged to no community, so their spirits were especially vulnerable.

These unfulfilled spirits would direct their anger and desires towards specific targets that often have more to do with their desires than in their previous lives. For example, those who died in childbirth attack pregnant women, new mothers, and children, for their rage is directed towards those who have what they don't have.

While many of the unfulfilled dead are bitter and angry, others are simply filled with longing. In the tale of "The Dead Mother," a woman dies, yet her spirit returns every night to try to suckle her baby and, in so doing, she ultimately kills her child by accident. Yet sometimes, these unfulfilled spirits could try to fulfill themselves in death. In Macedonia, for example, it was believed that some vampires actually returned to their homes and continued to live with their wives, continued to work their jobs, and so forth, just as if they were still alive (Conrad, 2001), which brings us to the next form of vampire.

Living

In Romania, the strigoi were people who had two souls, one of which would go out while they were still alive to drink blood, steal milk, and generally act like a vampire. Among the gypsies, women who became vampires could return to their husbands and exist as if they as if they were still alive, even having half-vampire children, although they would eventually wear their husbands out from their sexual voracity. Additionally, in Slavic countries, those who drained enough blood could return to their lives, or make new ones, getting married, and also having children who were half-vampires. Because of their dual lives, living vampires are, in many ways, much more shocking than even the dead ones. Their stories are very much like those of serial killers such as Ted Bundy or John Wayne Gacy, who everyone thought were normal, even as they stalked around committing murder.

These "living" vampires have a tendency to act very much like the wife-murdering Bluebeard; in fact, this might be where many of these stories come from. For example, the gypsies have a tale in which a vampire courts a young woman, then brings her back to his home, where she discovers that he plans to use girls hanging from meat hooks for their dinner. When she refuses to eat this "meat," he hangs her up as well; then not satisfied with this, he goes back and gets each of her sisters and brings them back to his home by pretending that his now dead wife wants them to visit.

In another gypsy tale, a man returns from the grave to live secretly with his wife and, after a while, she has a child with him. However, after eight years, she can no longer stand to keep his secret, and so she tells her brothers about him. They are then able to hunt down and kill her husband (Djordjevic, 1903). Sadly, this story doesn't explain why the vampire's wife is no longer able to stand her secret life; whether she loves someone else, her vampire husband is abusive, or if he is drinking the blood of their neighbors to sustain himself is anyone's guess.

Sometimes, people were even born vampires from the very beginning. For example, in Greece, if a deformed child's brothers and/or sisters begin to die of mysterious causes, then the deformed child's own mother might accuse him of being a vampire who was killing off his siblings (Lawson, 1910). Other living people chose to act the role of vampires, taking power and life from blood. A noble woman named Bathory became one of the most famous vampires by drinking and bathing in the blood of young girls in order to prolong her life and youth. Yet, despite her vampire nature, she was still very much alive (Melton, 2011).

Possessed and In a Nightmare

According to the Greeks, vampires began attacking their relatives first as a perversion of Christian values. "In other words, this most deadly of pagan pests, like the most lively of Christian virtues, begins at home" (Lawson, 1910).

In many ways, it seems that these vampires go about in death retracting and mocking their previous lives. They would blight the fields they had worked so hard to grow in life, and attack the people they had loved. One vampire named Grando attacked and raped his widow repeatedly, while also terrorizing former friends and neighbors (Veselica, 2006). Another woman in Greece testified that her husband came back to kill and attack people in his former village. It may be that these people might not have had control over their own bodies. According to the Greeks, there were many vampires that came into being because a devil had possessed their corpses. In this case, the soul of the human who had lived in the body previously was already in the afterlife, and it was something else dwelling in his/her corpse (Lawson, 1910).

It's also possible that other vampires are souls that exist in a nightmare world without a will. Those who do not have this will are unable to act rationally, to recognize those they loved in life. Many vampires may also be people who have been driven mad by their imprisonment in the ground, the pain of having died, and the suffering of rotting away. For many, this torture would have been maddening and it seems to have driven them into a nightmare state, for when they would rise as vampires, they'd haunt the places and people they knew in life, killing family, friends, and neighbors first as if they had no control over themselves. Indeed, the Celts greatly feared the dreams of the dead:

> On the occasion of witnessing an execution, there was a special rite to prevent dreams of the dead: to dream of the dead was the next step to their coming back as revenants. When Alex Mackintosh of Borlum was executed at Muirfield, we learn how "with mingled feelings of sorrow and horror, the multitude slowly and silently dispersed, many, if not most of the company, placing a small piece of bread under a stone, which, according to a superstitious tradition, would prevent after-dreams of the unfortunate Alexander Mackintosh." Blood innocently shed might readily call out for vengeance; for the soul was in the blood.
>
> In the etiquette of paying one's parting respects to the dead, before the corpse is buried, no custom is more tenacious in the Highlands than that of touching the body with the finger. To neglect doing so is thought to expose a person to dreaming of the deceased, and by consequence to the danger of being visited by the dead, and of being open to the dread haunting of the ghost. (Henderson, 2001)

In the tale of "St. Michael and the Vampire," a princess becomes a vampire. In an attempt to help his undead daughter, the king gives orders that all foreign merchants must read prayers over her body. One by one, the merchants are shut up in the church at night and, one by one, their bones are swept out in the morning. A young man, with St.

Michael as a helper spirit, is able to overcome the princess by creating a barrier of boards and scattering pears, then nuts, on the ground so that she stops to pick them up. As with many such tales, the boy must not only delay the vampire, he must also continue reading his prayers while never looking up, for to look up in fear at vampires is to be defeated by them. Finally, on the third night, the boy sprinkles himself with holy water, and covers himself with the smoke of holy incense. When the vampire girl jumps up, he sneaks into her coffin behind her with the image of St. Michael at his side. When the princess finally discovers that the boy has climbed into her coffin, the vampire princess begs him to come out of the coffin. However, he ignores her and continues to pray until at last daylight comes and she becomes human again. After this, the two of them are able to be married (Nisbet, 1894). This story shows that the princess wasn't in control of herself, for she could be cured by a shamanistic figure.

There is another important point to take from the nature of vampires in the nightmare state, for while they don't recognize those they attack, like the ghosts in "The Odyssey," it's possible that once they drain someone of their blood, they'll know who they just killed. So once they killed someone they had loved in life, they would be faced with the sudden realization of what they had done and what they were. So at first, vampires might simply be mindless killing machines, returning to what is familiar without knowing why. Only after they killed would understanding return to haunt them.

Vampire by Choice

Other people who became vampires were wicked people who refused to die and so chose very early on to take a life. In the story of "The Warlock," for example, an evil koldun (witch) gives orders that his three daughter-in-laws should, one-by-one, watch his dead body as it lies in state. Every night, he strangles each of these daughter-in-laws until the third one is smart enough to bring a cross with her, which she uses to kill him by laying it over his body (Ralston, 2007). Similarly, in the story of the "Headless Princess," a boy sees the princess removing her head in order to wash and comb her hair. The boy then shares the witch's secret with others, and through the revelation of her secret she begins to lose power, so that she wanes until she dies (remember that humans have power to hurt others through ill thoughts and looks). Before the princess dies, she asks that the boy be made to read psalter over her body for three nights. Her plan is to drain the boy of his life. Luckily for the boy, he knows an old lady who tells him that if he continues to read the psalter without distraction, the witch's corpse won't be able to touch him. For three nights, the witch uses her powers to conjure up horrors, to do anything she can to distract and frighten the boy, but he keeps reading the psalter and so is able to survive while she must stay dead (Ralston, 2007).

Fairies Need Respect

Fairies needed respect; they needed people to believe in them. In Lincolnshire, for example, the fairies (known as "The Strangers") grew angry because young people knew so little about them. So angry, in fact, that they caused the crops to fail, children to become sick, and money to grow scarce. More than this, they even caused men to become lecherous alcoholics and women to become addicted to opium. In short, the fairies reacted to people's disbelief in them by nearly destroying the people (Briggs, 1965).

When a woman named Nanny expressed the belief that the fairies were gone the fairies "decided it was time that old Nanny should be taught better, and should be made to speak more respectfully of them in the future; so they determined upon giving her an ocular demonstration of their existence." For this demonstration, the fairies actually appeared to her in an immense crowd forming a living pyramid (Crossing, 1890).

Those who failed to give offerings to the fairies, who failed to sing their praises and give proper respect, could often expect to suffer greatly. When the fairy in "Sleeping Beauty" was forgotten by the king and queen, she punished their daughter with a death curse. In "The Three Citrons," a fairy also cursed a king for forgetting to invite her to his wedding. Meanwhile, in the story of "The Little Wood Maiden," a woman's daughter receives a gift from a wood maiden, yet doesn't tell her mother, who grumbles about the item when she finds it, then later on, discovering the truth, cries:

> Oh, that was a wood maiden! At noon and midnight, the wood maidens dance. It is well you are not a little boy, or she might have danced you to death! But they are often kind to little girls and sometimes make them rich presents. Why didn't you tell me? If I hadn't grumbled, I could have had yarn enough to fill the house! (Fillmore, 2010)

It's perhaps this need for respect that causes the fairies to give something worthless to people that will turn into gold, for they want the person to respect them enough to accept any gift. This is also likely why fairies are often placated by gifts, respect, and kindness, why singing songs of their greatness so often works as a form of magical spell, by getting the fairies to aid the singer. In general:

> A distinct reverence was paid, a species of worship, traces of which lasted down to recent times. The clearest evidence of this is found in the Kormaks Saga. The hill of elves, like the altar of the god, is to be reddened with the blood of slaughtered bull, and of the animals flesh a feast prepared for the elves. (Grimm, 1882)

The people of Mari-El Russia, who have the last unbroken indigenous religion of Europe, also pray and make offerings to many fairy-like beings, sharing their feast with the spirits that live in groves of trees (Sebeok, 1956).

When a boy gave the Mermaid of Gob Ny Ooyl some apples, she thanked him with the following blessing: "The luck o' the sea be with you, but don't forgetful be. Of bringing some sweet Ian eggs for the children of the sea." Forever after, he never failed to get a good catch when out fishing. In Russia, the domovoy's family would try to gain his favor by offering him such things as porridge, tobacco, juniper, and bread and salt. While in England, children would offer Jack Frost a spoonful of kissel as they asked him not to destroy their winter crops (Keightley, 1892). Such respect had more than simply an emotional impact on fairies; at times, it could change their very nature. Ded Moroz, the current Russian Santa Claus figure, was at one time a cruel fairy that would freeze people to death, yet he would also give gifts to those who were polite to him. Thus he was a monster for whom respect could transform him into a gentle being. In the Russian *Cinderella* story, for example, a girl was sent into the woods to freeze to death by her wicked stepmother. As she sat in the cold, the Spirit of Frost leapt from fir tree to fir tree, snapping his fingers as he went. Then, as he came into sight, he started mocking the girl, but she always responded to his teasing respectfully even calling him "Frost Dearest." Ultimately he felt sorry for her and wrapped her in warm blankets to keep her alive through the cold, before leaving her with gifts that would make her wealthy. Later in the story, Frost freezes the girl's disrespectful sister-in-law to death for telling him that she's cold (Ralston, 2007).

The people of Russia would:

> Court the favor and satisfaction of the Domovoy by leaving him part of their meal, and by paying him homage with decorations of white linen along the passage to his favorite places in the house. When the Domovoy grew angry, people would offer it a cock, which would be killed at midnight, and then all the nooks and corners of the house would be washed with its blood, or bread and salt would be offered to the Domovoy. (Ralston, 2007)

The fates could also be convinced to give a child a better fate with offerings of a good supper and white cloth for their use (Gray, 1918).

There were many rituals to help people negotiate with and get on the good side of the fairies. Some of the best examples of these come from the Mari-El of Russia. In one of these ceremonies, conducted during the part of the summer when flies and other insects are numerous, the priest and some male assistants would go into a grove of birch trees. They would find a birch tree where the deities Aga Kurman, Aga Saus Aor Pasu Jer, and Surna Socektse were hiding among the branches. The assistants would make a fire and they would place loaves of bread on a white cloth spread under the tree, kneeling while the priest said a prayer. The priest would take a firebrand in his left hand and a knife in his right. After he had finished his prayer, the priest would strike the knife against an axe, which was on the ground at his feet. He would then brand the forehead and chest of a ram and ewe, which were tied to a post near the fire. Water was poured on the ram and ewe before they were sacrificed and skinned. The blood from each of these was poured into a fire for the fire spirit to share with the other spirits. The meat was cooked and the rest of the villagers would enter the sacred grove to partake in a feast. Pieces of meat were placed into bowls as an offering to the spirits, after which money was given to the priest by the people, who said a prayer to protect them and their grain against evil.

This ritual shows three important aspects about the fairies' desire for respect: first, that ritualized respect is effective for maintaining and building a relationship with the fairies; second, that it's important to show appreciation for what the fairies do by sharing food with them; and last, fairies enjoy watching and, to some extent, being a part of a human community. This last point is very important, as people often seem to forget that many fairies cared for and wanted to be a part of human communities. We see this clearly in nearly every festival of the people of Mari-El. For example, the festival of Aga Pajram involved a long celebration of feasting in the groves where the spirits lived. During the festivals to the keremet, the people would offer loaves of bread and animals to the keremet and their helpers, after which there would be two days of feasting and celebration (Sebeok, 1956). Even today, people bring greenery into the home at Christmas time, which people once did so that fairies would have a place to hide while viewing the families' celebrations.

Trade

There is, however, another aspect to the notion that fairies sought human food and approval. This is that fairies were often willing to trade with humans. One man in Shetland, who was worried that the wind would ruin his crop, so worried that he said he would give up his best ox to have the harvest done. The next morning, the grain was all cut and the ox was dead. The trow had taken him at his word, trading his ox for their help (Black, 1903). In another tale, a boy offers to give a phouka a warm coat if it will show itself to him, so it appears as a raging bull, but when the boy throws a coat over it, it becomes gentle as a lamb. This phouka then told him to come to the mill when the moon was up and he would gain good luck.

Emotionally Sensitive

In the 19th Century, an Icelandic clergyman wrote that certain rocks and stones were called the Stones of Landdisir (land goddesses). It was said to be unwise to make loud noises near them, and children were forbidden to play around them, as bad luck would come to those who did not treat them with respect (Davidson, 1989). We see these beliefs mirrored in the Celtic world of that time as well, where it was thought to be bad luck to disturb certain stones, as they were the homes to the fairies (Wentz, 1911). In other words, humans can impact rock spirits, which are sensitive both to noise and to being built upon. It may be that part of the rock spirits' relationships with humans existed in order to avoid these things. Such sensitivity is problematic when humans are able to be so destructive. The vaetter of Iceland grew angry when they saw one human murder another, and for a long time ships with dragon's heads were banned in the country for fear that they would disturb the stone spirits or give them the wrong impression of the human's intentions (Davidson, 1989). Some of the fairies of Ireland could also grow angry at the sight of blood and so become destructive poltergeists (Wilde).

Because of their sensitivity, rock fairies do more than offer rewards to humans who keep the peace with them; they punish those who fail to do so. When humans damage rocks or otherwise disturb them, the spirits of the land would haunt the humans, acting much as we'd expect a poltergeist to act, sometimes for thousands of years at a time (Wentz, 1911). During this time, they will damage crops, haunt houses, and kill or kidnap people. This danger posed by the spirits of the rocks made it extremely difficult to find a safe place to build or farm, or even play. Children playing near a group of rocks could, for example, be cursed. A farmer who moves a boulder could have his farm and house become haunted, etc. Further, the fact that a person's death could drive these spirits into a wild state may mean that many of the old tales that people think were about a ghost, may in fact, have been about the spirits of the Earth being corrupted by an act of violence and or pain.

Beyond simply being sensitive to noises, stone and earth spirits appear to be very emotionally sensitive. These spirits are most often referred to in the plural because they live in family groups (Davidson, 1989). So it would appear that the typical stone or earth fairy prefers to live a sedentary lifestyle with strong family ties. Further, their hatred of violence shows a love of living creatures, or at least those of human intelligence (they didn't appear to mind humans butchering goats or cattle or hunting for animals and even helped humans in these tasks). From this, we can presume that they cared about humans in much the same way that a motherly or fatherly figure might care about children in their neighborhood, or the way a human might care about a stray kitten.

Humans threaten the fairies' lifestyle, so it is perhaps for this reason that they come to humans in order to negotiate a deal to get the humans to leave them alone.

A Few More Fairy Activities

Kidnapping Children and Taking Slaves

To the fairies' way of thinking, the taking of human children would be a necessity, for they needed humans to strengthen their sickly line and to win victories in wars against other fairy clans. When such children were found by humans after living in Fairyland for a while, they had often been trained as smiths, presumably to forge iron so that they could wage war on other fairies with this magical metal. These children would also be expected to marry a fairy when they grew older so that they could have half-fairy children who would be healthier than the full-blooded fairies. Further, the taking of a human child gave an older fairy the opportunity to take the place of the human child, to be a child again.

Yet, as with nearly all things fairy, the act of kidnapping a child is a dual-sided sword. For while the fairies view it as a moral imperative, it is an emotionally destructive and cruel act for the mother of the child who was taken. In the story of one such mother from Brittany, she kissed her child before going out to get water.

> As she was coming back she saw a tiny, crested bird singing on a hawthorn bush, and this is what he sang: "Mariannik, be quick, be quick, For in the cradle is no Loik."
> "You silly bird!" exclaimed Mariannik, "Loik cannot

walk," but all the same, with a flutter at her heart, she hurried across the heath to the cottage.

She opened the door and felt at once that something terrible had happened. The fire had gone out. The cat's back was bristling. She hastened to the cradle where, instead of seeing Loik's round and rosy face, Oh, lack-a-day! she beheld a hideous dwarf with a dark and spotted face. He had a huge and gaping mouth; his hands and feet were evil, threatening, jagged claws.

"Merciful heavens!" cried Mariannik. "Who, are you? What have you done with my blessed child?"

The dwarf answered never a word, but grinned a wicked grin. (Mason, 1929)

Terrifying, overwhelming sorrow doesn't even begin to describe the emotions that such a moment is likely to bring. Other fairy changelings will live with their parents for years, acting strangely, never growing, and always leaving their parents to feel uncomfortable, uncertain. This is what horror movies are made of, and perhaps, given some fairies' nature as vampires, this could easily become such a horror story.

Yet there were some times when a fairy child was swapped for a human one, and in such cases, the fairy mother might want her own child back as well. In one instance, a mother and father lose their own baby when

> A young girl wearing a red handkerchief came in. She asked them why they were crying and when they showed her the changeling, she laughed with joy and said, "This is my own child that was stolen from me tonight because my people wanted to take your beautiful baby, but I'd rather have ours; if you let me take him, I will tell you how to get your child back."
>
> When the human parents agree to the fairy girl's terms she tells them that they can threaten to burn the fairy thrones on the hill to force the fairies to return the child (Briggs, 1976).

Hunting

The sound of the fairy dogs baying as they close in on the prey of the spirit world was once well known and greatly feared by the people throughout northern Europe. Hunting was one of favorite pastimes of nearly all fairies, whether friendly or harmful. Pwyll met a fairy king when the two of them were hunting and the two of them soon became friends. However, most people didn't have so much luck with encountering fairy hunters, for the souls of humans was often their game. One of the best descriptions of the wild hunt comes from the tale of a poor man journeying across the moor:

> A poor herdsman was journeying homeward across the moors one windy night, when he heard at a distance among the Tors the baying of hounds, which he soon recognised as the dismal chorus of the dandy-dogs. It was three or four miles to his house and, very much alarmed, he hurried onward as fast as the treacherous nature of the soil and the uncertainty of the path would allow; but, alas! the melancholy yelping of the hounds, and the dismal holloa of the hunter came nearer and nearer. After a considerable run, they had so gained upon him, that on looking back, oh horror! he could distinctly see hunter and dogs. The former was terrible to look at, and had the usual complement of horns and tail, accorded by common consent to the legendary devil. He was black, of course, and carried in his hand a long hunting-pole. The dogs, a numerous pack, blackened the small patch of moor that was visible; each snorting fire, and uttering a yelp of indescribably frightful tone. No cottage, rock, or tree was near to give the herdsman shelter, and nothing apparently remained to him but to abandon himself to their fury, when a happy thought suddenly flashed upon him and suggested a resource. Just as they were about to rush upon him, he fell on his knees in prayer. There was strange power in the holy words he uttered ; for immediately, as if resistance had been offered, the hell-hounds stood at bay, howling more dismally than ever, and the hunter shouted, "Bo Shrove," which (says my informant) means in the old language, "The boy prays," at which they all drew off on some other pursuit and disappeared (Hunt, 1908).

The vily of Eastern Europe also loved to hunt and would ride about on stags or horses in order to chase down both deer and those humans who angered them, shooting each with arrows. There were so many different fairies who loved hunting that they could be after any number of things. Some appeared to have abducted humans to be their slaves, others tagged humans to die of the plague, while others would hunt the wicked souls of the dead and other dangerous spirits. In nearly all cases, however, the fairies seem to have enjoyed hunting more than nearly any other pastime, except for possibly dancing and song. This means that it is impossible to completely quantify the nature of this hunt, as its purpose is dependent upon the fairies engaged in it. Many of these fairies were often kind, while others hated the cruel and malign spirits that haunted the world. Still others enjoyed nothing better than to hunt fairies and humans alike.

Interestingly enough, despite being the frequent target of the wild hunt, humans were very often the only ones who seemed able to thwart it. This is the reason that Little Wood Wives, the Hulda, and other beautiful forest fairies, who were also often the targets of the wild huntsmen, would seek human help. Many of these huntsmen, such as Woden, were believed to hold a special grudge against the lithe fairies and would kill them, then dress them like they were simply rabbits. The fairies' only defense against these huntsmen was to flee into trees which humans had marked with magical signs.

Fairy Food

The nature of food is magical, for humans who eat the food of fairies will oftentimes be trapped in Fairyland, becoming fairies until they can eat only human food for seven years. By the same token, fairies who eat too much human food risk being trapped in the mortal plane. Perhaps this is the curse of certain fairy refugees, that they were unable to access fairy food and so cannot return to Fairyland, but must continue to steal their sustenance from humans?

Regardless, it is commonly believed that fairies don't

typically eat human food the way we do; rather, they eat the ethereal part of the food, the spirit and goodness out of it. What is left behind is dry, moldy, slimy, or otherwise lacking in goodness. So when a fairy living underneath the fire pit would steal loaves of bread, he would leave them scattered about under the house for years. Scattered uneaten food is at times good evidence that there is a fairy and not an animal present, as animals would have eaten the physical part of the food. In such a case, however, someone might have difficulty realizing that they were the victim of fairy thefts as their cheese or bread or cakes would still be there, they just would be stale or dried out.

War

Fairies can be very warlike and very destructive. In *Fairy Faith in the Celtic Countries*, one man asserts that:

> There are other breeds or castes of fairies; and it seems to me, when I recall our ancient traditions, that some of these fairies are of the Fir Bolgs, some of the Tuatha De Danann, and some of the Milesians. All of them have been seen serenading round the western slope of Tara, dressed in ancient Irish costumes. Unlike the little red men, these fairy races are warlike and given to making invasions. Long processions of them have been seen going round the King's Chair (an earthwork on which the Kings of Tara are said to have been crowned); and they then would appear like soldiers of ancient Ireland in review (Wentz, 2011).

This book goes on to state that the potato famine of 1846-1847 was caused by a war between the fairies, during which many people saw fairies waging massive battles in the sky. Further, the fairies were said to have had a massive battle in the County of Mayo, where they appeared as swarms of flies coming in every direction and when the battle was over one could have filled baskets with the dead flies (fairies) that had floated down the river. Think about this for a moment. If each fly in these massive swarms represented a fairy, how many millions of fairies must have died in that war? How horrifyingly emotional would that experience have been?

Fairies were even said to almost always fight on Halloween. So intense were their battles that the frost and the lichens on the rocks would turn red from the fairies blood for some time thereafter.

Interestingly enough, fairies fight not only for their own clans, but for humans also. When the blight came on the potatoes of Munster, it was believed that the fairies of Ulster had overpowered the fairies of Munster and their fairy chief Daniel O'Donohue (Curtin 1895). The fairies of Munster then fought to defend the crops from those of Ulster, while the fairies from foreign lands would fight to blight them, while presumably also defending the crops and people of their own land.

Haunting

Fairies were very often the things that went bump in the night, even more so than ghosts. It wasn't ghosts that haunted people for building their houses on the wrong places but fairies. But it wasn't just out of vengeance that fairies haunted families and places; often it was a part of their malicious sense of humor. In Scotland, there was a bogle who was well known for haunting a bog "who was of a most mischievous disposition, and took particular pleasure in abusing every traveler who had occasion to pass through the place betwixt the twilight at night and cock-crowing in the morning" (Gibbings, 1889).

Fairy Backgrounds

Although most people classify fairies by where they live, such as within the household, in fields, in forests, etc., I would argue that a fairy's home is not its classification. After all, a cockroach and a cat might live in the same home, but that doesn't make them the same thing. Similarly, among fairies who live in human homes, we see that some of these fairies were part of the fairy court, but were banished for falling in love with a human, while others appear to have been banished for laziness and forced to work for humans until the humans saw them worthy to receive clothes. Other fairies who live in homes are the ancestral spirits of the family whose home they share, while some, like ghosts, are the first farmers on a farm. Others still appear to be refugees with nowhere else to go, who attempt to help a human's family in return for shelter, and on and on the list of possible backgrounds go.

What this means is that, while many of these fairies might have similar activities such as playing minor pranks on the family or sweeping floors, their reason for doing these things and the personality with which they are done is often completely different. If you were to write a story about a household fairy who was a slave to humans because it had been banished for being lazy, this would be completely different from a story about a fairy who was banished for loving humans and so went to live among them. Even the same activities can have different emotional backgrounds. For example, while the gift of clothing is important to nearly all household fairies, some few fairies demand it, others still are freed from their servitude by it, while refugees see it a sign that they are now too fine to work, that they are perhaps worthy to return to their lives.

Consider also that fairies typically either taught humans about or helped shape human culture. They are often the ancestral spirits to the humans of a given region, or they imitate human culture to some extent. So while many similarities exist between fairies across countries, their cultures are altogether different. For example, both the lars and domovoy are ancestral spirits that live with people in their houses, but the lars are from Ancient Rome and the domovoy are from Russia, so their lives and the lives of the families they lived with are very different from each other. As you can see, there are hundreds of different possible fairy backgrounds, so while I attempt to show some of the more common fairy backgrounds as a reference point, it's impossible to show all their backgrounds.

The Relationship between Humans and Fairies

Fairies and humanity are closely entwined one to another as shown by the tale of two fairy children, a brother and a sister. These fairy children lived in an underground world where they were out wandering far from home when, all at once, they found themselves standing under the sun. Dazzled and afraid by the bright light, the little green children began bawling and screaming until they were discovered by a kindly human. Eventually, they were taken in by Sir Richard de Caine at Wikes. Scared and saddened at finding himself in the human world, the fairy boy eventually died. However, over time, the girl began eating mortal food and through this became human herself, although she remained "rather loose and wanton in her conduct" (Hartland 1890).

What this and other stories shows us is that fairies could become human at times simply by eating our food and, as already pointed out, even a vampire who had died could become human again with the promptings of the right shamanistic figure. So although humans and fairies are very different, they are also closely related. Indeed, in Greek lore, humans were sometimes believed to be descended from the Nymphs of the Ash trees, who were Zeus's aunts, making us cousins to the deities and children of the fairies. In the lore of some Celtic people's, humans were descended from a deity the Romans compare to Dispater, the lord of the underworld, which is of interest because most fairies lived under hills and lakes in much of Celtic lore. As we'll see further, many humans became fairies when they died and other humans have become fairies just by living in Fairyland. In Greece, for example, the Queen of the Fairies offers to make one girl into a fairy:

"Would you not like to be a fairy?...and live with me in this garden where the sun never ceases to shine and where it is summer all the year?" (Gianakoulis, 1930).

In another story, all a girl would need to do is eat some candy offered to her by the fairies and she would become one forever. All of this begs the question: "If humans are so closely related to fairies, why is it that most humans know so little about them?" Why it is fairies seem to have magical powers that most humans (with the exception of some druids and wizards) seem to lack? I've come up with three answers to this question, although you will likely be able to come up with many more.

Fairies Fear Humans

In much of European lore, the deities rose up and killed the children of the first beings who, and in turn, had already oftentimes killed their parents as well. With such a violent past, it's no wonder that the deities worried that humans might rise up and kill them. This is why Plato held that Zeus split the originally four-armed and dual-souled humans and made them weaker, out of fear of the humans' strength. Fairies, too, desire to keep secrets from humans. For in the same manner that they will capture us to be their spouses, so will we take them out of greed for their treasure or to fulfill our own lustful desires. Indeed, there was a dwarf who told humans directly that we were mortal and weak due in part to our "faithlessness" (Grimm, 1882). What we see is that fairies believe humans to be their treacherous descendants, so it is possible that the secrets of many forms of magic have been concealed from humans simply to keep us from being even more dangerous.

Fairies Need Humanity

Briggs points out that one aspect of fairies is that they can never mature or be the hero, while humans, on the other hand, can mature and grow physically strong (Briggs, 1967). Saving the world from Armageddon requires something other than capricious or playful beings. Instead, it requires creatures that are not afraid to die, beings who seek out the warrior's life and are always striving for more – these are qualities that immortal and magic-bearing beings would have difficulty obtaining. Yet these are also qualities that fairies and other magical beings often need.

Germanic and Scandinavian myths also tell us that Odin will eventually need the souls of dead humans to help him in his final battle to prevent all things from being destroyed. So it is perhaps necessary for humans to be mortal so that we can join his army. This could also be his reason for creating us.

Odin is not the only one in mythology who needed humans. In the Welsh story of Prince Pwyll, the fairy king seeks out Pwyll in order to get his aid in slaying a monster that the fairies cannot kill (Griffis, 1921). Water dragons would seek out humans as far away as Japan in order to help them battle with unclean beings that they could not fight themselves. While one of Wentz's informants in Ireland states that:

> When the fairy tribes under the various kings and queens have a battle, one side manages to have a living man among them, and he, by knocking the fairies about, turns the battle in case the side he is on is

losing (Wentz, 2011).

Humans then are perhaps made to be a mortal form of fairy which is ignorant of magic, due to our short lives and because we are both feared and needed by the Other World. However, despite this separation, we are so closely related to fairies that humans can still gain the ability to perform magic and obtain immortality.

To Grow Up

The first fairies to become human may have done so in order to grow up, in order to grow beyond what they were. Fairies, after all, can never truly mature and can perhaps never really enjoy a moment for they have so many. Further, through our human nature, we appear to have many powers the fairies can never have.

Humans are Uncanny to Fairies

Briggs indicates that, in many ways, humans are uncanny to fairies; after all, humans can use iron and magical symbols, which thwart the fairies. The little Wood Wives of Germany, for example, were defenseless against the Wild Huntsman who would chase them down and slaughter them like deer. These Wood Wives would turn to humans for protection, for the humans could make the mark of a cross on the stumps of trees that would keep the Wild Huntsman away from the tree so that the Wood Wives would have a place to hide within (Grimm, 1935).

Humans in lore had many means of driving and keeping fairies away. On entering the forest, peasants would utter a protective prayer to keep the leshii (forest king) away. In ancient Rome, humans could drive away the spirits of nature with a broom, showing the power of civilization over nature. Later this idea would be replaced in part by showing the power of Christianity over nature, but the idea itself remains that civilization could overcome the spirits of nature, that humans had power over something magical.

When the Fairy Queen orders her servants to kidnap a child and leave a leprechaun in its place, they find that they can't lift the baby because of a simple needle in the child's clothes, which to the fairies appears as heavy as a massive beam of iron. Instead of kidnapping the child, the fairies settle with bestowing gifts on it, making it the grandest lady in the world, the greatest singer, and the best mantle maker. The Fairy Queen, however, promises that if the girl ever leaves her house, she will turn into in the form of a rat. So, although the fairies could still leave a curse, they can't move the power of iron.

In Scandinavian lore, the Bäckahästen was a fairy who could spirit away things of value, turn into a pile of sticks, a group of maidens, a pack of dogs, a child, or appear as a horse in order to trick children into riding him so that he could pull them into the water and drown him. However, even a child could thwart this powerful fairy by simply throwing a piece of steel between it at the water (Wigstrom, 1881). In another case, a man blocks open the doorway into Fairyland by sticking an iron knife into it so that no fairies or fairy magic could move it (Briggs, 1967), while a shepherd captured three powerful Yezinkas (hags from Czechoslovakia) because they are unable to move when they are struck by a human with brambles (Lawson, 1910).

As already mentioned in the section about why fairies are shy, many humans have the power of the evil eye; that is, we can cause fairies to lose their powers or to be cursed merely by looking at them. It's not just our ability to use magical items, then, that gives us power. It's also the fact that humans seem to have certain magical powers naturally, even if we're not aware of them. In Scotland, children run around rings, but are careful never to run around the same ring nine times in a row as this would give the fairies power over them (Atkinson, 1891). What we see from this is not that fairies have power, but that humans have a natural protection against the fairies, which can only be surrendered by performing certain acts.

When a young man's wife was kidnapped by the king of the fairies, he had workers dig up the fairy mound, although the fairies kept filling in their work. Eventually, however, it was discovered that putting salt in the hole they had dug would keep the fairies way. "Then the young lord knew he had power over Finvarra," the king of the fairies, and so he and his work crews dug on. Eventually, they could hear fairy music and they knew they were close. "See now," said one. "Finvarra is sad, for if one of those mortal men strikes a blow on the fairy palace with their spades, it will crumble to dust, and fade away like the mist." It was at this point that the king of the fairies, Finvarra, even with all his powers, had to return the young man's bride (Wilde, 1902).

Jacob Grimm pointed out that, physically, humans lie somewhere between the realms of fairies and giants. While fairies hold power and sway over us, they stand in awe before us (Grimm, 1882). It is relatively common in mythology for humans to capture leprechauns in order to steal their treasure, or to threaten the lives of tree fairies to force them to provide us with fertile fields. Furthermore, some reports also say that fairies abduct humans to strengthen their sickly line (Briggs, 1967). This shows that not only are humans physically stronger than fairies, but also we are close enough to bear children with them. Fairies themselves are not afraid of losing their powers by bringing human blood into their line because humans can gain the powers of fairies as Merlin did, but fairies may always be physically weak and never able to use iron.

Ancestral Spirits

I've already asserted that humans are descended from fairies, yet the relationship between humans and fairies doesn't end there, for humans and fairies often have children together. There are many stories, for example, of fairies such as the Water Woman of Wales, the Swan Maidens of Germanic Lore, the Sealkies of Scotland, and the Sky Maidens of Greece, which are compelled, at times, even forced to marry human men. For years, they live as humans, bearing children and perhaps even making friends before they divorce their husbands (or escape the enslavement he has brought them under). Once free, they return to Fairyland, likely still loving their children and perhaps even some of their human friends.

In addition to being descended from fairies, human souls often became fairies when we die. The fact that people once believed that some humans and, indeed, some of their own ancestors had become fairies gives us a shadowy window into understanding the reasoning of the beings of this strange world. For the dead have an obvious interest in the things, people, and places they loved in life. In the story of "The Three Spinners," a woman is told to spin a room full of flax in order to be married. Unable to perform such an impossible feat, she falls into despair until three old women appear to her and tell her that they are her ancestors. At this point, they proceed to help her in return for being invited to her child's christening (Grimm, 1812). The fairies' goal in helping the human girl in this story is clear. They seek, as many elders would, to help a grandchild or a great niece in finding love and happiness. That this is their goal becomes all the more clear by the fact that what they ask for in return is to be able to go to an important event for her child just as a doting elder would do.

Because there are so many doting and wise elders among fairies, ancestor worship was a common practice in ancient Europe. Mortals in many religions become gods or spirits which protected their descendants from harm and from their enemies. So many of the beings we would recognize as fairies are in the spirits of people's ancestors that walk the spirit world or remain behind to offer aid. In Russia, there was no doubt

> That the souls of the families' patriarchs watched over their children and their children's children; that the departed spirits, especially those of the ancestors, ought always to be regarded with pious veneration. When the family was in need, these ancestors should be solicited or conciliated by prayer and sacrifice (Ralston, 2007)

These patriarchs were not some distant beings, for they lived among humans and were closely connected with the fire burning in the domestic hearth. This fact accounts for the following:

> The stove, at the turn of the century in Russia, having come to be considered the special haunt of the domovoi, or house spirit, whose position in the esteem of the people is looked upon as a trace of the ancestor worship of olden days (Ralston, 2007).

A domovoi is a small, old man covered in hair who lives under the hearth or within the threshold of a house. The Slavic peoples were historically so close to him that each family would refer to him as "Grandfather." These household fairies exist all over Europe from England to Russia, providing protection against evil spirits, divination, blessings, and even, in some cases, helping directly with the housework. The ancestors that lived in the fireplace were so important to the people of Russia that:

> When a Russian family moves from one house to another, the fire is raked out of the old stove into a jar and solemnly conveyed to the new one, and the words "Welcome, Grandfather, to the new home!" being uttered when it arrived. All new animals are introduced to this "Grandfather," and food is laid out for them at special occasions.(Ralston, 2007)

Not all ancestor fairies are connected to the household, however. The previously mentioned bannik lives within the bathhouse while others live and aid in the fields and farm. Still others, such as the banshee, appear to live in the moorlands coming out only to watch humans and provide them with gifts or to mourn their passing (Ralston, 1872).

The Romans also believed that humans would often become fairies in death:

> M. A. Lefèvre shows that the Roman Lares, so frequently compared to house-haunting fairies, are in reality quite like the Gaelic banshee; that originally they were nothing more than the unattached souls of the dead, akin to Manes; that time and custom made distinctions between them; that in the common language Lares and Manes had synonymous dwellings;

> and that, finally, the idea of death was little by little divorced from the worship of the Lares, so that they became guardians of the family and protectors of life On all the tombs of their dead, the Romans inscribed these names: *Manes, inferi, silentes*, the last of which, meaning *the silent ones*, is equivalent to the term "People of Peace" given to the fairy-folk of Scotland. Nor were the Roman Lares always thought of as inhabiting dwellings. Many were supposed to live in the fields, in the streets of cities, at crossroads quite like certain orders of fairies and demons. In each place, these ancestral spirits had their chapels and received offerings of fruit, flowers, and foliage. If neglected, they became spiteful and were then known as Lemures. (Wentz, 1911)

In Italy, it was believed that the dead would also haunt the places they had died, and sometimes would even work with their descendants as familiar spirits. One cunning woman, for example, got her magical powers from her uncle (Magliocco, 2009).

In Serbia, white snakes were said to be ancestral spirits who lived under the threshold or hearth. Here, they were believed to bring good fortune to their families.

> Care was taken to protect the čuvarica, for it was believed that if it were killed, the master or another person in the household would soon die. As a mediator between the Underworld, Nature, and humans, this snake was thought to understand speech, to be able to teach man about medicinal herbs, and to induce fertility in wives and female livestock. Many legends associate man and snake, and metamorphosis of one into the other is common in South Slavic folklore. (Conrad, 2001)

While one of the oldest references to a banshee indicates that she is an ancestral spirit who, in one case, carries off the head king of Ireland in order to spend some time with her in her palace, where he seems to have passed a very enjoyable time (Wood-Martin, 1901).

Among the Saami and the Scandinavians, there was a

belief that the spirits of the dead dwelt in the mountains. The Saami particularly believed that the spirits of their ancestors lived happily in the mountains, riding about on reindeer which had been sacrificed to them, coming down to protect humanity against ill spirits. At times, however, these spirits would seek to steal someone's soul before their time had come, which would make the person sick. In these cases, the shaman would have to go retrieve the soul from them. There were other people whose souls had to live within the forests or hills for crimes they had committed; however, they could still eventually join the rest of the tribe in the mountains, or be appealed to for aid, depending on who they were in life.

Ancestors as Nature Spirits

Interestingly enough, many of these ancestral spirits went on to become nature spirits. Trees, for example, are said to embody the "ghost of the person buried under it" (Wentz, 2011). For this reason, it's dangerous and even cruel to cut down trees in cemeteries. The Yew tree is thought to have a root in each person in a cemetery and so contains each of their spirits. Trees over the bodies of two lovers are believed to entwine, helping them be together for as long as the trees survive (MacCulloch, 1911).

Beyond just trees, the Celts also held that the formation of a lake can result from digging the grave of a person.

> Here, we come upon the familiar idea of the danger of encroaching on the domain of a deity, e.g. that of the Earth-god, by digging the earth with the consequent punishment by a flood. (MacCulloch, 1911)

Humans then can become Earth-gods in death and ultimately the spirits of the lakes, if they so choose to grow into a flood.

A young man whose love died saw fairies dancing one winter's night on a hill where no one lives. When he climbed up the hill to get a closer look at these spirits, he sees his deceased love dancing, icicles dangling from her jingling like bells, for she has become a glacier spirit (Jegerlehner, 1907).

In the Russian and German version of the Cinderella

story (Lang, 1890), a birch tree grew from a mother's grave, and it is this birch tree that provided her daughter with the magical gifts needed to win the prince. In the German fairy tale, "The Juniper Tree," a boy is murdered and buried underneath a juniper tree. He is able to get his revenge because his soul is born out of this tree in the form of a bird (Grimm, 1912). As previously mentioned, the connection between the human soul and trees stretches as far west as Ireland where people believed the souls would manifest as trees and other plants. So trees, or at least their souls, are similar to human souls such that people believed we shared a connection to each other even if we're not always aware of it.

Recalling further that for over half the populations of Europe, humans were directly descended from trees in mythology. Tree fairies had a major advantage over most humans, however, for they could live for hundreds or even thousands of years longer than any human could. Further, giant trees inspire awe, reverence, and a sense of wonder that must have defined the most important of fairies and deities. Because of this, trees were also more closely connected to the other deities, fairies, and nature than humans typically were. Mistletoe, it was said, came down as a gift from the gods of the sky to crown the oak trees (Frazer, 2003). Such signs let people know which trees to respect and revere in an otherwise confusing world.

Indirect Ancestors

Many spirits, such as some banshees, may not have had children, but rather, they live alone on the moors and in their fairy palaces, but still watch over their families like a loving cousin or aunt, showing up during important occasions. They wail and cry to mourn the death of loved family members, and at times warn them when danger is coming. They come to the home when a new baby is born to offer blessings and gifts:

> There is a legend told of the Macleod family: (that) Soon after the heir of the Macleods was born, a beautiful woman in wonderful raiment, who was a fairy woman or banshee, (there were joyous as well as mourning

banshees), appeared at the castle and went directly to the babe's cradle. She took up the babe and chanted over it a series of verses, and each verse had its own melody. The verses foretold the future manhood of the young child and acted as a protective charm over its life. Then she put the babe back into its cradle and, going out, disappeared across the moorlands (Wentz, 2011).

In another tale, the banshee of Grants Meg Moulach would stand beside the head of the family and advise them on playing chess (Wilde, 1887). Not every family had a banshee, however: "Only families of historic lineage or those gifted with music and poetry, which are the fairies' gifts, are attended by banshees." Banshees, in these stories, most often took the form of a sweet, singing virgin rather than the scary ghost of modern film (Briggs, 1967).

It is clear, then, that banshees did far more than mourn the passing of their family members, but actively engaged in making the lives of their families better. When they had finished, they often returned to the moors, where the other fairies lived. That these beautiful poetic and musical beings would have influence over the other beauty and music-loving fairies can only be speculated, but it seems likely that such influences did occur.

Others still would aid those they knew in life, even if they hadn't had direct relationship with them. For example, there was a boy who was in a graveyard when:

> There came about him something in the shape of a dog, and then a great troop of cats. And they surrounded him and he tried to get away home, but he had no power to go the way he wanted, but had to go with them... and after a time they went into the fairy bush and left him. And he was going away and a woman came out of the bush, and called to him three times, to make him look back. And he saw that it was a woman that he knew before, that was dead, and so he knew that she was amongst the faeries. And she said to him, "It's well for you that I was here, and worked hard for you, or you would have been brought in among them, and be like me (Gregory, 1920).

How Humans Become Fairies When They Die

One might think that if fairies are dead humans, they would be happy when humans died. However, like the banshee, the domovoi could also be heard to wail when a loved one was about to die (Ralston, 1872). This is interesting not only because it denotes that the fairies were concerned about and loved their descendants, but because it also indicates that not all humans become fairies. If this is the case, then perhaps it is because fairies know the times in which a person will become a fairy; that they choose to let people die at some times, while saving them at others. So just as a birth needs to be timed, so too does death, in that it's bad to die too early, but also bad to live too long. This, however, leaves us to wonder what the catalyst is. Why do some human souls become banshees and domovoi while others do not? To understand this, we turn to an accounting of one of the closest relations between a human and a fairy we have, that of Elspeth Reoch, a young Scottish girl who was trained in magic and became the lover of a number of fairies.

Elspeth Reoch's first encounter with fairies occurred when she was twelve years old while waiting beside a loch for a boat, when two men approached her, one in black and the other in green tartan plaid. The man in plaid offered to teach her a spell that would allow her to see things as they actually were in return for a courtship, which ultimately led to a brief sexual relationship between her and the fairy. Her second encounter with fairies occurred two years later, just after she had a child by another man. At this time, a different fairy man came to her. This second fairy told her that he was a human who had died as the sun was going down, so that he was now neither dead nor alive but forever caught between Heaven and Earth. So it is that in this story perhaps we have our answer as to why some people become fairies when they die. People, according to this story, become caught in the in-between world of fairies when they die at a time of an in-between; during sundown, for example (Purkiss, 2007).

Further, according to Diane Purkiss, Elspeth's encounter with fairies also occurs during a time of an in-between when she is on the edge of the loch, at the boundary of two clans, between her family and another land. It also occurs when she is in adolescence, between childhood and adulthood. Her second encounter occurs when she has a child born outside of marriage.

"Her encounters with fairies occur at the two most common times for such encounters; at the threshold of womanhood and after childbirth" (Purkiss, 2007).

This time of in-between is a constant theme among fairies. For example, those who die in childbirth, another time of in-between, are some of the most likely people to become fairies; also babies who die before they can be named, while they are still between the world of the womb and the human world. Perhaps the reason fairies themselves often appear so young is that many of them are those who died on the cusp of adolescence between two moments of life. So just like the fairy Elspeth first encountered, they are stuck forever between being alive and being dead.

Beyond simply offering some clarity as to what circumstances cause humans to become fairies, this story also offers some insight into the simplicity of certain fairies' goal; that they seek out other humans like themselves, humans who are on the fringes. Fairies then, at least those fairies that are the dead, are attracted to two things: their descendants who they are trying to help, or those humans who have become like them by being on the margins, those who find themselves between two worlds. Of course in the latter casehowever not all such encounters are positive, as the fairies often seek to kill those just as they themselves died.

Trapped in Fairyland

Many humans had been kidnapped by the fairies as servants, slaves, or friends. Even so, they still had some influence over the fairies.

> One girl's mother was taken by the fairies and it was said of her that no child ever permitted her hair to fall as it pleased except this girl, and folks did say that whenever she tried to bind it to her head, the bright locks refused to obey her fingers, and slowly untwined

themselves until they became natural ringlets again. The girl was a sweet singer — and singing is a fairy gift — and she would wander about, lilting merrily to herself, while neighbors wondered, and young men lost their hearts. It was believed that the girl was under the special care of the Trows, for everything seemed to be smooth before her, and her golden hair was called "the blessing- o' them that loves her." (Fraser, 2003)

Others still are trapped in Fairyland, but seem to act very much like the fairies. For example, a woman named Katherine Fordyce appeared to someone in a dream to explain:

"I have taken the milk of your cow that you could not get, but it shall be made up to you; you shall have more than that if you will give me what you will know about soon." The good wife would not promise, having no idea what Katherine meant, but shortly afterwards, she understood it was a child of her own to which Katherine referred. The child came and the mother named it Katherine Fordyce; and after it was christened, this Trowbound Katherine appeared to the mother again and told her all should prosper in her family while that child remained in it. She told her also that she was quite comfortable among the Trows, but could not get out unless somebody chanced to see her and had presence of mind enough to call on God's name at the moment (Black, 1903).

In another case, one girl became a fairy when she made the mistake of eating fairy food. In order to try to escape the fairy realm, she haunted a castle and would steal human food, for if she could manage to eat only human food for seven years, she would be free of Fairyland.

The scholar Christiansen believed that fairies were the captors of the dead and not the dead themselves (Briggs, 1968), while I would contend that many fairies were the dead, yet he did have a point that fairies held many prisoners in their court.

According to Gibbing (1889) people see among the trooping fairies

> Faces of friends and relatives, long since doomed to the battle trench or the deep sea, have been recognized by those who dared to gaze on the fairy march. The maid has seen her lost lover, and the mother her stolen child, and the courage to plan and achieve their deliverance has been possessed by, at least, one border maiden.

So not only are the dead among the fairies, but it is possible at times to bring them back to life. This can also mean that many of them are not truly dead, that like the fairy in Elspeth's story, they are neither dead nor alive. Many children and adults are taken by the fairies, with changelings put in their place. Often, such changelings are made of wood or earth and only appear to be the person's dead body in order to dissuade anyone from looking for them. In one story, a man rescues his wife just as she is being carried off by a troop of fairies, which had "come through the window, thronging like bees from a hive."(Briggs 1967)

Not all fairies abduct people unwillingly, however. There are tales of people entering Fairyland on their own. In one tale, a fairy maiden attempts to lure the Prince Connla into Fairyland, stating that she is the one

> Whom neither death nor old age awaits. I love Connla, and now I call him away to the Plain of Pleasure, Moy Mell, where Boadag is king for aye, nor has there been complaint or sorrow in that land since he has held the kingship. Oh, come with me, Connla of the Fiery Hair, ruddy as the dawn with thy tawny skin. A fairy crown awaits thee to grace thy comely face and royal form. Come, and never shall thy comeliness fade, nor thy youth, till the last awful day of judgment. (Jacobs, 1892)

Three things should be obvious from this story. First and foremost is that fairies can love humans and can long to be with them. Such love can occur even when, as was the case with the fairy in love with Connla, the fairy and the human have never met, because at least some fairies have a huge advantage over humans in selecting their future mates in that they have some divination power; so to a fairy it can be blatantly obvious who they need to love and marry even when they have never met them.

Second, the story of Connla should tell us that fairies will lure the mortals they love to live with them in the fairy realm; that once such humans enter the fairy realm, they become immortal so long as they continue to live as the fairies do. Third, such mortals, despite being tempted by a beautiful, magical being and a "Plain of Pleasure," can still be emotionally attached to the mortal world. So they, or the fairies who love them, as well as the children of such unions and friends they make within Fairyland, will likely take an interest in mortal affairs from then on. So, here again, we see the world of fairies being directly affected by the world of humans.

The Forgotten Gods

Many fairies are supposed to have once been the gods that people worshiped that have now shrunk in power and strength and, at times, are even weaker than the humans who once worshiped them. How these fairies feel would, of course, depend greatly on what their purpose was for becoming deities in the first place. Regardless of this purpose, however, it must be a very hard thing to be suddenly ignored by humanity, especially for fairies, who tend to be very sensitive. It's no wonder than that it's often asserted that the child-eating hag Black Annis is a former Celtic Goddess. After all, it's not atypical for people to demonize what they once worshiped and for fairies to morph to fit human exceptions or to have dualistic natures that include a darker side. Yeats speculated of the fairies:

> Are they "the gods of the earth?" Perhaps! Many poets, and all mystic and occult writers, in all ages and countries, have declared that behind the visible are chains on chains of conscious beings, who are not of Heaven but of the Earth, who have no inherent form but change according to their whim, or the mind that sees them. You cannot lift your hand without

influencing and being influenced by hoards. The visible world is merely their skin. In dreams we go amongst them, and play with them, and combat with them. They are, perhaps, human souls in the crucible—these creatures of whim (Yeats, 1888).

To truly understand fairies who had once been deities, we have to look at the reasons these spirits had once been deities.

Cared for Humans

Many fairies cared for humanity and so became deities in order to help them live better lives. Even though they are no longer viewed as deities, many of these fairies still care for humans. For example, the Byelobog, one of the divinities of the Russians that retained his kind nature and became Bylun, an old man that assists travelers in finding their way out of dark forests and also assists reapers within corn fields (Ralston, 1872). Similarly, in Great Britain, there was a former deity who dressed in leaves and would help children who were lost in the mountains (Briggs, 1967). Other former deities seem to have become bitter and twisted, however. Danu, a goddess of the Celtic peoples, became not one, but many fairy beings, one of which is a hag known as Black Annis, which haunts caverns and hills from which she seeks to devour humans. Fairies, as you will recall, are very sensitive, and after years of working with people, of befriending them, people turned their backs on them. Worse, people turned their uncanny powers to banish and harm magical beings, on these former deities. "In a prayer of S. Columba's, (he) begs God to dispel 'this host (*i.e.* the old gods) around the cairns that reigneth'" (Macculloch, 1911).

Priests commonly traveled about the country, banishing and attacking these spirits. Yet things weren't so black and white, for many people still adored and worshiped the fairies in rituals and with offerings even into the past century, while many other deities had always been cruel and dangerous.

Spirits of Nature Humans Sought to Placate

Many of these deities returned to being simple natural phenomena. The Blue Hag of the Highlands, for example, appears to be the personification of winter. She herds deer and fights spring with her staff, which freezes the ground. When spring wins, she hides her staff under holly where the grass never grows (Briggs 1967).

The Tiddy Mun was a fen spirit, which caused pestilence and controlled the waters and the mists. Although the people still held affection for him, like all fairies and ancient deities, he could be dangerous if he was insulted. Once, when part of the fens was drained, the people had to pacify him with prayers (Briggs, 1967). That they pacified him with prayers is telling about his general role in the world. In essence, Tiddy Mun brought all the things that the fens were said to bring, from the fog to the diseases. Even with all of these problems, people still ultimately love the landscape around them, especially when such a landscape makes them unique from their neighbors.

The ocean deities too remained behind, continuing to manifest the sea. "Bucca" or "Bucca-Boo" seemed originally to have been a sea god. "Fishermen left fish on the sands for Bucca and in the harvest a piece of bread…along with a few drops of beer" (Briggs, 1967). As time passed, his role did shift, however, to that of a being that torments children. As we've seen, internal duality, that is making the same being good and bad, was common among the old religions of Europe. As time went on, the deities' abilities to do either of these grew less and less until they were left tormenting children.

Seeking Power from Humans

Recall that many fairies have ulterior motives in working with humans; they need us to fight their wars for them, to give them power through offerings, and more. While these fairies might have cared about humans to some extent, they would easily become bitter and angry when humans stopped giving them what they needed.

The Shrinking of Deities

Many of these "deities" were man gods, that is to say, they weren't much greater than humans and were oftentimes even afraid of humanity. Yet in many cases, they still seemed to become lessened once humans stopped following them. The lessening of deities became so extreme that Dirra, one of the gods of old, was captured by the Earl of Desmond as a fairy bride after she'd become a simple water nymph. It was not, however, just the Christians who lessened the deities of the peoples they'd conquered or converted. The Romans, upon conquering Gaul, turned many of the local gods into nymphs and naiads when their sacred pools, trees, valleys, etc. were taken over by Apollo. Then, as Briton was once more conquered by another religion, these beings were once again lessened to fees, fairies that stand no larger than a child.

Charles Squire maintains that many of the fairy beings of Ireland are the divinities of the pre-Celtic peoples who inhabited that kingdom, who were lessened when the Celts invaded. Specifically, he states that:

> The leprechaun, who makes shoes for the fairies and knows where hidden treasures are, the Gan Ceanach, or "love-talker" who fills the ears of idle girls with pleasant fancies when to merely mortal ideas they should be busy with their work; the pooka, who leads travellers astray, or taking the shape of an ass or mule, beguiles them to mount upon his back to their discomfiture; the Dulachan, who rides without a head, and other friendly or malicious spirits. Whence come they? A possible answer suggests itself. Preceding the Aryans and surviving the Aryan conquest all over Europe was a large, non-Aryan population which must have had its own gods who would retain their worship, be revered by successive generations, and remain rooted to the soil. (Macculloch, 1911)

It would seem strange to think that a divine being, a god, could be captured the way a leprechaun is; forced to become some man's bride through a simple trick the way many fairies are in legend. Emotionally going from being powerful to so weak would likely have been destructive for the immortal and sensitive fairies.

Jacob Grimm (1882) speaks of the White Maidens, who seem only to be able to appear in the daylight before fading away at night. These spirits of former deities would still seek to aid humanity in many cases, often showing them the way to treasure. Some of these would appear only once every seven years with the keys to the treasure.

> In the castle-vault by Wolfartsweiler lies hidden treasure, on account of which, every seventh year when may-lilies are in bloom, a white maiden appears; her black hair is plaited in long tails, she wears a golden girdle round her white gown, a bundle of keys at her side or in her hand, and a bunch of may-lilies in the other. She likes best to show herself to innocent children, to one of whom she beckoned one day from beside the grave below to come over to her: the child ran home in a fright and told about it; when it came back to the place with its father, the maiden was no longer there. On day at noon, two of the gooseherd's girls saw the white maiden come down to the brook, comb and plait up her tails, wash her face and hands, and walk up the castle again. The same thing happened the following noon, and although they had been told at home to be sure and speak to the maiden, they had not the courage after all. The third day, they never saw the maiden, but on a stone in the middle of the brook they found a liver sausage freshly fried, and liked it better than they ever did another. Another day, two men from Grunwettersbach saw the maiden fill a tub with water from the brook, and carry it up the hill; on the tub were two broad hoops of pure gold. The way she takes, every time she goes up and down was plainly to be distinguished in the grass.

Refugees

The Irish Queen was spirited away by the fairies as so

many other women had been before her, taken by a chieftain of the Tuatha De Danann. This time, however, the kidnapping of a mortal woman was a bridge too far, for the king declared war on the fairies, ordering the Tuatha De Danann's magical animals be encircled and confiscated and the mounds where they lived dug up. For years, he laid siege to the fairies' homes, leaving them starving and desperate, until at last they returned his wife. Yet even with the war ended, their power was still broken, and they were weakened forever after that (Wilde, 1902).

This was not the first time humans in Ireland waged war on the fairies; indeed, fairies had once lived above ground before the humans came, and in a massive war defeated them and sent them scurrying for the safety of the underworld, making them refugees in their own land. The Tuatha De Danann were unable to defeat the Irish in a test of arms because of the Irish people's powerful druids and deities. So now the fairies are forced reside in the hills and rocks of Ireland much as fairies do throughout Europe (Wentz, 2011).

Briggs asserts that:

> There seems no doubt that the children of the Goddess Don were the Dana O'sidh and there, conquered by the invading Milesians, took to the hollow hills and became the Daoine Sidh or the "Deeny Shee." The Fianna Fin and their contemporaries fought, love and mated with these Daoine Sidh. Originally of human or more than human size, they dwindled through successive generations from the small size of humans to the size of three-year-old children.

The idea that fairies are refugees within their own land, indigenous peoples who were defeated by humanity, is fairly common. In Cornwall, one man states that "Pixies were often supposed to be the souls of the prehistoric dwellers of this country. As such, pixies were supposed to be getting smaller and smaller until, finally, they are to vanish entirely" (Wentz, 2011).

This paints a much more terrifying picture of some of the fairies than we often imagined. According to this account, the pixies, who people often think of as cute, little, playful fairies, are small because they are shrinking into oblivion.

What's more, they have had to live for thousands of years with the knowledge that they will eventually disappear and that those humans who will remain are the descendants of the people who forced them into their horrible fate. It is no wonder, then, that such beings are caught between human-like sympathy and incredible bitterness because, while they must retain some human emotion, much of this emotion must be anger at being driven into their current state.

Many fairies are starving and bedraggled, they dwell in squalor, some even live under human homes, in invisible huts in backyards or in even worse conditions such as where humans throw their garbage. "There is a widespread story of a fairy woman who begs a cottager not to throw water out at the doorstep, as it falls down her chimney. The request is invariably granted" (Andrews, 1913).

Such fairies often create an illusionary world, a world filled with good food, yet they still depend on human food for their sustenance. They therefore steal bread, meat, fruit, and more from humans.

In Zealand, a man who was being robbed determined that a troll must be doing it and so he hid and waited for it to come and, sure enough, he saw a troll stealing his tile stove, so he jumped out and frightened the creature away. It was common in general for the hill folk to sneak into people's houses to steal bread and other items such as wheat, yet when fairies from Wales to Germany stole goods from people, they could easily be frightened away by a farmer (Knightly, 1892).

In one case, a fairy keeps coming to a woman's home to borrow the kettle, with the woman and the fairy each seeming to be uncanny to the other. Briggs states that

"One can see how well this could apply to members of a lurking conquered tribe and to the newly settled conquerors. Each one, as we can see, was formidable and uncanny to the other."

It may even be that many wilderness fairies (such as brownies, which can also haunt forests and pools of water) became house fairies because they no longer had anywhere else to go, but still felt the moral need to continue working.

In Ireland, it wasn't uncommon for someone to hear fairy children crying out that they were so hungry they will die, after which their mother promised to steal some milk from a cow. In one case, the farmer prevented this theft and so was punished with the death of his own son (Wilde, 1902).

In another tale, a man promises the fairies that they can use one of his cows to feed their children forever after. Later, when the man gets into debt, some men come to confiscate his cows, but are assaulted and thrown about by an invisible army. They run off, but return the next day with a group of police who are also attacked by an invisible force after which no one ever dares touch the man's cows (Curtin, 1895).

In an Austrian fairy tale, a poor girl freezing to death in the cold comes across a hut of fairies who demand that she sleep with one of them for shelter. The freezing girl, afraid of dying from the cold, ultimately agrees to go to bed with one of them. As she is lying there with him, a woman from a nearby village comes to trade with the fairies and finds the poor girl in bed with them. Disgusted that a human, one of her own, would sleep with such creatures, the woman brings the villagers back to the hut, kills the men, and sends the girl out to die in the elements (Keightley, 1892). Like the leprechauns, it would seem that fairies, in this case, were easily overcome by humans. This may explain the desire of at least some of the fairies to remain hidden, although this desire is contradicted by the fact that at least in some cases, fairies want humans to believe in their existence.

We must also realize that the woman in the aforementioned story felt no qualms about storming into the house of the fairies to discover the girl sleeping with one of them; for if the fairies had had time to hide the girl, they surely would have, since they must have known what the woman's reaction would be. What we have then is a story of beings who are ostracized, considered far less than human to the point that they are dehumanized. This is shown clearly in one German tale where a king chases down a "Wild Little Dwarf" as if he were game. Later, when the king complains that he didn't catch any animals that day, his men assure him that

> There is not so good a sportsman as you to be found in the whole world. You must not, however, complain of our day's luck; for you have caught an animal, whose like was never before seen or heard of. (Anderson, 1906)

The fairy in this story was compared to an animal to be captured and caged. Fairies often returned this cruelty in kind. In yet another German story, some travelers come across a group of fairy like beings living in a cave, huddling around fires to keep warm. Here, the fairies trap the humans and begin to use them for their meat, roasting them on spits (Krauss, 1883). Other fairy vengeance is more mischievous or subtle as the fairies must always remember that humans once defeated them, drove them into the caves, and so humans can still destroy them with iron, the evil eye and magical symbols, if we wish.

Still, not all relationships between humans and fairy refugees were bad. A farmer who lived in Emserwald, Germany had no friends or relatives nearby to stand as godfather for his child, so he entered the woods. Here he found a dwarf, whom he asked to take the role. The dwarf was very pleased to be asked, but he was too poor to give much of a gift to the child. When searching the cave where he lived, the dwarf found a coal-black root and told the farmer that if he was starving, he should distribute a little of this root to each member of his family. Years later, during a particularly hard winter, the family was starving and so they ate the root, which put them into hibernation until spring when there was food in the forests again. The fairies' gift, in this case, wasn't some treasure, but a means to avoid starving to death by avoiding the problem of poverty, which both the fairies and humans faced (Jegerlehner, 1907).

Another wild fairy of Scotland, known as the Gille Dubh, hid among the groves of trees. Although, truth be told, he wasn't much for hiding and many people saw the black-haired creature dressed only in leaves and moss. He was generally considered kind and lucky, which he proved by helping a little girl named Jessie Macrae find her way home after she'd gotten lost in the woods. Yet even this gentle fairy was treated like some animal and came to be hunted by the nobility of the land, when a Sir Hector Mackenzie formed a hunting party to shoot him. Luckily, however, the nobles in this case weren't good huntsmen for they never did manage to capture the poor fairy.

Eventually, living on the fringes was no longer acceptable for many fairies, especially as humans began to make too much noise or grew too aggressive, or as society changed in ways that the fairies hated. When this happened, the fairies often fled to other lands. The trolls, for example, eventually fled Denmark in hopes of finding a lonelier, quieter land in Norway (imagine then what will happen as more people move to Norway and they are forced to move again). A young girl and boy saw a scruffy, beaten, and misshapen group of fairies fleeing Scotland. And the pixies of Cornwall were driven further out into the country by the sound of church bells, which they could not abide (Briggs, 1978).

It wasn't just humans that fairy refugees might be hiding from, however, for the fairies were very warlike and would constantly invade each other's lands as shown by the story of a man who goes out into the woods, discouraged that the girl he loves will never return his affection. At this point, he is approached by a fairy who had been hiding from a fairy war in the form of a bird. The young man had left grain for the animals. Out of gratitude, the bird promised to help the young man build a relationship with the girl he loved.

Fairy Courts

Not all fairies are desperate and bedraggled, however; many live in societies very much like human societies. According to Henderson (2007)

> The social and political infrastructures of Fairyland were parallel to those of their human counterparts... they were organized into tribes and orders and held children, nurses, marriages, deaths, and burials. They lived under "aristocratic rulers and laws...

> The fairies... are counterparts of mankind. There are children and old people among them; they practice all kinds of trades and handicrafts; they possess cattle, dogs, arms; they require food, clothing, sleep; they are liable to disease and can be killed. They work similar jobs that mankind works. (Campbell, 1900)

Fairies often pursued occupations much like those of humans; mining for treasures, forging weapons, farming, herding animals, making shoes, and more. These fairy kingdoms were not in some distant land, rather, they were all around humans, in the sky, in mounds, in forests, in magical spaces made larger on the inside than the outside through the fairies power.

When these kingdoms of fairies were left undisturbed, they acted peacefully towards humans, and would sometimes even trade bread, cakes, and more with the people who lived near them. They would also utilize human midwives to help them bear their children, while also borrowing human halls for certain celebrations.

Along with places where fairies lived seemingly ordinary lives, there were castles and noble courts among the fairies. Indeed, some fairies lived in courts so wealthy and opulent that it would make the wealthiest kings and tsars cry tears of jealousy. The dwarfs, for example, have a court in which they are able to compete directly with the deities themselves, thanks to their supernatural ability to craft items of great magic. When the fairy court showed up to serve at King Herla's wedding:

> Everything that Herla had prepared was left untouched. His servants sat in idleness, for they were not called upon and hence rendered no service. The pygmies were everywhere, winning everybody's thanks, aflame with the glory of their garments and gems, like the sun and moon before other stars, a burden to no one in word or deed, never in the way and never out of the way. (Barber, 1999)

Many people who have seen the fairy courts have been so overcome by the opulence and beauty of them that after leaving, they long to return so much that they pine away and die. So those fairies that choose to live in and or are raised in the fairy court live in a world of extreme opulence, of constant parties, and never-ending dancing. I discuss this further in the section "The Other World as Heaven."

More often, however, fairies likely lived in smaller villages, or towns, with fantastic country fairs and magical gifts to be sure, but otherwise, very much like most humans of their time lived. The seven dwarfs Snow White encountered, for example, chose to live in a small cottage out in the forest. They were still social, still friendly, but they chose to live a much more isolated and quieter life than their peers.

Many nixies of German lore choose to live in small societies, alongside humans; even going to the human market to do their shopping. Although, at times their great beauty and the fact that the hems of their garments are always wet sometimes betrays their nature.

Similarly, the knockers, who dwell in the mines of Cornwall, work alongside humans and seem to live in smaller groups. Those fairies that choose to live apart from the fairy court are much like we would expect; perhaps a little warmer, more open to hospitality, and obsessed with hard work. This isn't to say that the knockers don't celebrate or dance; rather, it's to say that this doesn't seem to be the focus of their lives the way it is for some other fairies. That's what makes this background so difficult to qualify, and why writers need to add depth to this background by thinking about what job the fairy would have within a society, and what this job says about the fairy.

Solitary Fairies

Other fairies choose to live a solitary life, away from humans and even their own kind. These fairies tend to be far more feral, far more dangerous than others. The dwarfs that choose to live alone, for example, are often cruel and twisted, incapable of gratitude. In "Snow White and Rose Red," the heroines help a dwarf escape the clutches of an eagle and he curses them for it. Another solitary fairy, the Vodianoi of Russia, tends to be a loner, who acts very much like a serial killer. Other fairies choose to be solitary, not necessarily because they are overtly cruel, but because they prefer the company of animals. The Leshii, for example, were the kings of the forest. Semi-solitary fairies that tended to live like bachelors or hermits, they traveled the woods with animals (mostly wolves and bears, but all animals of the forest were under their command) and rarely with anyone else. They tended to live as the ultimate bachelors, gambling, drinking, and throwing wild parties that leveled trees. They were often grouchy and typically rowdy, even when they married and raised children. The solitary nature of this creature also begs the question "what it would be like to be the child of the king of the forest, the child of a creature that only likes to keep company with animals (or the occasional fling, which they might sleep with)?"

The Brown Man of the Muirs is another fairy who is the ruler of the animals, but he will never taste meat, instead choosing to live on nuts and berries. He grows furious with humans who hunt on his land, berating them, challenging them to fights, and ultimately cursing them to grow ill and die (Briggs, 1976).

Nature – Nurturing, but Dangerous

Most nature fairies are both nurturing and destructive, for they live in a world where nearly everything kills something to eat. Beavers chop down trees and rabbits eat undergrowth, with each of these actions killing the fairies in these plants. Wolves eat deer, and moose crush wolves. So, like the lions of the movie *The Lion King*, nature fairies must be both nurturing and destructive in order to survive in this environment.

There is some evidence to support the idea that the first peoples of Europe relied heavily on acorns to supply themselves with food. So, just as the Japanese greatly revere the kami of rice for providing them with life, the people of Europe would have revered the fairies of the oak trees for doing the same (Frazer, 2003). The trees' importance to humans was so great that, like wells, it was nearly impossible for the Christian priests to get people to stop worshiping them. Indeed, long after people started attending Christian churches, they were still hanging the heads of dead animals in an old pear tree. Just as they had done with the wells, the Christian priests had to settle at a compromise, initially hanging pictures of saints in trees so that it would appear that people were worshiping the saints not the trees. In one example of this:

> S. Martin of Tours was allowed to destroy a temple, but the people would not permit him to attack a much-venerated pine tree which stood beside it—an excellent example of the way in which the more official paganism fell before Christianity, while the older religion of the soil from which it sprang could not be entirely eradicated (MacCulloch, 1911).

Trees, it was believed, helped to control and cause much of the growth of the plants that humans and animals needed to survive. Indeed, nothing grows unless the fairies allowed it to. This was why May Day, winter festivals, and harvest festivals all involved the idea of trees, which themselves symbolize fertility and life. So great was the trees' power in making things grow and providing fertility, that in some parts of Bavaria, May Day bushes were set up in the houses of newly married people so that they would conceive. Women would also hug trees in hopes of becoming pregnant or hang chemises on fruitful trees, while the Wends would cause their cattle to run around the tree as a means of making them thrive (Frazer, 1922). Even to this day, we decorate pine trees and bring greenery into our homes in the wintertime to celebrate a major Christian holiday. In so doing, we continue to act out an ancient ritual of respect for the fairies, even if most people are unaware of what they are doing.

The Celts believed that the fairies lived under the earth, in part because this is where they could control the fertility of the world, where they could direct the activities of all living things. In Russia, the fertility of the earth was controlled by spirits that dwelt in water (or occasionally caves), known as rusalka. People would decorate their homes with fresh green birches (the 'Rusalka's Tree') and girls would go into the woods to decorate the trees with cloth, thread, and garland before dancing about the trees while swearing vows of eternal sisterhood. Like many nature fairies, however, the rusalka's naturally nurturing nature was tempered with a destructive bent, which would lead to famines, floods, and illness, and cause her to drown people in the cold waters (Rappoport, 1999).

Almost all water fairies throughout Europe were

obsessed with dancing and music, and with luring people into the water to drown them. Even so, it was the spirits of the wells that were the people's guardians and comfort. In one story, a group of horned witches keeps invading a woman's home, tormenting her and eventually forcing her to flee. After fleeing from her home, the woman collapses in tears beside a well, and it is here that a voice speaks to her, telling her what she must do to be free of the witches (Jacobs, 1892).

Well spirits and water spirits are often personified beings represented only as a simple voice that provides advice to humans in need. In the tale "Brother and Sister," a witch curses the streams of the forest so that anyone drinking from them will change into an animal, in order to curse her two stepchildren. The spring, however, warns the two children of the danger so that they can avoid drinking from the stream of water at first (Grimm, 1812). The voice in this story comes from the water itself. So, as before, the water of the ancient European world appears to be alive, not just in the form of a human, but in and of itself. What we see in this story is that just because this living water can be cursed and poisoned by a powerful witch, this does not mean that the water is a willing participant in the problem.

However, water does not always appear to care who it is helping so long as it is helping people who are alive, as this helpfulness extends to those who don't deserve it. Criminals are able to cross water for safety just as easily or perhaps more easily than innocent children can, as the latter are more likely to be subject to drowning by the fairies within the water. What's more, the advice of water fairies is given even to those who not only don't necessarily deserve it, but who would do evil with it. In the "Story of Gold Tree and Silver Tree," a Scottish variation of the "Snow White" stories, a trout in a stream takes the place of the mirror in advising the evil stepmother, telling her not only that Gold Tree is more beautiful, but also letting the stepmother know that her stepdaughter survived the queen's attempted murder, as well as where she is located. This information allows the evil stepmother to try to kill her innocent stepdaughter again (Jacobs, 1896).

In this story, the trout is the personification of the pool of water as fish are often representative of the fairies within wells and other bodies of water.

"Even now, in Brittany, the fairy dweller in a spring has the form of an eel, while in the 17th Century, Highland wells contained fish so sacred that no one dared to catch them" (MacCulloch, 1911).

> Odin also gained his great wisdom from a fountain known as "Mimir's' (Memor, memory) Spring, the fountain of all wit and wisdom" in whose liquid depths even the future was clearly mirrored and besought the old man who guarded it to let him have a draught. But Mimir, who well knew the value of such a favor (for his spring was considered the source or headwater of memory), refused the boon unless Odin would consent to give one of his eyes in exchange (Guerber, 1909).

Mimir, in this tale, didn't care what Odin was going to do with the knowledge, he only concerned himself with what he could get out of his gift. Thus, water spirits' goals would seem to be far more enigmatic than those of beings that were once human or are somehow connected to the mortal world. Yet it is obvious that they care about humanity to some extent; otherwise, why would they provide aid to those in need? One possible reason that the water seeks to aid humans could be that the water seeks respect above all else.

In one Russian tale, two rivers, the Volga and the Vazuza, get into a dispute over which of them is wiser and stronger in order to gain the respect of the other. Eventually, they agree to race to prove which is better. This race takes the form of a race to the sea in the springtime, so at least in this case their bodies are the rivers themselves. Russian rivers are well known in myths to demand respect of humans, drowning anyone who doesn't provide this respect while providing easy crossing for those who do. So it is apparent that these rivers greatly desire to be respected. The desire for respect, for sacrifices to it, can make water a cruel being at times.

> The malevolent aspect of the spirit of the well is seen in the "cursing wells" of which it was thought that when some article inscribed with an enemy's name was thrown into them with the accompaniment of a curse, the spirit of the well would cause his death. In some

cases the curse was inscribed on a leaden tablet thrown into the waters just as, in other cases, a prayer for the offerer's benefit was engraved on it. Or, again, objects over which a charm had been said were placed in a well that the victim who drew water might be injured. An excellent instance of a cursing well is that of Fynnon Elian in Denbigh, which must once have had a guardian priestess, for in 1815 an old woman who had charge of it presided at the ceremony. She wrote the name of the victim in a book receiving a gift at the same time. A pin was dropped into the well in the name of the victim, and through it and through knowledge of his name, the spirit of the well acted upon him to his hurt. Obviously, rites like these in which magic and religion mingle are not purely Celtic, but it is of interest to note their existence in Celtic lands and among Celtic folk. (MacCulloch, 1911)

Rivers themselves are dualistic by nature, for on the one hand, they provide water for humans to clean themselves, to drink from, to aid in the growing of crops, and to travel along. Yet at the same time, they are a destructive force that floods the land, destroying the same crops they allow to grow, the cities they allow to exist, and which drown the children they keep alive. It is not simply a matter of capricious opportunity however, as again rivers will travel far out of their way in floods to do these things. In another Russian fairy tale, the spirit of the stream takes the form of a king bear who seizes Tsar-Medved's beard as he's drinking and won't let go until he manages to trick the king into giving up two babies, a girl and a boy.

In Northern Europe, the rocks were perhaps the most nurturing spirits of nature. Here, the Bjergfolk actively involved themselves in human affairs, helping with farming and fortune telling. In Iceland, a man named Bjorn made an agreement with one such rock fairy called a bergbui, which appeared to him in a dream. The rock fairy provided him with a goat which helped to grow his herd rapidly, and who also sent the land spirits to assist his brothers in their fishing and hunting endeavors (Davidson, 1989).

Fairies of the stones were so active in mortal affairs, in fact, that their name in Iceland means both "harvest" and "seer," as they would provide counsel to humans in their dreams and even actively guard people's cattle. It may not simply be because of their kind nature that the spirits of rocks are willing to make such deals with humans, for these spirits are extremely sensitive. In the 19th Century, an Icelandic clergyman wrote that certain rocks and stones were called the stones of Landdisir (land goddesses). It was said to be unwise to make loud noises near them, and children were forbidden to play around them, as bad luck would come to those who did not treat them with respect (Davidson, 1989). Because the spirits of the land were so important to the people of Iceland, laws were passed requiring people to respect them, to avoid scaring or annoying them. So, by working with humanity, these fairies were able to keep themselves safe from harm.

Undead Nature Spirits

Just as humans have ghosts, so too do the trees. It is interesting, for example, to note that the Druids and Celts would use a sprig of rowan to keep away harm, since this shows that the fairies, or at least their power, remained even after a branch was plucked from a tree. This idea becomes even clearer as we think about the possible reasons for knocking on wood for luck. The idea that fairies live on in wood is not limited to the Druids, however. Swedish peasants would stick leafy branches into their grain fields in order to ensure an abundant crop. Further, large branches were placed on the roofs of houses at the end of the harvest season, decked out with grain in order to embody the tree spirit, which helped to improve the next year's harvest (Frazer, 2003).

> Circassians regard the pear tree as the protector of cattle. They would cut down a young pear tree in the forest, branch it, and carry it home where it was adored as a divinity. Almost every house had one such pear tree. In autumn, on the day of the festival, the tree was carried into the house with great ceremony to the sound of music amid the joyous cries of all the inmates who compliment it on its fortunate arrival. It is covered with candles, and a cheese is fastened to its top. Round about it they eat, drink, and sing. Then they bid the

tree good-bye and take it back to the courtyard, where it remains for the rest of the year, set up against the wall, without receiving any mark of respect (Frazer, 2003).

Perhaps the most interesting case of tree fairies living on in the wood comes from Scandinavia, where it is said that the fairies of the elder tree will continue to attack people from the furniture. In one disturbing story, the fairy of the elder tree, which appeared as an old man, came out of the floor, which was made of elder wood and sucked the breasts of three people, causing them to swell painfully (Keightley, 1892). The Celts believed that the coppices that spring from the trunks of felled oaks are haunted by angry spirits of trees. In one story, a moorland spirit with a white hand sprang from the coppices of birch trees. She would rise up at twilight and chase travelers, her clothes rustling like dead leaves. When she touched a man's head, he went mad. When she touched his heart, he died. This went on until at last one man finally banished her with salt (Briggs, 1967).

These last stories show even more clearly than the others do, that the fairies do not necessarily die when the tree does, or that at the very least, fairies can even jump into what otherwise appears to be dead wood. This means that many household fairies, many spirits of the forest, might be part of something that is no longer alive.

Domesticated Nature Spirits

As human civilization has expanded, many nature fairies have started to adapt to our farms and our suburbs by living in fields, in trees near our homes, and in our gardens. In one case, an obviously wild fairy known as broonie started to protect people and their grain, even casting spells on the crops to give a good harvest. In gratitude, the people made him some clothes, but broonie was still feral, so, as with so many other stories, he was offended that anyone should think he would need clothes and he ran off never to be seen again (Black, 1903).

In Croatia, there is another forest fairy known as a vedi, which are as tall as the trees, who live in small villages or cities within the forest. They act as mischievously as anyone would expect a forest spirit to act. Worse, they even enjoy suffering such that they will kidnap and torture people, releasing their victims just before they would have died from the pain and suffering. Yet the vedi who live near civilization have started to adopt human families, protecting them against natural disasters. Even these vedi are still somewhat feral, as they still harm and cause mischief for the neighbors of those they've adopted.

> This may be illustrated by the expression: "Dear God, let our vedi help us and don't let their vedi harm us." It was believed that after one pronounced such a prayer, the spirit would come quickly to the person's aid. (Conrad, 2001)

Similarly, the bauchan of Scotland would aid and protect the Macdonals of Morar for ages. Yet at the same time, he waged war on the community around this family, particularly enjoying attacking strong men after sunset who he would leave dead and often mutilated, although he never attacked women and children in this way. Rather than being domesticated, wild fairies often seem to adopt specific human families the way they would animals, while still hating the rest of humanity.

In Russia, a being known as the leshii (forest kings) have started to move into people's fields at farms, where they help the plants grow and they protect the animals much as they would in the forest. Of course, given that the crops themselves are natural plants, which have been altered to fit human purposes, it shouldn't be surprising that the fairies of these plants would be altered in addition. Few people have made a better or more extensive study of agricultural fairies than the writer of *The Golden Bough*, who points out that at one time, people would say that the grain-mother, goat, wolf, or whatever other form the grain fairy took, was running when the wind blew through the fields, thus personifying the field and all its actions. According to his, and the research of others, there are many thousands of rituals and ideas surrounding the spirits of nature who have been semi-domesticated; however there are a few common ideas among these.

The Spirit is Still Feral

Many people appear to have believed that the spirit in the grain was still feral, still dangerous, that perhaps it made the plants grow because that was simply its nature and not because it cared for humans. Indeed, fairies of the grain are often dangerous, which is also why parents tell their children to avoid going into the fields or the grain-mother will catch them. Further, many of these feral grain fairies look like animals rather than people. These more feral fairies will cause illness to those harvesters who stumble upon them. If, for example, a reaper is taken ill on the field, he is supposed to have stumbled unwittingly on the corn-spirit, who has thus punished the profane intruder. It is said, "The rye-wolf has got a hold of him; the harvest-goat has given him a push."

For this reason, people would try to drive the spirit of the grain away from their land, by beating at the last sheaf of grain when winter came and they no longer needed it around. Others even go so far as to try to kill the spirit of the fields. In this case, as the corn is being cut, the spirit flees before the reapers. The spirit then tries to hide in the last bit of uncut grain and either must be chased out by the last reaper or killed when the last reaper cuts the grain.

The Spirit Must be Befriended

Other peoples seemed to have a closer, or at least a cordial, relationship with the spirit of their fields. In these cases, it was believed that the spirit of the fields lived in the last bit of grain harvested; and there were a number of rituals designed to keep in the grain fairies' good graces. In some cases, the people would even turn the last of the grain into a doll in female form so that all the farmers could dance with it. *The Golden Bough* notes this repeatedly. In one specific case, it mentions that in parts of France, the last sheaf would be named the 'Mother of the Wheat', 'Mother of the Barley', 'Mother of the Rye', or 'Mother of the Oats', and would be made into a puppet dressed in clothing and given a crown and a blue or white scarf. In another case, the author notes that:

> A branch of a tree is stuck in the breast of the puppet, which is now called Ceres. At the dance in the evening Ceres is set in the middle of the floor, and the reaper who reaped fastest dances around it with the prettiest girl for his partner. After the dance, a pyre is made. All the girls, each wearing a wreath, strip the puppet, pull it to pieces, and place it on the pyre along with the flowers with which it was adorned. Then the girl who was the first to finish reaping sets fire to the pile, and all pray that Ceres may give a fruitful year (Frazer, 2003).

In this ritual, we see a clear continuation of the belief that tree spirits help create a fruitful harvest. In parts of Dumbartonshire, the maiden of the corn would be dressed in ribbons and hung in the kitchen for the entire year. In Styria, she would even be dedicated in the Christian Church, indicating the longevity of the people's respect for the fairies involved in the harvest, or at least in the tradition. Here, they also took the extra step of making the finest ears of grain into a wreath, which was twined with flowers and carried on the head of the prettiest girl in the village. The Slavs also made a wreath from the last sheaf known as the rye-mother, the wheat-mother, the oats-mother, the barley-mother, and so on, which would be placed on a girl's head and kept until spring when it would be mixed with the seeds the farmers planted. Other people drench with water the last girl who cut the last bit of grain. The fertility of the fairy is considered to be so strong that it is believed that the person who cuts the last sheaf of wheat will be married within a year (ibid).

The Spirit That Must Be Contained

Others still would try to capture the grain spirit by cutting the last bit of grain and keeping it prisoner in the kitchen, barn, or somewhere else so that the spirit couldn't escape.

Friendly Neighbors

There are also many fairies that live like friendly neighbors. For example when a poor farmer in Wales is thinking of selling his land to move to America he meets a fairy who tells him that his luck will improve if he leaves a candle burning when he goes to bed. The fairies sneak into his house and craft good bread, good beer and do more. They help his crops to flourish so that his luck is good from then on (Sikes, 1880).

Banished from Court

Stripped naked and cast out of the land of eternal joy, there are many fairies who live among humans or alone because they've been banished from the fairy court or human society. Certainly, some of these fairies must be bitter, angry, and dangerous, but it's difficult to tell from lore which of solitary fairies might have been banished from fairy court. Humans only seem to learn about the banished fairies which are friendly. For example, Fenodoree was a Manx Brownie who was banished from Fairyland because he'd fallen in love with a human girl and was dancing with her in the merry glen of Rushen during the sacred festival of the Harvest Moon, at which all the fairy court was supposed to attend. Once banished from the fairy court, he continued to live with humans, bringing luck and doing work in the houses where he lived (Briggs, 1967).

Similarly, another household fairy by the name of Hinzelmann came out of the Bohemian Forest because, as he said,

> Consequence obliged (him) to retire and take refuge with good people till his affairs should be in a better condition." He was extremely loyal and kind to those who provided him with shelter during his time away from the other fairies. Fairies tend, in general, to repay kindness many fold, so it shouldn't be surprising that they would work, provide divination, and other forms of aid to those people whose houses they chose to stay in to gain respite. Further, many fairies are friendly and

kind anyways. So when they live with another intelligent being for a long period of time, they begin to care about their adopted families as a matter of course. Hinzelmann is described as "quite friendly and intimate: he sang, laughed, and went on with every kind of sport so long as no one vexed him, and his voice was on these occasions soft and tender like that of a boy or maiden (Keightley, 1982).

A young troll was accused by a greater troll named Knurremurre of becoming too intimate with his wife, and so to avoid a fight, the younger troll turned into a cat and fled to live in a human village. There he lived as any cat would until at last a troll told the cat's "owner" to tell his cat that Knurremurre was dead. On hearing the news, his cat sprang up and exclaimed that he could go home, which he did with all haste.

The only commonly unfriendly banished fairies which are mentioned in any lore that I've read are those who were once human, such as the taran, who are the souls of unbaptized children who go about in Scotland, crying, "Nameless me, nameless me." Such spirits are forever caught outside of all societies, unclaimed by the fairy court and by human society, so they dwell apart, sorrowful and bitter.

Nature Elements

As the spirits that help plants to grow and animals to thrive, most nature fairies are naturally nurturing. So while they may not naturally aid humans, it's not too much of a leap to see them seeking to help humans. There are, however, other spirits such as the wind and the fog, which are not naturally so helpful. Indeed, many of these spirits are downright dangerous.

At one time, when the fishermen of Brittany were faced with fog, they would threaten to cut it in two with a knife. The Irish would battle the waves with axes in order to kill the fairy spirits within them to prevent the tides from rising too high

(MacCulloch, 1911). Fairies were found in every force of nature from the wind that blew to the heat and the cold. As shown by the previous examples, the relationship between people and the forces of nature was different from that of other fairies because people were more likely to feel the need to threaten or even do battle with the forces of nature, which means it's likely that many of these forces of nature were rather destructive and wanton. At the same time, however, these forces of nature could be appeased by people. In England, children would offer Jack Frost a spoonful of kissel as they asked him not to destroy their winter crops (Keightley, 1892). Further, some of these fairies such as the North Wind of Scandinavia or the Warmth from the Sun enjoy watching humans and can even feel sympathy for us the way a human might feel sympathy for a lost puppy or child. Such forces of nature would have spent thousands of years watching humans, following stories, and thinking about the nature of the world. So, while they might have difficulty understanding us, they would still be capable of caring for humans, in a way.

Half-Fairy

There are many fairies who are half-human, and while it's likely that such half-fairies are generally considered of a greater order in Fairyland, thanks to the normally uncanny nature of humans to fairies, it's difficult to know for certain the fate of children raised in Fairyland, as there are very few stories about them. However, we do have a number of stories about half-fairies who live with and were raised by humans. These half-fairies are oftentimes gifted with certain powers. For example, the child of the fairy woman Aine and the human Earl of Desmond shrank and grew in order to jump in and out of a small bottle to "surprise a woman." which means that, like any child, they grow up liking to show off, but have magic to help them do so. Unfortunately for them, these half-fairies seem to have a very troubled relationship with the fairy world. This troubled relationship might come from the fact that they or an ancestor of theirs was abandoned by the fairies. For in nearly every story about marriages between fairies and humans, the human breaks some taboo and the fairy leaves them. The purpose of this is probably to explain why the nearly immortal fairy is no long living with its descendants, but these stories also mean that the half-fairy's fairy ancestor left them, while their human ancestor disrespected their fairy ancestor. This situation likely creates resentment among the children of such unions for both parents. Further, while half-fairies tend to get along better with the fairies than most humans, their fairy nature means that they often either want the same things the fairies do, and so take them from the fairies, or else they play pranks on the fairies.

For example, a young woman who was believed to belong to the old breed of Bendith y Mamau (half-fairies), became the best of friends with a house fairy (bwca) that lived in the place she worked as a maid. As part of this friendship, they worked closely together, with him often helping her perform her daily chores, although she was never allowed to see him doing these things. Despite how good their relationship was, her fairy nature got the better of her and she couldn't resist playing a mean prank on the bwca. She put some stale urine in with his food. Furious, the bwca seized her by the neck and began to beat her and kick her about the house.

In another case, there was a boy in the County Mayo who never washed his feet, so they called him Guleesh Blackfoot (an indication that he was likely half-fairy). Upon being banished from his home for this, and for being lazy, he easily falls in with a crowd of fairies with whom he enters the Pope's home through a keyhole. He threatens the Pope to force him to reinstate a friend of his who is a priest. Guleesh then travels to France, where the fairies kidnap a princess whom he falls in love with and decides to make his own. So he "rescues" her by using his human powers to thwart the fairies (he crossed the girl to himself so that the fairies couldn't touch her). The fairies are furious with him, as they had intended the girl to be their servant.

Half-fairies live a strained life, not quite finding

acceptance among human or fairy societies, but easily making temporary friends in both.

Sample Fairy Characters

1-Glaistig (Scotland)

The glaistig's spirit is divided between two worlds for she is a spirit of the earth, dwelling in forests and hills on the one hand, yet she's a maiden of the water and fertility on the other. A beautiful woman with the legs of a goat, who haunts the forests of Scotland, dressed in long flowing robes to hide her animal half. Because of her dual nature, the glaistig was both revered and feared.

In one form, the glaistig is a kind being, although playful to the point of being childish. She spends much of the time dancing and singing in an endless stream of immortal parties, which, given her shepherd-like nature, might be similar to barn dances. Although playful and a bit mischievous, the glaistig loves to be helpful and especially enjoys getting praise for a job well done, which is why she so often helps herders with their cattle and farmers with growing crops in return for small gifts such as milk poured over the rocks where her spirit resides. The glaistig holds a romantic image of the pastoral life, which they consider to be beautiful and fun filled; a life in which humans live at peace with the beauty and serenity of nature. While not entirely true, this seems to be the vision, the dream that the glaistig seeks to make a reality.

Like many fairies, the glaistig is ancient and wise yet childish; being unable ever to fully mature and so is most likely to get along with children, which is why overworked parents sometimes use her as a babysitter, a task that she enjoys because she is more likely to make friends with children than anyone else.

In addition to beauty and serenity, the glaistig can also represent nature's more wild and destructive side. For despite her generally serene nature, the glaistig is prone to wild fits of rage and long tantrums as their emotional outbursts can last much longer than any human's could. At night, she often becomes a wantonly destructive vampire, luring men to dance with her so she can drain their blood. She might also lead people astray by covering the paths they are traveling on with rocks so they the get lost in the mountains.

2-Büt Aba (Water Mother) (Mari-El)

The Büt Aba loves serenity and beauty, which causes her to lead a fairly solitary existence in "clean" lakes and ponds. Further, water mothers have a very strict sense of how the world should work, which very few people can live up to; which means that people are constantly having to apologize and provide gifts to the Büt Aba for wrongs they don't necessarily remember committing, wrongs such as swearing, being lazy, loud, rude, and more. Such gifts typically include sacrifices of black sheep, black hens, and porridge.

Obsessed with cleanliness and purity, the Büt Aba is constantly cleaning the rivers and lakes where she lives, which in turn helps the villagers, who depend on clean drinking water, making her vital to a village's survival. Luckily, she does seem to have a naturally caring nature most of the time, one that allows her to thrive on praise and human affection. She loves to meet new people, and so when a new woman marries into the village, she always presents herself to the water mother with a gift of porridge, which also helps the woman avoid having the sensitive Büt Aba think she is ignoring her.

In addition, the Büt Aba basks in being center of attention at parties, enjoying feasts in her honor by the water where she lives. Similarly, she enjoys performances in her honor, such as when people role-play her making it rain. For this reason, she is very likely to make it rain, or perform other water-related tasks when people ask her during a festival in her honor and when people share their food with her. Of course, her enthusiasm in pleasing her adoring fans will sometimes go a little too far, and she'll make it rain far too much, at which point people will pull some of the remains of the food from the water. Since Büt Aba is usually happy to help keep the world flowing as it should be, she's usually, though not always, only too happy to cease the rain when asked. In addition to causing it to rain and making the water clean for drinking, she's known to give blessings and for helping fishermen get a good catch. This is why fishermen, understanding her desire to share in meals and receive affection, will also pour her vodka and porridge in return for an abundant catch.

The problem is that the Büt Aba's sensitive nature causes her to become easily depressed, which in turn causes Büt Aba to become slothful and lazy when she feels that people aren't paying enough attention to her or when people constantly act against her moral view of how the world should work. When depressed, she mopes sadly about her lake, allowing herself and her water to become unkempt so that the water makes everyone who drinks it sick. Worse still, her sensitivity can also lead her to become furious with those who make too much noise or swim carelessly in her waters. Such people are in danger of being pulled underwater or cursed with illness. Thus, outside of feasts in her honor, it's usually best to speak and act quietly around the water where she dwells.

3-Buffardello (Italy)

Originally nature spirits who lived in the trees (most often nut trees), the buffardello began to move into people's houses, where they caused mischief and stole from humans like little foxes. Indeed, they continued still appear as anthropomorphic goblins, who look like eighteen-inch-tall young children or old men with beards with some animal features, especially those of cats and foxes. Like many fairies, they almost always have a red hat, and when they are seen, more often than not, they are often dressed all in red;

although it's rare to see them as their feral nature means that they prefer to remain invisible around most humans. As nature fairies, the buffardello are still highly magical and have many abilities, including the power to control the wind and create illusions.

Like wild, rambunctious children who can get away with anything, the buffardello playfully run about homes, causing mischief and trouble wherever they go. Most of the time, they live like the foxes or cats, whose features they share, acting in a semi-solitary way in which they enjoy being around others, but don't necessarily care or spend very much time with a specific society. And like these animals, they grow curious about the growing cities and villages, so they soon began to move into these. Further, like cats, they subsist by hunting, but they don't just hunt for food as they enjoy teasing their animal victims before killing and draining their blood like a vampire would.

Despite the buffardello's childlike nature, they are often so ancient, they barely recall being young, and possibly never had a childhood at all, so they suffer greatly from a Peter Pan Syndrome. This desire to be young, to be childlike, means that they only seem to connect emotionally with children, for although the buffardello might delight in scaring children on occasion, they will sometimes play nicely with or sleep next to them like a cat or dog might. The danger is that, on occasion, the buffardello will kidnap these children, taking them off to their realm in the forest to live and play with them for months, years, or forever.

The buffardello thrives on chaos, as their childlike nature mixed with a lack of supervision means that they are able to get away with being much more mischievous than any human child could be, and even cruel at times. Their Peter Pan Syndrome leads them to crave attention, so even though they remain invisible to avoid trouble from humans, they laugh hysterically as they run wildly about people's homes. They especially love the sound of their footsteps echoing on stairs late at night, opening and closing windows, jumping on sleeping people's chests, making strange noises, moving furniture, ripping paper, throwing clothes about, turning on and off lights, and cutting people's hair and beards into patches.

At the same time, however, the buffardello suffers from

feelings of inadequacy and is anxious, nervous about human rejection to the point that they almost always remain hidden from people. However, they still feel a childlike love for girls and women and so will, on occasion, build up the courage to confess their love to girls or women by giving them gifts and blessing them with great beauty. Their anxiety means that they want to keep these relationships a secret and so will punish anyone who speaks of having a relationship with them. Such punishments can be extreme, as the buffardello suffers from extreme emotions, which cause them at times to fly into an uncontrollable rage, even killing those they once loved in a fit of anger. They may regret this action briefly, but are flighty by nature and so will often bounce along to their next prank or adventure a few moments later.

4-Banshee (Irish)

Fairyland is a place of delights, a place of music, singing, and dancing of continuous joy and feasting. Yet despite this, banshees take the time to come and give blessings to the children of their still mortal families, chanting poetic verses, and songs to protect and give gifts to those children, before returning to the moorlands. For banshees are gentle, kind to a fault, and extremely sensitive. Banshees feel emotional connections so deeply that they are unable to live happily in Fairyland, but instead choose to spend much of their time worrying about and fussing over the family they left behind when they died.

Banshees are extremely affectionate and their compassion is fervent to the point of becoming an all-consuming desire that lasts for hundreds, if not thousands of years. They are not fickle with their love, however, for they reserve this compassion for only a very select few, and they don't even help everyone among their human relatives.

Banshees seek serenity, harmony, and, above all, beauty. They are so idealistic that even through watching everyone they love die, over and over again, through thousands of years of pain and failure, they keep working for those they love. This all-consuming compassion, mixed with the banshee's ability to see the future, often leads to heartbreak, as the banshee must watch the death of those they love creep ever closer. The banshee's eyes grow red from crying over so many lost loved ones, and their wails of sorrow are often heard as the fateful death grows ever closer. Thus, banshees are defined by a deep sense of loss and a strong hope for better things.

Their love of poetry more than anything else is likely what gives them comfort and keeps them going, for even sorrow can be beautiful in its own way. So, just as the sorrowful song of "Danny Boy" can stir the heart, banshees too are given comfort by song and poetry. Thus, what they seek is to create a beautiful poem, a beautiful legacy through the blessings and advice they give, even as they work to craft a happier and better life for those they love.

As part of this legacy, banshees seek to pass on this gift of poetry to a select few, giving a gift that they hope will make the art of those they love most immortal, and the fruits of which they can enjoy for thousands of more years to come. Their love of sagas and their desire to set their family on a journey leads the banshee to speak in metaphors when giving advice, so they almost never give completely clear answers.

Their nature as spirits who no longer exist with the living, but who can't idle away their time in Fairyland, has led them to become somewhat solitary figures, even though they often dwell within their own palaces, which in turn causes them to become reflective of the world, and deep philosophical thinkers, even as they begin to live more and more in the fantasy world of their own minds.

5-Baba Yaga (Russia)

What am I? Who am I? Why am I here?

We have all asked these questions, we've all pondered these concerns at one time or another. And often, such concerns lead us to feel so solitary, so alone that we give a superficial answer or forget them. For Baba Yaga, who feels things much more intensely and for much longer than humans, and who has been given many responsibilities over nature, forgetting isn't an option.

Worse still, Baba Yaga suffers with these conflicted feelings even more than most, for she has been called the spirit of the moon, the spirit of the wind, a goddess of the forest, and the guardian into the land of the dead.

As the moon, Baba Yaga is both a queen of light and of the night and shadows. As a spirit of the wind, Baba Yaga brings comforting coolness to people on hot days, yet freezes them on cold ones. As a goddess of the forest, Baba Yaga is both creative and destructive, such that death and life both dwell inside of her. As the guardian to the land of the dead, she dwells at the point in the forest where it changes from the human world into the Other World of spirits. Thus, her home exists between the land of the living and the land of the dead. As a queen of the land of the dead and the guardian to the gates of the dead, it's her job keep the dead from returning to the world, and to protect the living from the dead. Although these two jobs seem similar, they are emotional opposites. For on the one hand, she will snatch away someone to devour, yet at the same time, she'll help someone rescue a lost love from other monsters that dwell in the spirit world. Thus, she is the Grim Reaper and the guardian of humanity at the same time, killing those who are unworthy to enter the land of the dead and keeping most people from returning to the land of the living. Yet those such as Vasilisa the Beautiful who passes certain tests and accomplishes certain tasks (most often with the help of the shamanistic familiar spirits), can escape from the land of the dead, should they fail in their tasks, Baba Yaga will devour them.

In one story, a young girl goes to find out where the geese carried her younger brother and finds him playing with golden apples at Baba Yaga's hut. The boy in this story doesn't appear to be mistreated by Baba Yaga, yet at the same time, those were often one of the birds that conveyed human souls into the land of the dead. We can presume that the boy is on the verge of death and that his sister is rescuing his soul; which makes this story scary enough, for the if the girl fails to rescue her brother from Baba Yaga, both of them will pass on into the land of the dead, never to return.

It may be that it's partially Baba Yaga's job to decide who lives and who dies, a terrifying job and mostly feared. Yet, at the same time, this job puts her in a position to do some good. For example, in "The Frog Princess," Baba Yaga helps a young man enter the other World and tells him how to defeat the evil being that has stolen away his wife's soul.

Although Baba Yaga dwells in an isolated hut in the

woods, she doesn't live alone, for she often spends her time with the riders of the day, the sun, and the night. Yet she still seems solitary, for she has a strong sense of the way the world should be, but just doesn't understand her place within I; which leads her to have a greater, although ambivalent obsession with purity such that she will help those who are pure of heart, but kill those who are not. Her conflicted nature, however, means that she herself is never able to find purity and so she is very irritable and sometimes enjoys wreaking destruction. Tearing through the forest and people's fields, she leaves chaos and death in her wake. She snatches children away from their mothers, devours people, and revels in the more cruel aspect of her nature.

The wickedness of her home and actions are a bit over the top, theatrical, as if she is exploring that side of herself, trying to convince herself to be darker than she naturally is. This darkness stems from bitterness and resentment at people's ultimate rejection of her, a dangerous side effect of her sensitivity to the feelings of others.

Her hideous appearance and people's obsession with beauty has led her to feel vindictive and vengeful against beautiful girls, which is why she treats beautiful girls as if they are worthless and lazy, bitter against their beauty and the love they receive from others. Yet Baba Yaga still clings to a romantic image of the world. So when beautiful girls prove their worth through cleverness and or hard work, she rewards them greatly. And when a brave young man calls her "granny" and seeks her help in finding his lost love, she is often more than willing to provide aid.

In addition to all her other conflicts, she must also deal with being a dragon-like being on the border between Asia, where dragons were gods, and Europe, where they were monsters. The Russian folklorist Alexander Afanasyev believed that Baba Yaga's name meant something akin to "serpent witch," or perhaps "serpent grandmother." Certainly, to some extent, Baba Yaga's generally negative, but occasionally positive nature with heroes, seems to show something dragon-like in her nature. So she is nature both kind and cruel. Like a child who brings home a baby bird he find injured on the ground in hopes of saving the little animal, yet shoots another bird with his slingshot, Baba Yaga is a bit immature and conflicted. Yet she is smart enough and ancient enough to understand her own conflict, smart enough to be tormented by the big question, "Who Am I?," a question that may have no answer. For nothing is ever clear in Fairyland.

6-Anguana (Italy)

Anguana love beautiful perfection, yet they must suffer with the knowledge that despite their great beauty, they have a single serious flaw, the foot of a goose or a goat, or the lower body of lizard, or a moss-covered back. This flaw, along with their own strong emotions, leads them to feel anxious about people, about being seen. Yet they are still curious about the world and filled with kindness. Indeed, the anguana have taught humans many of the secrets of civilization, helping humanity develop skills such as weaving and cheese making.

Above all else, the anguana value purity, which humans, with our short fickle lives, often violate. We are likely very befuddling to them. For while the anguana choose to dwell only in pure water, which they protect from harm and pollution, humans will often break their covenants of the past and pollute this water, even when it goes against our own interests. This makes the sensitive anguana vindictive and angry and causes her to feel ever-greater anxiety around the humans she can never truly understand. Most often, this leads her to live in pure water, away from the civilizations she helped to form. Yet there are few escapes from the civilization of humanity anymore, so with her young childlike nature, the anguana must dwell like an anxious girl near people.

Like most fairies, anguana have strong cravings for entertainment, which exhibits itself in almost continuous dancing and singing. Yet for the curious creatures, this simple entertainment isn't enough and so she will often follow people to listen to gossip and whispered secrets, which in her resentment, she will often use to harm people by revealing secrets about them or telling the perfect lie to make them fight with each other. Like a reality TV junkie, the Anguana watches the ensuing fights with a strange, anxious fascination, giggling and laughing with mischief.

Their love of beauty mixed with their own deformation can also lead them to feel resentment against human girls who are perfectly formed, a resentment that often boils over, causing the anguana to lash out, scaring these girls, teasing or making fun of them, or at times spreading discord by revealing secrets and spreading gossip about their target, or worse, murdering them wholesale.

7-**Ainsel**

A fairy girl in Northern England, Ainsel is playful and curious and, like many children, she instantly presumes that any other child she meets is a friend. However, she suffers from roller coaster-like emotions with extremely rambunctious highs and horrible lows in which she throws terrible fits. When she's happy, she becomes a bit wild, bouncing about from one location in which she shouldn't be to another. During these times, she enjoys taking risks, delighting in knowing that she's doing something she's not supposed to. The problem is that these adventures, like many similar childhood adventures, often end in pain, tears, and tantrums that wear on her mother's patience.

Sociable, always anxious to be the center of attention, she craves positive feedback from others, which leads her to be a bit of a show off. She is talkative, lively, and imaginative. So, as a natural artist, Ainsel uses her magical power to play games while creating art, forming animals out of ashes that prance about tiny illusions of trees and houses and humans.

Ainsel spends much of her time daydreaming, living in a fantasy world of her own, which, being magical, she is able to create in a clumsy, childish way. Yet she finds interaction invigorating, so she always seeks to pull others into this fantasy world of hers.

Her curiosity and playfulness, along with her constant attempts to make her own fantasy world, often get her into a bit of trouble, which is why her mother often scolds her after she hurts herself.

Extremely emotive, Ainsel's emotions change quickly, so she can grow furious at the drop of a hat, flying into rage-filled tantrums, and then suddenly becoming forgiving and happy again a few moments later.

8-Chuhayster (Ukraine)

A jolly, bright, and cheerful old nature spirit, the chuhayster might be a bit of a hermit, but he still enjoys being in the presence of others, so will at times sing and dance with other fairies. Despite these rambunctious moments, the chuhayster are generally very unassuming, preferring the quiet, solitary beauty of nature to the fun thrill of the fairy court.

Chuhayster live for beautiful moments and will explore their wilderness home, searching for quiet moments of contemplation and beauty. They love simple things, a bit of good food, the friendship and gratitude of others, the way the red sunset reflects off of green leaves, the smell of pine trees during the first snowfall, birds singing among elder tree blossoms, etc. Because they are lovers of beautiful moments, their deep, beautiful voices often echo through the forest as they sing about each new moment.

Their kindness and love of serenity makes them very tolerant of others, and even helpful to the woodsmen and hunters who must pass through their home. They also share the food that humans leave for them with the animals of the forest, which they love and care for as well. But the chuhayster cannot abide those who seek to harm other humans or fairies. Those that do are likely to incur the wrath of the chuhayste, for although the chuhayster is slow to anger, when they do grow angry, they hold grudges for a long time. They spend much of their time hunting down mayvak, a female forest fairy, which cuts off people's heads, and delights in hurting others.

9-Knockers (Cornish)

Although knockers are a nervous around the much larger and unpredictable humans, they still feel a deep sense of responsibility for the wellbeing of others, so long as those others work to take care of themselves. Knockers put a high value on relationships and working in harmony with others, and so in addition to living and working together, they allow humans to enter their homes to mine for precious minerals. For although they remain hidden from humans, they enjoy listening in on human conversations and can easily form a deep connection with those having them.

More than anything else, knockers love industry and hard work, which is why they live in mines where such work is commonly being done in conjunction with conversations, which are less likely to happen in factories. They see industry and hard work as the true path to make the world a better place, and gain joy out of the endless possibilities that come to fruition because of the seed they draw out of the earth, both for the fairy world and for the human world, as their compassion is large enough to cover both realms.

Their need to improve life for others and their constant dream of making a better world means that they have difficulty sitting still, and are almost always trying to accomplish something. This means that they are more reserved than the other fairies. Unable to join in the wild stream of constant partying that their kin love, they instead seek the quiet sanctuary of caverns deep under the earth. This doesn't mean that they are hermits or solitary by any means. Rather, it means that they prefer good company and conversation to meaningless frivolity, and a purpose driven life to an unimportant series of parties.

10-Monachicchio (Italy)

Living forever as children, Monachicchio are bubbly, silly fairies who are filled with an infectious cheer as they bounce happily from game to game. Despite originally being nature fairies, they are compulsively clean, so they are only willing to play in haystacks and barns for so long before having to wash up.

Although they are gentle and kind, spreading cheer, joy, and luck to the children they play with, they can be a bit bossy and each one feels that he has to be the leader of their little games, for they each want everything to be just so. This is why they so often seek out human children who they can lead about when they play their games. The Monachicchio's need to be in charge means that they often become demanding and rude if they don't get their way, and are even quick to anger, throwing tantrums, although they rarely become violent or cause any serious harm when upset. Instead, they become emotionally overwhelmed so that they cry and weep for long periods of time over very little.

They also love to show off, and are very prone to extravagance, which means they will seek out humans who they can impress with their simple magic tricks. With a voracious curiosity, they love to explore, sneaking about so that they can see opportunities to learn mischief or overhear conversations they couldn't otherwise. They don't have the anxiety around adults that most fairies have. Instead, they tend to find adults boring except when they can cause play pranks on them, as they love to watch people's reactions to their mischief and get a thrill out of doing things they aren't supposed to. Thus they remain invisible simply to annoy the adults, who can do nothing to an invisible fellow.

Some of their favorite pranks include tickling the feet of adults, pulling the covers off of sleeping people, or sitting on people to wake them up or make them snore. They also tie people's and animals' hair into knots. But most especially, they love to whisper sweet nothings into a girl's ear, and then lick the girl's face, giggling outrageously if she squeals and runs away. In addition to pranks, Monachicchio take childlike pleasure in life, with large appetites for food, drink, and fun.

11-North Wind

Like a cantankerous old man, the North Wind feels a strong sense of independence, a need to do things for himself, so he is easily irritated and angered. He loves his privacy, which in turn can lead him to feel isolated and alone. Despite his desire to be alone, he has an intense curiosity, an energetic interest in the world around him, which leads him to love to see new sights and experience new places. So he tends to be out and about to be doing things, as he craves constant stimulation and new experiences. Because of this interest, he knows nearly every place in the world, even going to places none of the other winds ever travel to.

He is a firm believer in love and has a romantic notion of the way the world should work. So when someone seeks help in reuniting with a lost love, he can become deeply caring and affectionate, fatherly even. In "The Tree Princesses of Whiteland," he goes out of his way to help a king recover his love from a wicked prince who is trying to take her from him.

Although he can be friendly, he doesn't really form long-term relationships, and most of the time he is gruff and often thoughtless as he zips about the world. He isn't easily tuned into what others are feeling and isn't very good at expressing his own feelings. So there are times when he can absentmindedly steal other people's food or damage their homes without even thinking about it or noticing what he's done, although he is open to criticism and is even sympathetic if he finds out he has done something wrong. In one tale, when he discovers that he took a poor boy's food from him, to make amends, the North Wind gives the boy a magical cloth that allows him to create an unlimited supply of food.

12-Lutin - Farfadet (France)

Lutins are lusty, sprightly fairies with strong desires for beautiful women or men and good wine and food. They live in a world of splendid parties and joyous revels. Childlike tricksters, they have a wicked and often mean-spirited sense of humor. They tend to be fickle little creatures, bouncing from one role to the next, changing from house fairies to nature spirits and back again one day to another. Still, the roles they take on come from a strong desire to be useful, and from a deep-seated sympathy for the "sad" little mortals who struggle through life. Thus, they will often busy themselves with helping humans herd cattle, bringing in the harvest, folding laundry, or consoling sad children.

They love hard work for its ability to improve not only a person's life, but the life of an entire community. They can't abide laziness and will punish those who are so disinterested as to not even really help themselves. In addition to helping a community with hard work, they also enjoy playing soldier, protecting houses from evil spirits and pests, such as mice, as they troop about through fields.

Despite their carefree exterior, they live with a lot of social anxiety, which they cover up by acting overly courageous and strong, and have a tendency to show off when they do come into view. Their anxiety also means they are very likely to seek praise for the work they've done, and can quickly grow vindictive and angry if such praise is not forthcoming. In one case, a man felt that he didn't need help bringing his crops in, so the lutin cursed the ungrateful ingrate with complete ruin, causing all his crops to wither away. This need for praise also means that they are very sensitive to insults, and dislike loud or awkward situations, and so they hate drunks who are prone to saying and doing stupid things. Given that no one can really punish the lutins, their dislike can take the form of cruel, mean-spirited reprisals that can get out of hand and all too often lead to serious injury or worse. Vindictive in the extreme, they dry up the fields of those who have insulted them or grow angry when they aren't praised for their good deeds.

The truth of the matter is that lutins long for childhood, not just to be young and truly carefree, but to be cared for by a family who loves them. So they will often use their magic to disguise themselves as children and swap themselves with babies in their cribs. What most defines lutins is that they yearn for an unconditional love they will never receive.

13-Leshy (Russia)

Tall creatures, appearing as satyrs or perhaps a bit like Bigfoot, leshy act like the ultimate bachelor (even when married) and feudal lords. Leshy live as the kings of the forest, gambling, chewing tobacco, drinking, and singing with each other. They throw parties so wild they uproot trees and leave wanton destruction in their wake.

Highly competitive, they will often battle with each other fiercely for the tiniest plots of property rights. Above all else, leshy value strength and courage, which is why they are most likely to be friends with the bears of the forest. Of course, part of their love for bears comes from the fact that these large animals can act as bodyguards for them when they are too drunk to protect themselves.

Arrogant to the extreme, the leshy see the lives of the animals of the forest as being entirely their property and so will travel about as their king, protecting them from human encroachment, but will sell the lives of these same animals to hunters for a bit of bread, some pancakes, salt, or a plug of tobacco.

They have a cruel sense of humor, enjoying leading

people to get lost in the forest, and then watching them as they try desperately to find their way out of the dangerous wolf-filled lands. They also wither crops and sicken animals.

They travel their domain, springing from tree to tree to survey their land; and at night when they sleep, they rock themselves in the branches as if they were cradles. For them, ownership of the magical realm is more important than the beautiful solitude of the woodlands, so as humans began to move into their territories, they started to become lords of the farms and crops as well. Thus it's very likely that now they are swiftly becoming lords of the suburbs and the animals that dwell there.

14-The Zwerg of Snow White

The zwerg are generally very social beings, living together in large cities under mountains or at least together in cottages in the woods. Warm, affectionate, caring, and enthusiastic about life, they strive to make the world a better place by using their vast knowledge and magical talents to give advice or magical gifts to the heroes of fairy tales so that they could complete their quests. Similarly, they also sneak into homes to help people clean, to leave gifts, and of course, on occasion, to help poor craftsmen who are struggling to get by.

The zwerg see a world full of possibilities, and have passion for making things better. They are enthusiastic craftsmen, which along with their kindness and enthusiasm, inspires others to work harder. This desire to make things better and their passion for hard work comes from a strong sense of morality, a belief that hard work is the greatest good, while greed and laziness are the greatest evil. They likely believe that hard work is what will ultimately allow people to live happily and without poverty, which they seem to detest. So they'll punish greed and laziness severely, at times even with death curses. This latter reaction is part of the extreme emotions that the zwerg seem to feel and are guided by.

So when Snow White shows up to the zwergs' home, they happily take her in and take care of her. She must, however, cook and clean and learn to work, even as a princess. In ancient Germanic lore, these zwerg would not have been goofy or odd; rather, they would have been beautifully angelic beings who may have been older than the forest itself. Of course, by the time the Grimm Brothers collected these stories many dwarfs of legend had changed form to appear much more ugly and twisted.

Zwerg are steady and loyal, which is why they have the secrets of magic and immortality. One such being tells humans that they aren't allowed to learn these secrets because of their duplicity and greed. These secrets of magic allow them to change shape, divine the future, and occasionally read minds. They can also use these powers to make magical items, such as a hat which allows them to become invisible. Their amazing craftsmanship doesn't just come from their magical powers, however, for it often comes from their love of hard work and their attention to detail.

Although they are social, and semi-commonly appear to humans, zwerg do prefer to remain hidden. They are, after all, the guardians of a treasure, so it wouldn't do to allow potential thieves to see their comings and goings on a regular basis.

15-Tomte (Scandinavia)

Contemplative and deep thinkers, Tomte love to know how things work. Always curious about the true nature of things, they enjoy spending time alone so that they can think and dwell on the nature of the world. Not as filled with fantastical thoughts as other fairies, their thoughts are much more reflective of the job they've chosen; that of farming and ranching, making them more practical.

Because of their practical view of the nature of the world, and their love of occasional moments of solitude, Tomte choose to dwell on human farms, apart from nature fairies, the fairy court, and the loudness of human cities. In addition, Tomte enjoy the slower pace of life in the country, tending to be traditionalists who dislike change. Even so, for specific tasks, they are flexible and creative in completing them.

A caring, helpful being with a strong love of farming and hard work, the Tomte enjoy helping to protect the animals and the family, while often performing chores. In many ways, they seem to be a fairly archetypical farmer, yet like many fairy folk, they suffer from a low self-esteem, which makes them easily offended and prone to wild mood swings.

Tomte are fairly direct, and seem to be unable to hide their emotions, whether good or bad. Because of their low self-esteem and their quiet nature, they have difficulty dealing with troubling emotional situations, often throwing a destructive poltergeist-like tantrum whenever they get upset. A commonly cited example of this is when a farmer put butter at the bottom of a Tomte's oatmeal instead of the top. Unable to see his butter, the Tomte became enraged and killed a cow out of spite. Only later, upon discovering his mistake, did the Tomte feel bad and replace the cow with one stolen from someone else.

Despite their quiet nature, when they are in the mood for fun, they are adventurous daredevils who enjoy taking risks. They go on little adventures to unwind, so they prefer the company of uncomplicated people, such as young boys who are often willing to aid them in stealing from and causing mischief at neighboring houses and barns. These adventures can quickly escalate out of control until someone gets hurt, as the Tomte tend to have a lot of pent up energy.

16-Tul aba (Fire Mother) (Mari-El)

With a deep reverence for the sacred, fire mothers have an obsession with purity; and for them nothing is more pure than the love of a family gathered around the warm hearth in which the fire mother dwells. So although they are quiet, they still love company, preferring to watch the goings on of a happy family. A bit serene, they are normally gentle, caring, and helpful. It is the fire spirit that brings the families' sacrifices to the other spirits and acts as a mediator between people and the gods, while also working to protect their family from evil spirits (they are able to leave the hearth in the form of a woman).

As gentle souls, fire spirits are extremely sensitive to anger, aggression, and impurity; so much so that if the fire mother is exposed to too much negative emotion or pollution, it can drive them crazy, causing them to become vindictive, cruel, and angry. When angry the fire mother begins to lash out at those around them, causing illness and, at times, even spreading out of control to burn away the household that has started causing them so much pain.

Gifts of black hens and the milk from a black cow, followed by a return to a serene and happy family state will often calm the angered fire mother, allowing her to once again relax and bask in the warmth of the affection around them.

17 - Pixie Vagabonds

While most pixies are finely dressed and live in beautiful palaces or mansions, there are some who live as vagabonds; dressed in rags they squat in homes, barns, and anywhere else they can find shelter. These pixies were banished for becoming too vain, for getting swept up by the endless parties and the glamor of their lives. So now, they must travel the world in order to gain an understanding of their place in it and the importance of hard work.

This humbling experience has caused them once again to become helpful, caring, kind and hard working. They spend their time helping farmers to bring in their crops, doing the washing and folding the clothes for old washer women, and the like. Still, their humble circumstances and their strong emotions mean that they are prone to wild mood swings, growing angry at the slightest offense or becoming intensely prideful with the smallest gift; such that even the gift of a set of clothes can once again cause these fairies to think once more of themselves as too good for work.

18 - Coleman Gray: A Pixie Child

One of the fairy children adopted for a time by humans, Coleman Gray is impulsive and energetic, living life in the here and now. Loving to have fun, he is adventurous, talkative, and inquisitive, as he flits from one moment to the next, gathering experiences the way a butterfly gathers nectar, never staying in one place for long or dwelling on what has been. So although he is caring and genuinely feels warmth for others, when he leaves his human family, he never returns or speaks to them again.

Still young, he is just beginning to develop an appreciation for the fine things in life such as beautiful music, songs, and dancing. But for now, he is primarily focused on whatever sounds fun at the moment, which is fine with most people because of the energetic enthusiasm he brings to his games. He is a lot of fun to be around.

Coleman Gray is intelligent, good humored, and outgoing, and his cheerful and friendly nature allows him to make friends easily. Although, at the same time, he often acts without thinking about how his actions might hurt others. Because of this, along with his childish nature, he engages in a lot of mischief, even more than a normal child would, which although never permanently harmful, can still hurt others in the short term. Luckily for him, the humans he's living with generally overlook his actions because of his fairy background.

He loves to be the center of attention, yet there has to be an underlying fear of humans that comes from the knowledge that they drove his people into hiding, and perhaps a certain amount of awe given to humans' great physical strength and untapped abilities.

Although he tends to act very wildly, he is also very tractable, and has a strong regard for his parents. He's still forming very specific principles with regards to what's right and wrong, but as these ideas form, he sticks obsessively to them, which is good because he, like most pixies, is naturally very caring, and is easily prone to worry when he sees neglected children or the elderly and sick. When he sees those who need help, he can't help but try to do something.

When he sees a poor child, he is prone to teaching them how to use the magic in morning dew to not only wash away the dirt on their faces, but to make themselves look more beautiful. He also has a tendency to want to help children escape to a happier place. His love of being helpful extends very heavily to his human family; although he is anxious to be seen helping them as he worries that others will judge the way he does his tasks. So he will often secretly clean the house or do the laundry when no one is looking. Yet despite the fact that he does these things in secret, he really does want to receive praise for his work as he thrives off of the good will and happiness of others.

The challenge he faces is that he does have a strong natural sense of justice and urge to punish those he sees as wrong. Like most pixies, he hates laziness and dirtiness above all else, yet he still has very little understanding of how the world works, which means that he can at times go overboard with punishing those who don't really deserve it.

Although normally humble, Coleman Gray is prone to sudden bouts of pride and extravagance. During these moments, he can become bossy and easily irritated, although such bouts usually go away after a short while.

19-Metsänväki (Finland)

Metsänväki are serene and highly sensitive. Their sensitive nature and their love of serenity make them somewhat reclusive, although it also means that they are highly caring, kind and helpful.

Lovers of the quiet beauty of nature and the poetry of life and death that exists in the woods, Metsänväki spend their time working to make the woods they live in ever more beautiful. They also pass the time in song and dance, working to perfect every art they can.

Their naturally caring nature leads them to help hunters obtain food, or to work to heal the sick. Yet they can't stand to be around too many human emotions and easily grow furious when their forest is violated by loud and disrespectful people. In their rage, they cause illness and will sometimes kill people.

Their sensitive nature also means that they are anxious about rejection and so rarely ever show themselves, even though they are stunningly beautiful. For even the gawking of people attracted by their angelic perfection embarrasses and makes them nervous. Yet such a quiet lifestyle often becomes too lonely for them and so they begin to yearn for company. Unable to connect with people or bring themselves to strike up a conversation with another, they usually just snatch away men whom they fall in love with from a distance, in hopes that they can marry these men without real fear of rejection.

20 - Peg Prowler

Peg Prowler is a refugee, a wilderness fairy now living like a fox that has encountered farms; she sneaks about, stealing chickens and haunting barns, when she's not living in her river.

Overly sensitive to the feelings of others, Peg Prowler has become ever more bitter, angry, and vindictive as time goes on. She recalls all too fondly a time in the distant past when she lived from dance to dance, working to help humanity in return for the sacrifice of a chicken or other animals. Now that humanity has started to ignore her and the other fairies, all her friends have fled into other lands, leaving Peg Prowler to feel a deep sense of loneliness; a loneliness that has driven her to drag people down into the water so that their ghosts might dwell with her in Fairyland. Yet most people's souls don't stay for long before going off to the spirit world, and so she must suffer the pain of being left over and over again by each new friend she makes. So every seven years, she seeks to find a new friend to take into Fairyland with her.

Her actions make people begin to fear her as a bogey, which in turn causes her to morph, becoming twisted and dark as people began to think of her more and more as a horror story. So while she's still playful at times, her playful nature is far darker now and she finds it funny to truly scare people, to vandalize property, to send people running and screaming.

She also still desires the finer things in life, so she spends as much time as she can in castles and mansions. Yet at the same time, such buildings remind her of what she's lost and make her feel forlorn and sad, so she must often leave these to cry along lonely roads and in her river.

However, even after all her suffering, there are a few moments when she tries to connect with people as she once did, by possessing a potential shaman to act as a mediator between her and the human world (see Witches and Cunning). But the last time she tried to attach herself to a child, people didn't understand what was happening and so they exorcised her, leaving her more frustrated and angrier than ever.

Witches & Cunning

The man lay drenched in sweat; every nerve in his body screamed with agony. His stomach hurt so much he kept hoping he'd wretch it out of his body. He was so sick that his soul had already left him in the form of a bird, which was singing a mournful, supernaturally beautiful song outside his window. They both knew that he was going to die, that his soul would never be fully reunited with his body. That's when he felt a hand take his, felt himself getting up and, in that moment, the pain was gone, washed away like it had all been a bad dream. He was certain he'd died at last, as he was led by an ethereal woman to stand in a heavenly court before the queen of the fairies. She demanded that he return to his body and return to the land of the living in order to heal the sick, help the poor, and make the world a better place. A few moments later, he was back in bed, recovered from his illness, but he was never free or alone again. From that day on, the fairies were his constant companions and his masters, for his life belonged to them now.

The shamans of the European traditions go by many names: witches, cunning, hexe, and more, but they all act as mediators between the human and the spirit worlds, most often as servants to powers greater than themselves. Yes, there are other magical traditions in Europe such as alchemists, ritual wizards, and others who use formulas and herbs to perform magical feats, but these were not witches, even if a witch also learned these forms of magic. A witch was very specifically someone who worked with spirits for good or for ill.

The cunning (good witches in parts of Britain) to whom people went for cures to illnesses and to find lost treasure, as well as evil witches people feared would put curses on them, didn't always have power themselves. Rather, they used their relationship with fairies to perform seemingly supernatural feats. Witches are in essence "those who have a close and oftentimes intimate relationship with fairies." This means that the boy in Wales who plays with fairy children daily is a witch, as is the girl who becomes the object of a fairies affection in Italy. Both these people are able to receive gifts and magical aid from the fairies and so seemed to be supernatural, even if they didn't always have powers themselves.

This also means that what defines a witch as good or evil were the fairies with whom they had a relationship. Those who worked with good fairies tended to do good things, and those who worked with evil fairies tended to do evil things. According to Yeats:

> Witches and fairy doctors receive their power from opposite dynasties; the witch from evil spirits and her own malignant will; the fairy doctor from the fairies, and a something--a temperament--that is born with him or her. The first is always feared and hated. The second is gone to for advice, and is never worse than mischievous. The most celebrated fairy doctors are sometimes people the fairies loved and carried away, and kept with them for seven years; not that those the fairies' love are always carried off--they may merely grow silent and strange, and take to lonely wanderings in the "gentle" places (Yeats, 1888).

But as we've seen, the activities of fairies are never so black and white, which means that most witches were altogether gray. Further, many, if not most witches, had no choice which fairies they worked with, as more often than not the fairies, good or bad, chose them to be their mediators with the human world.

As mediators between the human world and the world of fairies, people often came to rely on these witches. In some places, people even used to enjoy going to the wise man's home. People would travel for miles to visit the white witches of Cornwall to obtain their protection, charms, spells, counter-spells, or to keep them safe when they traveled long distances. Such activities weren't restricted to only the poor or people of the distant past. Noblemen, ship captains, soldiers, and more would all visit cunning folk in such numbers that people would have to wait for a long time to take a turn to see them. Many of the books on witches and most of my sources discuss witches after the famous witch-hunts, which shows that not only did the cunning survive the worst of the witch-hunts in many countries; they did so openly while often maintaining a certain amount of respect. This is not to say that witches didn't fear for their lives during these hunts; many cunning folk were secretive in part because of them. What it means is that it didn't matter the time period; there were always some people who respected good witches.

Defining Magic

Magic in Europe was most often believed to come from otherworldly beings, indeed, in ancient Europe there was typically very little or even no distinction between religion and magic. The Romans, for example, defined magic as prayers and religious formulas performed for selfish ends. They believed that to use such religious-magico prayers for purely selfish purposes was disgraceful, and frowned greatly upon those who earned money from clients to say prayers on their behalf. Priests and real religion were supposed to benefit communities, families and groups of people, or to be said on behalf of those in need without expectation of compensation. Despite society's disapproval, people did use religious-magico practices and prayed for their own success and safety all the time.

Worse still were those who used religious-magico practices in an attempt to manipulate the gods, to constrain them through ritual rather than giving them their proper respect. Of course, the line does blur here because many publicly accepted rituals still did try to restrain the gods and, in many ways, priests of Rome could be likened to lawyers; negotiating and carrying out contracts with the deities. The Romans also feared strange religions and odd ideas, even before they were Christian, and a user of magico-religous powers who sought money, even if the money was for others, would have been considered more of a magical figure than a religious one.

The Greeks had a definition of magic that was closer to that which most fantasy writers today use. Initially, the Ancient Greeks stated that magic was the use of a tool that had special powers (such as a wand), the use of herbs to perform supernatural things, and the use of secrets, which were told exclusively to a person by a deity (most often Hermes). This last point is especially interesting not only because of Hermes's relation to the shaman deities of the north, such as Odin, but most especially because of his relation to the fairy-like creatures I've been discussing in this book. In both these cases, witches, cunning folk and similar users of magic would often receive secrets from either shamanistic spirits/deities or fairies, which they could not share with anyone, lest the magic stop working.

The Ancient Germanic and Celtic people seem to have had very little if any separation between what was magical and what was religion. Indeed the Germanic peoples lead deity (Woden, Odin, etc.) was both a shaman and a deity of the magical arts. Certainly, the Germanic peoples had formulas and methods, which weren't necessarily prayers, but they had certain religious connotations inherent within them.

Despite their differences, however, all the people of Ancient Europe had a definition for what was "evil magic." And all of them outlawed such practices to one extent or another. Evil magic was defined as the use of evil spirits and or the use of spells for evil purposes. Interestingly enough, this definition seems to be very similar to that of the later Christians, who defined sorcerers and witches as those who worshiped and used devils, pagan deities, or spirits. Even among the medieval

Christians, there was, at times, a clear distinction between those witches who used evil spirits and peoples, such as the cunning, who used good spirits. Further, even throughout medieval times, magic took on a religious definition, for among the Christianized people of the Middle Ages, there were believed to be two types of magic: high magic and low magic. High magic was used by magicians and the like to get closer to the nature of the divine, to get closer to God. This was the most common and important type of magic for the educated; even alchemists were as much or more obsessed with this idea as they were with any earthly treasure.

The Encounter

The person wishing to acquire the witch's knowledge must go to the sea-shore at midnight, must, as he goes, turn three times against the course of the sun, must lie down flat on his back with his head to the south, and on ground between the lines of high and low water. He must grasp a stone in each hand, have a stone at the side of each foot, a stone at his head, a flat stone on his chest, and another over his heart ; and must lie with arms and legs stretched out. He will then shut his eyes, and slowly repeat the following Incantation : — O, Mester King & a that's ill, Come fill me wi the warlock skill, An I sall serve wi all me will. Trow tak' me gin I sinno ! Trow tak' me gin I winno ! Trow tak me whin I cinno !
Come tak' me noo, an tak me a', Tak lights an liver, pluck an ga', Tak me, tak me, noo, I say, Fae de how o' de head tae de tip of de tae ; Tak a dat's oot an in o' me, Tak hide an hair an a tae thee, Tak hert an hams, flesh, bleud, an buns, Tak a atween de seeven stuns I de name o de muckle black Wallawa ! The person must lie quiet for a little time after repeating the Incantation. Then opening his eyes, he should turn on his left side, arise and fling the stones used in the operation into the

> sea. Each stone must be flung singly ; and with the throwing of each a certain malediction was said (Black, 1903).

In lore, there were always some few who sought out the fairies in hopes of becoming a witch. In Russia, for example, there were some people who sought the goodwill of the unclean dead by offering them eggs (Ivanits, 2992). Yet, in most stories, these people are either attacked by the spirits or grow so frightened when they encounter them that they flee. There are very few records of people gaining power by seeking out the fairies, even though it was sometimes considered to be very easy to become a witch. Walking around the church backwards at midnight could give a person the power to shape change, for example (Jacobs, 2011). This was also dangerous as, oftentimes, those who would walk around churches in the wrong way would be kidnapped by the fairies.

In the unique case of Ann Jefferies, a servant girl who did bold things that even boys were afraid to do, had the fairies come to her after she sought them out:

> Turning up fern leaves, and looking into the bells of the foxglove to find a fairy, singing all the time. "'airy fairy and fairy bright; Come and be my chosen sprite,"
> She never allowed a moonlight night to pass without going down into the valley, and walked against the stream, singing: 'Moon shines bright, waters run clear, I am here, but where's my fairy dear? (Hunt, 1903)'

At first, the fairies ignored her, then one day, after she'd finished her chores for the morning in the household where she worked as a servant, she was sitting in the garden, when six little men in green with "charming faces and bright eyes" came.

Anne's case is fairly rare, however. More commonly a person inherits their relationship with the fairies from someone else (a mother, an uncle, etc.) or they are chosen by the fairies during a time of grief. As Purkiss puts it:

"In most cases, these are stories of a woman who meets a man dressed in green or black who asks her to serve him. Eventually, she gives in and they seal their agreement with sex...."

Among the people of South East Europe, it was believed that certain witches would fraternize with the spirits of nature. However, these witches would wear pillows over their genitals to protect them from the nature spirits' lust (Conradn, 2001), which is not to say that all such relationships involve sexual intimacy. However, the sexualization of the relationship between fairies and humans fits a historical pattern in Europe, as in Greece, where Hermes and other male deities were only served by female seers; while the female nymphs were only served by male seers, which were often believed to be their spouses (Larson).

More often, a relationship that was desired, however, was a relationship that came out of hardship:

> Fairies are the fantasies of the dispossessed. They do not come from wealth and privilege. They come from the deeps of misery. People whose lives are a perpetual struggle to survive suddenly faced with one burden too many..... A fairy story is a story about hitting rock bottom – in that sense a story about dying... (Purkiss, 2007)

So very often, the first encounter took place when the future witch lie dying or found herself in a time of desperation.

> Saint Selvija from the village of Sveta in the vicinity of Demir Hisar offers an interesting example. Despite being married for ten years, Selvija was not able to give birth. According to her story, that period was "a great burden" for her... The story continues to state that because she was not able to have a child, her husband stopped loving her and started trying to force her to leave. She refused to do so as she had no other place to go. In the last four years of her "childless experience," Selvija stopped eating everything, even bread. In this period of self-starvation, she often prayed to God to give her a child, vowing that she would be his servant. One day when, in an extremely weak and depressed condition, she sat down to rest, St. John appeared at her door and instructed her to go to a certain monastery where there was healing water that would

make her healthy and able to have children: and finally, she had a girl... After having her children, Selvija became "weak" again until one day she fell into a coma. She was "like dead" for three days and three nights. That was the first time she visited both Heaven and Hell. After coming back, she started to heal and continued to heal until the end of her life.... (Petreska, 2008)

Similarly, when one "Living Saint" was seven, she nearly died from smallpox when a storm broke out, and then St. George entered the house in a bright light to tell her parents not to be afraid (Ivonav, 1992).

While the desperation theme was common in the making of witches, not all of them had to die to encounter the spirit world. In a Slavic fairy tale, a man's wife divorces him after many years of marriage so that he falls on hard times and begins to starve to death. Dejected and alone, he wanders into the forest, where he encounters a wolf who asks him where he is going and, after a few moments of conversation, the wolf joins him on his journey. In yet another Slavic tale, a snake jumps out of a tree and says to a farmer, "You're a poor man, and I will help you. If you bring me a bowl of milk every day before sunrise, I'll give you a coin" (Krass, 1883).

In England, a starving man named John Webster was returning home from work with a heavy heart, for he couldn't think of a way to get food for his wife and children. That was when he met a fairy (who appeared as a woman dressed in fine clothes) who offered to help him escape his poverty. Meanwhile, Bessie Dunlop meets the fairy Tom Reid when she is starving to death and weak from having just given birth to a child, yet she still has to drive the cattle out into the field and home again by herself because her husband and child are even worse off than she is. Adding to all of this, one of her cows has just died, leaving her even more impoverished than she was before. As with most such stories, the fairy offers her comfort and aid so that she can get through her hard times (Wilby, 2006).

In the German fairy tale, "Puss and Boots," a boy's father dies, leaving him so poverty stricken that he thinks his only recourse is to eat a cat and then starve to death; until the cat speaks to him and promises to make him rich (Jacob

Grimm believed this cat to be a household fairy). In the story of "Godfather Death," a poor man has no means to provide his son with a christening and so is desperately seeking any aid he can find when he encounters Death, who offers to stand as godfather for his child (and who later aids his child in performing magical healing).

The miller's daughter in "Rumpelstiltskin," encounters the fairy Rumpelstiltskin when she has been locked away by her "fiancé" with the order that she weave straw into gold. At this time, she is between her father's house and that of a potential husband, between being free and a prisoner, and it is then when the fairy appears to her. In "The Old Woman in the Wood," everyone that a young girl is traveling with is murdered by bandits and, although she manages to escape, she is lost and soon finds herself starving. Sad at the loss of everyone she knows and so weary from starvation that she can't go on, she at last sits down to die. That is when a white bird comes with a magical key to a tree filled with food.

Finally, in the story "The Pebble," an old man laments that:

> Sorrow keeps me awake every night. But all these tales must be only fancies, and the benevolent fairies in these mountains, who used to help the poor when they were near despair, are most likely long since gone, or else my trouble would have brought them to my relief. And with men, oh! with men there is no pity!" During this lamenting, a giant, shadowy form brushed past him in the twilight, whispering in his ear, "Do not despair." He looked up, but saw nothing save the shadow of the oak under which he sat, heard nothing save the sighing of the evening wind in its branches. (Lauder, 1881)

When people first encountered these beings, they often saw them as clear as day, and often didn't realize right away that what they were seeing was even a fairy or spirit, although just as often, encountering the spirit was a terrifying experience.

When Essex witch Elizabeth Bennett first met one of her familiars, she was so afraid she cried out: "In the name of God, what art thou...?" While Cornish cunning woman Anne Jefferies was "so frightened to see six persons of small stature, all clothed in green jump over the garden hedge that she fell into a kind of convulsion-fit (Wibly, 2006).

A man named David Hunter flung the firewood he was carrying and ran terrified into his house when he encountered the fairy for the first time (Seymour, 1913).

What's important to realize in all these cases is that the fairies approached people because they wanted to be involved in humanity. They wanted to change the course of history, help the poor, or harm people and cause mischief. Whatever the reason, these fairies sought out human mediators to take action in the human world on their behalf, even providing secrets and magic to their followers and allies. Even powerful beings, such as the queen of the fairies and the lords of evil fairy courts, or the king of the forest (often called the devil in fairy tales), want something from humanity and will send out their servants to work with witches as familiar spirits. Other times, the familiar spirits seem to be acting of their own accord and for their own ends. Although there do appear to be a number of times when the fairies have no real goal other than friendship with the witch. Regardless, a person typically became a witch after he or she experienced his or her first encounter with the "Other World."

It was common during this first encounter for the relationship between fairies and witches to be formalized with their familiar spirit taking the witch to the fairy court to stand before the devil or the fairy queen. A witch named Isabell Haldane was taken when she was lying in her bed and carried to a hillside, which opened up for her to enter. She stayed there for twelve hours in the fairy court before being brought home again by a man with a gray beard.

Although Isabell says very little about her experience in the fairy court this first time, most people were given assignments to spread mischief or to help the poor. As previously mentioned, helping the poor could involve fermenting a rebellion against the nobility, but more commonly, it involved healing the sick and poor with magic. Although not all relationships between the fairies and witches were so ennoble or noble, there were many times when a fairy just helped a person make a little more money (Suart, 1843).

Even when a visit to the fairy court wasn't part of this first encounter, there was typically some form of exchange to be made. For example, one cunning was told that she would learn many secrets if she would become the consort of one of the fairies she met, while the cat in "Puss in Boots" requested a fine pair of boots in return for his service.

Less commonly, this first encounter involved a person helping a spirit and so was rewarded, not with a simple gift, but with lifelong service from the fairy. For example, a man in Lithuania was returning home from the fields when he heard a chicken clucking. Finding the rain-drenched animal looking pathetic, he took it home, and only later realized that it was actually an Aitvaras (a powerful fire spirit which looks like a rooster or heron), who would later try to please him by stealing gifts from his neighbors.

In addition to being chosen by the fairies, some people inherited their powers from another witch. In the aforementioned story of "Puss in Boots," the boy in the story received his magical cat as his inheritance from his father. A witch named Margaret Ley was also given a spirit by her dying mother. In a rather strange case, one woman appears to have received her spirit from a teacher of sorts, someone she called her master, who blew the spirit into her mouth (Wilby, 2006), while in Russia, people believed that some witches were outright forced to inherit their powers when they accepted something from a dying witch. In Medynskii, a young boy inherited an army of spirits when he accepted a pitcher of water from a dying witch. Similarly, a little girl was tormented by an army of spirits, which sought to force her to work with them after she accepted a roll from a witch (Ivantis, 1992).

In the case of Alison, her brother returned from Egypt to find her on the verge of death, so he healed her and took her to Fairyland. There, he introduced her to witches and the Fairy Queen (Linton, 1883). In an odd take on this idea, a man named Andrew Man was promised power by his mother, then, some twenty-eight years later, the Fairy Queen came and killed all his cattle: "and it was then that their guilty, albeit poetic and loving intercourse, began." From this time on, he also gained many powers (Linton, 1883).

In some cases, the fairies will ask someone for help, oftentimes in kidnapping someone to be their slave; someone to work in their household who the fairies cannot take from their homes because of a priest's blessing, iron, or some other power, which only a human can bypass. In one case, a troop of fairies began destroying a farmer's cattle, then, when the farmer was desperate, they came to him with an offer:

> I am very badly off from the want of a wife and a housekeeper, and what I wished was that yourself would come here till I spoke to you. I have the woman made out these four or five days, and we were to go for her tonight, and I want you to go with us. We have strength enough of our own men, but we can never take her without help from this world. You'll not lose by assisting me. I'll be your friend ever and always for the future (Curtin 1895).

In this, and most similar tales, the young man betrays the fairies because he falls in love with the young woman he kidnaps for them, although the tales do beg the question of "what if the young man didn't betray the fairies, but aided them and so gained their trust and friendship?" The answer simply put is that he would then become a wicked witch, one who helps the fairies perform their evil deeds and in turn gains help from the fairies.

The Witch's Life

Most witches lead fairly normal lives within their society, living as nearly any other person would, while often (but not always) keeping their witchcraft a secret. They get married, have children, and work jobs of all kinds. Indeed, witches could be beggars or nobles; they could be servants, farmers, blacksmiths, and more. Many witches became merchants of magical services, selling their spells for money. Still others became thieves, using their powers and fairies to steal what they needed. Since a witch could be anyone, they could have nearly any personality, so I begin my discussion of them by discussing a few experiences they might have had and some of the relationships witches had with their fairies.

There is an interesting push and pull between familiars and witches, one that comes from the sometimes conflicting personalities and goals of each. There are, after all, many different traits and backgrounds for fairies, so their goals and their reasons for working with the witch can vary greatly. For example, a witch named Bessie Dunlop worked with a fairy named Tom Reid who had been a man before dying and entering the service of the Fairy Queen thirty years earlier. Because of Tom's background, many of his relatives were still alive and so he had Bessie delivering messages to these relatives for him, in addition to the work he had her do for the Fairy Queen (mostly involving helping the poor and healing the sick) (Wibly, 2006). This is extremely different from the experience a man named Tom Tiver had with the fairy Yallery Brown, who didn't seem to understand humans at all and eventually ruined his life (Jacobs, 2004). This, in turn, is different from the multitude of people who were forced to work with evil spirits against their will.

The one thing in common for most of these stories is the fact that the fairy initiated the relationship. It was typically the fairies' goals that mattered first and foremost in the relationship between the witch and the fairy. And if the witch didn't want any part of the relationship, the fairy could torment them until they gave in. Because it was usually the familiar, the fairy, who initiated and to some extent controlled the relationship with the witch, a case could be made that the story of a witch is really the fairy's story – that the fairy's character should be developed first in order to understand why they would approach a witch, what they would want from the witch, and how they would treat the witch. In this last point, we typically see three primary relationship types between a fairy and their witch. In the first type, the witch is enslaved by the fairy, in the second a partnership forms between the witch and the fairy and, in the third kind, the fairy cares for the human so much they essentially work for them.

A few more things to keep in mind:

Fairies and Witches are Often Mischievous

During the Medieval Era, practical jokes were likely the most wildly appreciated form of humor, and great pleasure was taken in the sight of men and woman injuring themselves as a result of some prank or another.

Take hocking, for example... a group of lads lay a noose on the ground and wait for an unsuspecting passerby to step into it. Then they hoist him up, suddenly, by his ankles, often bashing his head on the ground in the process.

Meanwhile, boys in London would commonly steal the hoods from and play other pranks on members of Parliament (Mortimer, 2011).

In many ways, I see the trickster nature of fairies as a natural extension of the mischievous nature of many humans, especially in an era when violence and violent humor were often celebrated. Because of this, the activities of many witches were very much like cruel pranks. They would, for example, lie in wait with their fairy companions outside of weddings in order to curse the new husband and wife so that they got into fights that the fairies and the witches could watch and presumably laugh at. Social discord was often believed to be caused by witches throughout Europe, and one can easily imagine them impishly laughing as they watched people scream and yell at each other. Turning people's emotions upside down was a common way for witches to cause mischief. In one case, a witch cursed another lady by sending her visions of naked men (Linton, 1861).

Other witches were well known for coming into people's homes to ride them around like horses, leaving them exhausted. Even the shooting of people with invisible darts that cause pain and illness might at times be the result of a bad sense of humor. What's important to understand is that witches are very clearly still human, still part of the culture in which they live. Male witches in Russia and Celtic lands, for example, would often use their powers to seduce girls or to blackmail them into having sexual relationships with them in much the same way that the nobility of the past did. In

Ireland, a witch punished a man who had rejected her by trapping his soul in the land between life and death (Kennedey, 1891). Still another witch would aid other women by getting the men they loved to leave their girlfriends for them (Linton, 1861). Other witches lived as farmers and centers of their community, giving alms to the poor and healing the sick, but otherwise, they acted as any other kindhearted member of the community. The difference between witches and a normal person then comes down to the witch's relationship with the fairies and their power. Power, after all, is very corrupting; people who can get away with more will often do more, and thanks to their magic, witches are much less likely to get caught than other people.

Witches Are Usually Born From Suffering

Where witches came from emotionally is important, and although some witches were princesses, wealthy nobles, and merchants, most of them appear to have originally been desperate. Sometimes, their desperation lead them to hate society before they ever encountered the spirits. To understand the minds of these desperate witches, we must begin to understand where they came from and what their place in society was before they became witches.

The story of "Hansel and Gretel" is a good place to begin. In one of the original stories told to the Grimm Brothers, Hansel's and Gretel's mother is still alive and it is she, the children's own mother, who makes the decision to abandon them in the forest. But how harsh can we actually be on Hansel's and Gretel's mother? She was a woman who likely died of starvation shortly after sending her two children into the woods, which means it's likely that she'd already started to hallucinate, had started to lose her ability to reason by the time she made this horrifying decision. Many faced with starvation have even eaten their own children, and at one time, children weren't as highly valued as they are now. The anthropologist Tian-Shanskaia, for example, tells the story of a Russian peasant woman over a hundred years ago who was distressed when she was going to have her third child because she couldn't imagine how she would feed it. She lost weight in the course of her pregnancy.

> Dark spots appeared on her face and she aged so rapidly that no one would have guessed that she was only twenty-two years old. It was with a feeling of relief that she buried her second son, who died of diarrhea.

Tian-shanskaia goes on to say;
"Those who have too many children are cursed by their family members (especially their mother-in-law, the children's grandmother) who may say 'Better that your puppies died off.'"

In a story from the Caucasus Mountains, a fisherman's son frees a beautiful fish when it asks him for help. As punishment, his own father turns him out of the home to wander alone in the woods. Here, he saves a deer being chased by a hunter, then a crane being hunted by an eagle, and so he gains ally after ally even after being rejected by his own family.

None of this is to say that children weren't generally loved; rather, it's to point out that the world was a lot more desperate than many of us can imagine. "Langland sees the poor, chard with children and the chief lords rend," spending their small wages on milk and meal to make porridge to glut the maws of their children that cry after food. Also, in winter, they suffer much hunger and woe (Cels, 2004). When the father in "Godfather Death" goes out to find someone to stand godfather for his child because he doesn't have enough money for a christening, he chooses Death to be the child's godfather because only Death is fair; he kills both the poor and rich alike. Fairness to this man is not caring who suffers, so long as everyone does so eventually.

Even without starvation, women, who were the most likely people to become witches in much of Europe, lived as second-class citizens in a way that would shock most people of today. Many men in Europe's past would beat their wives frequently with anything they could get a hold of. In Russia, it wasn't uncommon for men to drag their wives by their braids:

So that their heads make a thumpity thump noise on the steps. In one extreme case, a man rolled up his wife's "braids around his hand and beat her head on the front steps, on the benches, and on the wall until she lapsed into a coma. (Tian-Shanskaia, 1993)

It's true, of course, that these are extreme cases, that such suffering wasn't necessarily commonplace; however, becoming a witch wasn't commonplace either, and those who did become witches usually did so during a time of suffering greater than most people had to endure. It's no wonder, then, that oftentimes the people who became witches had no one to rely on but the fairies (Purkiss, 2007), which means that witches would have cared far more about their relationship with the fairies than most people could care about any relationship they had with another human. The witch's hardship could also mean that they were bitter and angry against society, making them easy targets for evil fairies who were trying to manipulate them.

More common than abuse, however, were those who became witches because they were suffering from a loss or potential loss of love. What records we have of witches often speak of women being approached by the fairies when they were mourning the death of a husband, a child, or the illness and starvation of those they loved. This would indicate that the woman had lost hope, which meant that they once had it, that they had a love they were concerned about losing. In the story of one man who became a cunning, his youngest child died and so:

> The mother finally died of grief, and the other children died because of the loss of their mother, and the father was left alone. It was some time after this that the little folk returned and helped him become a wealthy farmer and a well-respected witch by sharing with him all their secrets (Wentz, 2011).

More evidence for love, or at least being part of a social order is the fact that children in fairy tales who gain supernatural allies often return home at the end of the story to share their wealth with their parents. Oddly enough, even at the end of "Hansel and Gretel," the brother and sister returned home. It would seem that despite, or perhaps because of the harshness of daily life, it's likely that a certain closeness was common. After all, in many parts of Europe, travelers could often expect some place to stay, as people would let them into their homes as a form of alms. People and communities were tightly knitted together; that was how they were able to survive the harsh conditions placed upon them by the nobility and the environment in which they lived. So while suffering is often the catalyst that makes someone a witch, it's important to keep in mind that this is by no means the only aspect of the witch's life. After all many, if not most, of them choose to help those in need.

Some Witches Chose to Live on the Fringes of Society

In Manx, there was a tale of a wizard who only kept company with evil spirits and would punish any who came too close to his home, no matter the reason (Sophia, 1911). Because hardship drove many witches to be witches, they oftentimes wanted revenge against specific people or society in general, and witches are some of the few people who can truly take revenge and get what they want through theft. The milk of their neighbor's cow, which is likely the most valuable thing their neighbor owns, is theirs for the taking. Some gold coins from the greedy nobleman who mistreats the serfs are also theirs to be had. Elspeth used her powers of divination to blackmail other women; women who were unfaithful, or women who got pregnant out of wedlock (Purkiss, 2007). It's easy to imagine nearly anyone giving into the temptation to mete out bits of vengeance against those who wronged them and occasionally stealing to get what they want, especially when pressured by overly emotional and highly sensitive fairies.

Someone who is cut off in traffic might swear and curse and berate the person who can't hear them, as if their anger will change something. They will have little effect on the person who "wronged" them. For a witch, however, this anger can have a very real effect. The witch can bring curses against those they perceive as having wronged them, those they are jealous of. The spoiled rich kid who flaunts his wealth can be made to vomit, the person who bumps into them can be made to itch fiercely for a time, and so on. The witch Dorothy Ellis used her spirit to lame and kill her neighbor's cattle when they angered her. Another witch named Jonet felt wronged by being one of the poorest people in her parish, so she became a witch that cursed others. Other witches used their familiars to destroy beer, to cause sickness, or even death (Wibly, 2006).

It would be easy enough for a witch to go overboard with these curses; after all, a sense of powerlessness can make some seek to take power in any way they can. It can also cause bitterness, resentment, and anger, which can all flair up at various intervals. For example, in England, a witch named Bitty Chidley, who lived as a beggar, went to a family who generally gave her what she asked for; however, the lady of the house on this particular day was busy and so refused. Because of this, Bitty cursed the woman's cattle (Hartland, 1890). So despite this family's normal generosity towards Bitty, she was still quick to curse them for a small slight. By the same token, the sense of power, the ability to get away with nearly anything, can be corrupting as well, so there is a fine line that witches have to walk. In the Ukraine, even good witches known as babky would often avoid other babky for fear that the others might secretly be using black magic and evil spirits (Philips, 2004).

In Yorkshire, witches were believed to travel the countryside spreading evil, forcing girls to marry those they didn't want to, killing husbands, causing babies to be born lame, and more. One witch named Peggy, who had a tall hat and red cloak, "cast a spell against one Tom Person, and every head of cattle he possessed died." Tom was forced to move, and his cousin got the farm. Luckily, Tom's cousin, Peggy, was friends with him, so rather than curse him, she blessed him to always prosper. At the same time, two women's cows were made to give poor milk because of Peggy's malice. Yet, despite seemingly being an evil witch, Peggy had a son and she had friends. Yet she cursed people she didn't like, so she wasn't purely evil or purely good; rather, she was human. Humans, however, are easily corrupted by power, so it's no wonder people feared and perhaps avoided her (Blakeborough, 1898).

Further, the spirits themselves sometimes take things

too far, killing those they were just supposed to nip. This is one of the primary reasons why witches were so often pushed to the fringes of societ;, because whether they were good or bad, helpful or dangerous, people feared that they would cause harm. The witch in the story of the "White Stag," for example, lives in the woods and no one goes to see her unless they really, really need something (Lauder, 1881). The temptation to put a curse on someone, after all, might just prove too great one day. This fear may also have led many witches to live on the fringes of society, to remove themselves from the temptation to do harm. Imagine how the witch must have felt when her spirits killed someone they were just supposed to "nip."

Other witches likely chose to live on the fringes because they no longer fit into society. Their primary companions are fairies, after all. And fairies often live in the wilderness, away from humanity, even if they want to be involved in human affairs. So a witch whose closest friends are such fairies could be expected to dwell as they do, away from other humans. For example, a man named Archedamos was an acolyte for the nymphs who lived out in the wilderness and was likely proud of the work he did for the nymphs. Out there, he was able to worship and speak with the nymphs as he chose:

> The cult he oversees seemingly has no civic, tribal, domestic, or deme affiliation. His marginality is typical of visionaries across cultures, who either belong to an outsider class in the first place or deliberately remove themselves from the mainstream. This separation, however, does not imply complete disengagement from society. The nymphoept, like possessed persons in other cultures, had a recognized social role that was enhanced by his withdrawal and isolation. (Larson, 2001)

Here in the wilderness, Archedamos was free to build homes for the nymphs, to tend their gardens in peace, and to give prophecies to whoever the nymphs deemed worthy, without society's judgment.

It might even be dangerous for some witches to continue to live with society, as they constantly had to take precautions against ordinary people. When two Finnish magicians were hired to find a lost amulet, they insisted that they first be closed alone inside a house so that they could astrally project without interference. As we'll see in the section on Spirit Journeys, sending their souls out of their bodies was a common way for witches to gain power. Yet during this time, they were vulnerable; if someone moved their body or spoke to them, it could often mean their death. So it was safer for them to isolate themselves, to avoid the risk of having others around when they were performing a dangerous piece of magic (Lecouteux, 2003).

Yet living away from society, doing secret things, and utilizing spirits to do who knows what carries its own set of risks. People can't help but have grown a bit suspicious, a bit concerned, which would have further isolated the witches. This situation was made worse at times by the people's conversion to Christianity, although the church's stance was sometimes that there were no witches and so many were tried as secular rather than religious criminals for using evil spirits and placing curses on people. In a time when a child as young as seven could be hung for theft, placing a curse on others could be a serious crime, and the witches had very little recourse when trying to prove their innocence. Thus, they often had to be suspicious of authority, concerned that someone might have them taken away and tortured.

Slave, Servant, and Battered

A witch's relationship with the spirits is never black and white, for all fairies are both creative and destructive to some degree. Even the saints were often cruel and vindictive. Elijah would destroy people's fields for working on his day and the Virgin Mary would send curses; while even evil fairies would heal the sick and Death himself would stand godfather for a child. Fairies were born out of a very, very gray world, and because of this, many people were horrified at the thought of becoming a witch, of being forced to do a familiar's bidding for very little return. Often, witches lived in isolation, rejected by society, impoverished, or were forced to do terrible things by the spirits that they came to serve. This is why there were some witches that would try to get out of their arrangement with the spirits. One Russian sorcerer, for example, asked his granddaughter to lock him away during her wedding so that he wouldn't be forced to curse her or her new husband (Ivanits, 1992). Similarly, the familiars of a Huntingdonshire witch named Elizabeth Chandler would just show up against her will and, indeed, she often prayed to God to deliver her from them (Wibly, 2006).

Oftentimes, many people who became witches were broken by the fairies, enslaved to their will. Possession and torment were common features of people's early encounters with the spirit world. Imagine if, in any exorcism movie, the evil spirits that had possessed the victim had forced a deal upon them to let the person live semi-happily if they allowed the fairies to use them to spread evil. In lore, the spirits in such a situation would often torture a person until, at last, they gave in; and once the person did so they would have very little control.

Recall from the section on "Robin Hood and the Queen of the Fairies" the story of the woodsman who was overcome by spirits and driven mad into the forest for two years before emerging to do the will of the spirits. This man was forced to give up his whole life in service of the spirit. Imagine how much more difficult this would have been if he'd been a rich nobleman who was forced to live in poverty and steal from the rich, his former friends and family, to give to the poor. He might have tried to resist for a time, but eventually, he would have had to give up everything he owned and everyone he loved in order to serve the fairies will.

In Lithuania, a man found a rooster-shaped spirit known as an Aitvaras. He soon became upset because this spirit would rob from his neighbors and torment those around him. In order to try to be rid of the spirit, he at last left it in the house, which he burnt down. However, the Aitvaras rose from the fire like a phoenix and continued to follow him. When Janet Trail encountered the fairies;

> "They drave me down, and then I was beside myself, and would have eaten the very earth beside me." Being asked the cause why she was so much troubled by

them, she answered that the principal of them had bidden her do ill, by casting sickness upon people, and she refused to do it (Stuart, 1843).

Elspeth Roth was still a young teen when she was tormented by a fairy man every night, until at last she agreed to let him lie with her (Purkiss, 1967). In the end, when an ordinary person is faced with the power of a spirit, good or bad, there is very little they can do to escape the fate that the spirits have laid out for them. Yet there were some who resisted and suffered for it. Many cunning who refused to do evil deeds for the fairies would be pushed, hit, tossed into ditches, and beaten by the fairies. Worse still was the treatment Isobel received at the hands of her fairy familiar who was "temperamental and physically aggressive. He was quick to anger, controlling, sexually predatory, and physically abusive." She and other companions of hers were further beaten if they dared be absent from coven meetings. In hearing Isobel's story, one can't help but think of a battered woman being strung along in an abusive relationship (Wibly, 2010).

Alison was taught witchcraft by her own brother, a brother who had saved her life and brought her to see the queen of the fairies. Yet despite the fact that it was her brother who taught her the witch's craft, she was later abused and tormented by these fairies. Many fairies began coming lustily to her.

> But the Fairy Folk were not kind to Alison. They tormented her sorely and treated her with great harshness; knocking her about and beating her so... they leave her covered with bruises. She was never free from her questionable associates, who used to come upon her at all times and initiate her into their secrets, whether she would or no (Linton, 1861).

Not all witch's spirits would force them to perform evil deeds; many forced them to help their community. For these spirits, sacrificing the happiness of a single person to save hundreds through healing and other aid was justified. Still, regardless of the reasons, like many forced into this position, the witches would often come to believe that they loved their abusers, the fairies; believing it was their own fault that the fairies were punishing them. More than this, they could begin to believe strongly in what the fairies made them do. Those forced to work for their community might become elevated within their communities and so proud of what they were able to do. Those forced to perform evil acts could become hostile and dangerous, very similar to the effects seen in some child soldiers. Regardless of what the enslaved witch was forced to do, depression and anxiety were common for enslaved witches.

The Love

In other cases, the fairy would fall in love (or, at least, lust) with the witch. The daughter of one cunning woman claimed that she had become cunning when her mother arranged for her to lay with an elf man; while many other witches would have sexual relationships with various fairy lords (Wibly, 2010). Meanwhile, Anne Jefferies had many different male fairies constantly vying for her affections, and even acting jealously if she paid more attention to one of them than the others. (Hunt, 1908)

A young girl named Katherine Jonesdochter had a fairy called "Bowman" come and lay with her, and he continued to do so for forty years. In return for being his sexual partner, the fairy gave her magical secrets (Briggs, 1967). In ancient Greece, the relationship between nymphs and their followers, or Hermes and his followers, was in many ways similar to marriage, which is why Hermes had primarily female diviners and nymphs only had male diviners (Larson, 2001).

In other cases, the fairy's love of a human was more childlike. In Italy, for example, the fairies known as Buffardello would often fall in love with woman and pretty girls and would try to make them happy. While such fairies might try to steal a kiss on the check, sexual relationships were very rare. Some fairies are often very much like children.

In a darker take on these tales, a girl begins a secret relationship with an evil spirit, which she keeps secret from her family until she ultimately makes a pact to kill her brother so that she and the spirit can live together as a married couple in the forest (Zeluna.net). So even evil fairies could fall in love with mortal women, although this love was corrupting.

The Pet

For a being thousands of years old, with incredible powers, and perhaps a bit of arrogance, humans are very much like any animal. But just as many humans love animals and will take in stray cats, will raise money for animal shelters, and more, many fairies who view humans as animals "love" them. They find humans cute, amusing, and perhaps a bit noble in our own way, and some witches must surely be "adopted" by these fairies. Living as a pet would be very difficult for many people, especially those who love their freedom. Many fairies would use their pet (the witch) to aid other humans, often in limited ways. Such fairies don't necessarily want to change the course of humanity or to change our nature, but they do feel sorry for us. So like an old lady who puts out food for stray cats, or people who leave food for birds and deer in the wilderness, these fairies care about humanity, but don't want to interfere too much with our "natural" environment.

Even so, it can be a lot of work to help others, especially when one is starving oneself, and the fairies are likely to take a firm hand with the witch if necessary. They will train and manipulate the witch with a system of punishments and rewards much the way someone would train a dog. While such training is far less brutal than the psychopathic enslavement some witches suffer, it would still be difficult for many people to accept this. With fairies being so often dual-natured, there is always the risk that the witch will anger the fairy too much, so they'll become destructive and cruel in their nature.

Friends

One shouldn't make the mistake of thinking that a witch's relationship with the fairies was always negative. Oftentimes, witches and fairies became close friends. Indeed, it was the desire for friendship that led many fairies to approach witches in the first place. Often, the witch and fairy were so close to each other that the witch's relationship with the fairies superseded many, if not all others. Such witches might seem isolated and withdrawn, living at the edge of society, but the truth is that they are very social, and have very close long-lasting friendships with the spirits.

Sible Hedingham would call her spirit to her in much the same way that one might call a beloved pet. In other cases, the witch and her familiar spirit would argue with each other like an old married couple; while Elizabeth Sawyer had a familiar who took the form of a dog that would wag his tale when she would pet him (Wibly, 2006).

The cat familiar from the story of "Puss in Boots" called the person he worked with "Master" and made plans to help him get married. In the story of the "White Stag," a witch who lives at the edge of society tells someone who has come seeking her advice that she'll ask her ravens. She then opens the window and calls the birds with a single piercing whistle and a few unintelligible words. When the ravens come, she addresses them: "Ye good ravens, ye are as old as the Harz and primeval forest, and ye know all things; hence, ye shall tell me the history of the White Stag" (Lauder, 1881).

In Cornwall, there was a woman who was asked about some lost horses. She turned her back on her client and began to speak to herself in Cornish (presumably she was talking to her fairy partners). She then turned back to her client and gave him some herbs that would drive out the evil spirits in his stables.

In a rather amusing tale from Hungary, "The Fairy Elizabeth," a fairy comes to her future husband in the form of a white pigeon and tells him, "If you ever want to meet me, seek for me in the town of Johra, in the country of Black Sorrow." At first, he can find no one who knows where this is; eventually, he finds an old woman (witch), who doesn't know where the land is either. However, while:

"They were still consulting somebody knocked at the

window and the old woman called out, "Who's that?"

"It's I, my dear queen," replied a bird; and she began to scold it for being so late; but still she let it in, hoping that it might tell them something. Lo! It was a lame woodpecker.

"Why are you so late?" she demanded, and the bird replied that it was because it had such a bad foot. "Where did you get your leg broken?" inquired the old woman.

"In Johara, in the country of Black Sorrow."

"You are just the one we want," said the old woman; "I command you to take this man on your back without delay and to carry him to the very town where you have come from."

The woodpecker began to make excuses and said that it would rather not go there, lest they should break the other leg also; but the old woman stamped with her foot, and so it was obliged to obey; and at once set off with the man on its back, whose third horse had already died. On they went over seven times seven countries, and even beyond them, till they came to a very high mountain, so high that it reached to Heaven. (Zeluna.net)

I love this conversation and this story, not only because it shows a relationship between a witch and familiar where the witch is in charge, but because there seems to be some level of friendship, an almost teasing relationship between the familiar and the witch. In many cases, fairies seemed even anxious to help. In Russia, for example, it was believed that a witch's spirits would hide in the area around where they lived, waiting to be called upon. The fairy Yallery Brown was anxious to help the person who rescued him, yet because this person didn't know how to deal with the fairy, he tried to get rid of him, thereby angering Yallery Brown. Yet one can even easily imagine that if the man had handled things better, rather than trying to banish the fairy, they could have formed a close relationship. After all, at first, Yallery Brown was originally anxious to help.

Other fairies loved to play with people and were very much like children. As already mentioned, the Buffardello of Italy would often play with girls and other children. In the

Scandinavian countries, there are many stories of the house fairy, the Tomte playing with boys, as he enjoyed causing mischief just like they did. In these cases, they would often go on raids to rob the neighboring farms, or play pranks on other people together, much like unruly children. In Wales, a boy befriended some fairies and would play constantly with them, so when his family got into financial trouble, they helped him uncover a secret treasure. This childishness of fairies also means that many witches would treat the fairies like unruly children.

Further, since many fairies are ancestor spirits, a witch's fairies are oftentimes ancestors. In Italy, one witch said that the spirit of her uncle was the one who helped her to diagnose illness while her father came to help and reassure when she was pregnant (Magliocco, 2009). In the German version of *Cinderella*, it was Cinderella's mother whose spirit had come to live in a tree that gave her magical gifts and advice. Obviously, in these last cases, the relationship between a person and the fairy spirit helping them depends on their relationship with the family members who have become fairies, but one can imagine that in most cases, the relationship would be primarily positive.

Even in such a partnership, familiars might begin to turn violent. However, in such cases, the witches could scold and control them much "as if they were wayward children." When one witch discovered that her familiar had hurt someone more than she intended, she scolded the familiar saying, "Thou, villain! What hast thou done? I bid thee to nip it but a little and not to hurt it" (Wibly, 2006).

Perhaps the oddest fairy relationship is between a rough and tumble man named Callum, of the Scottish Mountains, and a gruff spirit named the bauchan. In these stories, Callum often opposed the fairy's schemes, as the fairy sought to cause trouble for his neighbors. This meant that the two would often fight with each other. One day after fighting with the bauchan, Callum discovered that his magical handkerchief was missing. He rushed about desperately searching for it until he found the bauchan busily rubbing the handkerchief on a flat stone.

> Ah! you are back; it is well for you, for if I had rubbed a hole into this before your return, you were a dead man.

No doctor on earth or power could save you; but you shall never have this handkerchief till you have won it in a fair fight." "Done," said Callum, and at it they went again, and Callum recovered his handkerchief (Campbell, 1890)

Yet despite all their fighting, the bauchan still helped Callum. After a massive snowstorm had snowed in Callum and his wife, Callum began wishing he could get his firewood, and no sooner had he done this than the grinning bauchan tossed a giant tree beside his door. More than this, when Callum had to travel to America, the bauchan beat him there and helped him clear the trees and rocks from his farmland. Here at last, the bauchan stops teasing and fighting with Callum (Campbell, 1890). So, to my mind, this relationship between the Callum and the bauchan seems a bit like the relationship between the two old men in *Grumpy Old Men,* in which both fight and play pranks on each other, but they can't actually imagine living without the other.

Finally, there were many relationships between fairies and humans that centered around art and music. One such example was an orphan street urchin in Edinburgh who met with the fairies every day to play the drums for them, and joined them in flying about the world (Henderson and Cowan, 2001).

Social Center

Many fairy doctors would become the center of their society, beloved by the people. For example, when a cowherd named Maurice Griffin gained the power of foretelling and curing the sick people, the parish priest was at first concerned about him. But after speaking with him, the priest came to accept him and even used his services. Further, Griffin became beloved of the man he worked for because of his powers, and he was even given his master's daughter as a wife. Soon, people began to come from all around to seek his help.

In "The Doom," when a man is sick and on the verge of death, a wise old woman tells the family, "Send for the fairy doctor". Similarly in the tale "The Farmers Fate" it is the fairy doctor who at last is able to help a farmer struck by a mysterious condition:

> However, riding home one evening after sunset, he was suddenly "struck" and fell insensible to the ground. They carried him home and laid him on his bed, where he lay for several days, his eyes fixed and staring without any motion of the eyelids, and no indication of life remaining, except his colour, which never changed.
>
> All the doctors came and looked at him, but could do nothing. There was no fracture nor injury of any kind to his frame; so the doctors shook their heads and went their way, saying they would call again in a day or two. But. the family objected to delay, and sent at once for the great fairy doctor of the district. The moment he came, he threw herbs on the fire, when a fragrant smell filled the room like church incense. Then he pounded some herbs and mixed a liquid with them, but what the herbs were, no one knew. And with this mixture, he touched the brow and the lips and the hands of the man, and sprinkled the rest over his insensible form. After this, he told them to keep silence round him for two hours, when he would return and finish the cure. And so it happened, for in two hours the life came back to the man, though he could not speak. But strength came gradually; and by the next day, he rose up. (Wilde, 1902)

Lady Wilde further describes the life of one fairy doctor as follows:

> He never touched beer, spirits, or meat in all his life, but has lived entirely on bread, fruit, and vegetables. A man who knew him thus describes him—"Winter and summer his dress is the same--merely a flannel shirt and coat. He will pay his share at a feast, but neither eats nor drinks of the food and drink set before him. He speaks no English, and never could be made to learn

the English tongue, though he says it might be used with great effect to curse one's enemy. He holds a burial-ground sacred, and would not carry away so much as a leaf of ivy from a grave. And he maintains that the people are right to keep to their ancient usages, such as never to dig a grave on a Monday, and to carry the coffin three times round the grave, following the course of the sun, for then the dead rest in peace. Like the people, also, he holds suicides as accursed; for they believe that all its dead turn over on their faces if a suicide is laid amongst them."

Though well off, he never, even in his youth, thought of taking a wife; nor was he ever known to love a woman. He stands quite apart from life, and by this means holds his power over the mysteries. No money will tempt him to impart his knowledge to another, for if he did he would be struck dead--so he believes. He would not touch a hazel stick, but carries an ash wand, which he holds in his hands when he prays, laid across his knees; and the whole of his life is devoted to works of grace and charity, and though now an old man, he has never had a day's sickness. No one has ever seen him in a rage, nor heard an angry word from his lips but once, and then being under great irritation, he recited the Lord's Prayer backwards as an imprecation on his enemy. Before his death he will reveal the mystery of his power, but not till the hand of death is on him for certain.'" When he does reveal it, we may be sure it will be to one person only--his successor. There are several such doctors in County Sligo, really well up in herbal medicine by all accounts, and my friends find them in their own counties. (Yeats, 1888)

The Fairy's Purpose

Fairies rarely work with a witch without some specific purpose in mind, and this purpose, their reason for working with a witch, often determines what they will have the witch do. It's important to keep in mind, however, that they don't necessarily choose the best person for any given purpose. So a person with any character traits, background, personality, and dreams could be forced to work towards any one of the fairy's purposes.

Aid the Poor

One of the most common demands placed upon people by the fairies, especially those who die and return, is to help the poor. Such people are given the ability to heal the sick and afflicted, to give blessings, and insure good harvests. Yet they do these things for the poorest of people and oftentimes are even forbidden from taking any financial reward for their efforts at all. This means that these witches can work long hours while often living in destitution. Those witches who can get pleasure from helping others, who can accept sharing the suffering of the poor as a spiritual experience, will find peace and even happiness with this job. Others, however, would not be cut out for this work. Imagine, for example, a greedy person or a person who was emotionally weak being forced into this job. Even if a witch is caring, living in poverty, working so hard for no reward could be nearly impossible for many people. These witches often find themselves in conflict with the spirits that control their lives, a struggle which could lead the spirits to grow violent and perhaps evil. So it's a careful road the impoverished witches must walk.

Merchants

Some fairies clearly seek to help witches become wealthier for a number of different reasons. This sometimes means that they will do labor for the witch, steal for them, or give them magical aid so that they can earn money through their charms. Other times, merchant witches are able to manipulate the spirits so they can use them to help them act as magical merchants. Such witches often find lost and stolen goods, perform love divination, and even more menial tasks in return for monetary reward. However, these fairies may also heal the sick for the witch and help the powerful, making this a potentially lucrative job.

Depending on the society in which they lived, those living as merchant witches would have had to walk a fine line. In Ancient Rome, for example, manipulating the spirits was frowned upon and at times bordered on the edge of illegal. In most all societies, merchant witches would be subject to suits by people who accused them of wrongly claiming that they were thieves. Worse still, a merchant witch could be accused of causing plagues so that the witch could make more money curing them, or of taking money to put curses on people (which some of them did do). The penalty for murdering someone with magic in most past societies was death, and it was difficult for a witch to defend against such a charge; so witches could be persecuted no matter what society they lived in. However, at the same time, many of these merchant witches were highly respected members of society. Ultimately, regardless of their society, whether people loved or hated them often depended on whether people thought that a witch was performing malign magic in the community, and whether or not people thought the merchant witch was responsible.

Community Defenders

In a world filled with evil spirits and wicked witches, some witches are needed to protect their communities against blight and illness. In the Baltic States, such witches would send their souls out of their bodies in the form of wolves which would battle against other witches that wanted to ruin its crops. Similarly, witches in Italy would send their souls out into the air to protect their village's crop against spirits who wanted to blight it. Although most of these witches inherited their position, they were like drafted soldiers in many ways. These witches are soldiers without a choice, but risk their lives engaging in secret battles with evil spirits. They are thrust into a dangerous world and may easily become emotionally overwhelmed. Those who succeed in this role must learn to control their emotions, must learn to feel a sense of calm before the storm. Further, because these witches are allied with, and depend on the good will of the fairies to survive, these witches would likely become enforcers of tradition and lovers of ceremonies, as these traditions and ceremonies are often set down in order to keep the good will of the fairies that aid them in their battle.

The Hero

There are many times when a person might be called on to fight the fairie's wars for them. Prince Pwyll, for example, was called on by the king of the fairies to slay a monster that the Fairy King could not defeat. Others are called to help humanity in its struggle against giants, dragons, and, of course, other humans. These are warrior witches, and oftentimes, they had to learn to be brutal warriors very quickly, for they often faced brutal enemies.

Tormentor

There are evil fairies; cruel, malign monsters who seek to harm humanity. Such fairies might call upon ordinary people as a cruel joke, possessing and tormenting the witch into servitude, forcing them to kill, curse, and cause mischief for the fairies. These witches are oftentimes the true prisoners of the fairy's will. They are frequently brainwashed through fear and pain. Such witches would suffer emotionally until they finally broke and accepted their place, beginning to revel in the suffering they caused; although for many, this would never happen.

The Friendship

Many fairies choose to partner with humans because of friendship or love. Some fairies were saved by the witches; others felt a close kinship to them or fell in love with the witch. Still other fairies loved to play with children, and so children have the opportunity to befriend and gain secrets from the fairies. These playmates of the fairies would be like any child, and their relationship with the fairies would be similar to this, except that a child who plays with the fairies is always in danger of being carried off or of incurring the wrath of the fairy's darker aspect.

Given that fairies often needed human help, they would seek to serve humans who had given them aid in the past. For example, in one tale from Brittany, a man named Jegu gains the friendship of a fairy of a pool of water after providing food for this fairy when it was hiding in the form of a bird from a war with another tribe of fairies (Masson, 1929).

Another girl dances every day as she watches over her family's sheep at the edge of the forest and here she encounters a fairy who has enjoyed watching her dance, because the fairy loves dancing as well. So the two of them begin spending their days dancing together and the fairy gives the human many magical gifts (Wraitislaw, 1890).

In yet another tale, two children forced to work for Baba Yaga share their food with the talking animals of the witch's home, and so these spirits help the children complete every chore Baba Yaga gives them (Blumenthal, 1903). Fairies often appreciated human gifts, as in another case: a poor man was walking to the market in order to buy a sheep when he heard some invisible fairies bemoaning the fact that they had not cloth with which to cover their child. Concerned for his safety, the man pulled off his plaid and tossed it to the saddened fairies, who at once began to celebrate. Although this man never did see the fairies, they blessed him to prosper thereafter (Gibbings, 1889). So one can easily see how he could have become a witch if the fairies had wished to communicate with him. In another story, related by Gibbings, there is a boy who lives about a small town as a street urchin, playing with the other children by day, performing fortune telling and telling some tales of the fairies for money. Some nights, he also plays the drums for the fairies and travels about the world with them, eating of their rich food and drinking with them. This is a boy who is a skilled drummer and so became friends with the fairies, who give him not only the gift of telling the future, but of a "cunning much above his years."

Excerpt from: "The Three Princes, The Three Dragons and the Old Woman with the Iron Nose"

> Ambrose received a present from his fairy godmother, which consisted of a black egg with five corners, which she placed under Ambrose's left armpit. Ambrose carried his egg about with him under his left armpit for seven winters and seven summers, and on Ash Wednesday, in the eighth year, a horse with five legs and three heads jumped out of the egg; this horse was a Tatos and could speak...
> At the time when the brothers went out to fight the dragons, Ambrose was thirteen years and thirteen days old, and his horse was exactly five years old. The two elder brothers had been gone some time, when he went into the stable to his little horse, and, laying his head upon its neck, began to weep bitterly.
> The little horse neighed loudly and said, " Why are you crying, my dear master?"
> "Because," replied Ambrose, " I dare not ask my father to let me go away, although I should like to do so very

much."
"Go to your royal father, my dear master, for he has a very bad attack of toothache just now, and tell him that the king of herbs sends word to him through the Tatos-horse with three heads, that his toothache will not cease until he gives you permission to go and fight the dragons ; and you can also tell him that if you go, there will be no more dragons left on this earth ; but if you do not go his two elder boys will perish in the stomachs of the dragons. Tell him, also, that I have assured you that you will be able to make the dragons vomit out, at once, all the lads whomsoever they have swallowed; and that his land will become so powerful when the lads, who have grown strong in the stomachs of the dragons, return that, while the world lasts, no nation will ever be able to vanquish him." Thus spoke the Tatos colt, and neighed so loudly that the whole world rang with the sound.
The little boy told his father what the Tatos colt had told him...."

Scholar and Oracle

Those fairies who seek to improve humanity often have messages to give them. These fairies seek out people to be their oracles, and/or wandering scholars who can change the philosophy by which humanity lives. These oracles are called upon by the fairies to spread some message, some moral ideal of the fairies, or to aid humanity by foretelling the future. Although the oracles themselves often live what seems to be a very hard life, as they are forced to give up everything they know and oftentimes they live away from the rest of humanity, it's important to bear in mind that they aren't solitary or lonely. Oracles are always with the fairies and spirits, and are often the lovers of these magical beings. Oracles themselves were often times extremely beautiful. For example, in Germany:

When the old heathen gods and goddesses were still worshiped in the Rhine country, a certain priestess of Herthe took up her abode in an ancient grove, where she practiced her occult arts so successfully that the fame of her divination spread far and wide, and men came from all parts of Europe to learn from her what the future had in store for them. Frequently, a warrior left her abode with a consuming fire kindled in his breast, which would rob him of sleep for many a long night, yet none dared to declare his love to her, for, lovely though she was, there was an air of austerity, an atmosphere of mysticism about her which commanded awe and reverence, and forbade even the smallest familiarity (Spence, 1915).

Fairy is a Slave or Servant

Not all fairies are in control of their relationship with the witch. For example, in a Mari-El tale, a woodsman gets ready to chop a tree when the trees spirit begs him for its life. He agrees to spare the tree, but only if it begins to serve him; then whenever he wants something else, he goes out to the tree with an ax. Although this Mari-El man manages to get the better of the tree spirit and live happily ever after, such enslavements typically doesn't work out nearly so well.

In a similar tale, a fisherman catches the king of the fish, who tells the fisherman that if he's set free, he'll fill his nets daily. Bound by his promise, the king of the fish does just this, and much more. In fact, when the fisherman's ship is capsized by a storm:

> The Fish King appeared, and, holding a flask to the drowning man's lips, made him drink a magic fluid, which ensured his ability to exist under water. He conveyed the fisherman to his capital, a place of dazzling splendor, paved with gold and gems. The rude caster of nets instantly filled his pockets with the spoil of this marvelous causeway. Though probably rather disturbed by the incident, the Fish King, with true royal politeness, informed him that whenever he desired to

return the way was open to him. The fisherman expressed his sorrow at having to leave such a delightful environment, but added that unless he returned to Earth his wife and family would regard him as lost. The Fish King called a large tunnyfish, and as Arion mounted the dolphin in the old Argolian tale, so the fisherman approached the tunny, which hollowed his back and shaped it as a selle (Spence, 2010).

Before dismissing the fisherman, however, the Fish King presented him with an inexhaustible purse (Spence, 1917).

This story is interesting because, just as the tree in the Mari-El tale, the Fish King clearly starts out as a servant; however, by the end of this story, he's clearly a friend to the fisherman, for he isn't obligated to save him. When reading stories like this, I always wonder what happened in the interim to change the relationship between the fairy and the human.

Other times, the fairy will make an agreement to exchange work with the person. For example, "the devil" might agree to work for a person for seven years if the person will work for the devil after that.

A Few Witch Archetypes

Witches are often very different from our stereotypes of them, in part because people rarely understand the depth of their relationship with the spirit world, and oftentimes with individual fairies. Further, while the wicked witches are easy to identify in fairy tales, other witches are more difficult to see. Few people, for example, would realize that Cinderella is a witch, even though she summons the spirit of her dead mother. Fewer still would realize that the Viking warriors, known as berserkers, were witches, although they were possessed by animal spirits (thus their berserker state) and would even send their souls out of their bodies to do battle in the form of animals. Jack from "Jack and the Beanstalk," might very well have been a witch. He journeyed into the Other World so readily and got a magical gift from the fairies. Of course, it's possible that this was the only time he'd ever receive help from the fairies or enter the spirit world, which would mean he was just a person the fairies helped. But if the fairies continued to work with him and he continued to go on spirit journeys, then that would make him a witch. As you can see, there can be thousands of different types of witches, so my goal with these archetypes is not to cover all the possibilities, but to help change the perception of what a witch is. In order to do this, I've taken some of the key ideas in a few fairy tales, lore, witch trials, and other similar sources and mixed these with different personality traits and character archetypes in order to create what I hope are interesting and unique archetypes for witch characters.

Sweet Damsel

Examples: Cinderella, Two Eyes from "One Eye, Two Eyes, and Three Eyes," Farmer's daughter from "Baba Yaga II," the girls from "Snow White and Rose Red."

These witches are often described as pious and good, sweet and innocent, as well as hardworking. However, they are also often the target of bitterness and jealousy. Many people, after all, often hate sweet innocence and make fun of it. Further, because of their beauty and the fact that so many others naturally love them, those who feel they are in competition with them often despise these witches. Cinderella's stepmother and stepsisters called her a "stupid goose" and they stole her clothes and sent her to work in the kitchen all day. Two Eyes' own mother told her that she did not belong to her and pushed her about, and only fed her scraps like a dog. Yet through it all, Cinderella and Two Eyes remained kind and gentle, so it wasn't innocence that made them kind; it was, in reality, in their nature to be so. The reality is that one of their biggest advantages is that, while they have material needs, they are able to think of spiritual means of achieving these. When Cinderella's father goes off to the fair, he asks Cinderella and his stepdaughters what they want and, of course, his stepdaughters want beautiful dresses. But Cinderella has her mind on a more magical prize, so she asks her father to "break off for me the first branch which knocks against your hat on your way home." Cinderella takes this branch of a hazel bush and plants it in her mother's grave and, over time, this branch grows into a tree, from which the spirit of her mother can communicate with and aid her in the form of a bird. Still, material concerns do matter to them. Cinderella does ask her mother for help finding love, and Two Eyes asks her magical goat for food, as she is given so little that she would nearly starve to death if not for this magic.

Another major advantage that sweet damsels have is

that most spirits and people automatically seek to help them. Two Eyes received knowledge from an old woman who may have been a witch or a fairy; while the Farmer's Daughter, who was left to work for Baba Yaga, received help from spirit helpers in the form of mice. More noticeably in many of these tales, it doesn't take very long for a prince to fall in love with the sweet damsels. So on the one hand, these witches have a hard life, thanks to jealousy and resentment that many people feel towards them, while on the other hand, they are beloved and lucky because of their beauty. They might be hard working, or at least willing workers, but it's not through their work or their cleverness that they succeed; rather it's through their relationship with the spirit world, through their witch's powers.

The Wise Warrior

Examples: Diana, Artemis, Odin, male practitioners of shamanistic magic in Germanic Lore and Väinämöinen

Wise warriors are aggressively brilliant and obsessed with knowledge. Extremely independent and freedom loving, they not only don't seem to care what social conventions they have to break, they seem to enjoy breaking them. Male wise warriors will often engage in magic and activities legally reserved for women, while female wise warriors will often engage in practices normally reserved for men by their societies. This is because there were spells that were limited exclusively to men or women, except when they cross-dressed. Unfortunately, this breaking of social conventions could often lead to serious consequences for the wise warrior, who was very likely to get into trouble with their society and at times be arrested, banished, or even executed for what they were doing.

Even though wise warriors don't typically follow society's rules when those rules would confine them, they do have a strong set of convictions, which come from the important goals they are trying to achieve. Many wise warriors are involved in the struggle to protect the world and humanity from hostile other worldly forces, to protect their nation from outside invaders, and/or to protect the weakest members of society. They have an overwhelming need to take action and to constantly be doing something, which means that they will often instigate war, even when others seek peace. Their devotion to their vision and their goals also means that they are willing to sacrifice a lot of themselves, often suffering great pain and going on dangerous spirit journeys to gain the knowledge and skills they need to help protect others and achieve their vision. Odin, for example, sacrificed one of his eyes and hung himself from the world's tree to learn the secrets of runes and divination. Their constant taking of spirit journeys can lead them to isolate themselves from other humans in order to prevent others from moving their bodies while their souls are away.

Wise warriors are often skilled in the arts of divination, able to see much of what is going to happen and what they must to make a better future. Their ability to see the future, to peer into the spirit realm, means that they see great calamities, dark enemies, and horrifying possibilities as well. Many of them have even seen their own deaths, an eventuality they deal with through stubborn determination and poems. This, in turn, means that they are often very skilled poets, spending many weeks with their fairy companions on spirit journeys, practicing this art, singing of battles, of honor, and likely even of loss; as most of them would have seen friends die, and must prepare for their own inevitable ends.

The primary purpose of their spirit journeys, however, is typically to gain knowledge; knowledge that is mixed with their cunning and guile, that would put many con men to shame. They use this cunning and knowledge to manipulate others in the rare cases when war isn't the best option, or to get others to agree to war.

Despite the fact that these witches seem like they should be serious, their knowledge of the future, along with their constant struggle, means that they need to cut loose more than most. Because of this, they love wild parties, great feasts, and to hunt, chasing difficult prey. Hunting is often an especially important pastime for them as the chase allows them to work towards some goal while enjoying the peace that can be gained in nature.

Relationships

Wise warriors are fiercely loyal to the spirits they serve, although the most important spirits to them are their companions, who are typically a mixture of brilliant thinkers who can help them seek knowledge, and strong warriors in their own right. The most famous ones have spirits of bears, ravens, horses, and deer as companions.

The wisdom of wise warriors means that they often make great leaders; however, they are rarely leaders of massive numbers of people or kingdoms. Rather, they tend to be leaders of small groups of like-minded individuals who seek to make the world a better place through battle.

Robin Hood

A subset of the wise warrior, these were those witches that were called to lead rebellions and overthrow dictatorial systems while helping the poor. They, like the wise warriors, were not usually followers of social norms, with many men working for "The Fairy Queen" wearing dresses. Similarly, they loved adventure, hunting, to be out doing something. As natural leaders, they easily attracted fairly large numbers of followers, and they were likely selected by the fairies for this ability.

Rebels have an important place in Europe's lore, as shown by the popularity of characters like Robin Hood. Even most of the gods in pagan Europe rebelled against the tyranny of giants, their parents, or their king. The Tuatha De Danann of Ireland, for example, eventually banished their king, Bres, because of his cruelty. They then had to fight a second war with him when he returned with an army of demonic creatures (Davidson, 1989). This means that many fairies feel a natural affinity for rebels fighting against wicked tyrants or an unjust system. An unmarried prophetess named Veleda, for example, was an important part of the Rhenish rebellion against the rule of Rome. It was said that she enjoyed influence over the tribes, and because of her sacredness and power, she was too important to mingle with ordinary people; so only her family would convey messages between her and the Romans who came to negotiate with her (Aldhouse-Green, 2005). Although Veleda's experience was unique in record, as most leaders of rebellions went out into society purposefully to mingle with and help the poor, she still begins a long history of Germanic, Celtic, and Slavic rebellions lead by shamanistic figures.

Possessed Warriors

Examples: Germanic Beserkers

I must begin discussing berserkers by clearing up a common misunderstanding of what they are. Berserkers aren't always wild, chaotic brutes. It's true, of course, that many of them were greatly hated, and their brand of witchcraft was even outlawed at times. However, the berserk state comes from the berserker being possessed by a spirit known as the dyr-fylgja so that they can join in a battle with the ferocity of an animal, as well as supernatural strength, speed, and immunity to damage. Other berserkers project their souls out of their bodies in the form of wolves, bears, bulls, or other powerful animals in order to help their comrades. Being possessed by a spirit and projecting one's soul from one's body requires an incredible amount of mental discipline, which comes from contemplative meditation. Far from being chaotic, the berserker is disciplined and highly mentally organized, which would be necessary to achieve meditation in the middle of a battle. Further, berserkers would follow the rules with regards to duels and oaths. Kings would try to attract them to their armies.

Of course, berserkers were still brutal and vicious warriors, as shown by many sagas and tales about Vikings and Germanic warriors. Edill, for example, was said at the age of seven to have split another child's head to his teeth with an ax. It is perhaps this brutality and their uncompromising nature that causes the spirits to seek out these witches in the first place. After all, the spirits who work with berserkers appear to be warriors themselves, given the way they make the berserkers act when they take them over. But brutality doesn't mean berserkers are crazy. They are warriors and they follow their leader to the death. The fact that they are willing to give themselves over to the spirits, to enter the berserker rage, requires a lot of trust. And while a warrior might be wild and berserk while possessed, even losing control to the point that they kill their own comrades, what a person does while possessed is about a conflict between themselves and the spirits possessing them, it doesn't define the character of the person.

Like any who are possessed by the spirits, they would have struggled with a lot of pain and agony. Taking the spirits into oneself is difficult, while taking spirit journeys is akin to dying. For them to do these things so frequently and so willingly in the midst of battle requires that they be willing to dedicate themselves to a higher purpose. And while they may not have divined the future, they know that the world is filled with darkness and enemies that seek to destroy that which they love. They are dedicated to fighting this. In this sense, they are very much like the wise warriors; however, unlike the wise warriors, they don't flaunt society's conservative conventions; although they are murderous at times, and so are just as likely to break more serious laws.

Berserkers, like many of their culture, love poetry, songs, and beauty. A lot can likely be learned about them by looking at the highly religious and very violent knights who were descended from them. These knights may have loved combat and seducing woman, but they also tended to love things like ballads and flower arrangements. Further, berserkers are made immovable in part by their deep concern for their clan, whom they love and to whom they are heroes. They tend to have families at some point, becoming dependable and loving parents. Of course, the fact that failure isn't an option, along with their passion, often makes them stubborn, even about small things in arguments.

Adventurous, Luck Born, & Tricksters

Examples: The Hero of "The Three Golden Hairs," "The Drummer," Ambrose from "The Three Princes, "The Three Dragons," and "The Old Woman with the Iron Nose," Hermes, Jack from "Jack and the Bean Stalk," and "Jack and His Comrades," the girl from "The Old Dame and Her Hen," as well as Boots from many tales, including "Boots and the Troll," and "Princess on the Glass Hill."

Adventurous witches and tricksters are some of the most liminal of witches, for they can enter the spirit world so easily, it's often difficult in stories to tell that they've left the human world behind them. They are fun loving, freewheeling witches, who are quick to accept any challenge placed before them, whether rescuing a hen taken into the world beneath a mountain or stealing three golden hairs from a devil, they willingly set forth on some of the most dangerous and strangest adventures in fairy tales.

Adventurous witches and trickster witches are very similar to each other; both are born lucky, with an easygoing nature and the ability to get along quickly with both people and magical beings. Indeed, they are so similar that it is almost impossible to tell if the character of a story is meant to be a trickster or a lucky adventurer. Yet there is one clear difference between the two, which is that adventurous witches aren't very often clever, strong, or skilled (although they can be any of these things). When given a seemingly impossible task, the adventurous witch won't come up with a way to achieve it; rather, the spirits will do it for them or tell them how to do it. Tricksters, on the other hand, tend to use cunning and guile to accomplish their tasks, rather than relying only on help from other spirits. Yet true to their liminal natures, any one witch can, in the same story, appear to be both adventurous and a trickster. In the story of "The Drummer," for example, the drummer tricks a giant into thinking that an army is coming to kill him. Afraid, the giant promises to do anything that the drummer wishes. Whereupon:

> "You have long legs," said the drummer, "and can run quicker than I. Carry me to the glass-mountain, and I will give my followers a signal to go back, and they shall leave you in peace this time." "Come here, worm," said the giant." Seat yourself on my shoulder; I will carry you where you wish to be." The giant lifted him up, and the drummer began to beat his drum up aloft to his heart's delight. The giant thought,: that is the signal for the other people to turn back."

So the drummer is able to trick his passage into the spirit world. The drummer then steals a magical saddle, which can transport him to the top of a glass mountain, from two men. However, when he is given a task on the top of the glass mountain to empty a pond with a thimble, he works for a while, but eventually gives up and lies down. That's when a resident of the spirit world comes and does the work for him.

So his ultimate success doesn't come from anything he did; rather, he only succeeds because a fairy of the glass mountain comes to his aid.

The Adventurous Witches

"It's time for me to go out to seek my fortune," the adventurous witches will often tell their parents while they are still young. These witches don't think very much about danger and are always anxious to prove themselves, certain they can succeed where everyone else has failed. Ambrose, for example, wanted so badly to go out and seek after the dragons, which had killed his older brothers, that his familiar, a horse named Tatos, cursed his father with a toothache until he allowed Ambrose to go.

Such witches tend to have been chosen to be heroic and to do good deeds by fairies early in their lives. As a result, they've often been lucky all their lives. Because of this, they are optimistic and generally cheerful. So cheerful, in fact, that it's almost impossible for others not to like them when they meet them. However, because of their freewheeling, easygoing nature, most people simply presume that they are fools who don't realize how hard the real world is, which is likely partly true. They were born lucky, after all, and they always seem to find luck easily enough so they've never really struggled the way ordinary people have.

Adventurous witches are bold risk takers. They will ask the most feared monsters, such as Baba Yaga, to prepare supper for them with very little introduction at all, and oftentimes, such creatures will do just what these witches want them to. They, like many other witches chosen by the fairies, have a strong need to be up and about, to see new places, and do new things. They are spontaneous and optimistic and are not only willing, but often eager to set out on dangerous quest; enter the spirit world, find lost knights, save princesses, and more. This can lead to problems, as they are prone to jumping headlong into dangerous situations, to ignoring some warnings of danger. Thankfully, their spirit companions are often there to help rescue them from these situations.

The reason these witches were chosen by the spirits to

do good likely stems from the fact that they are very generous and kind. When the hero of "The Drummer" picks up the shift of a fairy girl, he's the only character I know of in fairy tales to return it with no strings attached, because he's not the type to take advantage of someone – except, of course, when he steals from a giant or some other magical entity. Their caring nature means that they are likely prone to give advice to others. Unfortunately, since they are so carefree, and tend not to think much about little things like consequences and the future, this advice isn't always good for people who don't have fairies to help them out. That is, unless they have found out what needs to be done from the spirit world beforehand.

Despite their freewheeling nature, the adventurous witch's primary goal is to accomplish the task they've set out to accomplish. So they are happy to take advice from any who can give it. This often puts them on good terms with the spirits who seek those willing to take their advice. Adventurers are also very likely to end up gaining new spirit allies by saving them from some danger (hunters, animals, other spirits, etc.). This means that they often build a strong bond with these spirits, who tend to be of a fairly utilitarian nature. That is, they are good in many different situations, such as fish, birds, squirrels, foxes, etc. and fairies who can retrieve items or help them figure out problems.

Tricksters

Tricksters are very much like the adventurous witch, and indeed, they can often be said to be the same thing, for one of their biggest advantages in interacting with both worlds is the fact that people and spirits are quick to trust them. For example, in the story of "Jack and the Bean Stalk," Jack is easily able to convince the giant's wife to let him into his house. Even after stealing from the giant, Jack is still able to trick the giant's wife into letting him back into the house a second time. The trickster is not only clever, but also eloquent, quick talking, witty, and often, very funny. Because of this, many people find them entertaining to be around and think their antics are hilarious. Of course, those who are the butts of their "jokes" or who become targets for theft, despise them for these very traits. This means that tricksters often get into trouble with the powerful, yet at the same time, even more powerful spirits think their antics are funny and so shield them from the wrath of those on which they've played tricks

This protection is important because tricksters are easily bored and love to seek out new challenges, often plying their wit against that of others with riddles or by playing pranks on them. They have strong appetites for pleasures, including fun, wine, food, and sex. This in turn often leads them to use their talents to steal. Because they are very caring individuals, one of the hallmarks of tricksters is that they typically steal from tyrants or destructive spirits. More than this, they are just as likely to use their talents to benefit those in need as they are to help themselves. They are very likely to risk their lives to rescue those who are imprisoned or in danger in the spirit world, or in places few others can enter. So tricksters do live by a moral code, one of their own making perhaps, but this moral code almost always involves helping those they feel sorry for or who very clearly need help.

Their fun loving and caring nature means that they make friends easily and are quickly able to win the trust of spirits and people alike. Both humanity and the spirit world are lucky to have them because they steal secrets that save villages and benefit people, as Hermes so often did. Jack, from "Jack and his Comrades," uses his familiar animal spirits to help him steal from some robbers so that the money that they took could be replaced to its rightful owner. Meanwhile, the shaman figure from "The Devil with the Three Golden Hairs" was asked by many villagers to help them discover why their tree had stopped bearing fruit, their well had dried up, etc. He managed to discover these secrets by gaining help from the "devil's" mother, who asked the devil in his sleep the answers to these questions.

Their ability to move in and out of dangerous places and to get along with nearly anyone means that tricksters are often asked to help guide others through dangerous places or steal magical objects. Boots from "Boots and the Troll," for example, was asked repeatedly by the king to steal silver ducks, a quilt of gold and silver, and more from a troll; which he did in typical trickster style, through a mixture of cleverness, deceit, and quick talking.

The Luck Born

The luck born are similar in many ways to the adventurous witch. 'Luck born,' however, have either completed their quest and so are now living 'happily ever after,' or never had to go on an adventure to achieve wealth and success. Instead, these witches have established themselves as leaders of the community they settle into, sometimes as kings, but more often as wealthy merchants and farmers. In nearly all cases, they become peacemakers, helping people make peace not only with each other, but with the otherworldly forces around them. They are generally very accepting of everyone which, along with their warm and kind nature, means that they are always willing to give alms to those in need. Typically, the luck born were chosen by the fairies in order to make the world better through their kindness, so many will heal the sick for free and perform other similar services.

Like the adventurous witch, luck born are confident and optimistic; after all, everything seems to go their way. They have a tendency to enjoy the finer things in life, such as good food and good wine. Further, luck born tend to gather a set of sophisticated friends around them, a task made easier by their natural ability to develop friends. Although they are very aware of other people's feelings and use this knowledge to help others and become the center of attention, they are still very secretive, as the spirits so often require of their servants. Still, they aren't isolationist and are typically married and have children, whom they will most likely pass their secrets onto. They are also likely to have some very interesting stories to tell, especially about their early adventure (if they had it) that led them to their wealth. They often form a very sophisticated social circle around themselves, of both spirits and humans. Others likely wonder how they can keep track of so many people's names, birthdays, likes and dislikes, and be so unaware of much of the rest of the world.

Bold Musician

The bold musicians are talented musicians who have a strong love for not only dancing and the finer things in life, but were spontaneous enough and bold enough to jump headlong into a fairy's dance to play music, offer musical advice, and generally help the fairies have a good time.

As self-made witches, bold musicians aren't likely very powerful, and they most likely don't have a lot of knowledge of herbs, charms, or other things, but they're really not that interested in that. They do make friends easily, and their shared love of music with the fairies means that the fairies often help them and will happily do favors for them.

They love new experiences and new places. Lively and fun, they love to be the center of attention. Because they get along so well, and don't really care much for debate, they are generally the peacemakers among their friends; a task made easier by the fact that they are very observant of other people, and can easily sense when things are wrong.

Charming and smooth talking, they could easily become important and capable leaders of society, but that rarely ever interests them. Unlike the luck born, they weren't given their gifts; they made them through their easygoing nature, and so they usually stick to that by enjoying the moment.

Spirit-Forged Witch

Examples: the Völva, the Heroine from "The Seven Raven," Freyja,

In many societies, these witches were greatly honored and revered such that Jacob Grimm even claimed that these women could receive a place much higher than that of heroes. Even lords would give up their seats to these women, or at least that's how it was in societies that still respected the shamaness's role. In these Old Germanic societies, the shamaness was so important that it was rare for her to stay in one place for very long; rather, she would travel from village to village and town to town in order to help as many people as possible.

Spirit-forged shamanesses usually become shamanesses in the most intense and brutal ways imaginable. Many suffer greatly and even die in order to enter the spirit world and learn its secrets, as well as the skills they need to make the world a better place. At times, this suffering and death was purposeful, with the shamaness having agreed to be tortured with blades and or fire so that she could enter the spirit world. Then after learning what she needed to, the spirit-forged witch's soul would return to her body with a sudden gasping yawn.

Even the spirit journey they undertook after their pain and suffering could be extremely harsh, involving dangerous, other worldly wildernesses and difficult ritual spells which required great sacrifices. For example, the girl in "The Seven Ravens" cut off her own finger to use as the key to enter the glass mountain (land of the dead), after having already suffered through the heat of the sun and the bloodthirstiness of the moon, and a long harsh and lonely wilderness.

After being "spirit forged" through fire and hardship, these witches became commanding figures, for they had been to the land of the dead and returned. Even without speaking, many people are instantly drawn to them after these journeys. Even in societies where the shamanesses were exalted, they could be greatly feared, for they were dangerous, cunning, and mysterious. Their close relationship with death, and the fact that they were so often companions with the spirits of the dead, often meant that in many ways they represented death.

In addition, the spirit-forged witch was easily angered. In order to become witches, they had to suffer iron and fire, and starvation and sorrow, so there could be no compromise with them. Even Thor wasn't as stubborn as Freyja was. The very earth could quake with their anger, causing people to cower before them.

They are very much concerned with traditions and ceremonies, and are often the center of these. In addition, they believe strongly in propriety, diligence, and hard work. So diligent that they have very little patience for weakness; they will drive wars and kill deserters.

Still, they are involved in much more than war, for the spirit-forged create abundant harvests and good weather. They bring hope and luck to the people. Despite this importance, they tend to live apart from people, often being pushed to the fringes of society, even when they are respected and beloved. It's important to keep in mind, however, that this doesn't mean they are solitary; they just prefer to spend their time with like-minded people and spirits. So they often meet with each other, flying off to massive celebrations. They will even get married to great heroes who have also faced death many times; heroes who, like them, have been "forged" by danger and hardship. When married, they spin the fate of their lover in combat so that his enemies are powerless against him. Other times, they hover over him, granting him strength, or attacking their enemies' ability to function.

Still, regardless of any human relationships they might have, the spirit-forged's real relationship is most likely with the spirits. They often ride giant wolves or cats. The greatest and most powerful spirits often seek to support them, respecting what they did during their spirit journeys to gain the powers they have.

Threshold Guardians

Examples: Hecate, The Living Saints of Bulgaria, and the Heroine from the "Six Swans"

Threshold guardians spend their time on the threshold of realities between the spaces of humanity and the spirits, more specifically, between their community and their ancestral spirits, commonly seen at crossroads, the time between night and day, in graveyards or the forests near their homes. Here, they seek to befriend and placate what spirits they can or fight off those they can't. Although they are normally kind, they spend so much time in the land of the dead that their nature alters and people begin to fear them and their odd behavior, which often leads them to be discriminated against.

In many ways, one could think of guardians as being like the guard dogs of their communities. Indeed, Hecate, the most famous of the guardians, often took the form of a dog while on spirit journeys and traveled with dogs. Like a guard dog, threshold guardians are protective, loyal, and kind. Above all else, they love their families and their communities, which thanks to the witch's unique nature, means that their ancestor spirits are close friends as well.

Like dogs, they have highly attuned senses, which extend into the magical world and the future as well. This means that they are able to divine coming dangers to prepare for them and warn those they love. They don't only use their senses to detect danger. They spend much of their time in the spirit world and around their homes in the form of hares, cats, dogs, and other animals in order to learn what is happening, make allies, and root out dangers.

They enjoy their time in the Other World because of their friendship with spirits, especially the spirits of the dead, ancestral spirits who are beautiful and kind. They love to make people comfortable and happy, whether living or dead. So while they are necromancers, they are the necromancers who summon up ghosts as friends; rather than dwelling on death, they dwell on eternal life in all its stages. Cheerful and bright, they are the most beloved of witches to the spirits.

Relationship with People

Perhaps the most beloved of witches, other people are often happy to be around them. As healers and protectors of their communities, they are often greatly loved and highly regarded. Most threshold guardians live for their families and their communities (living and dead).

Just as threshold guardians don't differentiate between spirits and people, they also don't concern themselves with social class or power. They tend to think of everyone as equals and speak with them or judge their actions equally. The threshold guardians themselves are chosen by the people from all walks of life; some might be wealthy while others might be beggars, but they are all equal when they meet.

Their unconventional nature and their lack of respect for authority does lead to problems, as some are known at times to aid the fairies in abducting children in order to help fight the secret wars in which the fairies engage. They are very concerned with family and most of them will have children, although their secretive nature means that they don't always share what they do with those they love.

Relationship with Spirits

Threshold guardians were very likely to be chosen by ancestral spirits and so they usually work closely with the spirit of a dead uncle, grandmother, or similar relative. This means that their closest relationship may be with their familiar spirits. These spirits often introduce them to other spirits, including a queen of the fairies, with whom they are very likely to serve. Threshold guardians were frequently chosen both because they had an ancestral spirit who could show them around the spirit world and because of their kind and caring nature. This means fairies that care about the communities of humans are very likely to care greatly for threshold guardians. However, fairies, by nature, are oftentimes dualistic, so threshold guardians are often called upon by them to do things the human community would frown on. This can create strong moral dilemmas for some threshold guardians, ones that they may never truly solve.

Mischief-Maker

Examples: The many witches of folk belief who would blight fields, ruin cows, turn flour into manure, cause husbands and wives to fight, and more for no apparent reason.

Unlike the trickster, the mischief-maker isn't friendly or caring. Worse still, they don't feel remorse or guilt. Working with callous spirits who, like them, lack much empathy, they love to play pranks on humanity. Most of their pranks become ever more horrifyingly cruel as they try to outdo each other, and to show off for the spirits they work with.

Childish and prone to tantrums, they have trouble dealing with stress of any kind and either try to ignore problems or deal with them by causing ever more trouble. This makes them vindictive and dangerous, likely to take revenge for the smallest slights. Mischief-makers tend to be implosive and irresponsible; they don't think much about the future and so, often get themselves into trouble financially and otherwise.

Although sneaky and secretive at times, they love to show off. Like the fairies they serve, they love wild parties and have strong appetites for food, wine, and sex. Because of this, mischief-makers often attend parties with other witches and spirits who share their lifestyles. Although they aren't necessarily clever, so their pranks tend to be fairly simple and unimaginative, most of the time they simply repeat the same prank over and over again, or they copy another witch's pranks. Their lack of creativity and cleverness, as well as foresight, often means that they are easily deceived by others.

Many mischief-makers may even have been chosen for their lack of cleverness and their mental weakness, as this made it easier for the spirits to break and bend them to their will. Mischief-makers are likely very much like pets or slaves of the spirits, although some might have been naturally psychopathic.

Relationship with People

Mischief-makers oftentimes seem like ordinary members of their community. They hold typical jobs, have families, and would generally be considered normal, although their appetites and boredom also mean that they often spend a lot more money than most and so easily get into financial difficulty. They have a tendency to be easily angered and lack many social inhibitions, so they are also very likely to get into trouble frequently. Such trouble usually involves their relationship with members of the opposite sex, the likelihood that they will engage in a fight, become abusive, etc.

Relationship with Fairies

Although the spirits with which mischief-makers work lack empathy for the most part, they also attach themselves very closely to those they work with. More than this, their love of mischief means that they usually want to work with humans, so they are emotionally invested in the mischief-maker.

However, since there are so many fairies that seek to help humanity, they are often at odds with much of the spirit world. This adds to their paranoid and secretive nature because direct confrontation usually isn't their style. They are bullies who like to pick fights with those weaker than they are and secretly hurt those who might be able to fight back.

The Wicked

Examples: Wicked Stepmothers who are witches, as well as those witches in lore who would recruit new witches for the devil.

Whether princesses or peasants, wicked witches feel trapped by social norms, and by their place in society. They are very smart and are often able to quickly read and understand people, a skill they use to manipulate and deceive others. Far from not caring what others think, the wicked seeks to force their place in history, to gain the acknowledgment from the world of spirits and or in the human world. Their grandiose sense of self-worth means that they are power hungry. They will stop at nothing to achieve their ends.

Wicked witches tend to be charismatic and charming and enjoy the company of others, especially those with whom they share a common interest. Yet at the same time, they must surely fear and mistrust other wicked witches, so their life is fueled by a mixture of paranoia, anxiety, and a need to connect.

Their trademark act is to bargain with people in order to gain more power. Often this means bargaining for the souls, for the soul is where a person's power lies. Though really, they will bargain for anything that brings them closer to achieving their goals. They enjoy mind games, enjoy feeling a sense of power over others and so will sometimes bargain and manipulate people simply for the feelings of power they get from tricking others to give up what they love.

Wicked witches approach the desperate and power hungry with deals, offering to give these people what they want, for a price. They console those who are sorrowful, provide for the wanting. They then begin to work on these people, seeking to alter the way they think. The primary goal of wicked witches is to get other people to commit to serve the spirits they serve, either as slaves (in the afterlife), warriors, or other wicked witches. This way they can gain more favor with powerful Forest Kings, queens of the fairies, dragons, and similar beings.

Devious and brutal when they see what they want, they allow nothing to stand in their way and will often slaughter thousands through curses and worse. Oftentimes, the desperation, the famines, wars, and diseases that make so many willing to bargain for their souls are caused by the wicked witches.

Relationship with Spirits

The relationship between the spirits and the wicked witch runs the gambit of such negative relationships with the spirits as being viewed as servants or, worse, slaves. The spirits they serve are often abusive, predatory, and cruel. This means that the wicked witches frequently find themselves on the receiving end of the spirit's assault. This, in turn, can drive them to work harder to please the spirits, to think of themselves as failures. Even when wicked witches have a close relationship with the spirits they serve, they and the spirits still view each other primarily as tools to achieve their ends. This can mean that they will come into conflict with each other and adds further fuel to the wicked witch's paranoia.

Relationship with People

Although they could have come from any social class, the charming and persuasive wicked witches end up in the highest tiers of society. They are queens, kings, princess, wealthy merchants, and more. In these positions, they typically hide who they are from all but those they revile so much that they attack because they can't bear to see them happy, or those they see as competition for their power, who they also attack directly.

Wicked witches use their position to make themselves as happy as money is capable of making them, as no matter how much they have, they are always obsessed with gaining more. Wicked witches are masters of morphing their appearance, of changing the way they seem to others. So when they approach someone with a bargain, the person rarely, if ever, realizes who's approaching them. Often, to those they help they are heroes, saviors at first. Some people don't realize that they've been tricked until the fairies take them away to be slaves in the spirit world.

The Psychopath

Thrill-seeking serial killers, psychopaths are very often the worst result of the horrifying and unstable world in which they live. They typically had abusive parents, lived in an often-cruel society, and survived in constant desperation, which eventually led them to break psychologically. This break is very often fueled by the psychotic fairies, who seek to use the psychopath in order to gain their own sadistic pleasure. Psychopaths are fascinated by fire, by blight, starvation, suffering, disease, and death. Sadistic and cruel, they work with the spirits to torture animals and people alike. What they aren't fascinated by is other people, whom they usually don't like to be with, and so they live in isolation. However, they are often charming and know when they need to act nice in order to get what they want.

They are methodical planners and patient, they so are able to wait a long time between actions to avoid letting people know what's happening. They can also spend years cultivating and developing the connections they need to spread a massive plague. For them, death and suffering are victories, so they are likely to collect trophies from their exploits, the skulls of those dead from plagues they spread, starvation they created, and more.

Relationship with People

Psychopaths either live completely isolated places, or else they act as fairly ordinary people. So while people always suspect the isolated psychopath of being evil, they are shocked if they learn what the social one is. Many psychopaths live seemingly normal lives, getting married and even having children. Oftentimes, these children will inherit the psychopath's spirits and so will become psychopaths themselves.

Despite their cruel and uncaring nature, psychopaths need approval, and so will often act temporarily in ways that would help them get this approval, although more often than not, they have started to get their approval from the evil spirits they work with or other psychopathic witches.

Relationship with Spirits

Psychopaths are incapable of a real healthy relationship, but they crave approval, and the cruel spirits they work with provide this. This drives them to be crueler than nearly any other human could be. Their need for control leads them to develop a fantasy world where they are the ones controlling the spirits they work with, and not the other way around. At the same time, the spirits are usually all too happy to let them think they are controlling things, so long as the witch provides them with opportunities to help wreak havoc. However, sometimes the spirits aren't content with this relationship, so they begin bullying and abusing the psychopath to make certain the witch knows that the fairies are in charge.

The Lost

Desperate people who are trapped by their low place in society, the lost are often easily won over by the fairies with promises of secrets and power. At first, they might be happy at having a secret, childishly playing with the Other World as if they were writing a story, rather than living their lives. Their need for acknowledgment often leads them to reveal their nature clumsily by threatening to curse people for minor offenses. Other times, they will reveal themselves by blackmailing people with secrets they learned through their divination powers, or from the spirits themselves. However, when faced with the reality of the fairies' dual nature, they often regret their impulsive decision to become servants to the fairies and so try to resist their demands. This, in turn, causes the fairies to torment them, which often leads to further depression and a sense of powerlessness. This feeling of powerlessness means that the lost will almost always give into the fairies' demands.

The lost feel a strong need to be accepted and they eventually lack any will to resist the spirits, which means that they can often do terrible things for the fairies in return for minor favors. Worse still, their bitterness and resentment at their place in society can lead them to do some very horrible things on their own. Still, the lost aren't psychopathic, per se, and may even feel guilt after cursing others – guilt which they try to make up for by blessing and healing others.

The lost try to balance their lives between evil and good, but they are never really able to do this, so they quickly come to feel even more isolated and lonely. Their need to be accepted means that, on the surface, they usually follow social conventions. They work, get married if that is typical for the society in they live, etc. They always wish for a better place, for something better, but they are afraid to do anything that would make waves, except when their frustration boils over in short outbursts of anger.

Relationship with Other People

The lost normally try to get along with other people; they try to act friendly and kind. Often lonely, they seek out others to do things with, to give them acceptance. However, they are moody, bitter, and easily angered; so it's rare that people want to be with them for very long, as they will often lash out angrily. This anger can lead them to threaten people with witchcraft or even become physically abusive. This causes rumors to spread about them and may lead angry mobs to attack them.

Relationship with the Spirits

The losts' relationship with the fairies with whom they work is often like that of an abused and battered lover, for they often have a bad sexual relationship with the fairies who are quick to anger and abuse them. The fairies that approach them typically needed to feel a sense of power as well, so the lost, with their low self-esteem, offer the perfect outlet for the fairies' need to control things, as they were weak and easy to manipulate. However, the fairies often become bored with their relationship with the lost and so leave them. There are always other fairies, however, and the lost almost always find themselves in another bad relationship, despite promising that they will never again end up in that situation.

Mystics

Examples: Pagan Hermits, Philosophers, and Hermit Monks

These witches have a strong love for the powerful spirits that they serve. They are more than happy to give up their lives for the fairies; in fact, they don't even view doing so as a sacrifice. They tend to have a rich inner world and so live private, secretive lives, not letting very many people "in." Yet they themselves are very warm, gentle, and kind. They are keen observers of human nature and so are highly attuned to the feelings of others, although with the exception of occasionally providing help, they tend keep their own feelings hidden most of the time. Often this causes them to live semi-hermitic lives, which can become problematic because they are prone to bouts of depression and sudden overzealous religious streaks that can lead them to hurt themselves as they seek to enter the spirit world through agony or by taking the pain of others on themselves.

These witches have a clear idea of the way the world should be, a vision that they believe will be obtained through the spirits. They spend most of their time striving towards this vision with an intense passion. Because of their kindness and their dedication to making people's lives better, their community and whole regions can come to rely on them, which sometimes thrusts them into leadership roles they aren't always comfortable with. However, their dedication means that they will sometimes take on these leadership roles with gusto when that is the best way to accomplish their goals.

Lovers of beauty and cleanliness, they are nevertheless very minimalistic in their choice of lifestyle and decor. They don't seek after the "finer" things in life, choosing instead to seek out spiritual fulfillment by helping others. Sacrifice is a way of life for them, an emotional need.

Although intelligent and capable, they tend to be slow learners and so very often need a hands-on approach for a very long period of time to understand new concepts. This means that they are frequently taught about the spirit world when they are on the verge of death so that they can take a long spirit journey. For many of them, their experience with the spirit world begins when they die and come back to life, something that has a profound effect on their view of mortal life, which they are more easily able to accept as nothing more than a transition period, a learning experience.

Relationships
Very much beloved, mystics still often live apart from the hustle and bustle of daily life, spending much of their time in meditation or working to heal the sick, make harvests rich, and do other good things.

Very often, mystics become the people who help communities to maintain traditions, and so might be viewed by revolutionaries and young people as old fashioned and out of touch. Other times, the mystics can see certain traditions, especially those that lead to poverty and corruption as being the root of evil in society. Both these things can lead to social problems at times, as the mystic can defend their view with passionate zealousness, which leads to conflict and anger,

The spirits who work with these witches love them, just as the mystics love the spirits. These witches have a deep, abiding respect for the fairies and the knowledge they have, and the spirits are awed by the mystic's ability to do what needs to be done and love others, no matter what.

Smiths

Fairies fear nothing more than they fear iron, for it has the power to destroy their magic, to kill them, and to banish them. Those humans who work it often have a magical power all their own, one which many fairies covet. They will kidnap children to train them to be smiths who can work iron. For with iron, the fairies can win wars against others of their kind and they can reshape the "Other World;" but so can the smiths who use iron.

Smiths are hardworking and dedicated. As risk takers, they love challenges, love to push their limits. Contemplative and thoughtful, but not necessary interested in abstract concepts or ideas, smiths prefer to tinker, to manipulate things to try to understand them and improve their skills.

Far from just working metal, smiths are able to forge destiny, to shape magic, and gain favor from the fairies. This makes smiths some of the most powerful of witches. Further, the spirits of the dead and fairies are often unable to harm a smith directly in Celtic lore, and so wicked spirits will simply avoid contact with them (Gregory, 1920).

Relationship with People

Although they aren't very good at expressing themselves and they tend to be quiet, their generous and helpful nature often makes them a center of their community. So, in some cities of the past, smiths were not only a necessary part of the community, they might have been some of the only skilled laborers in town. This gives them an automatic position of power and of envy. Their typically calm demeanor often smoothed over people's natural resentment towards those who find such success, and certainly folktales don't have nearly as many negative portrayals of smiths as we do of millers and similar people. Only those who feared magic seem to hate smiths and their powers.

Relationship with Fairies

Fairies both fear and stand in awe of smiths, for only smiths truly have the power to craft things that they fear, and they make doing so look so effortless. Fairies can be close companions to the smiths. In fact, sometimes, the fairies even trained smiths in their art, and other times the fairies granted them the skills they needed to perfect the craft. Smiths, with their soft-spoken nature and kindness, enjoy the company of fairies to a point. Yet their work with iron likely makes it difficult for the fairies to spend too much time around them.

The Hardworking

In Fairyland, it is often the hardest working who survive, for fairies respect and even demand hard work. Thus, those who stumble upon Fairyland and work hard are often rewarded by the fairies and have the opportunity to make friends with them. In addition to being hard working, these witches are polite and respectful of authority, as well as generous and kind. All are traits that allow a person to not only survive, but often thrive in Fairyland.

Although patient with their work, these witches easily lose their temper with those who don't respect and follow the guidance of the spirits. They may even learn from the spirits to curse those who don't work hard. Still, they are very good friends to have; they love to help others and are often involved in their community, although they only take leadership positions when those are thrust upon them. These witches will work hard and diligently to maintain their friendships. Celebrations, ceremonies, and tradition tend to have a great meaning for them, so they almost never forget important details or events in their friendships.

Relationship with People

It's fairly easy to like the diligent and generally warm-natured hard workers, although they aren't showy, keeping their appearance and homes clean and practical. This lack of showiness often means that, while people rely on them and while they maintain long friendships with people, few people consider them "best" friends.

Relationship with the Fairies

Fairies often reserve some of their best gifts for the diligent and hard working. They love those who set out to accomplish things and do so in a timely manner without complaint. More than this, the respectful and generous way in which the hard workers treat the fairies quickly endears them to each other.

The Good Neighbor

Quiet and reserved, these witches have an interest in security and living peacefully. They are serene, preferring contemplation. This is contrasted by a strong sense of duty, a loyalty to those around them that keeps them as a part of the world and the community in which they live. They are good people who can always be depended upon to do right by their community.

They believe strongly in traditions and laws (that make sense) and avoid breaking long established moral codes; tending to push the community to keep these long established traditions as well, which can put them at odds with people who seek change.

They are incredibly knowledgeable, at least when it comes to facts, although they do have difficulty understanding ideas that are different from their own. They have a strong sense of duty, and feel that it is their job to help those in need. Strong believers in the importance of honesty and promises, they'll always do what they say they'll do.

They are perfectionists in their own lives, who are uncomfortable expressing affection and emotion to others. This means that it's often difficult for them to form close relationships with anyone but the fairies whom they respect. As a result, most of these witches never get married, but when they do, they take their roles as spouses and parents very seriously and are often wonderfully loving, even if they aren't very good at saying it. More often than not, however, their community becomes their family. They quietly attend community gatherings, enjoy watching the people in their community grow and thrive, and do all they can, from healing the sick to helping the crops to grow, in order to make their community a better place.

Using Magic

Whether they wish to or not, no matter what they had hoped or dreamed for their lives, witches were chosen by the fairies to use magic. So witches must perform magic and they must engage in the rituals the fairies demand of them. Therefore, magic is a double-edged sword for many. On the one hand, it is a gift, the power to manipulate the world in ways that most mortals will never know. On the other hand, it is a power that isolates the witch, something which the fairies use to bend them to their will. It is also, however, the means by which witches can bind and force the fairies to do what they want. The essence of magic is both a struggle and a partnership between men and the supernatural forces that control the world.

The Magic of Man, Gods, and Fairies

In many tales, the gods and fairies don't seem to have withstood much more than the witches and shamans. True, some might have been able to change their size and form, but so too could many great witches and wizards. What's more, as already mentioned, many deities feared humans, and others such as the Tuatha De' Danann of Ireland had even been defeated by human druids. Oftentimes, fairies, and deities gained most of their supernatural powers from the same things that mortal witches did. Odin called up spirits to help him the way any shaman would, while others utilized their great knowledge of herbs. For example, the deities were immortal because they ate from a magical fruit tree, and fairies used magical herbs for many things. When Athena, the goddess of wisdom, wanted to bring a woman named Arkhne back to life, she had to use magical herbs from Hecate (a goddess of magic), for she didn't have the power to do this by herself. Often, it seems that the primary power of the deities came from skill and knowledge greater than that of most humans, but not necessarily greater than all humans. The forms of magic I present to you are not just used by witches; they are also used by fairies and deities as well.

Blood Magic

There is power in blood, for blood is tied to a person's life, to their soul. This is why, in so many fairy tales, the blood can speak for the person from whom it comes. In one story, a wicked witch plans to murder a girl who tricks her into killing her own daughter instead. In order to escape before the witch finds out what happened, the girl takes the head of the witch's now decapitated daughter:

> And dropped three drops of blood on the ground, one in front of the bed, one in the kitchen, and one on the stairs. Then she hurried away with her lover. When the old witch got up next morning, she called her daughter, and wanted to give her the apron, but she did not come. Then the witch cried, "Where are you?"
> "Here, on the stairs; I am sweeping," answered the first drop of blood.
> The old woman went out, but saw no one on the stairs, and cried again, "Where are you?" "Here in the kitchen, I am warming myself," cried the second drop of blood.
> (Sweetheart Roland, Grimm Brother's Tale)

Far from rare, this idea of three talking drops of blood is practically ubiquitous throughout Northern Europe's fairy tales; and people would use their own blood to pretend they were in places they weren't and so trick giants, witches, and more. Blood may also be the means by which a changeling of clay can be made to replace a person. In "The Magic Maiden," an abused girl finds herself among the fairies and, after begging to be able to stay with them, they take three drops of her blood and inject these into a clay doll.

> Her own clothes had been put on the clay doll, which was to be sent to the village in her stead. During the night, the doll had grown bigger and bigger, till it was the very image of Elsa. It ran about like a human being. Elsa was frightened when she saw the doll so like herself, but the Lady, noticing her terror, said, "Fear nothing! This clay doll cannot hurt you. We are going to send it to your parents. The wicked woman may beat it all she wishes, for the clay doll can feel no pain." So the clay image was sent to her parents (Olcott, 1928).

Blood, it seems, has two primary powers: the first is to offer a vital connection to the person whom it is from; the second is to offer life. Thus, blood can be used as a means of healing or as a surrogate for the person. These powers mean that the spirits can often use blood to insure that a person follows through on their bargain, which is why oaths with spirits must be signed in blood; and the means of summoning many spirits includes offering three drops of one's own blood. Further, in Finnish mythology, three drops of blood could be added to a specially prepared sculpture; when this was done, the "para" would come to life and serve the person who supplied the blood as a magical familiar (often able to steal milk and cheese for them).

This connection between blood and a person could have many uses. In "Koshchei the Deathless,"

> Prince Ivan dismounted, let some drops of blood run from his little finger into a glass, gave it to his brothers, and said, "If the blood in this glass turns black, tarry here no longer; that will mean that I am about to die." Then he took leave of them and went his way.

While in "The Goose Girl," a princess'

> Aged mother went into her bedroom, took a small knife, and cut her finger with it until it bled. Then she held a white handkerchief to it, into which she let three drops of blood fall, gave it to her daughter, and said, "Dear child, preserve this carefully; it will be of service to you on your way."

These drops of blood not only speak to the princess, telling her what her mother would want her to do, but they also offer her magical protection. Once she loses them, a wicked serving maid is able to take the princess' place. Finally, in the Welsh fairy tale, "Two Cat Witches," a man cuts an evil witch's hand so that as the blood flows out of her, so does her magical power. In this way, the man was able to make the evil witch harmless.

Magical Items

There exists in fairy tales many strange magical items by which witches and fairies gain their magical powers. In "The Nix," two children are trying to escape slavery at the hands of a nixie when the wicked fairy begins to chase after them:

> When the children saw this, the boy threw behind him a comb, which made a great ridge with a thousand times a thousand teeth, but the nixie managed to keep herself steady on them, and at last crossed over. Then the girl threw behind her a looking glass, which formed a hill of mirrors, and was so slippery that it was impossible for the nixie to cross it. Then she thought, I will go home quickly and fetch my axe, and cut the hill of glass in half. (The Nix – Grimm Brothers Tale)

This idea of throwing objects to create mountains, hills of mirrors, forests, lakes, and more is extremely common in fairy tales, not only in Europe, but as far away as Japan. This may be because fairies gain much of their magic through the crafting of magical items, rather than through actual spells. Alps (elves) in Germany become invisible, thanks to their magical hats. Fairies fly by means of bundles of various plants on which they sit; similarly, the Greek shaman Abaris would ride about on a magical arrow, which was likely an item that helped him on his spirit journeys (Blackburn, 1991), just as fairies used thistles to fly. Many other beings use special boots to allow them to move at incredible speeds. In "Sweetheart Roland," a witch has a pair of many-league boots, with which she can cover an hour's walk with every step she takes. Her daughter, whom she's chasing, however, has a magical wand that allows her to change herself into a duck and her sweetheart into a lake. Witches could also make enchanted clothes, which protected the wearer against injury. Swords could make those holding them greater warriors, and more.

Aid from the Fairies

Among ordinary people, there are thousands of chants, such as little poems that are meant to ask the fairies for aid. There are also sacrifices and gifts that can be offered to the fairies to try to secure their blessing. Such chants and sacrifices don't allow one to become a witch, however. At best, such actions secure the goodwill of the fairies most people won't ever see. Witches are unique because they do see and converse with the fairies; for them, gaining magical aid, such as help with healing, protection, divination, and so forth is about bargaining with friends, with acquaintance, with servants, or with one's master. How the fairies react to the witch's pleas depends on their relationship with the fairy as well as what the fairy is able to do. A witch whose spirit helper is their uncle will have a different experience gaining magical aid than a child who is friends with a few fairy children.

Sometimes, a witch's relationships with the fairies they knew wasn't enough to do everything, however. Any given fairy is limited in their abilities and their willingness to assist in some tasks. During these times, the witch would often choose to seek the aid of a fairy with whom they didn't have a relationship. In Sweden, witches would call Bjära (fairies that appeared as hares, cats, and birds) to help them steal milk from their neighbors. Similarly, although Odin carried Mime's head with him to gain insights and secrets, and had two ravens that could fly about the world and bring him back new; but he still called up the spirits of the dead and earth to learn even more.

The rituals for calling these spirits could be fairly complex, requiring not only the right words and offerings, but the right timing as well. Witches in South Eastern Europe, for example, typically called spirits at night, or the time between day and night, for this is the time of spirits. Such spirits were also invoked in places that were important to them; at the edge of villages, crossroads, places that lay between or that acted as other worlds such as the water and forests (Petreska, 2008). Other rituals were performed in places that were associated with cleanliness and purity, such as bathhouses in Eastern Europe, places that are often still associated with vestiges of paganism (Vadeysha, 2005).

It's important to bear in mind that when the witch seeks out and speaks to the fairies, she is, in fact, speaking to beings with wills and emotions of their own. Beings, who like anyone else, want to know what's in it for them. So, while a witch might be able to bow down towards beautiful elves and ask for a handout like a beggar, she is more likely to come with some offering or overture of friendship. By the same token, those seeking out evil spirits will come with a plan to do something that the spirits would find fun, or some gift for them.

Still, there are many witches, especially in folktales, who seem to be able to develop a rapport with the fairies instantly. For example, the hero in "The Devil's Three Golden Hairs" or in "Jack and the Beanstalk" convinces the otherworldly spirit, the giant or the ogre he lives with, to let them stay for the night. Others convince Baba Yaga to cook them dinner, get spirits they've never met to help them complete impossible tasks, and more, just based on their charisma and or magnetism.

Beyond simply asking for help from the fairies, there are some people who become possessed by them to gain powers. While possessed, the fairies give the witch strength in battle. Other times, the fairy is able to use the person as a mouthpiece to give messages and divine the future.

Among the Welsh, there are certain individuals called

"awenyddion," who behave as if they are possessed by devils. You will not find them anywhere else. When you consult them about some problem, they immediately go into a trance and lose control of their senses, as if they are possessed. They do not answer the question put to them in any logical way. Words stream from their mouths, incoherently and apparently meaningless, and without any sense at all, but all the same will express; and, if you listen carefully to what they say, you will receive the solution to their problem. When it is all over, they will recover from their trance, as if they were ordinary people waking from a heavy sleep, but you have to give them a good shake before they regain control of themselves...." (Davidson, 1989)

The Berserkers of the north were possessed by animal spirits, giving them the beastly ferocity of bears and wolves. With the strength given to them by the spirits, these warriors could bite through steel, become immune to nearly all weapons, tear people's throats out, and more (Fee, 2004).

While the witch Ljot went to attack some brothers who had kidnapped her son in the most hideous form. She had thrown one foot over her head and went backwards upon hand and foot, with her face sticking out behind; her eyes were hideous and demon like.... (Keyser, 1854)

Had Ljot spotted her victims before they spotted her, they would have been driven mad; however, their attendant spirit was powerful and it helped them to spot her first.

Gifts and Secrets of the Fairies

Many magical secrets that a fairy shared with a witch had to remain secret, as revealing how the magic worked would rob it of its power. An example of one of these secrets comes from Elspeth, who would boil an egg and then drink moisture from its shell to gain knowledge of the truth of things (Purkiss, 2007).

We don't know many of the secrets that fairies shared with witches, as they were secret and witches almost never revealed them. To do so was to suffer the wrath of the fairies, and to drain the secret of its magic. The Italian cunning said specifically that they would not share their secrets for then they would lose the ability to use the magic, and the person they shared it with would gain nothing from it (Mogliocco, 2009).

Only those the fairies approved of could learn these secrets, and it may be that because humans had the ability to spoil and ruin things with their ill will and thoughts, some people would naturally destroy magical things. For this reason, the fairies would only be able to share their secrets with those who would not drain the secrets of their potency, people who, for whatever reason, couldn't simply hurt the magic with their thoughts.

Spirit Journeys

Much of a witch's power comes from their ability to send their soul from their body to journey about this or the Other World.

> All magical or Platonic writers of the times speak much of the transformation or projection of the sidereal body of witch or wizard. Once the soul escapes from the natural body, though but for a moment, it passes into the body of air and can transform itself as it please or even dream itself into some shape it has not willed. (Gregory, 1920)

What this means is that a witch has a dream form, which is, in essence, like a fairy, a form that can change shape, size, become invisible, and perform many other magical feats. This also means that the witches didn't disappear each night when they worked their mischief; rather their bodies remained behind as if sleeping.

> They go often to Elfhame or Faeryland and the mountains open before them and as they go out and in they are terrified by the "rowtling and skoylling" of the

great "elf bulls." They sometimes confess to trooping in the shape of cats and to finding upon their terrestrial bodies when they awake in the morning the scratches they had made upon one another in the night's wandering, or should they have wandered in the images of hares the bites of dogs. Isobell Godie, who was tried at Loclilay in 1662, confessed that, "We put besoms in our beds with our husbands till we return again to them... and then we would fly away where we would be, even as straws would fly upon a highway. We will fly like straws when we please; wild straws and corn straws will be horses to us, and we put them betwixt our feet and say horse and hillock in the devil's name. And when any see these straws in a whirlwind and do not sanctify themselves, we may shoot them dead at our pleasure." (Gregory, 1920)

Oftentimes, the witches in lore gain many of their abilities in the spirit world based on the clothes they wear. This is certainly true of much of Eurasia, where the shaman who wears a wolf outfit will be able take the form of a wolf while those who wear an eagle outfit will take the form of an eagle. If any of these items of clothing are stolen from their soul when it is out, they will be trapped, unable to change form. Thus, the shaman's soul wears whatever their body is wearing and gains power from these magical items as well.

> On such occasions, the human body was believed to lie as if dead or in an enchanted sleep, while the soul, enclosed in the form of a whale, a seal, a falcon, or any other animal that might be found best adapted to the object of its magic journey, roamed abroad in other places. It was then necessary to be careful not to speak the sorcerer's name nor wake up the sleeping body, for by doing so the whole charm was destroyed and the spirit was compelled to turn back to its own proper habitation again (Keyser, 1854).

Other times, those on spirit journeys are also able to ride upon magical beings in order to travel supernaturally fast and to places that are impossible for a human to reach. When trying to reach the Well of D'yerree-in-Dowan, a prince meets with an ancient fairy, who gives him a little gelding the size of a goat. At first, the prince doesn't believe that such a tiny animal can carry him; however, when he gets on it, it runs as fast as lighting to the witch-fairy's brother hundreds of miles away. Her brother gives the prince gifts and carries him across the river to the Other World so that he can complete his quest (Hyde, 1890).

The witches sometimes sought out the fairies; not in the human world, but in their world. For example, in Macedonia, healers would fall into trances. Their spirits would set out to speak with the saints so that they could learn how to cure ailments or gain other help (Petreska, 2008). Other times, the witch would send their souls from their bodies to search for some lost item, to attack people, to do battle with evil forces, etc. The list of reasons for sending one's soul on a spirit journey and the spirit world itself is so complex that I have dedicated an entire chapter to this subject later in this book.

The witches of Europe had many means of entering into trances: some would meditate, dance about, sing, drum, or play music. Väinämöinen, the shamanistic hero of Finland, for example, would duel with other witches, such as Youkahainen, by chanting songs and sagas. Indeed, Youkahainen challenges Väinämöinen to battle by saying that He that is the sweeter singer, He alone shall keep the highway. At which point:

> Grandly sang wise Väinämöinen, Till the copper-bearing mountains, And the flinty rocks and ledges Heard his magic tones and trembled; Mountain cliffs were torn to pieces, All the ocean heaved and tumbled; And the distant hills re-echoed. Lo! the boastful Youkahainen Is transfixed in silent wonder...

> And alas! for Youkahainen, Sings him into deeps of quick-sand; Ever deeper, deeper, deeper, In his torture, sinks the wizard, To his belt in mud and water. Now it was that Youkahainen Comprehended but too clearly What his folly, what the end was (Crawford, 1888).

The berserkers would also chant verses as challenges in battle, likely as a means of becoming possessed or sending their souls forth in the forms of animals to do battle.

Others would meditate, lying down as if going to sleep in order to enter the spirit world, during which time they would become comatose. Finally, drugs were often used to help stimulate spirit journeys, but many considered these to be a low form of magic, one only fit for those too weak to enter a trance on their own.

The Evil Eye and Emotions

Much of a witch's power came from their own ability to affect things with their emotions, especially their negative emotions. If a witch looked at an animal with jealousy or anger, it might become lame, lose the ability to give milk, or even sicken and die; and they could do the same to humans. Many witches could kill (or at least sicken) anyone they disliked with a spiteful look or word. The idea of the evil eye is so common, it leads one to wonder if the reverse were possible – if kind looks and blessings could bring someone luck. This is rarely if ever mentioned, however, as fear of the negative consequences of this power were much greater than any hope for positive ones, a fear that increased because so many people didn't have control over the harm they did.

> One young girl was much dreaded in the country in consequence; for anything struck by her, beast or man, became instantly paralyzed, as if turned to stone. One day, at a hurling match, she threw a lump of clay at the winner in anger, because her own lover had failed to win the prize. Immediately, the young victor fell down, stunned and lifeless, and was so carried by his mother. Then they sent in all haste for the young girl to restore him to consciousness; but she was so frightened at her own evil work that she went and hid herself. Finding it then impossible to bring her, his friends sent for the fairy doctor, who, by dint of many charms and much stroking, at last restored the young man to life. The girl, however, was in such dread of the curses of the mother, that she fled, and took service in a distant part of the country. And all the people rejoiced much over her departure from amongst them. (Wilde 1887)

Others were said to be so powerful in their evil eyes that they could cause the earth to quake or a person to die with a look.

Magical Herbs

There were some herbal remedies that were not secret. An Italian cunning named Massimo was able to freely discuss the traditional use of dozens of plants with folklorists studying the magical healers of his country where cunning would use plantains for bruises, horsetails for coughs, blackberry leaves for sprains, and certain spider webs for bandages (Magiliocco, 2009). In Eastern Europe, garlic and bundles of elder are often used to keep evil spirits away. While in Britain, even things as odd as toads, frogs, and spiders might be rubbed onto certain skin disorders or swollen joints to heal them. There were often so many herbal remedies that no one person could know or remember them all, so the cunning would often discuss these with the fairies. Even stranger is the idea that one could cure a toothache with the dust from a priests grave (Wood-Martin, 1901). In essence, herbalism worked because the objects being used in it had power of their own, power that one tried to draw into specific uses.

Many seemingly herbal charms are fairly complex. For example, those wishing to see a vision of their future loves could bake a cake with dust from graves, water from nine different sources, and a drop of blood from one's own third finger. This resulting mixture had to be laid at the crossroads (perhaps as an offering?) (Blakeborough, 1898).

> Herb doctors are in much esteem among country people, and gain their knowledge from supernatural sources. They don't learn: "it is given to them." The following are two cases cited by the old man.
>
> In former times, all the people had great faith in old women who were herb doctors. These women became doctors, not by learning different herbs, and studying, but by a supernatural power, and this power came to

them always without their expecting it.

One woman of great name as a doctor got her power in this way. Three women were going to a village a mile out of Dingle. On the road, they came to a small river, and there was no way to cross, but to walk through the water. All at once, a fine lady stood before them, spoke very kindly to the first woman, and asked would she carry her over the river.

"Indeed, then, I will not: I've enough to do to carry myself."

The lady asked the second woman and received a like answer, but when the third woman was asked she said: "I will carry you and welcome, and why not?" So she took the fine lady on her back, carried her over the water, and put her down on the dry bank.

The lady thanked her very kindly, and said, "When you wake to-morrow morning you will know all plants and herbs, you will know what their names are, and what virtues are in them."

Next morning, when the woman woke she could call all plants and herbs by name, she knew where they grew, and knew the power of each, from that out she was a great doctor.

Another woman was at the seashore one day. After a time, she turned to go home, and while on the way felt afraid, she began to tremble suddenly, and grow sick from dread. She felt that something unnatural was near her, looked behind, and right there saw some great dark form. The moment she looked, it vanished, but from that out, she knew all plants and herbs and was a very great doctor (Curtin, 1895).

Magical Charms

Charms are prayers meant to gain protection, healing, luck, and more. As written prayers, charms are one of the most common means by which ordinary people attempt to gain help from the spirits. As always, relationship matters in gaining aid from the fairies, so witches who have good relationships with the fairies are far more effective at asking them for favors. It's also likely that people believed, to some extent, that the witch would imbue the charm with some of their own power as they chant or make it.

Charms are most often objects the witches find or things they make that are imbued with magical properties. In Russia, the most common magical charms at the close of the nineteenth century were scraps of paper with bits of writing on them. Such charms can include words from the Bible, pleas to spirits, and more. Similarly, in England, charms were also often written on paper and sewn into cloth, put in amulets, and sealed into wax. These charms could be placed at entrances to a house to keep out harmful spirits, invite in luck, buried in the field to aid the fertility of the plants, carried by the person to help stop toothaches, and much, much more.

Charms seem to have been primarily a written request to the spirits for help and blessings. In order to fight off the evil spirits that cause illness and other problems, for example, one would place charms with verses from the Bible on the cheeks or necks of the afflicted (Abbott, 1903).

Other charms were spoken as rhymes to grant protection, healing, or curses. In this way, charms were often very much a mixture of herbal magic and prayers. One would apply honey and pepper to injuries, while praying to god in a set way. It was also common to chant and or sing a charm while milking a cow, for example in Scotland people would chant:

> COME, Mary, and milk my cow, Come, Bride, and encompass her, Come, Columba the benign, And twine thine arms around my cow. Ho my heifer, ho my gentle heifer, Ho my heifer, ho my gentle heifer, Ho my heifer, ho my gentle heifer, my heifer dear, generous and kind,

For the sake of the High King take to thy calf. Come, Mary Virgin, to my cow, Come, great Bride, the beauteous (Carmichael, 1900).

Among the Germanic people, such charms were known as galldr and they could include magical songs and runes. In one use of such charms, Egil's wife tried to poison him, but being suspicious, Egil tested his drink for poison with magic by carving runes into his cup, then cut himself and marked these runes with his blood, which in turn caused the horn to burst so that he would not drink from it. While it might seem that anyone could perform such charms, it's important to keep in mind that charms were about a relationship with the spiritual beings. This means that ordinary people, who didn't have the relationship with the spirit world that a cunning had, couldn't simply make up one of their own and expect it to work as well.

Sympathetic Magic

All things contain some level of magic in them, especially when these things encounter strong emotions. This is why the evil eye can be so effective. This means that people can make it rain by wishing for it to rain, while splashing water on nicely dressed girls in a village ceremony, as the strong emotions and desires involved in this activity were believed to be able to influence the weather by example. In much of Europe, a boy and a girl would roll around in the field together (or actually engage in sex) in order to pass their fertility on to the crops that people hoped to grow.

Voodoo dolls work in a very similar fashion, with things done to a rough replica of a person believed to affect the person by example and emotion. Similarly, stones with large holes in them could help give an easy birth by allowing babies easy passage through the birth canal. Stronger still were spells that used items specifically related to a person or object. Thus, using a sliver from a house would make it easier to affect the house for good or ill, while a piece of hair would make it easier to affect a person for good or ill.

The cure recommended by folk-physician for the bite of

a mad dog is to apply to the wound a tuft of hair cut off from the dog that bit you. This is a relic of the ancient and once worldwide homeopathic doctrine, according to which the cause that produced the harm can also affect the cure (Abbott, 1903).

In Estonia, the witches knead stalks of rye together, and repeat a spell over them; unless the knots are soon found out and burnt, the crop is sure to fail. They tried to copy the features of the man they were going to bewitch in the wax or clay puppet; they solemnly baptized it, gave it sponsors, and anointed it. When they pricked it with a needle, the man felt a sharp pain; if they pricked the head or heart, he died. They tried to have an Easter candle out of the church, to do the work by. Sticking needles into a wax-figure occurs in Kemble's (Grimm, 1882).

In addition, words, runes and charms, such as those learned by Odin, seemed to have worked as a form of sympathetic magic in addition to or instead of being a prayer to other powers. Here again, however, it seems that those magicians who learned to harness their emotions properly could gain more impact from sympathetic magic than could ordinary people.

Cleverness, Cunning, and Charisma

Although not strictly magical, the witch was often able to discern how to trick fairies, how to defeat them, and so could obtain the desired affect without magic. Perhaps the most famous example is in the folktale "The Brewery of Eggshells." In this story, a mother's baby is taken by the fairies and replaced with a changeling, which, needless to say, made the mother "very unhappy." But she had no idea what to do about it until she met a cunning woman who told her to boil empty eggshells and nothing else. When the mother followed the cunning woman's advice, the changeling was so surprised that he revealed who he was, and so she was able to force him to return her baby.

In addition, many witches are incredibly skilled liars and very charismatic. It was said that Odin was such a good liar that people believed everything he said. Further, witches could be very convincing; such as "The Drummer" from the tale by that name who was able to trick two people into handing him a magical saddle, which he stole so that he could transport himself to the top of the Glass Mountain.

Supernaturally Skilled

Many deities, witches, and other people are said to be supernaturally skilled. They are able to craft things that are magical, or work so skillfully and fast they seem magical. In "The Four Skillful Brothers," one of the brothers learns to be such a skilled tailor that he can sew a boat together after a dragon has ripped it apart. Rumpelstiltskin is able to weave an astounding amount of straw into gold in a short period of time. Other fairies are able to do an impossible amount of farm work in a short amount of time, build a magical boat which can be folded up and placed in a pocket, create lightning bolts (or hammers that act as lightning bolts), etc.

Wishes

Granting wishes for others that the fairies can't grant for themselves also seems to be a power that fairies occasionally possess. For example, the fairy, which a Mari-El man threatened with death, couldn't use its magic to harm the man or help itself, but it could alter the way other people thought in order to bring harm to the man who had threatened it. Another man forces an Elle Maid to make him supernaturally strong despite the fact that she is clearly physically weak, as she is unable to defend herself against a mere mortal.

Journey into Spirit World

Take a deep breath, but don't let it out until you close your eyes. Now do this a few more times, keeping your eyes closed and letting your breath out a little slower. For just a moment, you feel a sudden calm, a strange and odd sensation as your mind clears ever so slightly. For that brief moment, you have almost touched on the world of fairies; almost, but probably not quite. Most of us will never experience the spirit world of the shamans, the witches, and the cunning; and yet, at one time, people believed this world was all around them. For fairies lived not just in the forest, but also under the threshold and hearth of their houses, in the fields where they farmed, in the rocks, and on hills overlooking their village. Oftentimes, what we find is that the spirit world isn't a place, it's a state of mind. Those who have studied shamans called this state of mind "ecstasy." It can be entered into by the most skilled of witches with a simple rhyme, a moment of meditation, a whispered prayer. Others must spend hours chanting, must go catatonic, dance and sing wildly, make themselves suffer, or perform a complex ritual.

Typically, people's first spirit journey takes place when they are sick and nigh unto death. For example, a Roman citizen named Stephen was so sick he had stopped breathing. His family had even already called an embalmer when his soul returned from its journey to his body. Some people have even deprived themselves of food, sleep, and even beat themselves in order to force their souls to enter the spirit world: for it is very difficult for a healthy person to enter the spirit world, but it does happen to those who dream at times (Lecouteux, 2003).

In one saga, a warrior sends his soul out of his body in the form of a giant bear that battles his enemies with a strength that his physical self couldn't match. Witches, too, originally sent their souls traveling the world while their bodies lay in a state of catalepsy, thus the tales of witches attacking people while in the form of a cat, a wolf, a hag, etc. were originally tales about an evil shaman who could send their souls from their bodies to wreak havoc on the world. When witches would fly to their celebrations and meetings, they originally weren't always believed to be flying; rather, they were sending their soul away from their body to journey faster than they could physically. So, despite the dangers, the advantages of sending one's soul from one's body are many, for souls can change shape, become invisible, squeeze through impossibly small cracks (but it couldn't pass through a solid wall), fly (at times), and be stronger and faster than any human could be. Further, the shaman/witch could send their soul forth in the form of fog, clouds, and other natural forces.

However, a shaman's soul is not invincible, for the souls can still be hurt, sometimes in more or less the same way as the person's physical body can be. Further, the shamans' souls have corporeal form and so, whatever happens to the soul, will happen to the person's body. Thus, if a witch's soul in cat form has its foot cut off, the witch will also lose a foot, and if the shaman's soul dies, so too will they. There are even stories of people killing the witches in storm clouds, tornadoes, and other natural disasters with things like knives and arrows. Further, the witch's soul could even be captured. In one story, every time a knight has a baby, it is strangled the day after its birth. So after the fourth child was born, a lot of people came and encircled the baby, but they all eventually go to sleep, except for one pilgrim. An old woman approaches the cradle and starts to strangle the child; however, the pilgrim seizes her and awakens the other people. The villagers recognize the woman as one of the village matrons, so she is brought before them to stand side by side with her double (Lecouteux, 2003).

Even within the spirit world, many of the same rules often apply to the shaman's soul that we would expect to see apply in the physical world. In folklore, when a shaman sends their soul into the spirit world, this soul still appears and acts as if it were human or some animal. The spirit world, in these cases, is pictured as having an up and a down, as well as having solid ground, rivers, trees, and so forth, just like in the stories of *Alice in Wonderland* and *Peter Pan*, where very little time has passed when the shaman's séance ends.

The real danger from a spirit journey comes from the fact that during it, a person's body is still vulnerable to attack and, if it is moved, the soul may not be able to find its way back. This may be another reason why witches live in isolation, to avoid having people move their bodies while they take such journeys.

> In Slavic belief, the soul is a being quite distinct from the body, which it is free to leave even during life, so that there are many stories of human souls coming forth from the bodies of sleeping persons and either dwelling in trees or, in the shape of white birds, fluttering about in the world and finally returning to their normal habitations. It is inadvisable to go to bed thirsty, lest the soul, wearied by its search for water, may weaken the body. If a man faints, his soul leaves his body and uneasily flutters about the world; but when it returns, consciousness is likewise restored. Some individuals have lain like dead for three days, during which time their souls dwelt in the Other World and beheld all that might be seen either in Heaven or in paradise. A soul that leaves the body when asleep and flies about in the world is called Vjedogonja or Zduh, Zduhacz ("Spirit") by the Serbs; and not only the souls of sleeping persons, but even those of fowls and domestic animals, such as cats, dogs, oxen, etc., may be transformed into Zduhaczs. These genii, regardless of nationality, sex, or age, assemble on mountain-tops, where they battle either singly or in troops, the victors bringing to their countrymen a rich harvest and success in breeding cattle; but if a man's soul perishes in this fight, he will never awake (Gray, 1918).

Similarly, in England, Anne Jefferies had a convulsion when she first entered the spirit world, showing that lapsing into a coma and epilepsy to enter the spirit world is fairly ubiquitous throughout Europe.

Time in the Spirit World

While nothing is ever certain about time in the fairy world, those who travel to it with their physical body tend to come back years later, despite having only spent a few moments in the spirit world. For example, in the tale, "The Elves," collected by the Brothers Grimm, a servant girl enters Fairyland and stands godmother for a fairy child for a few hours, but when she returns, seven years have passed in the human world. On the other hand, those who project their souls into the spirit world can think they are gone for days, even though only a few moments have passed for their bodies.

Cosmology of the Spirit Worlds

Although there are many different cosmologies in Europe and so potentially hundreds if not thousands of different spirit worlds, these spirit worlds can be broken into six basic categories, which include:

1-Isolated wildernesses, such as forests and bridges between realms

2-Parallel worlds that are much like our own

3-States of mind that allow one to see the fairy world in which the shaman's spirit journey takes place in our own world

4-Heavenly courts, such as the realm of the gods and

fairy queens

5-To Hell, where people are punished for their wrongdoings in life

6-Strange realms, often meant to illustrate some metaphysical and philosophical point

The witch's experience in these spirit worlds, what happens to them, is largely dictated by their purpose for entering into the spirit world, and here we see eight primary reasons that witches enter the spirit world. These are:

1-To gain treasure

2-To battle against evil forces, recover something that was stolen, or save someone who has been taken into the spirit world

3-To gain knowledge and magical aid

4-To gain philosophical enlightenment

5-As slaves of the fairies

6-As servants of the fairies

7-As guests of the fairies

8-Are lost in the fairy world

Forest, Wilderness, and Bridges

The spirit world is often surrounded by a vast wilderness. Baba Yaga, for example, lives deep in the forest, where she is the guardian to the gates of the dead. Similarly, the witch of the forest in "Hansel and Gretel" appears to have lived in another world that may even have been the land of the dead. Other spirit worlds were often depicted as being across a body of water with a bridge or else with a boatman or a duck to carry people from one side to the other.

> In Slavic lore, the bridge between the human world and the land of the dead is often depicted as a bridge that is thin as a hair so only the righteous can cross it to meet with deceased relatives.... (Petreska, 2008)

Other times, this bridge was depicted as a rainbow or the Milky Way. This bridge is often given such names as "Mouse Path," as the mouse is a common form for the human soul to take when it leaves the body (mice and moles are liminal beings, living underground and above ground). In other stories, the land of the dead was an underwater city that the soul had to swim to. Still other times, it was a steep hill made of glass or iron, which had to be climbed to reach paradise or those who were imprisoned in the Other World (Ralston, 2007).

The stories of journeys into the spirit world often suggest "long lonely journeys through cold and darkness, over rushing rivers and high mountains" (Davidson, 1989), although fairies didn't always dwell in distant places. Oftentimes, the fairies would dwell in hills, underground, in crystal palaces under lakes and rivers, in the sky directly overhead and more (Henderson, 1879).

People could even stumble upon these wilderness fairylands by accident, as easily as falling into a well. In the story of "Belly Beg, Tom Beg, and Fairies," Tom Beg is taken into some mist and soon finds himself "in a green glen such as he'd never seen before, although he knew every glen within five miles of him." It was here that he encountered the fairy host who was riding in a parade, which was more splendid than anything Tom had ever seen before.

Parallel Worlds

Those reaching the spirit world often find that it's very

much like our own world. In the Russian Tale of "The Girl in the Well," a girl falls down a well to find herself in a spirit world filled with villages and cowherds who need her help with the simple task of cleaning up after herd animals. This means that she is able to find work that pays exceptionally well and so make a fortune doing something relatively easy. In a similar German fairy tale, a girl falls down a well, where she meets a fairy named "Mother Hulda," who offers her work in return for a great reward.

From these and many other stories, one gets the impression that the Other World often serves as a dream for the underemployed to finally get paid what they are worth, or to get the jobs they want. So a modern-day person entering the Other World might be able to become heroic and rich by being an accountant or garbage truck driver as no one in Fairyland wants to do these two jobs, but they all need help with them. In other cases, a person pulled into Fairyland in the modern day might become a rock star, an actor, or gain success in some other art with which they were struggling to be discovered in our world.

The key point is that people throughout Europe saw the afterlife as being very much like human life, except with a few basic changes based on the purpose for the visit to this land. Ivanov states that:

> Afterlife reports confirm the stereotypical folk vision of the Other World as a village where the dead live in families and neighborhoods, where the topography sometimes reminds the sojourner of the cemetery in his native village. The righteous eat and drink what was brought to their graves during memorial services, while sinners sit hungry to one side. This segregation is often further elaborated in terms of the Christian distinction between Heaven and Hell.

Sometimes, the spirit world is so similar to the human world that one can only identify it in fairy tales through the means by which the character reaches it (such as falling down a well) or by some other detail. For example, those born with a caul on their heads are likely to become shamans in European lore. So when this detail is included in a fairy tale, it makes it easier for us to see the spirit journey inherent in these stories.

For example, in "The Devil with the Three Golden Hairs," a baby is born with a caul on his head. Because of his connection to the spirit world, he is "fated" to marry the king's daughter when he turns fourteen. Being none too pleased about the thought of some peasant marrying his daughter, the king sets the child adrift in the river in hopes of drowning him. As with most actions taken to avoid fate in stories, this sets into motion the events that will lead to the young shaman marrying the king's daughter. When the shaman gets older, the king tries to prevent him from marrying his daughter by sending him on a difficult and dangerous quest, to retrieve three golden hairs from the devil.(To do this, the boy must enter the spirit realm, so one must wonder if the king gives the boy this task because he knows that he can enter into the realm of the dead. Perhaps in an older tale, this is in fact the story of a king or chieftain testing a shaman's power.) On his journey, the boy encounters villages that are very much like any one would see in the human world. So if it weren't for the fact that he was born with a caul on his head or the fact that he needed to cross a river with the help of an immortal boatman, one might never realize that he was in the spirit world. One of the biggest differences between the human and the spirit world is that in the spirit world, the devil can be a neighbor that the people see, an ogre or dragon can rule the lands in which the "spirits" work, and all manner of magical creatures are much more apparent. Further, as previously mentioned, someone can make a much better living doing menial tasks than they could hope to make in the human world.

The Heavenly Court

There is a perfect land, a land of beauty and happiness; it is in the king's palace, and peasants dream of this land every day. Yet even the king's palace can't compare to the beauty of the fairy court or the court of the gods. This court is:

Described as a place of happiness and beauty where sickness, death, and decay are unknown; trees there bear rich fruit, while their leaves make music and birds sing in their branches; there is abundance of gleaming gold and silver, and everywhere lovely women, welcoming goddesses of the Sid. It is they who lure human heroes and the sons of kings to this fair land... (Ellis Davidson, 1989)

The courts of the fairies and the gods are a dream and fantasy for the living, a place of feasting and merriment where witches are often served delicious foods and are able to dance freely with beautiful fairies.

In the *Voyage of Bran,* a maiden from the Other World tells Bran and his court of a land of women across the sea that is more beautiful and wonderful than anything they could imagine. It is a land with "Wealth, treasures of every hue," filled with sweet music and the best wine for drinking. It has chariots of gold, silver, and bronze.

Anne Jefferies Anne traveled to a spirit world that had:

Temples and palaces of gold and silver. Trees laden with fruits and flowers. Lakes full of gold and silver fish, and the air full of birds of the sweetest song, and the most brilliant colours. Hundreds of ladies and gentlemen were walking about. Hundreds more were idling in the most luxuriant bowers, the fragrance of the flowers oppressing them with a sense of delicious repose. Hundreds were also dancing, or engaged in sports of various kinds. Anne was, however, surprised to find that these happy people were no longer the small people she had previously seen. There was now no more than the difference usually seen in a crowd, between their height and her own. Anne found herself arrayed in the most highly decorated clothes. So grand, indeed, did she appear, that she doubted her identity.

Fearing the Heavenly Court

To enter the Heavenly Court is to die, to be trapped in a state of meaningless, to never be able to move on or grow up.

For warriors, for kings, and many others this is true suffering. When Bran was sailing for "The Land of Women," he came to the "Island of Joy," where a "large host was gaping and laughing." Unable to converse, these people continued to laugh no matter how hard Bran called out to them from the ship, so he sent one of his men to the island in hopes of getting directions, and that man too began to gape stupidly at Bran and his former comrades, only able to laugh without thought. This moment illustrates clearly the horror of constant bliss, of unabated meaninglessness. Think for a moment about Pixar's movie *Wall-E*, in which all humans have essentially become slugs, unable to act or do anything but eat, chat on computers, and entertain themselves. In this story, there is nothing inherently wrong with society. No one is eating these people or enslaving them secretly; they are choosing to be the way they are. Yet most of us hate seeing people living so meaninglessly. Thus, for many, a heavenly place is tantamount to a nightmare world.

When Bran and his men finally reach the "Land of Women," it's as wonderful as they imagined, and they stay a year there in bliss. Yet a year of bliss is all they can stand, before they get homesick and seek to return, but as is often the case, there is no returning from "Heaven," from the Other World; for while only a year has passed for them, many hundreds have passed for Ireland. So if they set foot on Ireland, they will age and decay instantly (Meyer, 1895).

Other times, the Heavenly Court is used as a means to deceive people, especially those who are kidnapped by the fairies. In one Greek tale, a man named Petros is spirited away by a cloud drawn by three white horses and a throng of fairies.

> The earth seemed to slip away from him and drop down, down. There was no sensation of motion, only a great wind in his face, and hills, trees and streams whirling beneath him... At last, after what seemed days and days of riding without motion on the horse's back, Petros saw ahead a mysterious shore. A city of mist rested upon it and was faintly reflected in the cloudy sea on which they floated. A palace of pearl could be seen from afar, like a pile of foam glimmering in the faded light. The great silver gate of the city at the very edge of the sea admitted them through the banked

cloud walls to the pearl-studded path to the palace.

Petros was assisted to the ground. Throngs of fairy maidens in white, with chains of pearls entwined with flowers, greeted him in song and led him to the palace. The path lay between gardens of white roses, roses of thirty petals, of a hundred petals, of a thousand petals, whose perfume hung heavy above them. The maidens parted, bowing on either hand while Petros passed up the sixty-six silver steps that led into the hall.

Fairies in blue, in white and in gray, colors of the sky, surrounded him. Strange notes, sweet as the murmur of the Eurotas, fell upon his ears. The inner walls of the palace were festooned with cloud-like draperies caught with pearls. In the center of the main hall was a crystal fountain and beyond it, as behind a shimmering veil, the fairy queen sat upon her throne. Petros was dazzled, but the queen smiled reassuringly and spoke in the gentlest of voices (Gianakoulis, 1930).

This whole set up, however, is for the Fairy Queen to try and take the one thing that is protecting him from the fairies' influence: his ring. When the queen asks for this ring, it's obvious from the story that if he gives it up, something very bad will happen. Given the ability of fairies to alter perceptions of an individual with glamour, it seems likely that in most cases, the Fairy Court is meant to be an imitation of exactly what a person would want, what they would desire. So how it would appear would likely vary from person to person.

State of Mind

While two shepherds were watching a herd of cattle, one of them falls asleep, and a few moments later a tiny red mouse the size of a cricket crawls from the man's mouth. Curious, the other shepherd follows this mouse through fields and swamps to a lightning shattered tree (lightning shattered trees were often the homes of gods or spirits chosen by gods in lore), which the mouse crawls inside of. After a moment, the mouse leaves the tree and returns to the sleeping shepherd's mouth. On waking, the shepherd tells of a dream in which he ran through fields and swamps to find a hidden treasure inside of a tree (Grautoff, 1916).

While the shepherd's spirit journey wasn't undertaken purposefully, it does illustrate that sometimes there was great wealth to be had within our world, known at times as the Middle World, which had secrets to be learned and battles to be fought. There are also fairies to be met at crossroads, in the forests, and on mountains. The witches of Russia would often send their souls flying over the countryside to Bald Mountain for their meetings with the fairies who lived there. When Aine had some girls look at the hills through a hole in a magical stone, they saw that the hills were teeming with fairies (Ellis Davidson, 1989). Midwives in tales will accidentally get magical ointment in their eyes while applying this to the eyes of fairy babies and, because of this, they will be able to see the fairies wandering in markets and other places. In the tale of "Old Gwilym," an old man heard some music on a road he took every day when he walked home. When he looked up, he saw brightly lit houses he'd never seen before and fairies who were dancing and singing.

Witches who can send their souls from their bodies are able to deliver messages to faraway places, fight wars as animals or ghost like beings, or they can find lost items, and more, thanks to astral travel through our world. Sometimes, these astral travelers act as the fairies of tales. In one village, people would prepare meals for the "Good Ladies," who were in fact women of the community who actually projected themselves to travel about while still in their beds (Lecouteux, 2003).

Hell

Hell is a place of suffering, where the wicked starve as they are forced to watch the spirits of good people eat their fill, where people burn in lakes of fire. Yet at the same time, it is also envisioned as a playground for evil beings such as devils, dragons, ogres, and other wicked spirits; beings which are by no means infallible, for many people have tricked their way out of Hell, or have rescued a love one from Hell. In spirit journeys, however, the primary purpose of Hell is to illustrate some lesson about the nature of sin and evil to the person who is undertaking the journey.

Hell, in fairy tales, is more like a fairy realm, with semi-moral beings that hate immorality, but still enjoy cruelty at times, and so choose to be cruel to the immoral. In the story of "The Fiddler in Hell," a fiddler accidentally falls into Hell, where he meets a greedy, wealthy man who pleads with him to help him escape by digging up his money and distributing it among the poor. The devils then find the fiddler, who plays on his fiddle until the strings break, at which point, because the devils enjoyed his music so much, he's able to trick them into letting him go home to get more strings.

In the story of "Why the Sea is Salt," a merchant makes his way to Hell to sell a bit of bacon because meat is scarce in Hell. Once he gets there, the devils swarm about him and try to outbid each other for that little bit of meat. Having already been advised by a woodcutter, however, the man trades the bit of bacon for an old quern, which could grind an unlimited supply of food. In the tale of "Stephen the Murderer," a man goes to Hell and blackmails the devils into helping him find a ring that they stole from his mother. Hell in fairy tales, then, is sort of a mixture of ideas about the fairy world, about the Christian afterlife, and the pre-Christian afterlife.

Strange Worlds

There are, of course, some spirit worlds that don't easily fit into any category, which may have some semblance to the human world, but don't quite mesh with it. For example, in the fairy tale "The Stars in the Sky," a girl sets out to get the stars and, on the way, she asks the Brooklet, the Mill-Dam, and a Good Folk (a fairy) how to reach them, but they can only say where they shine, not how to reach them. The girl begins to cry. Taking pity on her, the Good Folk says:

> "If you won't go home to your mother, go forward, go forward; mind you, take the right road. Ask Four Feet to carry you to No Feet At All, and tell No Feet At All to carry you to the stairs without steps, and if you can climb that--"

"Oh, shall I be among the stars in the sky then?" cried the lassie.

"If you'll not be, then you'll be elsewhere," said the Good Folk, and set to dancing again.

From there, the girl is carried by a horse who serves the fairies to the edge of the sea, where she meets a fish who also works for the fairies. The fish then caries her along a silver path in the water towards a stairway to the stars. Unfortunately, the more she climbs this stairway, the further down she sinks, until at last she falls out of bed (Jacobs, 2004).

Healers seeking to banish the illness out of someone's body will use the power of the word to banish the spirits:

> To spaces which were believed to be alien to man. They were spaces that were not culturally conquered and thus outside the village community... The verbal declarations clearly show that the disease is cast off into a world where humans are not present. Most frequently these unhealthy, lifeless communities are described as villages without roosters, where no dogs bark, no cats, meow, literary, villages which have been abandoned... They were places where no one could travel and from which there was no return. Places such as Moan Forest and Neverland, for example, are locations where there are no attributes of human culture or symbols of a healthy community bustling with life, and the human body is a widely known practice.... On occasion, the Other World is described as better than the one the ill person occupies and the

illness is urged to go to this more attractive realm. (Petreska, 2008)

Similarly, dangerous spirits in Finland are often banished to strange lands as well:

> The evil beings I send away, the kehno I incite away, destructive beings I force away, malicious beings I drag away, to sproutless clearings run to waste, to lands unploughed, to swampy dells, to untraversed swamps in which frogs spawn, where muck-worms crawl, to a nameless meadow, unknown by name, where from the earth no herbage sprouts, from the sward no grass exalts itself. If there thou findest not a place, thee I conjure away to the head of the waters of Sumukse, to dark Sariola, to the mist of the sea, to the haze of the lower air, to the feather-tip of a swan, right under the tongue of a pintail duck. (Abercromby, 1898)

The Purpose for Entering the "Other World"

To Gain Knowledge

Bodvar's mother had such a restless sleep that he asked her about it and she told him, "I took a witch's ride to many places this night and I learned with certainty things I did not know before" (Lecouteux, 2003).

The spirit world is a place to gain knowledge, to learn magical secrets. Magical healers who enter the spirit world often encounter some supernatural creature who orders them to return to the world of the living and perform some mission, such as to heal the sick or to spread disease. Those who rejected this mission were often punished. One woman claimed that her children had died because she didn't want to work as a healer. Opposite this, another woman who accepted her job as a healer was able to bear several sons as a reward (Petreska, 2008).

In Russia, a young man entered the world beneath the earth to become apprenticed to some nixies who lived in a house made of green rushes – "in fact, everything was green," from the people and the food. Here, the man is apprenticed to work with the nixies. During his three years of service, he suffered greatly at the hands of the nixies, but in the end, he became handsome and learned how to take the form of any animal he wished (Nisbet, 2010).

The Cunning folk of Britain entered the spirit world to learn and perform magic. Here:

> Under the supervision of the presiding supernatural figures, magical skills and magical objects could be acquired and/or communal magical activities performed. While evil witches at these meetings would receive gifts that would harm people and spread disease. They would travel out to sink and destroy ships, curse people with waxen images, etc. Good witches, on the other hand, would gain the secret to healing the sick or the means to counter the actions of evil spirits and witches (Wibly, 2006).

To Protect the Village, Save Someone, or Recover Something that Was Stolen

In the Baltic region, there are tales of people who would send their souls out in the form of wolves in order to battle with evil witches, which would steal the seeds from and blight the crops of their village. Similarly, the benandanti of Italy are shamans who would send their souls from their bodies in order to do battle with witches that attacked the villages' crops (Although there is the flip side of this, in which evil witches took the spirit journey to try to destroy the village).

In the tale "Childe Rowland," a shamanistic character had to save his sister who made the mistake of walking widdershins around a church or a hill, and it is this which leads that person to being pulled into Fairyland. In this case, the protagonist is told by Merlin that he has to behead everyone he meets in Fairyland, and he ultimately must battle with and defeat the elf king (Jacob, 2004).

In Ireland, a young girl finds herself faced with a corpse who she knows she has to follow. As she journeys after him, he passes through a cavern of horrors, but her fairy helper puts wax in her ears so she won't have to hear them. Then the fairy makes her sticky shoes so she can climb a mountain of glass. At last, she plunges to the bottom of the ocean where she rescues the corpse and brings him back to life (Kennedy, 1866).

To Gain Metaphysical and Philosophical Understanding

Like Scrooge in *A Christmas Carol*, many people were guided by spirits and fairies on a journey to gain some philosophical or metaphysical understanding. In a German fairy tale, a dwarf-like fairy known as a graumannchen grants a fisherman's wish to make him king some five hundred years in his past. On this journey, the man discovers that life in the past is not so romantic or wonderful as he'd hoped, and later he is nearly killed by the enemies he gains as king. He misses his wife and his children. With his lesson learned, he asks the graumannchen to bring him home, where he then lives out his days in contentment with what he has. He's so content that he doesn't even seek the treasure he buried before leaving the past, but chooses to live out his days as a poor fisherman, leaving it to his son to dig up the treasure (Lauder, 1881).

More commonly in both Christian and Pagan Eurasia, someone would enter the Other World to gain an understanding of the suffering of sinners. That is, to learn about the torments of Hell and how to avoid these. On such journeys, a person's soul is usually met by an angel, who guides them to see the bliss of Heaven where there are beautiful gardens and cheerful children, as well as the torments of Hell, where the sinful boil in cauldrons and are eaten by dragons (Petreska, 2008). Many such journeys will involve understanding how to avoid the fate suffered by those in Hell, or will show the poor how their tormentors will suffer later. As with *A Christmas Carol*, the primary lesson in many of these stories seems to be that the greedy and heartless rich are doomed to suffer.

The danger of greed and the importance of valuing something other than money were central lessons for many spirit journeys. In one tale, a monk enters the fairy realm, where a white swan turns into a beautiful virgin, who asks him what he desires. The monk responds that he wishes for the jewels of the earth, inducing her to fury so that she hits him with her keys and causes him to flee in horror. Similarly, a shepherd who finds his way into the spirit world is given the opportunity to take anything he wants, but is warned to "choose wisely." Instead, he chooses the gold and jewels although he is warned that these treasures are not the most valuable. He leaves Fairyland with nothing but these anyway and finds that the jewels have turned to worthless rocks.

Other times, the person on the spirit journey meets sinners who offer advice. For example, one girl sinned against her father and asked the person on their spirit journey to warn her little brother against being rude against his mother. Sometimes, the lesson of being a good parent was illustrated by showing a drunkard of a father in Hell and a pious kind mother in Heaven (Wigzell, 2003). This idea of punishment and morality isn't just Christian, however, as it is featured in tales about the Ancient Greek afterlife, including that of a shaman named Er. After dying in battle, Er's soul entered the spirit world for twelve days before returning to life. On his journey, he heard that the souls of those who went to Heaven tell of the wonders and beauty of the place. He also heard from the wicked that went into the Earth cried with despair, and were required to pay tenfold what they had done in life before being released. It was even worse for tyrants and murderers, who would never be released from torment. Oddly enough, however, Er went on to discover that when people got to choose what they were reincarnated as, those from the Heavens often chose to be someone fated to be a sinful person the next time around, while those from Hell often chose to live a better life for their next attempt

To Gain a Love or Some other Treasure

In contrast to the idea of learning some lesson, the spirit world was also place to gain treasure or find a wife. At the end of "Hansel and Gretel," after the children have defeated the witch, they find a great treasure and are able to return home on the back of a duck, which takes them over a body of water. In the Russian story of "The Girl in the Well," the girl returns home with great riches that make others envious of her. In "The Three Citrons," a young man is told by the spirit of a girl to travel to the Glass Mountain, where he finds fruit that contains his future wife (Kirby, 1894). Meanwhile, Prince Bayaya gets help from a magical horse to enter the spirit realm, where he defeats a dragon and marries a princess (Fillmore, 2010). Similarly, in the story of "The Princess on the Glass Mountain," a princess sits atop a glass mountain and none shall marry her but the one who can climb the mountain. Many try, but the mountain is slippery as ice, so they all fail until a prince who had saved a dwarf from prison gets magical gifts such as a magical horse and armor. With these, he is able to climb the Glass Mountain, thereby entering the spirit world (Dasent, 1906).

Other heroes managed to steal from the spirit world. For example, a man named Colcheragh rode swiftly after a fairy party to their court, where he eventually gave a toast with a beautiful silver cup. Then, "Cup in hand, slammed the door behind him, and ran for his life." However, in truth, he got very little for this theft; for he could never again leave his house after dark for fear that the fairies would take revenge (Morrison, 1911).

As Workers or Guests of Otherworldly Beings

Many people in the spirit world are there to serve the fairies in some capacity. While some of these poor unfortunate people are slaves, others are well-paid servants and others are honored guests. For example, in Germany, one hardworking girl was asked to stand as godmother to a fairy child. So she went and played this part, dancing and having a fun time with the fairies before they stuffed her pockets full of money and returned her home, although seven years had passed.

In "The Devil's Sooty Brother," a starving soldier meets a fairy, who offers to give him seven years of work that will make him wealthy. But the man must agree not to wash or groom himself for the seven years of service he gives to the fairy. After working hard for the fairy/devil for seven years, he was paid with a knapsack full of gold. In the story of "Broceliande," the fairies hire some poor girls to watch over their cows for them and even ask one of these hardworking girls to stand godmother for their child.

In addition to servants and godparents, it was very common for the fairies to seek out midwives to help their wives give birth. These midwives were always well paid and returned home after their service, although in lore, many of them accidentally got fairy ointment in one of their eyes and so the fairies would poke this out. Nevertheless, fairies tended to keep their bargains and overpay those who worked for them.

A girl named Cherry from Zennor is out looking for a job when she is suddenly overcome and "sat herself down on a stone by the roadside, and cried to think of her home, which she might never see again." This is when a handsome man comes, who is searching for a nanny for his little boy. At first, Cherry doesn't realize that she has found herself in Fairyland when she goes to work for this man, although there are many strange things about the mansion where she cares for the man's child. Whenever she asks the boy about these, however, he threatens to tell his aunt, the head of the household, that she was asking things she shouldn't. Eventually, curiosity gets the better of her and she peers into the room where she was told never to look. There, she sees her master in the form of a tiny fairy, kissing and reveling with beautiful fairies. Overcome by jealousy, Cherry lets slip what she's seen and so is banished from the fairy's home (Hartland, 1890).

As Slaves of Otherworldly Beings

Many people are kidnapped by the fairies and forced to work as slaves in the fairy realm. These people can usually only escape the fairy realm with the help of another. Knowing that outside people can aid in the escape of their slaves, the fairies will leave behind changelings of wood, mud, or some other substance that has been glamoured to appear like and act similar to the person they took so people won't come to rescue their slaves. Luckily for some of the prisoners of the spirit world, they can still appear in the mortal world for brief moments. Some of these people will steal human food in order to avoid eating fairy food (which would trap them in Fairyland for seven years or forever each time they eat it). Others will appear to humans to request help. In one case, a woman's husband thought she was dead because the changeling the fairies had left behind appeared as a corpse. However, after some time, her spirit appeared to him:

> Do not be disturbed, dear husband," said the appearance; "I am now in the power of the fairies, but if you only have courage and prudence we may be soon happy with each other again. Next Friday will be May-eve, and the whole court will ride out of the old fort after midnight. I must be there along with the rest. Sprinkle a circle with holy water, and have a black-hafted knife with you. If you have courage to pull me off the horse, and draw me into the ring, all they can do will be useless. You must have some food for me every night on the dresser, for if I taste one mouthful with them, I will be lost to you forever (Kennedy, 1891).

In the Tale of "The Drummer," a shamanistic figure spots some beautiful girls swimming in a lake, and steals a shift from one of these. However, he is kind, so when the girl comes in the night begging for her shift back, he returns it, but only after learning that the girl was the daughter of a king who was taken captive and is now never allowed to leave the glass mountain, except for her daily baths in the lake. With her shift returned, the girl flies back to Fairyland and the drummer sets out to find the glass mountain and rescue the girl.

In another story, a young woman must rescue her love from Fairyland. In this story, a young knight named Tamlane is taken from his love by the fairies to be the knight to the Elf Queen. After serving in Fairyland for many years, he finally manages to get away for a brief moment into order to tell his love how to free him.

"To-morrow night is Hallowe'en, and the fairy court will

then ride through England and Scotland, and if you would borrow me from Elfland, you must take your stand by Miles Cross between twelve and one o' the night, and with holy water in your hand you must cast a compass all around you....."

"You must spring upon me suddenly, and I will fall to the ground. Then seize me quick, and whatever change befall me, for they will exercise all their magic on me, cling hold to me till they turn me into red-hot iron. Then cast me into this pool and I will be turned back into a mother-naked man. Cast then your green mantle over me, and I shall be yours, and be of the world again." (Jacobs, 2004)

Many attempts to rescue someone from Fairyland end in failure, however, and the fairies will at times punish the person who attempts to be rescued with death, making this a dangerous thing to try, which may be why so few who are taken ever try to escape. Further, many people move on after a person is taken and don't want to go to the trouble of rescuing them. In one case, a young woman is taken by a cat with a human's face, although everyone believes she'd died because of a changeling left behind. After some time has passed, her husband remarries. Yet at the end of a year, the man's neighbor comes to give the news that the woman is still alive in Fairyland. She had been creeping out like a ghost to steal the servants' food in order to avoid eating fairy food, which would trap her in Fairyland forever. However, because her husband is remarried, he ignores her pleas to rescue her. So at the end of seven years, she becomes a captive in Fairyland forever. She is, however, a very angry captive and she attacks her former husband's new wife and child whenever she can get away from Fairyland in the form of a ghost, and eventually kills the wife and child with sickness.

To Live

Some people are taken to live in the fairy realm, often as wives or husbands, or children of the fairy folk. Others, however, are taken to be friends to the fairies. There is very little information about these people that I can find, other than that they still do help those they cared for in life, and likely live within a heavenly court; and that they are often asked to aid the fairies with their supernatural powers and their ability to wage war.

References

Abbott, G. F. (1976) *Macedonian Folklore.* Folcroft, PA: Folcroft Libr. Ed

Abercromby, John (1898) *Magic Songs of the West Finns.*

Aldhouse-Green, Miranda and Aldhouse-Green, Stephen (2005) *The Quest for the Shaman: Shape-Shifters, Sorcerers and Spirit Healers in Ancient Europe.* New York, Thames & Hudson.

Andrews, Elizabeth (2011) *Ulster Folklore.* Gutenberg.org: http://www.gutenberg.org/files/37187/37187-h/37187-h.htm#Fairies_and_their_Dwelling-places3

Asbjørnsen, Peter Christen, Jørgen Engebretsen Moe, and George Webbe Dasent. (1900) *Popular Tales from the Norse.* London: G. Routledge

Atkinson, J. C. (1891) *Forty Years in a Moreland Parish.* London: Macmillan and CO.

Bain, R. Nisbet (2009) *Cossack Fairy Tales and Folk Tales.* Gutenberg.org: http://www.gutenberg.org/files/29672/29672-h/29672-h.htm

Balfour, M. C. (1904) *Examples of Printed Folk-lore Concerning Northumberland.* London: David Nutt.

Barber, Richard (2004) *Myths and Legends of the British Isles by Richard Barber.* Rochester, NY: Boydell Press

Biti, Vladimir & Katusic, Bernarda & Lang, Peter (2010) *Märchen in den südslawischen Literaturen*

Black, George Fraser (1903) *County Folklore Vol. III – Orkney & Shetland Islands*. London, UK: David Nutt.

Blackburn, Barry (1991) *Theios Anēr and the Markan Miracle Traditions*. Tübingen : J.C.B. Mohr

Blumenthals, Verra (1903) *Folk Tales From the Russia*. Rand, Mcnally & Company.

Bottrell, William (1873) *Traditions and Hearthisde Stories of West Cornwall*.

Briggs, Katharine Mary (1967) *The Fairies in Tradition and Literature*. London, UK: Routledge

Briggs, Katharine (1968) *Folktales of England*. Chicago: University of Chicago Press

Briggs, Katharine Mary (1976) *An encyclopedia of fairies: hobgoblins, brownies, bogies, and other supernatural creatures*. New York, NY: Pantheon Books.

Briggs, Katharine Mary (1978) *The Vanishing People.: Fairy Lore and Legends*. New York, NY: Pantheon Books.

Brown, Norman Oliver (1947) *Hermes the Thief; The Evolution of a Myth*. Madison, WI: University of Wisconson

Bruchanov (1991) *Грузинские народные сказки*. Ростовское книжное издательство: http://skazki.yaxy.ru/52.html

Bunce, John Thackray (2005) Fairy tales their orgin and meaning. Gutenberg. Org: http://www.gutenberg.org/files/8226/8226-h/8226-h.htm

Campbell, John Gregorson (1900) *Superstitions of the Highlands and Islands of Scotland*. Glasgow, England: James MacLehose and Sons.

Carmichael, Alexander (1928) *Carmina Gadelica Hymns and*

Incantations. Edinburgh, UK: Oliver and Boyd

Chaucer, Geoffrey (2011) *Caterbury Tales*. Amazon Digital Services, Inc.

Conrad, Joseph L. (2001) *Male Mythological Beings Among the South Slavs*. Folklorica

Crawford, John Martin (1888) *The Kalevala*.

Croker, Thomas (1834) *Fairy Legends and Traditions of the South of Ireland*. LONDON: John Murray.

Crossing, William (1890) *Tales of the Dartmoor Pixies*. Amazon Digital Services, Inc.

Curtin, Jeemiah (1895) *Tales of the Fairies and of the Ghost World*. Boston: Little Brown & Company.

Czaplicka, Mari Antoinette (2004) *Shamanism in Siberia*. Kessinger Publishing.

Daniels, Cora L. M. & Stevens, C. M. (1903) *Encyclopaedia of Superstitions, Folklore, and the Occult Sciences of the World*. Chicago: J. H. Yewdale & sons Company

Dasent, George Webbe (1906) Popular Tales from the Norse and North German. London: Norrcena Society

Dequiqnet, Jean-Mari (2011) *Memoirs of a Breton Peasant*. New York: Seven Stories Press

Djordjevic, Tihomir R. (1903) *Die Zigeuner in Serbien: ethnologische Forschungen*.

Douglas, George (1901) *Scottish Fairy and Folk Tales*. New York: A. L. Burt Company, Publishers

Ellis Davidson, H. R. & Ellis Davidson, Hilda Roderick (1989) *Myths and Symbols in Pagan Europe: Early Scandinavian and Celtic Religion*. Syracuse, NY: Syracuse University Press

Emerson, P. H. (2003) *Welsh Fairy-tales and Other Stories.* Gutenberg.org: http://www.gutenberg.org/files/8675/8675-h/8675-h.htm

Fee, Christopher R., & Leeming, David A. (2004) *Gods, Heroes, & Kings : The Battle for Mythic Britain: The Battle for Mythic.* New York: Oxford University Press

Fillmore, Parker (2010) *Czechoslovak Fairy Tales.* Gutenberg.org: http://www.gutenberg.org/files/32217/32217-h/32217-h.htm

Frazer, James George (2003) *The Golden Bough : a study of magic and religion.* Gutenberg.org: http://www.gutenberg.org/dirs/etext03/bough11h.htm

Gianakoulis, Theodore P. & Macpherson, Georgia H. (1930) *Fairy Tales of Modern Greece.* Boston, MA: E. P. Dutton & CO

Gibbings, W. W. (1889) *Folk-Lore and Legends, Scotland.* Gutenberg.org: http://www.gutenberg.org/files/17071/17071-h/17071-h.htm

Gjorgjevic, Tihomi R. (1903) Die Zigeuner in Serbien: ethnologische Forschungen. Budapest: Thalia

Grautoff, Otto (1916) *Die Baltischen Provinzen: Märchen und Sagen.* Felix Lehmann Verla.

Gray, L. H. (1918) *The Mythology of All Races Vol. III.* Marshall Jones Company

Gregory, Lady (1920) *Visions and beliefs in the west of Ireland.* New York and London: G. P. Putnam's Sons.

Griffis, William Elliot (2005) *Welsh Fairy Tales.* Gutenberg.org: http://www.gutenberg.org/cache/epub/9368/pg9368.html

Grimberg, Carl (1924) *Svenska Folkets Underbara Berättelser.* Stockholm, Sweden: L. J. Hjerta.

Grimes, Heilan Yvette (2010) *The Norse Myths*. Boston, MA: Hollow Earth Publishing.

Grimm, Jacob (1882) *Teutonic Mythology*. Londan, UK: George Bell and Sons.

Grimm, Jacob and Grimm, Wilhelm (2008) Gutenberg.org: http://www.gutenberg.org/files/2591/2591-h/2591-h.htm

Guerber, H. A. (1988) Myths and Legends of the Middle Ages. Crescent

Gyula Pap (1896) The Folk-Tales of the Magyars. Zeluna.net

Hartnup, Karen (2004) *On the Beliefs of the Greeks: Leo Allatios and Popular Orthodoxy*. Leiden, The Netherlands: Brill Academic Pub

Hartland, Edwin Sidney (1890) *English Fairy and Other Folk Tales*. London: The Walter Scott Publishing Co.

Hellman, Roxanne and Hall, Derek (2011) *Vampire Legends and Myths*. New York: Rosen Publishing Group

Henderson, Lizanne & Cowan, Edward J. (2001) *Scottish Fairy Belief*. Google eBook

Henderson, William (1879) *Notes on the Folk-Lore of the Northern Counties of England and the Borders*. London: W. Satchell, Peyton and CO.

Homer (1999) *The Odyssey*. (Samuel Butler. Trans) Gutenberg.org: http://www.gutenberg.org/ebooks/1727

Hunt, Robert (1908) *Popular Romances of the West of England; or, The Drolls, Traditions, and Superstitions of Old Cornwall*. London: Chatto & Windus.

Hyde, Douglas (1890) *Beside the Fire : A Collection of Irish Gaelic Folk Stories*. London: David Nutt.

Ivanits, Linda J. (1992) *Russian Folk Belief.* Armonk, NY: M.E. Sharpe.

Jacobs, Joseph (2004) *English Fairy Tales.* Gutenberg.org: http://www.gutenberg.org/files/14241/14241-h/14241-h.htm

Jacobs, Joseph (2011) *Folklore, Volume 13.* Ulan Press

Jegerlehner, Johannes (1907) *Was die Sennen erzählen: märchen und sagen aus dem Wallis.* Budjdruckerel Buhler & Werder

Jettmar, K. (1986) *The Religions of the Hindukush 1: The Religion of the Kaffirs.* Aris & Phillips

Keightley, Thomas (1892) *The Fairy Mythology.* London, UK: George Bell and Sons.

Kennedy, Patrick (1866) *Legendary Fictions of the Irish Celts by Patrick Kennedy.* London Macmillan and CO.

Keyser, Rudolph (1854) *The Religion of the Northman.* New York: Charles B. Norton.

Kirby, W. F. (1894) *The Hero of Esthonia.* London: John C. Nimmo

Kucharz, Christel (2009) *The Real Story Behind van Gogh's Severed Ear.* ABC News. http://abcnews.go.com/International/story?id=7506786&page=1

Kukharenko, Svitlana P. (2007) *Animal Magic: Contemporary Beliefs and Practices in Ukrainian Villages.* University of Alberta: https://journals.ku.edu/index.php/folklorica/article/viewFile/3784/3622

Lady Isabel and the Elf Knight: http://www.springthyme.co.uk/ballads/balladtexts/4_LadyIsabel.html

Lang, Andrew (1897) *The Pink Fairy Book.* Gutenberg.org http://www.gutenberg.org/files/5615/5615-h/5615-h.htm

Larson, Jennifer (2001) *Greek Nymphs: Myth, Cult, Lore.* New York, NY: Oxford University Press

Lauder, Toofie (1881) *Legends and Tales of the Harz Mountains.* London: Hodder and Stoughton.

Lawson, John Cuthbert (1910) *Modern Greek folklore and ancient Greek religion: a study in survivals.* Cambridge University Press

Lecouteux, Claude (2003) *Lecouteux, Witches, Werewolves and Fairies: Shapeshifters and Astral Doubles in the Middle Ages.* Rochester, Vermont: Inner Traditions – Bear & Company

Leland, Charles Godfrey (1892) *Etruscan Roman Remains in Popular Tradition.* New York, NY: Scribner's Sons.

Linton, E. Lynn (1861) *Witch Stories.* London: Chapman and Hall

Lonnrot, Elias (2010) *The Kalevala.* Gutenberg.org: http://www.gutenberg.org/cache/epub/5186/pg5186.html

Macculloch, J. A. (1911) *The Religion of the Ancient Celts.* Edinburgh, UK: Morrison & Gibb.

Magliocco, Sabina (2009) Italian Cunning Craft: Some Preliminary Observations. *Journal for the Academic Study of Magic.* Vol 5

Masson, Elsie (1929) *Folk Tales of Brittany.* Philadlephia: Macrae, Smith, Company.

McCall, Andrew (1979) *The Medieval Underworld.* H. Hamilton

Melton, J. Gordon (1998) *The Vampire Book: The encyclopedia of the Undead.* Canton, MI: Visible Ink Press.

Meyer, Kuno (1895) *The Voyage of Bran, Son of Febal.* London: David Nutt.

Morrison, Sophia (1911) *Manx Fairy Tales.* London: David Nutt

Mortimer, Ian (2008) *The Time Traveler's Guide to Medieval England.* London: Touchstone

Narvaez, Peter (1997) *The Good People: New Fairylore Essays.* University Press of Kentucky

Olcott, Frances J. (1928) *Wonder Tales From Baltic Wizards.*

Petreska, Vesna (2008) *The Secret Knowledge of Folk Healers in Macedonian. Folklorica*: Vol 13

Petrovic, Sreten: СРПСКА МИТОЛОГИЈА http://svevlad.org.rs/knjige_files/petrovic_mitologija.html#vampir

Philips, Sarah D. (2004) Waxing Like the Moon: Women Folk Healers in Rural Western Ukraine. *Folklorica, Journal of the Slavic and East European Folklore Association.*

Purkiss, Diane (2007) *Fairies and Fairy Stories: A History.* Stroud, Gloucestershire: Tempus

Ralston, W. R. S. (2007) *Russian Fairy Tales.* Gutenberg.org http://www.gutenberg.org/files/22373/22373-h/22373-h.htm

Rhys, John (1901) *Celtic Folklore: Welsh and Manx.* Oxford: Clarendon Press.

Riordan, James (1991) *The Sun Maiden and the Crescent Moon: Siberian Folk Tales.* Northampton, MA: Interlink Publishing Group

Rodgers, Charles (1884) *Social Life in Scotland, From Early to Recent Times.* Edinburgh, UK: William Patterson.

Savina, Magliocco (2009) *Italain Cunning Craft: Some*

Preliminary Observations. Journal for the Academic Study of Magic.

Sebeok, Thomas Albert (1956) *Studies in Cheremis: The Supernatural.* New York: Wenner-Gren Foundation for Anthropological Research

Seymour, John D. (2013) *Irish Witchcraft and Demonology.* Gutenberg.org: http://www.gutenberg.org/files/43651/43651-h/43651-h.htm

Sikes, Wirt (1880) *British Goblins Welsh Folk Lore, Fairy Mythology, Legends and Traditions.* London: Sampsons Low Marston, Searle, & Rivington.

Spence, Lewis (2010) *Legends & Romance of Brittany.* Gutenberg.org: http://www.gutenberg.org/files/30871/30871-h/30871-h.htm

Spence, Lewis (2005) *Hero Tales and Legends of the Rhine.* Guternberg.org: http://www.gutenberg.org/files/16539/16539-h/16539-h.htm

Stuart, John (1843) *Extracts from the Presbytery book of Strathbogie.* Aberdeen, Printed for the Spalding Club

Tacitus, Cornelisus (2012) *The Germania.* Gutenberg.org http://www.gutenberg.org/files/39573/39573-h/39573-h.html

Taylor, Timothy (2007) The Real Vampire Slayers. *The Independent.* http://www.independent.co.uk/news/world/europe/the-real-vampire-slayers-397874.html

Tian-Shanskaia, O. S., & Ransel, D. L. (1993) *Village Life in Late Tsarist Russia.* Indiana University Press

Vadeysha, Masha (2005) The Russian Bathhouse: The Old

Russian Pert' and the Christian Bania in Traditional Culture. *Folklorica, Journal of the Slavic and East European Folkore Association*

Veselica, Lajla (2006) *Croatian 'Dracula Revived to Lure Tourists.* http://www.mg.co.za/article/2006-04-24-croatian-dracula-revived-to-lure-tourists

Wigzell, Faith (2003) The Ethical Values of Narodnoe Pravoslavie: Traditional Near-Death Experiences and Fedotov. *Folklorica, Journal of the Slavic and East European Folkore Association.*

Wentz, W. Y. Evans (2011) *Fairy Faith in the Celtic Countries.* Gutenberg.org: http://www.gutenberg.org/files/34853/34853-h/34853-h.htm

Wibly, Emma (2006) *Cunning-Folk and Familiar Spirits: Shamanistic Visionary Traditions in Early Modern British Witchcraft and Magic.* Sussex, UK: Sussex Academic Press.

Wibly, Emma (2010) *The Visions of Isobel Gowdie: Magic, Witchcraft and Dark Shamanism in Seventeenth-Century Scotland.* Sussex, UK: Sussex Academic Press.

Wigström, Eva (1881) *Folkdiktning : Visor, Folktro, Sägner, Och en Svartkonstbok.*

Wilde, Jane F. E. (1902) *Ancient Legends, Mystic Charms & Supersitions of Ireland.* London, UK: Chatto & Windus.

Wlislocki, Heinrich von (1891) *Märchen und Sagen der Bukowinaer und Siebenbürger armenier.* Google eBook: http://google.com/books?id=dk0TAAAAYAAJ

Wood-Martin, W. G. (1902) *Traces of the Elder Faiths of Ireland; a Folklore Sketch; a Handbook of Irish Pre-Christian Tradition.* London: Longmans, Green, and CO.

Wratislaw, A. H. (1890) *Sixty Folk-Tales from Exclusively Slavonic Sources.* London Ellion Stock.

Young, Ella (1910) *Celtic Wonder Tales*. Maunsel & Company.

Yeats, W. B. (1888) *Fairy and Folk tales of the Irish Peasantry*

Made in the USA
Lexington, KY
23 March 2017